CLEVER GIRL

DRIVEN WOMEN

LARALYN DORAN

THREE DOGS DAY

CLEVER GIRL

Copyright © 2023 by Laralyn Doran.

This book is a work of fiction. Names, characters, businesses, organizations, places, events and incidents either are the product of the author's imagination or are used fictitiously. Any resemblance to actual persons, living or dead, events, or locales is entirely coincidental.

For information contact Laralyn Doran at:
P. O. Box 234
Monrovia, MD 21770-0234
www.LaralynDoran.com

Book and Cover design by Deranged Doctor Designs
Photography: Lindee Robinson
Editor: Elaine York

ISBN: 978-1-7353474-4-8 (eBook)
ISBN: 978-1-7353474-5-5 (Trade Paperback)
First Edition: February 2023

For my Husband

1

GUS

"Good afternoon, Harper," I said as she marched into her corporate office at Merlo Motorsports, simultaneously tossing her phone on her elegant executive desk and shoving my boot-clad feet off it.

Harper Merrick scowled as I replanted my feet on her desk, daring her to do it again—a challenge a brother would give a sister. I flashed her my most amiable yet, taunting smile, but she didn't miss a beat and wasn't impressed with my boldness. We've been friends all our lives, after all.

"The new guy isn't going to work out," she stated, and with the grace that belied her tone, she dropped into her leather executive chair. Crossing legs almost as long as mine, she pinched the bridge of her nose and let out a very unfeminine groan of frustration.

This was a typical expression these past few months as Harper and my other best friend CJ were trying to get a new stock car team off the starting line. Recruitment was challenging for any new start-up, but employee retention seemed to be their Achilles' heel. The latest departure was one of several.

"Jacks or CJ?" I asked. The cause for lack of retention could usually be narrowed down to Jacks, the veteran crew chief who came out of retirement just to help this fledging new team and fired anyone whom he deemed unfit without discussion—or our notoriously hot-headed best friend, Charlotte Jean "CJ" Lomax, the talented driver who was the face of the team, driving them to quit.

I repositioned my feet and weaved my hands behind my head. Her frustration or concern level was high enough that my movement didn't even elicit a condemnation.

I'd been waffling back and forth between being envious of not being part of this new endeavor and thanking my stars I got to sit back and enjoy the fireworks as they tried to get this team off the ground.

She flashed another scowl my way. I grinned. She scowled some more. Today was a day of entertainment.

"Just goes to show being the head of a female-centric stock car team wasn't all glitz and glamour," I said.

"Don't you have your own team to run?"

What made things more interesting was I, Gus Quinlan, worked for a rival team and was CJ's fiancé's crew chief. It wasn't easy walking the tightrope between friendship and competition. Especially because my employer, Merrick Motorsports, was owned and operated by Harper's father—the man to whom I owed my entire career.

Yes, we are a bit of a tangled bunch. Holiday dinners were interesting.

Harper propped her deep red stilettos on her desk, mirroring my stance, but even in her impeccable suit, she couldn't possibly pull off the coolness factor like I did. She wasn't capable of my level of relaxation—of course, I had a veteran staff and not half the issues she did. I gave myself a mental pat on the back.

"If anyone would've told me running a stock car team was akin to teaching preschoolers to share new toys, I wouldn't have bothered. She wiped her hands over her forehead and raked them through her long blonde hair.

Ah, so today's drama was due to CJ.

"Did he quit or did CJ run him out of the building?"

"Does it matter?" She tossed up her hands in frustration. "He's gone, and I still need a new lead engineer."

"He was too soft-spoken to deal with her. What does Jacks say?"

"Jacks keeps reminding me he's got a foot out the door," she sat straight up and threw her hands in the air, pointedly staring at me. "And that I promised to find him a new crew chief. But if Jacks doesn't back up the people I bring in, he makes it clear they don't have his blessing. But, just letting CJ have free rein to run him out was his way of giving the new guy his walking papers and avoiding an argument with me about it."

I dropped my head to hide my grin, "I could still learn a thing or two from the old man."

"That old man is as wily as a fox," she grumbled. "Very passive-aggressive of him. He knew I'd be begging him to hold off until I found someone else, and he didn't want to wait." She stared up at the ceiling and softly said, "You know you'd solve all my problems if you just came over and worked for us. CJ would listen to you—"

She glanced over, and I gave her my standard side-eyed stare, calling her out on what she knew was a lie. On a good day, there was a fifty-fifty chance CJ would consider what I said to her.

"Well, she'd listen to you more than anyone else. And Jacks trusts you—"

I shrugged. "You know I would if I could. But I have a contract with your father over at Merrick for another season, and I really don't think CJ would want me abandoning Grady and leaving your brother to find him a new crew chief." I rested my right hand on my chest. "Besides—"

"You're loyal to my father..."

I gave her one nod because she knew this. The minute her brother was in charge, I was gone. I was slipping that into my next contract. No way I was working for that pompous ass. But her father, I owed my career to that man.

"So now I have to fill two major positions—lead engineer and crew chief." She threw her hands in the air, let out an audible sigh, and sat up straight.

"We had a real decent season. I may be able to sweet-talk one more season out of Jacks if he can pass it by his wife. But I really have to take his threat of leaving seriously. Originally, he was only supposed to

3

be here for a year. If you can't take his place, I need you to help me find someone who can come in as lead engineer, at least to back him up."

This was how Harper got people to do things for her. "In case you forgot. I don't work for you. I work for your competitor—your father and brother—who love you but wouldn't take too kindly to that idea. Junior would lose his mind if I was recruiting for you."

She walked in front of me and leaned against the desk. "I don't need you to recruit, I just need you to rack your brain. We've basically looked through all the Cup teams, and either CJ or Jacks nixed them, gave me a 'hell no,' or ran from me when I approached them.

"Obviously, we need someone smart and eager. But they also need to be young and strong-willed enough to hold their own with CJ and not someone who will rock the boat. We just got this ship sailing in the right direction. I don't want to capsize it with the wrong person.

"Shouldn't you be using racing metaphors instead of sailing ones?"

"Come on. Help me." I swear she was about to stomp her foot and start whining if I didn't take her seriously. "This could be your future team one day. Who would you want to work with?"

I closed my eyes, sat up straight, and held up my hand to stop her. We'd come to the reason I was actually here—to help out an old friend.

"That's why I'm here. I have a friend…I was going to suggest her before, but I thought she was happy where she was. I heard she was pretty entrenched in Rex Richardson Racing. But rumors are spreading that's not the case any longer.

"She?"

I ignored the one word she picked up on. "Not sure if she'd be willing to move to

Charlotte—" I scratched the side of my head.

"She?" Harper repeated herself, her eyes growing bigger with interest. "Is she an engineer?"

"Yes. She's—"

She crossed her arms over her chest and sighed. "Gus, I'm not hiring one of your ex-girlfriends for you—"

I held out a hand. "Slow your roll…she's just about one of the most

4

talented, intelligent engineers I know. In fact, when Junior finds out I have connections to her and am pointing her your way, he's going to possibly fire me. She's living in Chicago, and has a fantastic resume, but recently separated from Triple R due to some personnel issues."

I leaned forward, as if imparting a secret, "Harper, if I heard correctly, she was on the team that helped design and test the Next Gen car."

Harper cocked her head, "Go on—"

"I haven't spoken to her recently, so I'm not sure of the circumstances. But, seriously, this girl—err, um, woman, is sharp. She's probably one of the smartest people I know. She's got a backbone, and I think she'd be a good fit for Merlo."

Harper turned to her computer and logged in, ready to move on with her day and whatever her next crisis was going to be. "Well, okay. Sounds good. Why don't you give her a call and see if she wants to come out, and we can set up a meeting? Let Megan work out the details."

"Uh. You forget," I stood ready to leave. "I don't work for you. I'll leave her name with Megan, and maybe she can track her down--"

"Wait, I thought you said you knew her?"

"I do—"

"And you never dated her?" She stared up at me from her computer.

"No."

"Did you ever sleep with her?"

"No."

"Then why won't you call her and set up an introduction?" She hadn't been my friend

since we were kids without learning when I was hiding something, but I still tried to cover.

"First of all, your father would have my head if he knew I was recruiting someone of Mia's caliber to your team and not our own. Second of all," I paused, checking my phone as if I were ready to leave. "It's been a few years since I talked to her and...I think she's been avoiding me."

Harper rolled her eyes and kept working on her computer. "So, another broken heart. I don't want that complication here, Gus."

"I swear it was never like that. We were in some college classes together. Actually, you may remember meeting her. I brought her to a race once, and showed her around. Tommy met her. He liked her." An ache echoed inside me. Faint, but still present whenever Tommy's name was mentioned.

Harper studied me.

"Honestly, we just lost touch." I shrugged, "I have no idea why, but I…"

"Probably did something stupid. You weren't the sharpest crayon in the box back then," she said. "Especially with girls."

That's it. As always, she fell back on the old insult of me being a womanizer. "I'm serious," I grabbed my jacket to leave. "Just have someone reach out to her…or don't," I said, feeling in my bones this was right. I wasn't sure what was going on with Mia, but the rumors flying around didn't sound good, and they certainly didn't sound like her.

I'd like to help her. While Mr. Merrick was responsible for helping me with my career, I wanted to pay it forward because if it wasn't for Mia, I probably wouldn't have made it out of college.

2

GUS

Let me preface this by saying two of my best friends are women, so I truly believe that men and women could be friends and relate just on that level. From the time we could race go-karts, CJ could out-race me seven ways to Sunday, and I took pride in that fact and always had her back. Harper was sharp as a tack, and my mother raised me on her own and was one of the strongest people I know. I didn't just love women— I respected the hell out of them.

I was also a heterosexual male who not only appreciated the artistry, power, and sound of a powerful engine but was also awe-inspired by a woman's form bent deep under the hood of a stock car. The imagery of a beautiful body draped under the hood of a monster of a machine, fine-tuning it, making it purr…

Come on…anyone could see the sexual innuendos there.

Typically, I stayed away from women who worked on the circuit. It made things complicated. I learned my lesson early in my career and regretted breaking my rule every time I was tempted to deviate.

However, walking into Harper's garage a week later, all reasoning escaped me. A hood was up on one of the Cup cars, with three men standing around as a yet-to-be-identified-but-definitely-female mechanic was waist-deep under it. The gorgeous female backside was clad in tailored pants instead of coveralls, and her red heels were noticeable when she went up on her toes, raising a leg and reaching for something deep inside the belly of the beast. To be clear, I wasn't the only one appreciating the view.

"I must say coming to your garage is more enjoyable than hanging out at my own." I tilted my head, hands on my hips, watching her shift and lean in farther as if searching for something.

"Hmm?" Harper was distracted by something on her phone.

I gestured through the observation glass to the garage below us. "New mechanic?"

She peered over and searched the garage floor. The smirk she tried to hold back warned me of something to come.

"Well, kind of..." She gestured to the woman, now beginning to straighten. "Walk with me. It's why I called you."

"I thought you were buying me lunch or missed my witty banter," I said, my hands coming off my hips and smoothing down my shirt.

"Of course, if that's what your ego needs today." She turned back to her phone.

"Hey, asshole." The voice came from behind Harper, but I knew it well.

"Hey, Dixie—what's happening?" It was a nickname she'd been labeled with years ago. The jackass drivers on the circuit, jealous of her talent and resentful of her being there, used to paper her car with Dixie cups representing the only type of "Cup" trophy she'd ever win. Boy, were they eating their words. They either bottomed out, changed careers—like me—or were still struggling, bitterly, to reach her level of skill and accomplishments.

"Not much. How's my man doing these days?" She strode over and searched the garage floor for what I was looking at. She zeroed in on it and adopted the same smirk as her buddy Harper had. She turned to me and cocked an eyebrow. "Has something caught your eye, GQ?"

I called her Dixie. She called me GQ—Gus Quinlan. When the magazine put me on the cover, the teasing was relentless. The money I got for that cover was a down payment for the house, though, so screw them. I was young, and it was more publicity than I really wanted, so it will never happen again.

"Well, now that you mentioned it, I was just asking—"

"We were just getting to that," Harper interjected. She put her arm around me and said, "CJ would like you to join us or observe it from up here."

"What—oh, no…I need the audio also."

I pushed Harper off me. "What the hell is your problem? Why are you being so cagey? Is this what happens when your boyfriend is out of town? You get handsy—and weird. No need to introduce me to anyone. I'm sure I will cross paths with her eventually." My voice was laced with confidence and calculation.

CJ stepped up and poked me in the chest with her finger. "Listen to me, August Quin—"

"Uh-oh, she's pulling out the full name—" Harper muttered.

"You better not screw this up for us or I'll junk-punch you. Hands off."

Ah, more of a challenge. I put my hand to my chest as if pretending to clutch my pearls with mock innocence. "I don't know what you are talking about."

"I don't think we'll have to worry about it," Harper said conspiratorially to CJ and walked us to stairs leading down into the bowels of Merlo Racing.

"Why? Is she married?" That was a line I never crossed. If they had any type of commitment with someone else, they were off limits. I followed them down the stairs as Harper answered the all-important question.

"No, just got out of a relationship, and she's quite beautiful," Harper said once we got to the bottom of the stairs and walked toward the glass doors that led to the floor of the garage. "That's why CJ is threatening your ability to procreate if you mess this up."

I held the door for the two of them, and they walked ahead of me. Harper was tall, but I was taller, and CJ barely reached my chin. So it was easy to see over them as we approached the lusciously curvy woman who had her back to us. She was wiping off her hands and talking to Jacks as Harper reached them and got their attention.

The mystery woman turned slightly to Harper, giving me a view of her profile, and I stopped in my tracks.

Come to think of it, I knew that ponytail…the mane of curly hair. But those curves—those didn't add up…

"That's the reaction I was waiting for," CJ murmured as a phone clicked and a flash broke my concentration. CJ was staring at her phone, tapping buttons. "Oh, yeah. That was worth skipping lunch with Sadie for."

My brain caught up with the program. Ponytail, new employee… my brain caught up. The woman wasn't a mystery to me.

Mia.

Familiar heavy feelings stood on my chest as if I were run over by my own race car. My mouth moved a few times before sound was possible.

"You called her," I managed to get out.

Harper stood next to me, proud stance, with a hand on her hip. "I did. Looks like she's getting along well with Jacks and the boys."

Yep. She had everyone's full attention, that's for sure. And now she had mine.

"Why didn't you tell me? I would've—" I stared down at myself. What was I going to say to finish that sentence, *"I would've dressed up?"*

Jeans and an older shirt and my boots. Standard everyday wear, they were clean.

Was I nervous?

"You would've what?" CJ leaned closer to me, a mixture of curiosity with a spike of amusement.

"I would've come over sooner," I said and started to walk toward Mia, a smile plastered on my face, and I prayed it appeared confident and not as insecure as I felt about seeing her again. It bothered me that she cut off all communication with me and never seemed interested in reconnecting whenever I tried.

Not knowing why someone chose not to be friends with you was… unnerving. It wasn't like we had a fight. It wasn't as if we had a relationship and broke up. She just kind of disappeared.

I peeked back over at her and found her staring at me as she spoke to one of the mechanics. There was curiosity as she studied me before the barrier of indifference slammed down, and her face went blank.

I dropped my head.

Maturity had slimmed her face and rounded her curves, but I could still see the serious girl with the ponytail, who'd lived in t-shirts and jean cut-offs instead of new form-fitting clothes and heels. Experience and confidence had her standing a bit straighter, a bit prouder, and it outlined her beauty. She was undoubtedly a woman, but she was also the girl I once knew.

She was Mia St. James.

I couldn't stop the smile coming through, even if she seemed less than happy to see me.

It showed in the slight hesitancy to move toward me, the tightness of her smile as she approached me—she wasn't as excited to see me as I was to see her.

It was as if I was finding someone I'd lost—because I had.

"Hey, Gus."

She held out her hand for me to shake.

Either CJ or Harper whispered, "Oh…this ain't awkward."

Screw this. She can tell me why she's prickly later. I turned on the charm. Stepping closer, I reached for her hand, softly taking it between both of mine as two lovers would. I stared at her from beneath my lashes, leaning forward and brushing my lips across her cheek, drawing back slowly and deepening my voice. "Hey there, Mia Darlin'."

She pulled her hand out of mine and shoved my chest, her other hand on her hip. She fought the laughter, but the smirk wouldn't be denied. "What have I told you about calling me darlin'? And wipe that stupid grin off your face. Your charms and good looks don't work on me, remember?"

I threw my head back and laughed, dragging her in for a true hug.

She softened in my hug and patted my back, accepting the greeting as I rocked her back and forth.

Harper and CJ walked up behind us, one of them commenting, "Oh, yeah. She'll fit in just fine."

3

MIA

"I'm kind of pissed at you," my best friend Shyla said.

"Why?" I popped my head out of my closet as she was about to sit down on what used to be our bed—mine and the backstabbing asshole's. Thinking better of it, she grabbed a chair from my vanity and pulled it over to watch me disassemble my life.

"You were the one who told me to go for it."

"I told you to move on with your life." She had her ebony hair in a high ponytail and tightened it. "I told you to get a fresh start."

With the dramatic flair that was part of her charm, she flung out her arm. "I didn't mean for you to do it several states away."

I folded clothes and placed them in moving boxes. "Well, it's not like jobs in the racing industry are in every town." I walked back into the closet, past his things. His scent permeated the entire room—making me angrier by the moment. I couldn't stay here much longer, or I wouldn't be held accountable for my actions. "Besides, I need to get out of Chicago."

She sighed loud enough for me to hear and rubbed her hands over her face. "I know."

"Everyone thinks I'm the bad guy in this—that I'm the jilted coworker, throwing a tantrum because he was promoted over me." I pointed at my chest, the anger ramping me up again. "No one is ever going to believe it's because of me that he's even got a job still. That it was me who saved his ass, covered for him numerous times."

"I know." Her tone was weary because these were phrases I'd been chanting for the last two months while I was living with her—licking my wounds, trying to piece my life back together after it imploded while I just stood by.

"And then to have him stack the odds more in his favor—to ambush my chances of ever getting ahead in that company—" I began pacing. "No, I need to get the hell out of Chicago. Screw that...I need to get out of Illinois. North Carolina may not be far enough. I know people on the Formula One circuit. I'm considering jumping continents—"

"Don't you dare." She stood, now eager to help me calm down and change the subject before I made any other rash life decisions. "North Carolina will be doable. I can handle North Carolina."

I dropped the clothes I was folding and stared at my best friend. Shyla was the closest thing I had to a sister. It was because of her I had the determination and strength to stand up for myself and demand more.

I threw an arm around her shoulder.

"I don't know if I've ever thanked you for—"

"Don't you thank me. That's what sisters do—we hand you the ice cream, we support you as you put yourself back together." She turned to me, holding my hand, swinging it back and forth, then narrowing her eyes, "And if necessary, we plot the revenge and give you an alibi." She pointed at me, "I'm still down for the revenge and alibi. You're leaving town anyway—why not go out with a bang." Her smile was devious that if you didn't know her, you'd question her flippancy.

I shook my head. "Let's just get out of here."

She sat up and motioned around us, "But we have access to all his stuff."

"No, I just want to go—"

"Just a little Nair in the shampoo—"

"Some Ex-lax in his protein powder—"

I laughed.

"What about hot sauce in—"

"Shyla, girl. I love you, but I just want to leave.

I stood and went back into the closet. "I'm not doing anything that will give credence to his claims of me being petty and jealous. Plus, I have to believe Karma, or his own incompetence will catch up with him."

Her disagreement was noted, and we both cleared shelves and drawers. Although, the Nair in his shampoo may have happened if I had some with me. Keith would've figured out the Ex-lax in the protein powder and probably charged me with poisoning him—he loved drama, after all.

"So, what was it like seeing Gus after all this time? Tell me about Mr. Sexy-Pants himself. Is he as gorgeous in person? Was it like looking into the sun? Do his photos do him justice? You know he was named one of the sexiest bachelors in sports, right?

I stopped what I was doing and turned to her, "Is that a thing?"

"Well, it should be."

"Yeah, well, if it was, he'd probably be it."

"Oh, do tell."

"Oh, he's just as charming as ever. It's not fair that one man was given so many gifts."

"Did you sample the gifts?"

"No, I told you it's not like that with us...

"Why isn't it?"

"Because he's never seen me as anything more than a friend— maybe even a little sister or a pet. You've seen the women he dates." I put my underwear in my suitcase, bemoaning the lack of silk or thongs among them. It wasn't granny panties, but Keith didn't exactly inspire lingerie. "If there was an antithesis of me, that would be who he dates."

"Girl, you are hot. And it's the 21st century. You could always change the score and make the first move."

"I'm not jumping Gus."

"No...you're more subtle than that. Have I taught you nothing?"

I paused my packing as I thought back to all her lessons...

15

"Flirt with him—you have the cute wolf in sheep's clothing, seductress under the cape-thing."

"Never been into the *Red Riding Hood* fetish."

"Shut up. You know what I mean. And when you wore glasses, you completely had the

sexy librarian thing down—I bet he loved the sexy librarian.

"He never showed it—"

"You were barely legal? Were you legal?" She shook her head, changing the direction of the argument. "Before you were saddled with dickhead, you weren't even aware of your effect on men."

I forced a chuckle, "You realize most of the men I'm around during the day don't have a lot of options when it comes to women they get to look at, right? If a man is starving, a cracker is a gourmet meal."

"Give yourself some credit—"

I held up my hand and went to grab some more clothing from the drawer.

"I'm trying to look forward and think of this nightmare as a positive turn of events—"

"Positive turn back to Gus Quin—"

"No," I said, drawing out the word with a firm tone. "I'm being offered a position with a woman-centric race team that is focused on building a diverse company and looking for people to help in that process. Plus, they have the Driven Women Initiative, and I really want to be involved with that program. I shrugged, "Maybe Keith being a self-serving dickhead was actually a blessing in disguise."

"Plus," Shyla said, her face alight with anticipation, "He's going to be livid when he finds out you landed on your feet so fast. I think deep down he liked having you here under his thumb because he was able to keep you from ascending past him." She picked up the box to take it out to the car. "God, I'd want to be there when he finds out where you're going—who you're going to work for—Harper Merrick, Jackson Grove...I'm not even into stock cars, and I know that's royalty."

Her point had merit I would probably ponder later.

"Does he know about your past with Gus?"

"He knows I know him. But not much else."

"Well, at least you won't be working for Gus."

"No, just his best friends," I said, and tried to remember all the stories he used to tell me

when we were studying in college about his crew back at home.

"What was he like back then when you met him?"

"He was wicked smart—still is. He just has the attention span of a gnat—especially with women."

She bent her head back to look at me, "Maybe he hasn't found the right one to keep his attention."

I shrugged. I had no idea.

Shyla switched subjects, staring at the now-empty side of my closet. "There has to be something we can do to aggravate asshole."

"I don't care enough to exert the energy," I said wearily. "I need to take charge of my own life and career. I'll leave a note to forward anything else I may have left behind to you." I stared at the boxes that accumulated by the door. Thinking out loud, I said, "He still has the key to the storage unit downstairs. I don't have anywhere to put things yet, so I'll get them later. No need to make a stink about it now."

Shyla went to grab her keys. "Do you think he's going to cause you any more trouble?"

I shook my head. "He's gotten what he's wanted. Plus, I'm out of his hair." I brought out the last box from the kitchen. "I have a feeling he's going to have his hands too full trying to hold things together to worry about me."

Shyla was quiet as she stared down at her hands.

"What?"

"Do you really think he just used you?"

Now I was quiet.

"I know you don't want to hear this. But I do think in his own selfish way he did care about you—"

"Maybe, but I think he cared about furthering his career more."

4

GUS

"Hello?" My mom's distinctive voice came through the car speakers as I navigated traffic on the way to the shop.

"Hey, Mom." It was early morning, and my caffeine hadn't kicked in yet, but I needed to catch my mom before the day got away from me, and we were forced to play phone tag all day long.

"Hello, sweetheart. How's my favorite son?" I was her only son, but she always said I was the equivalent of raising an entire team of boys.

"I'm good." I was driving to the office and summoning my patience to deal with Junior and all his smugness. Because, of course, all of Grady's success—all of our success—was due to his leadership. Grady's increasing popularity led to an increase in sponsorships, which made him look good. He failed to understand that Grady's face was the face of the team—not his.

I shifted back to my mom when she asked, "What do I owe the pleasure of this early-morning call?"

"Just wanted to hear your sweet voice to start my day."

"It's a bit early for the BS, honey. Spill it. What do you want?" Clearly, Mom hadn't had her coffee yet, either.

"Okay, straight to the point. Harper is hiring a new engineer. A woman I knew from college—she's been living in Chicago. Do you remember me mentioning Mia St. James?

"Mia! Your Mia—of course, I'm still mad at you that I never got to meet her before you ran her off."

I was at a stop light and rolled my eyes at myself in the rearview mirror. "Mom, I didn't—never mind. It's not important. She wants to move down here as soon as possible.

"Oh, fun. Sure, honey. No problem." I heard the drawer in the kitchen open and slammed shut as my mom got out her pad of paper and pen. "Do you know what she's looking for? Does she need a single-family home, does she have children?"

Jeez, I never asked. I guess I just assumed.

"I don't think so. I believe she's single. There was mention of a breakup, and she's living with a friend now. I don't think there would be any contingencies."

"Hmm. Okay. I'll see what's around and wait for her call. I will warn you, if you talk to her, the market is super-hot right now, and if she sees something she likes, she needs to act fast."

"Sounds good. Will let her know. I'll get her number from Harper and send your info to her. Suggest she call you today. Thanks, Mom."

I put on my blinker to turn into Merrick's parking lot.

"Happy to help. So—" I almost escaped.

"Mom, we're friends. That's it. In fact, I'm not even sure we are friends—"

"What's she doing in Charlotte? How did she end up with Harper?"

I had to wrap up this call. I couldn't be overheard talking about Merlo business walking into Merrick's offices. And I didn't want to get into something with my mom that I didn't even understand myself.

"No. She's going to be a lead engineer for Merlo."

"Oh. So, obviously smart, an engineer, not your employee. Hm. Sounds like an interesting girl—"

"Mom."

"Okay. I got to go. I'm late to meet a client. Love you. I'll let you know how things go with your Mia. Bye!"

Click.

There was a reason Mia and I got along so well. She was very similar to CJ and Harper. She was a strong, smart, opinionated, and engaging woman—and yes, she's got a smile that lights up a room. No wonder CJ and Harper liked her. My mom has been lamenting for years because I never had any chemistry with CJ or Harper. She's been moaning about how they are engaged, wishing it could've been to me —but that's because she loves them and wanted me with someone I can settle down with.

Crap. My mom also loved Mia, even though she had never met her. She loved her because Mia kept me in line. She knew how much time Mia devoted to me—not only helping me study but focusing on my future.

I got out of my car and froze. Mia and my mom—talking.

About her future in North Carolina.

Shit.

This may have been a bad idea.

After getting Mia's number from Harper, I texted her my mom's information and offered her services in helping Mia find a place to live. She texted back a quick thank you, and I was satisfied with yet another good deed, feeling my part was done. Without thinking too much about it, I saved Mia's number in my phone, just in case.

My mom called later that afternoon while I was in my office and didn't even say hello.

"I love her." It was how she greeted me.

"Excuse me?" I said, closing the door to my office.

"Your Mia—" I could hear her smile in the tone of her voice as she ran through the conversation with Mia at breakneck speed. "She's not like your usual women…not that I've met many of them. But I hear things—"

I held up my hand as if she were in front of me. "Mom, Mia is a friend. Not a girlfriend."

"She's a girl—" she said.

"—and she's a friend." I finished her sentence. "That's it." My tone was clipped.

"Hm. Okay, fine." She acquiesced too easily. That didn't bode well for me—or for Mia.

"Mom, I haven't seen her in years. We are barely acquaintances. Please don't make this awkward."

"You had longer than that to try to win over CJ or Harper—you love those girls, and you let them slip right through your fingers—"

"Mom, I never felt anything for them—we've been through this."

"But—"

"Mom."

"I just don't want you to be—"

"I know, Mom."

Alone. Like her. She didn't want me to be alone.

"Well, anyway." She let out a big, disappointed sigh before gearing up to business mode. "I'm sending over the listing to Mia. As I told her, the market is tight. She'll need to act quick. Not even sure if she'll have time to fly down and see them. If she sees something she likes, she may have to put an offer in sight-unseen."

"Okay."

"I'll send you a listing also. I circled a few that I thought were worthwhile. I told her I can do a virtual walkthrough with her if she sees anything on the list she likes—but it would have to be today."

"Alright, send it over to me. Maybe I can give her my two cents."

"No problem, honey." I could hear the smile in my mom's voice. "Let me know if you hear from her."

Why was I inserting myself into this? Because I assumed Mia didn't know many people in the city. Well, she knew Harper and CJ, but not enough to ask them to help her find a place to live. Besides, they were busy with their own business. Harper was slammed getting sponsors situated for the upcoming season, and any spare time was spent with Cal, Grady's brother. CJ—when not at the track—was in la-la-engaged land of preparing for a wedding with Grady.

Anyway, with everyone coupled up these days, I had time to spare.

My mom battled a broken heart and was a woman cast aside to raise me on her own.

The tears of pride in her eyes when I received a college degree—something she always wanted but never achieved—was partly because Mia kicked my ass in gear.

I can at least help her find a house.

It was also probably a good idea not to leave those two alone together for any length of time.

I scrolled through my contacts and pulled up the number Harper gave me for Mia. I won't lie. A new energy rushed me. I was happy to do this—it would be good to have her back in my life.

Gus

Hey, this is your friendly southern tour guide…My mom said she sent you the real estate listings. See anything you like?

I stood still for a moment, actually waiting, expecting a quick reply. That was kind of arrogant of me. That she would immediately see my text and respond.

Hours later, right before lunch, her text came through.

Mia

I texted your mom about a specific one that interested me. She's going to get back to me.

BTW, thanks for setting this up with her.

Mom sent me the listing Mia indicated, and I decided to go check it out. A three-bedroom colonial with a decent size backyard and a large, two-car garage that was coincidentally near my own house. I walked into the house; Mom was chatting and laughing with Mia, who was streaming through on her iPad. My mom's face lit up, making her look young enough to be my sister. Her highlighted blonde hair was shoulder-length, her make-up looked like a professional had applied it, as was her tailored pantsuit. She took her career seriously—even if it wasn't the one she originally planned on having.

"Oh, hi, honey." She turned the iPad around with a flourish so Mia could see I was there.

I smiled at the surprise in Mia's voice as I grabbed the iPad out of my mother's hand.

"Gus?" Her tawny-colored eyes were wide, and a hand smoothed over her swept-up hair and then fiddled with the hoodie sweatshirt she was wearing.

"Hey, darlin'. How are you two beautiful ladies doing this fine day?" Dialing up the southern twang again.

My mother rolled her eyes. "No wonder you're single," she muttered. "Don't blow this sale for me, son."

Mia's giggle grew with my feigned offense, but it was her smile that put me at ease with joining them.

"What are you doing there? I thought your mom was showing me the property."

My mom grabbed the iPad from me. "I'm here. My son just suddenly decided he was interested in Charlotte real estate, or he doesn't trust me not to take you for a ride."

"Gus, I'm sure you have better things to do with your time," Mia said.

I walked in the kitchen checking out the appliances but yelled back, "Nothing except listen to Junior Merrick crow about how his brilliance is going to lead us to a championship season." My mom turned the iPad around so Mia could view the kitchen. "It was a good excuse to get out of the office." I poked my head into her view. "So, this is much more appealing."

"Okay, well. Come here, Gus, make yourself useful." Mom handed me the iPad.

I made an exaggerated smile, dramatically widening my eyes, and zoomed in on my face in an attempt to break the ice more and make Mia give me another smile, while my mom started her spiel. "This house was built in the early 1990s. It has two floors, central air, gas heat. All the specifics are in your printout. Three bedrooms, two-and-a-half baths. Recently refurnished with new engineered hardwood floors throughout the first floor—"

I slowly walked from room to room and bathroom to bathroom. Giving extended commentary my mom couldn't exactly hear. "This is where they found the first body under the floorboards."

In one of the bedrooms, I said, "You really can't even smell the meth lab chemicals anymore."

"Oh, and look, you can't even see the elderly naked couple next door since they put in the privacy fence." Then we walked into the other room, and I pretended to cover the camera. "Yikes. Well, maybe it's not as high as it should be." My face appeared in the camera view. "I take that back...from this angle...uh. Yeah. You may want to put in some large evergreens or something."

She was subtly covering her mouth, but I saw it in her eyes. She was laughing.

Then I remembered Mia had two laughs. One was the library laugh —polite, demure, cute.

The other was hilarious, and anyone around her couldn't help but smile when it let loose.

I still hadn't heard that one yet—but I was working on it.

"Michelle?" Mia shouted out to my mother. "As riveting as your son's tour is, what is the situation with offers on this one?"

"Went on the market yesterday. If we want to avoid the weekend rush, I'd move fast."

"Gus, take me outside. Let me see the garage."

"Your wish..." I turned the screen around as if I were escorting the person herself.

We walked out back through a screened-in porch to a deck that stepped down to a small stone patio and onto the beautiful, well-maintained grass yard bordered by tall trees belying the age of the house and property. "It really is a nice house, Mia. No bullshit."

"I know. I just hate doing this from here."

I opened the door that led to the garage. "There is a door to the garage from the kitchen as well, but—" I walked into the back of the garage that jutted behind the house at least another eight feet. I flicked on the light. "Mia," I said in a whisper.

The light illuminated the vast space and we both went quiet. From the street, the garage appeared normal size. But it was much more. Two large bays, extra deep, and a work area lined with built-in shelves and a workbench. And skylights...in a garage...with windows on the side for

24

natural light. It was a garage of a person who enjoyed spending time in it.

Simultaneously we both yelled.

"Mom!"

"Michelle!"

"Yes?" My mom came strolling in, cell phone in hand.

She took in the garage, the iPad, and then me. She leaned against the door frame, crossed her arms, and amusement in the form of a cocked smile took hold as she waited for the words.

"Make an offer," I said.

"Gus, sweetheart. This is Mia's decision."

"Mom, if Mia doesn't take it, I'm going to."

The disembodied voice practically shouted, "Oh, hell no, pretty boy. That place is mine."

I turned the iPad around and brought it close, so she was face-to-face with me. With her furrowed brow, wild, high ponytail, and all-natural, squished-up face, she made me think I was the next bully she was going to take down. She was adorable. She thought I was serious. Time to poke the bear.

"Then you better get your ass down here and claim it."

Mia and my mom discussed details and my mom said, "Alright, let me make a call," and disappeared back into the house. It left Mia and me alone in a vast garage with the reason we were talking now concluded.

Silence.

"So..."

A topic came to me, and she jumped when I blurted out, "How's the packing going?"

Wait, was that too personal? Is she at her ex-boyfriend's house packing things up? And would that be difficult to talk about?

Crap. Nice going, idiot.

She shrugged, "It's pretty much done. I don't have a lot. We—I—well, my ex and I lived together, so a lot of the stuff, furniture and such, was his. I guess I'll have to do some shopping when I get down there."

I nodded. "I'm sure my mom can give you some idea of places to get things. Are you excited about working at Merlo?" I leaned against the workbench, propping the iPad up on the table.

"Yeah, I am. A bit nervous. I've heard about Harper and CJ, and I admire them, but they can be a little intimidating."

I let out a chuckle because CJ can be a lot when you meet her. Harper, only when you cross her. She's more subtle than CJ about her take downs, but you still end up on the floor. "They may come across strong, but they are soft and squishy inside. Hell, they put up with me all these years."

She nodded, looking down at her lap. "Just a bit unnerving to move to a new place without knowing anyone."

"Trust me, within a week, you won't feel like that anymore," I said, putting my hand to my chest, I turned up the arrogance, "Besides, you know me."

She shook her head and opened her mouth to reply. An unknown expression was fighting to cross her face when my mom came walking out.

"Okay, so I gave them your offer to take to their client. The only stipulation they made is they need at least thirty days to move. The house they bought won't be ready until then."

"I can't wait that long to move down there," she said, concern and anxiety raising the pitch of her words.

My mom held up her hand and said, "It's fine. We can make arrangements to get you down here. When does Harper want you to start?"

"Basically, yesterday. The off-season is short. I don't have a lot of time to acclimate to the team. I was going to leave to fly down Thursday, and my friend was going to oversee the moving of the rest of my things after we closed on the sale." Mia's concern wasn't going anywhere.

I watched my mom, she surveyed me, glanced back at Mia, and she started to bite her lip. When she tucked her hand under her chin and began studying me more earnestly, I knew—I just knew—she was up to something, and I needed to brace. Before I could puzzle together what it was, her face lit up and she threw up her hands. "I know!"

Here it comes…

"You can stay with Gus until it's ready."

"What!" Mia almost shouted over the iPad.

"Excuse me?" I practically growled at my mother.

"Sure, this is perfect. You're right around the corner," She pointed at me, just to make sure Mia knew who she was talking about, insert eye roll. "Both Merrick and Merlo are within a few miles of here. You can show her where all the local spots are and help her get acclimated."

"I don't think—" Mia's words were almost shrill in pitch.

"Mom…" Mine was almost baritone, and a crowbar couldn't have unlocked the tightness of my jaw.

"Oh my God, this is perfect," she said, turning to Mia. "Just think what you can save in an extended hotel stay." Then she turned to me and waved me off, "You're never home anyway."

She turned to both of us, although she side-eyed me the entire time. "Besides, you said you two were once friends. Wouldn't you do this for CJ or Harper, Gus?"

I would. I would do this for them. She had a point. Damnit. Why did she always have to have a point when I didn't agree with her.

Mia was biting her thumbnail and had her face turned from the screen.

"Mia," I said, and tried to sound chipper, encouraging. "My mom is right. I'm never home. Even in the off-season, I'm at the office, garage, or racetrack most of the time. You'll be busy like that as well. I have four bedrooms, two with their own bathrooms, and lots of space. You'll probably never see me. You're welcome to stay there until your house is ready."

"See." My mother clapped her hands. "Southern hospitality at its finest." She pinched my cheek as if I were five. "Perfect solution." And before she could hear any disagreement, she practically ran out of the garage saying, "I'll call the seller and tell her we have a deal and draw up the papers. "You two work out the details about your roommate arrangement."

She popped her head back in and said, "By the way, congratulations, Mia!"

With her head turned so Mia couldn't see her on the iPad, my mother winked at me.

I rubbed my hand over my face and gave my best reassuring smile to Mia.

Shoot me now.

5

MIA

I drove into town Thursday evening with whatever I could fit in my car. Shyla was going to come down with me, but given that I was a guest a Chez Gus, I thought adding another woman was pushing my luck.

I wasn't convinced he was completely on board with this arrangement. However, given that this relocation and purchasing the house was costing me a chunk out of my savings, I had to agree it made sense financially.

After arriving late, I found Gus waiting for me with his front porch light on. Pulling into his driveway, I just about fell out of the car, and it must have shown on my face.

"Jesus, Mia. You really shouldn't have made that trip by yourself," he said, coming over to the car in a sweatshirt, plaid lounge pants, and slippers. With his five o'clock shadow and ruffled hair, he may have fallen asleep on the sofa waiting for me, and I was feeling too guilty to argue with him.

"I'm fine. It was just the last hour, or three, that did me in." I reached in and grabbed my purse and the small overnight bag I had in the front seat.

"Pop the trunk," he said, moving behind my car.

"Gus, it can wait until tomorrow. Let's go back inside…it's freezing."

"Let's just get it in. That way you will feel more at home with your things."

I popped the trunk, and he lugged out the two full suitcases and led me up the path to his house.

It opened to a large split-level foyer and had a driveway that ran across the front and around the back, presumably to a state-of-the-art home garage…since I didn't see his cars, and I assumed anything car-related with Gus would be state of the art.

He held open the front door for me while toeing off his shoes in the front hall and pushing them to the side. Then he gestured for my jacket, placing it on what appeared to be a well-worn designated hook behind the door. I was touched at such a domestic, almost boyish thing to do—something his mom would've ingrained in him—and realized how personal it was for Gus to have me in his home.

I walked over to the floor-to-ceiling back windows overlooking a patio, and where I could catch a glimpse of the building in the moonlight. "I'm too tired tonight to appreciate it now, but you will show me everything back there tomorrow."

In response, he flashed the smile that probably broke a thousand hearts.

"Promise." I put as much authority in that reply as I could.

"Absolutely. It's my turn to show off," he said, the smile turning smug. "Wait until you see what I have inside."

I grabbed his arm, swinging him around. "You didn't."

His cocky eye raise was confirmation, and if it wasn't so late and I wasn't so tired, I would've run out there myself. "You got the Camaro?"

He nodded before continuing through the house. "1969 Camaro Z28…It's the one I bought before Tommy died. We were going to work on it together."

The house wasn't fancy, and it wasn't a sparse bachelor pad. I could tell his mother's influence was around. He had plush furniture and some decorative items that weren't frou-frou enough to be considered feminine. There weren't any scented candles or throw pillows, but there were framed photos on the wall and a few knick-knacks. Hardwood floors and beautiful throw rugs helped dress up the neutral tones.

"It took me a few years to start working on it once he was gone, but I'd like to say she was worth it."

The kitchen was open to the rest of the house. Stainless steel, gray cabinets, and beautiful countertops, but very clean and efficient. I halted briefly near a door that would lead out to the garage—the temptation of the Camaro was calling to me.

"Later," he said, giving me a nudge. "You need all your senses in full form to appreciate her."

He walked into the kitchen. "Can I get you a bottle of water?"

"Yes, please," I said as I glanced at some of the photos on the wall. He handed me a bottle and walked me into a family room with a large leather sectional with an equally styled leather recliner that took up the space and faced one of the most giant flat screens I'd ever seen. It was also flanked by a stone fireplace.

I took a sip of the water and muttered to myself, "Nice," as we continued to the back, where I assumed the bedrooms were.

"I'll also drive you around tomorrow and show you where all the neighborhood essentials and hot spots are located."

"Great," I scanned the hallway, taking everything in, trying to see what else I could learn about the new Gus.

"And, of course, we have the engagement party tomorrow night."

"Yes, I remember," I said with a touch of anxiety. When I came down to meet with CJ and Harper, within minutes of accepting the position, CJ invited me to her engagement party. "Nothing like jumping in the deep end and meeting half of the stock car racing industry in Charlotte. Plus, free food and booze."

Gus turned to me, his hand on the back of his neck. "Here's the thing, I'm actually seeing someone, and asked her to the engagement party a few weeks ago, so…"

"Hey, seriously. I'm a house guest, not your ward." I shook my head and put up my hand. "You don't have to babysit me or anything. You do you."

I mean, really, should I be surprised?

Oh God, is he going to bring women home while I'm here? Not that it's my business or anything, but how thick are these walls?

"But, um…how's your girlfriend going to feel about me staying here with you?"

"Oh, we're not serious or anything," he said, waving his hand, as if what I asked had no significance. "It'll be fine."

If I was dating Gus, no matter how casually, I'd be "not fine" with this…at all.

He walked me around, pointing out the rest of the house. Powder room, dining room, coat closet, and back to the bedrooms.

"That's my room," he gestured at a door but didn't open it. "And here," he walked a few steps down the hall, "is the guest room, as promised. It has a bathroom attached, so you have complete privacy."

Thank God we don't share a wall. At least that should help keep out some of the sounds coming from his room.

He tapped on the door frame. "Anyway, let me know if you need anything… Oh, wait. Do you have something to sleep in? I could get you a t-shirt or something." He turned to walk out as I took off my shoes after sitting on the bed. *Something? What did he mean something? Did he keep a drawer of women's nightgowns? Come on, Mia, now you are buying into it all.*

"No, I'm good. I have some pajamas in my smaller bag."

"I have extra toothbrushes and things in the bathroom, so help yourself." He gestured. "And I left towels on the bed." He pointed at plush navy towels.

"Thanks."

He turned to leave. "Okay, well, good night, then."

"Hey, Gus," I said, wanting to add something before he left.

He reached the door and turned, "Yeah."

"I really appreciate you helping me out like this." Man, I was never good at accepting help, let alone acknowledging it. "I know it was probably you who put my name in Harper's ear, and I appreciate that too." I went to twirl the absent ring that was now on the dresser I shared back in Chicago with Keith and then clenched my hands. "The opportunity came at the right time and I—well… Thank you for letting me stay here." I attempted to sound teasing, "I hope I don't cramp your style."

He gave me a mock brush-off, "You can see I have the room. It's not a big deal." Both of us seemed to run out of things to cover, the house was suddenly very quiet. He knocked on the door frame once and said, "Well, good night," before grabbing the door to close it behind him.

"Good night, um…" My voice cracked. I cleared my throat. "Good night, Gus."

He popped open the door just as I was bending down to open my suitcase, a hesitant glance that almost seemed boyish. "Hey, Mia..." He bit his bottom lip as he paused, "I—I'm glad you're here."

"So am I," I whispered where he couldn't hear me, so I simply replied, "Thanks, for everything."

He nodded and left.

A good night it was. Let's just say my dreams that night were… well, they were far from good, they were…well, let's just not think about them.

6

MIA

Hey, Roomie—running some errands, coffee is fresh. Will bring home some breakfast/lunch. Relax. -G

Great thinking. That was sweet of him.

I fixed a cup of coffee, settled into his comfy sofa with it, and sat with my thoughts for the day ahead, including what I was going to wear that night. I basically dumped a bunch of options into one of the suitcases, but I was still stuck, not knowing what kind of atmosphere it would have.

Charlotte gave me the feeling of ol' south, and most would think engagement parties would be preceded with engraved invitations and a fancy sit-down dinner. I'd heard CJ Lomax and Grady McBane charted their own path and I didn't have an engraved invitation to clue me into anything.

I texted Harper for more info because I really didn't know what to expect.

Harper called me within minutes with a greeting and a warm welcome to Charlotte. "As for the party wear, it will run the gambit, from cocktail dresses to jeans, I'm guessing. Just planning the engagement party has been enough to convince me that when Cal and I get married, I'm running off to Vegas."

"Why?"

"Well, my mother considers CJ her adopted daughter and therefore has inserted herself into the planning of the wedding. When you meet my mom, you will understand the battles that have been waged, where CJ won, and where she lost."

"Oh, my."

"Yeah, CJ and Grady have decided to hold the wedding out of town to minimize the attention and have been very quiet about the details. My mom was hoping for a big, splashy, extravagant society wedding, but that much attention may have turned CJ into a runaway bride, so Grady gallantly took on my mom, and she shut up."

"I understand."

"Grady has his way. He's the only guy I know more charming than Gus—but don't tell him I said that. I mean, they're both pretty to look at. The difference is Gus has an aloof confidence that things will go his way, but Grady enjoys charming people into thinking it's all their idea."

"Oh…" I mean, what do you say to that?

"Of course, you know Gus, so you'd understand that, right?"

"I guess—"

"Then there's my Cal." She sighed. "My man just has to look at someone, his voice just drops an octave and well…swoon." She giggled. My soon-to-be boss giggled. I imagined anyone from Triple R giggling, and it almost made me giggle.

I was already looking forward to the evening and getting to know my new co-workers in a casual atmosphere. I had a feeling there were going to be many differences in this new position.

"Anyway, my mom couldn't dismiss the distillery-slash-brewery. If she did, she risked being nudged out of the wedding preparations."

I mocked with dramatic pitch. "Oh…the politics."

"You have no idea."

"Okay, well, that doesn't help me plan my outfit." More concerned than ever about the right attire. "Not to sound like we are in high school, but what are you wearing?"

She gave a soft laugh and ran down her possibilities, and then asked me what I had with me. We decided on a form-fitting deep *merlot*-colored dress with a boat-neck and three-quarter sleeves—I sold her on the color—and a pair of high-heeled boots.

"Are you coming with Gus?" she asked as we concluded our fashion debate.

"Oh, no. He's got a date, so I'm driving myself."

"Oh. Right, I forgot he was seeing someone. Kara or Keelie or something."

I ignored that his friends didn't even know the name of the woman he was dating and held back from prying. "He gave me the directions. It seems easy enough," I said because who he was dating wasn't a big deal. Probably tally, leggy, and beautiful—he had a type.

"No, no. Cal and I will come pick you up on our way—"

"Harper, no—"

"I insist. We'll be by to get you around 6:45, okay? I promised CJ I'd be there early to help with interference if she needed it."

"Harper, it's sweet, but really I don't want to be in the way."

"Oh, please. I'm not going to have you, the new member of our crew, walk in by yourself barely knowing a sole. What kind of boss—slash—hostess would I be? Besides, we can catch up in the car and I can give you the dirt on everyone before we show up. Once we get there, I can introduce you to some key people, also."

"Harper, really. I don't want to impose on your night with Cal."

"You won't be. Besides, if he were listening, it would already have been decided. Six-forty-five and call me with any other questions Gus can't answer...or...you don't want to ask."

"Okay."

"See you then."

I settled in on the sofa in my sleep shorts, sweatshirt, and my hair still in a ponytail, with my latest novel and Gus's afghan thrown over me—as I would any other Saturday evening I was relaxing at home. It was a gray day outside and Gus's house was relaxing. The colors were muted, the sofa was comfy. If the red brick fireplace had a fire, it would be perfect.

I burrowed farther into the sofa and sighed at my latest book boyfriend as he and the lucky heroine were finally…finally giving into the desire they'd been denying for the last two-hundred pages. I bit my lip. It was so worth it. Not for the first time, I wished a man like that really existed, or at the very least, they would be willing to learn from romance novels.

Because, damn. I realized how long it had been since anyone came close to making me feel that desired. That…excited.

I pushed the blanket off me a little. Was it hot in here?

I drifted off with steamy thoughts and heated dreams. However, things cooled as I was pulled back into reality, opening my eyes to find a pair of legs next to me—more specifically, long legs in faded jeans and clearly male anatomy near eye level.

I quickly shot my gaze upward to stop fixating on that area, only to be fixated by his blue eyes. Damn I kept forgetting how strong a pull those bad boys had on me.

"Hey." I sat up so quickly the book fell out of my lap and onto his feet.

A smirk quickly replaced another expression I didn't quite catch as Gus bent down to pick up the book before I could. "What are you reading that has you so flushed, dear Mia?" He studied the cover. "The Billionaire's Contract?" he said, turning the book over to read the back. "You read this?" The tone was judgmental.

And the heat on my cheeks wasn't just embarrassment. It was indignation. "Yes, so."

He side-eyed me and stared at the cover again. I glared and made to grab the book. He stepped away, flipped through the pages, and landed on the area I was reading. Of course, that was the moment his jeans-clad body jarred a memory of the vivid dream I had from the night before—one I didn't wish to relive in his presence.

The heat wasn't just on my face—it was nuclear in all parts of me. I jumped off the couch in hopes that my flush would be considered a form of exertion. Hell, even book shame would be better than him knowing how turned on I was at that moment. I grabbed the book back. "What I read isn't any of your business."

He let out a laugh. "You just surprised me, that's all. I didn't take you as a girl who read—"

"Romance?"

"Well, yeah."

My hand was on my hip now, the book dangling from my hand. "Why not?"

He shrugged and picked up the take-out bag he left on the table. "I don't know. I always took you as more of a non-fiction, biography, or maybe classic literature person."

I rolled my eyes. "You're so...so—"

"What?"

"Wrong. Judgmental. Ignorant." I stalked back to my room with my book.

"Don't be mad." His voice carried down the hall to my room. "I brought egg sandwiches and donuts. I wasn't sure what you wanted."

I put the book on my nightstand, slipping a bookmark in where I left off for later. I took a deep breath, chastising my awakening libido.

I was hungry so my indignation—and my future inappropriate dreams—would have to wait, and I strutted to the kitchen. My Rex Richardson Racing sweatshirt was oversized and hid the fact that I wasn't wearing a bra and long enough to hide my boy shorts. Gus's eyes went to my bare legs when I walked in wearing my puppy slippers.

"Puppy slippers, really?" he said.

"Boy, aren't you judgey today." I sat at the breakfast counter, crossing my legs and purposefully dangling my puppy-slipper-clad foot.

He handed me a wrapped sandwich from the bag. "Mia St. James...dirty romance novels and puppy slippers. Aren't you a contradiction?"

"How do you know it was 'dirty'? And don't use that word, use 'spicy'. How did you know it was spicy?"

He made a cup of coffee for himself and, with his back to me, with a hint of amusement, said, "I could just tell." He turned around, blowing on the hot coffee, and leaning against the counter. His eyes roamed over me—my warm cheeks, my braless chest—and then back at his coffee before adding, "A man can tell."

Could he tell I was braless? Wait…was he actually looking?

He studied his cup. "It's weird…you know—"

"Weird?"

"Having you here."

I shifted in my seat…was he having second thoughts? Maybe being here was too much of an imposition. "Why is that?" I took a bite of the sandwich and then tried hard not to choke.

"Because you're here. In my kitchen, in puppy slippers, and still haven't told me why you ditched me years ago without even a goodbye."

Ah…the uncomfortable discussion that was several years over-due…It took me a few tries to swallow the sandwich. I'd prepared for this…what I would say, the expression on my face, etc. Still, I attempted to deny, "I don't know what you're talking about."

"You left without saying goodbye. We were friends, good friends, I thought. And one day…'poof', you were gone. Not a word—"

I found my voice, and I evened it out. "You knew I was leaving. You knew where I was going. I didn't just disappear—"

"But you did. We got back to campus after we came home for the race that weekend, and you just packed up and left. Not a word."

"You knew I transferred to Michigan. It was an amazing opportunity—"

"You left before the end of the semester."

"I was done with my exams and classes. My professors signed off." I couldn't keep a small amount of defensiveness from creeping into my voice as I stood. I wanted to walk into my room, but he would've just followed me.

"You didn't come to me—"

A small, bitter laugh burst out of me. It was borderline bitchy. "My life didn't revolve around you, Gus."

The words hung in the air, heavy. I had to lighten things up—I didn't want to revisit this time. With my back to him, I closed my eyes. "I didn't mean to ditch you, my father called, and found a last-minute discounted ticket. I knew you had an exam that morning, so I left." I shrugged. "I'm sorry if you took it personally. It wasn't meant to be. I'm not one for goodbyes. You knew I was leaving. We'd discussed it all weekend at the race." I turned, finally resolved in my defense to face him. "I figured that was enough. I'm sorry if I hurt your—"

He held up his hand. "It's fine." His expression was tight. It wasn't fine, but he was leaving it alone.

I let out an audible breath. Dropping my shoulders, I sat back down and took a big bite of my sandwich. "Regardless, I appreciate everything you are doing for me now and I'm sorry if my actions were misunderstood. I am glad to be here." My smile was genuine. My eyes met his warily and I nodded. "And I'm sorry your mom put you on the spot by having me stay here. But it really does help."

He nodded again. "It's not a problem." He put his coffee down and began to clean up the
counter.

Silence fell until I started a new line of conversation.

"I spoke to Harper and I'm going to go to the engagement party with her and Cal this evening." I took another bite of my sandwich.

He nodded, "Sounds good. I'm going to work in the garage in a little while if you want to come take a look."

I stopped chewing and forced myself to swallow half of what was in my mouth so I could get out, "Is the Camaro there?"

A brow lifted in invitation, a quirk on one side of his lips in acknowledgment of the temptation.

Damn. Even the spiciest novels didn't hold a candle to watching Gus bent under the hood of a muscle car…in those jeans—

He turned his back on me to pick up a donut, and I took that opportunity to subtly fan myself with the neckline of my sweatshirt. Was it warm in here?

I had to admit…with this kind of view on a daily basis, I won't need spicy novels for quite a while.

7

GUS

It was an uncommonly mild November evening, even for Charlotte. And I was enjoying the large veranda, leaning against an outside bar, nursing a scotch. I took a sip of the drink, not allowing CJ to ruffle my feathers, which was her mission in life.

"Did you scare your date off already?" my best friend said, joining me.

I pointed out Kellie, surrounded by Mr. Merrick, Junior, and some other men from Merrick and their top sponsors. "Nah, she's just working the room." As always.

"So, how's the roomie?" CJ said.

I shrugged. "Fine. Are you going to run her out of town or will she last through Christmas?"

She turned around, mimicking my stance, facing the veranda doors, peering inside and people-watching with me. "She's cool."

That was a high compliment. I lifted an eyebrow and stared down at CJ.

"What?" She gave me her side-eye stare.

I shook my head. "Nothing. I gave up on you being able to make friends with other women."

Her backhand snaked out and connected with my midsection. I let out an "oaf" and scolded myself. I knew better.

CJ gestured to the crowded room with her beer bottle. "I'm a friendly person. I can be nice."

I just nodded because it was her party. I was just kidding. CJ had a heart of gold under a tough exterior built up out of years of being cut down by absent parents, the trauma of losing her first love, being bullied and stalked by a vindictive nemesis, and having people from every facet of her life telling her she wasn't good enough. It was why there were very few people she trusted, and she was fiercely loyal to those she did.

"Seriously, though, are you good with Mia being at your place?" she glanced at her beer bottle before taking a sip, lacing a casual tone in her question, but it was the reason she sought me out—to check on me.

"Yeah. She just moved in, so I haven't had a chance to get on her nerves yet."

We had a good time this afternoon in my garage. I didn't usually like having anyone in my sanctum. It was my Zen room. A place I went to clear my head and relax. But today was fun. We put on some music, and she sat propped on the worktable as I showed off the Camaro Z28 I rebuilt and asked questions about what I'd already worked on, replaced, and what was on my punch list to do next.

I had forgotten her father owned a shop back in Chicago, and she was more than familiar with the restoration business. Even dabbled in it as a hobby herself.

Before thinking about it, I offered to her, "There are a few auctions coming up this year. I like to check them out when I'm in town…if you're interested."

Mia had paused before nodding her head, "Yeah. That would be fun. Maybe you could help me find a new project once I get settled—something for me to mess with in my downtime?"

We talked about what kind of cars she worked on before—mostly domestic. What she'd be looking at. "You know…I'd always wanted to restore one of those old Bronco trucks—"

CJ shook me out of the memory of this afternoon's conversation, but not before I realized how I was looking forward to helping her track down one of those. I'd reach out to some of my contacts this week.

I finished my drink to hide my distraction.

"We...I appreciate you doing this. I know it's cramping your style, but don't screw this up for us, okay." She glanced up at me and then back at the sea of people, "We need her to stick around."

"What do you mean?" My good mood dimmed. "What do you think I'm going to do? Leave the toilet seat up one too many times?"

CJ rolled her eyes. "No—"

"Well," I turned toward her but continued to lean my elbow on the bar, trying to maintain my casual attitude. "What makes you think I would be the one to run her off and not the person with a record of running off most of her crew."

CJ wasn't feeling casual anymore. She straightened. "I don't run off my crew. They leave when they can't handle how high the bar is set."

I threw back my head and forced a laugh. "Is that what you call it?"

Her lips thinned, and the color raised on her face. Screw it. She started this argument, and I had a fairly good idea of where this was going.

"Yeah, but I'm not living with her," she gritted her teeth, "and I don't have a history of having women fall in love with me and then break their hearts." She walked away and toward an opening at the other end of the bar, flagging down a bartender.

I stomped behind, gritting my teeth once I was in front of her again. "First of all, I'm seeing someone. I don't cheat. I'm always monogamous."

She rolled her eyes and harrumphed. She grabbed a beer from the bartender and circled me until my back was facing the bar.

I held out my fingers. "Second, I never give any of the women I date any expectations, I'm always up front with them, and I never set out to break their hearts." It's why I only recently started dating Kellie because I knew she wasn't the hearts-and-flowers type of girl. She was all about her career. "Third—" and this is the one I needed her to understand. "Mia and I aren't like that. We have never been."

Grady's shadow fell over us as he walked over, snaking an arm around his fiancée.

"And why is that?" CJ's hand covered his, but she wasn't letting go. She was digging in. "She's beautiful. She's smarter than—"

Grady, sensing the tension between us, cut in, kissing her cheek and holding her back against his chest. "Hey there! I was told you aren't milling around enough. Harper told me to come get you before her mom gets her hands on you again."

He waved down a waiter for some of the appetizers on his tray— probably to stuff in our mouths before we started to make a scene.

"I was just asking Gus why he never went after Mia. Since they're 'friends'." She mockingly used freaking air quotes.

"I can be friends with women, CJ. I'm friends with you and Harper, aren't I?"

The waiter displayed his tray and Grady stood between us to grab a few things. CJ craned around him, trying to still stare me down, which, given the size discrepancy between the two of them and him holding her was slightly entertaining to watch. She opened her mouth, gearing up to start in with me again. "You practically grew up with us—"

"Charlotte, honey, have you tried a mini crab cake?" Grady sweetly shoved one in her mouth.

What she didn't point out, what both of them were gracious enough not to mention, was when Grady came to town, I had confessed to wanting a chance to take our friendship further. My loyalty to my deceased friend, Tommy, her first love—was tangled up with feelings I thought I had for her. There were blurred lines, and for a little while and I thought I'd been jealous over their chemistry and obvious feelings for each other.

I never made a move on CJ in the years since Tommy's death, and in hindsight, I realize it was because I never really wanted to. I was waiting for her to become more to me—and she didn't.

Seeing her with Grady now, I'm so thankful I never made that mistake, and never risked our friendship.

CJ chewed the crab cake, shaking her finger at me, silently berating me, and I crossed my arms over my chest, bracing for when she swallowed and continued.

An arm snaked around from behind, "Gus, babe, I need a drink," Kellie said. "Can you get me a dirty martini, Grey Goose, and two olives?" She pulled me back, opening our growing circle of people and breaking the intimate argument CJ and I had been having.

I pulled Kellie forward, drawing her into the group farther. Kellie's arm wrapped around my waist, and she leaned in to nuzzle herself under my neck.

Mia was walking toward us, so deep in conversation with Cooper Sullivan, Grady's long-time best friend and best man, she almost ran into Grady and CJ. She threw her head back and laughed at something Cooper said right before they noticed us.

"Sure. I'll get it for you. But first, I want you to meet Mia St. James and Cooper Sullivan." I motioned to Mia to draw her attention from the amusing Cooper. "Mia is the friend from college I told you about. She's going to work for Merlo and staying with me until her house is ready."

Kellie straightened, but her smile didn't falter as she studied Mia and Cooper, standing close together as if they *were* together. She reached out her hand, maintaining contact with me and shook both of theirs, exchanging greetings.

"Gus, I have to say you are the first man I have known that has as many women friends as you do—it's a good thing I'm a secure person," she gave an elegant laugh and waved her hand as if dismissing any jealousy, she could possibly have.

A glance at Mia told me nothing of what she was thinking. She just hid her expression behind her copper mug, discovering it was empty.

"I think Mia needs another 'Jackass,'" Cooper said with his hand seemingly supporting her on her back. Mia smiled more radiantly than I thought I'd ever seen her before. Definitely, since she'd been back, and I was more than curious about what caused it. As if it was their own inside joke that he tossed over to the rest of us, "They are Moscow

45

Mules made with local ingredients. The bar named them Charlotte Mules—but I shortened them to Jackass."

He winked at our "Charlotte Jean," aka CJ, as if it was in honor of her.

She gave him the one finger salute, but I was too busy studying the position of Cooper's hand in relation to, what I think, was Mia's intake of the Jackass drinks.

"Oh, I think I've had my share of those," she muttered, tilting her copper cup.

I turned to flag down the bartender again. "When did you get back in town, Cooper? I thought you were in Chicago?"

"I was. But I wouldn't miss my boy's engagement party." He grabbed Grady's shoulder with his other hand, shaking him. "Besides, as his best man, it's my job to make sure he doesn't do anything to mess this up."

Grady brushed off his arm. "Keep it up, and you won't be in the wedding."

I gave the bartender the orders and watched as Cooper engaged Mia in private conversation. Both making the other smile and laugh. I hadn't seen her laugh like that since she'd been in town.

I should be happy he was pulling that out of her. It reminded me of a younger, doe-eyed Mia. She wasn't doe-eyed anymore. There was a sharpness to her now. But as she laughed with Cooper, I did see her relax more than she had with me.

Maybe she had had too many of those drinks and this was her loosening up. I should probably keep an eye on her. Of course, Cooper was a good guy, and I knew she was safe with him...but—

"I couldn't be his bitch boy forever," Cooper said, nudging CJ with his shoulder, his eyes settling on me, but he was still addressing her. "That's your job now."

CJ glanced around. "These guys like to believe Grady has calmed me. And that I'm under his spell—"

"Nah, CJ, we know better." Cooper leaned down to Mia and said, "I was Grady's former babysitter before CJ decided to take on the task of leashing—I mean—maturing him."

Mia graced him with another mega-watt smile.

"So you're going to work with these crazy women?" Cooper's eyes were taking in everything about her. Put your tongue back in your mouth Cooper...God, the man was too obvious.

"We're indoctrinating her—so don't go telling stories outside of the circle yet. We haven't done the ceremony that will bind her to us," CJ deadpanned.

Mia didn't miss a beat and fired back, "So, is there a safe word or something I can still use to back out?"

"Yeah, it's boys rule, and girls drool," Grady said. CJ looked over her shoulder, elbowing her fiancé. They shared a look, and CJ's face immediately transformed—softened.

His eyes were locked on her's, and there was no way anyone couldn't see the love the two had for each other. Not lust or chemistry. A true bond—teasing friendship, respect, and the need to just be near each other. He held up her hand and kissed it softly, then said, "Come on, Charlotte." Grady was the only one able to get away with using CJ's given first name. "We must mingle." And he led her away without protest.

I wondered if I'd find that. If I'd want to find that with someone. Seeing those private moments between two people who were meant to be together sometimes made me wonder if I was better off alone instead of holding out hope of finding it.

"I never thought I'd see the day..." Cooper said, as the couple walked off hand-in-hand. "What about you, G-man?"

I nodded, "Yep." I took a sip of my drink. "But happy for them."

"What? Of the two of them settling down?" Mia said.

Cooper nodded. "Yes, thank God, because I was getting too old to manage the drama that followed Grady."

Mia gave a little laugh and nodded to Cooper, "Oh, so you're that friend. The responsible one. The designated driver. The Debbie Downer who was always thinking about the next-day consequences."

He rubbed his hand over his chest and winced. "Jeez, you make me sound like a very boring person."

She smiled more, pretty much cutting me out of the conversation, "Nah, you just sound like me."

He beamed with satisfaction. "Finally, someone with a level head." He threw his head back to thank the heavens. "I've been waiting all my life for you."

"You're laying it on a bit thick, man." Both glanced over as if reminded I was even there. I finished my drink, ready to get another. That's when I noticed that Kellie had disappeared. Guess I should've noticed that.

Cooper, again ignoring my presence, closed the distance with Mia. "I wasn't expecting to meet someone like you this evening."

"Oh, now I see it." Mia leaned back and crossed my arms.

"What?" Cooper's smile made me question just how much I trusted him with Mia.

"You've been hanging around Grady long enough to pick up on his legendary sweet talk."

Yeah, I better break this up. He is a student of a master after all, and she's still getting over a break-up that was obviously bad enough for her to move out of state.

8

GUS

Just how many drinks had Mia had? Was she making rational decisions? "Mia, are Cal and Harper driving you home, or can we give you a ride?"

Her smile fell. "What?"

I shifted. "Do you need a ride home?"

"Now?"

"Well, soon?"

"You want me to ride home with you and Kellie?" Her head dipped, and she looked up at me as if I had three heads.

I shrugged, seeing the miscalculation and how ridiculous it must sound. "Well...if you need a ride."

She put up her hand and there was a slight drawl in her voice that wasn't there earlier—say, when she was sober. "No, thank you. I'm good."

"It's fine, Gus. I'll drive her home."

He must have read my thoughts because he added, "She's staying with you, right?" His message to me was he did plan on bringing her home. To my home—not his home.

I opened my mouth for the diatribe I had ready to shoot out.

"That would be great, Coop." Coop…when did she start calling him Coop? "Last thing I want is to be a third wheel with any of these love birds. It's bad enough I'll be in the same house as them this evening." She held her hand to her mouth, and mock whispered, "Guess I better find my noise-canceling headphones."

"You could always stay at my place—"

"No." The word was so vehement the people around us all turned to stare in our direction.

Kellie chose that time to hook her arm in mine. "What's going on over here?"

Mia, initially stunned by my outburst, cocked out her hip and leveled her eyes at

me, filled with disbelief and amusement as she answered Kellie. "I just told Gus that Cooper would take care of getting me home tonight—"

Cooper's grin was of the shit-eating kind, and he rocked back on his feet, hands in his pockets, proof he spent more than a decade as wingman to Grady McBane.

I compared him to his mentor, who stood almost the same exact way, but with a sense of amused pride about ten yards away, watching over the scene. "I offered to let Mia stay at my place so you and Gus could have your privacy this evening—"

"I just meant it wouldn't be necessary…" I concentrated on reining in the frustration I was wielding. Who cares if Cooper is hitting on Mia? She's a grown woman. In a sexy dress. With a broken heart. Staying at my place. She's my responsibility. That's why I'm frustrated. Because I wasn't sure of my boundaries—or my responsibilities—here.

Kellie patted Cooper's arm as a flirtatious southern debutante, "You're so considerate, but we stay at my place, anyway. His bachelor pad isn't exactly my taste."

Mia cocked her head and flicked her hair over her shoulder, studying me. "Good, that's settled." She turned to Cooper, looping her arm through his. "I'd love to catch a ride with you, Cooper. Let these couples have their night together. You and I can have all the fun."

Fun? What fun?

Kellie pulled out her phone and checked the time. "We should probably go, Gus. I have my trainer coming tomorrow morning at 7:00."

I continued to glare a hole in Cooper's back as he and Mia walked by the four pairs of eyes that were watching everything and studying me. As if watching from center court at a tennis match, CJ, Harper, Grady, and Cal stood aside as Cooper's hand went to Mia's back as he escorted her across the room and then back at me. I tried to school my expression, but it was too late. Harper and CJ narrowed their eyes. Grady and Cal exchanged a look.

She was new to the city. She was my friend. She'd been drinking, and she better make it home in one piece.

"Okay, that's fine." I put my hand on Kellie's slim lower back. "Let's go."

"So I have a conference in LA next week. We should pull out our calendars and see what we can match up," Kellie said—practical, straightforward. We were pulling out of the parking lot in the Camaro. I rarely drove this car except on special occasions. Mia would've appreciated it. She loved just sitting in it this afternoon, looking under the hood and listening to everything I did to rescue it—but all of it was lost on Kellie.

Lost in my memories as I made my way through the tangle of streets, Kellie touched my knee to get my attention. "I have a corporate dinner for some clients on Tuesday next week. I was hoping you could join us. It's with Charisma Auto Supplies, and I know they'd love to meet you. Maybe you could even snag another sponsorship out of it."

This was the one thing that sucked about dating someone who ran with industry professionals. Ultimately, I was trotted out like a prized stallion. It sounded arrogant. You'd be surprised how people would react, not just to a driver but to anyone connected to a successful race team. While Kellie may not be impressed with my job title, she knew some of the men she works with were. It was not lost on me that she knew how to take advantage of it. Up until I started dating her, she worked on hotel and cosmetic accounts.

I'm not an idiot.

I shifted in my seat. My elbow rested on the door and I leaned into it. "We'll see. I have to check if I'm in town," I said, turning onto the highway leading back to her side of town.

"I thought Tuesday was a safe day. I thought that was a down day before resetting for the next weekend."

"Yeah, but sometimes I have my sponsorship commitments scheduled by PR and marketing."

We were at a light when her phone dinged and she pulled it out of her purse. She focused on the screen but was still seeking more of a commitment. "Can you check for me?" She dropped the volume of her voice, making it raspier and more seductive.

I briefly closed my eyes to stop them from rolling. This was becoming routine.

But that was the point. We'd been dating for a few months, except for a bit of dog and pony show occasionally, we got along great. Sex had been decent. She's intelligent, respected, and holds her own in any crowd. I usually enjoyed her company.

I reached for her hand, squeezed it, and said, "I'll see what I can do." Then put the car in gear and started to pull away from the light.

She gave me her beauty pageant smile and returned to her phone. "So, tell me about this roommate situation. Who is she and how long will she be around?"

"What? Mia?" Startled by the abrupt question, it took me a moment to catch up. "Oh, someone I know from college days. A friend who helped me get into engineering school. She was just hired as a lead engineer at Merlo and needed a place to stay while waiting for the house she bought to be available."

"But why stay with you?"

"My mom. She arranged it."

That stopped the typing. She put her phone in her lap and turned in her seat to face me. "Doesn't your mom know we are seeing each other?"

"Yes, of course." I held up my hand before this evolved into a "Doesn't your mother like me?" question. Because, truthfully, my mother doesn't have an opinion. Which I think is worse than not liking her. She is apathetic to her because she doesn't think she will be sticking around. Man, my friends and family have so much faith in me.

"Mia and I are old friends. We have never been anything more than friends. Like Harper and CJ kind of friends."

"So you never…"

I shook my head before she finished. "No, it's not like that with her."

Kellie sat still a moment, staring out the front window as I wove in and out of traffic. She waved off a thought and said, "Yeah, she's not your type." Dismissing any thought of Mia and me together and returned to her phone.

"Harper," she pointed her perfectly manicured finger at me while still holding her phone. "She's your type. If Harper was staying with you, you and I would have a problem. But…" Kellie let it hang while digging through her purse.

"But what?" I gripped the steering wheel a bit harder, wishing she'd let it go.

"You managed to just be friends with Harper—who is so gorgeous, I would put the moves on her myself—but you never even kissed her." She shook her head. "I don't know why I even brought it up." She waved me off. "I guess it was the idea of your season starting—all the young girls throwing themselves at you—it's got my green-eyed monster rearing its head and I don't share well. But I'll be good. I'm sorry I was being ridiculous."

———

"Good morning, Sunshine," I said to Mia, who was curled up in one of my oversized chairs in the family room, as I walked in the door after my run.

"Really? You're one of those guys?"

I walked to the fridge and used the water dispenser to fill my water bottle. "What does that mean—those guys? If you mean incredibly fit with amazing abs and a fantastic ass. Then, yes. I am one of those guys. Sorry, though, you'll have to take my word." I winked at her.

"Ugh. It's too damn early for your ego," she said, readjusting herself on the chair with a messy ponytail, oversized, well-worn sweatshirt that dropped to her thighs encased in a pair of yoga pants, and those damn chunky puppy slippers. A pair of dark glasses were perched on top of her head.

She blew on her large cup as she snuggled deeper into the chair, laid her head back, closed her eyes, and sighed.

"Did you have fun last night?"

"Yes, I did, actually." She lifted her head slowly as if it cost her neck a great deal of effort and slowly opened her eyes to me. "Maybe a bit too much."

"You weren't here when I got home." It popped out of my mouth before I thought too much about it.

"Yes." She pulled the glasses down and studied her phone.

"Well..."

"Well, what?" Her brow furrowed in concentration, and then she began biting her bottom lip.

"The party was over soon after I left, wasn't it?"

"Uh-huh."

"Where did you go?"

"Huh?" She began typing.

"Mia, did Cooper bring you home last night or how did you get home?" Irritation seeped into my tone, even though I knew he did. His truck pulled up an hour and a half after I got home from dropping Kellie off. I made an excuse to Kellie about not being sure if Mia had her key.

I wouldn't say she was happy, but it was to Kellie's credit that she didn't seem too upset by me leaving to run home and check on Mia. And shouldn't she have been?

"Gus, what's wrong?" She tilted her phone down, peering over her glasses to study me, reminding me of how we used to talk in college.

I finished my water and turned back into the kitchen, presumably to fill it up again. "Nothing, I just wanted to make sure you made it home, okay?"

She soft-footed it into the kitchen and was standing behind me. "I have an older brother and a nosey father, and I know when I'm being interrogated." She crossed her arms over her chest, pulled off the glasses, and hitched out her hip. "Yes, Cooper drove me home. We stopped to get something to eat because he was starving and didn't eat much at the party. We got to talking and then he drove me here."

I turned my back. Feeling ridiculous. Cooper was a good guy. I knew this. I nodded. "Okay. Good."

A ping went off on her phone, she pulled the glasses down again, studying her screen. "That little bugger," she said to the phone, but the amusement in her eyes brightened her whole face, awakening her.

"What?" I said. I came behind her and peeked over her shoulder to see an app opened that looked like a grid of a Scrabble board.

"Cooper showed me this Word Scramble game," she said as she played around with a slew of letters on a virtual board.

"What's that?"

"It's the board game where you have seven letters to make up words on the board for points," she said, the tip of her tongue sticking out just enough to see the edge of it. "And Cooper is killing me, but just wait until I get the hang of it."

She turned, forgetting my interrogation, and headed back into the living room, burying herself in the oversized chair and curling up with a blanket, a ghost of a smile lingering. A ping sounded, and her shoulders shook with a slight chuckle.

Me and my nosiness were completely forgotten.

"I don't have much to eat. I was thinking of going to the grocery store later. Want to come? Maybe I could show you around town a bit since you are starting Monday?"

There was a delay of silence.

"Mia?" I peeked back into the room and found her face hidden by the phone.

She waved a hand absently. "Yeah, that sounds good...what time?"

"Maybe an hour?"

"Okay. I need to take a shower. An hour works." And then to herself…or maybe to the phone, she yelled, "That's not even a word."

She was making friends. That's what she's supposed to do. I shook my head, not understanding where the protectiveness was coming from —but this whole thing with Cooper was very inconvenient.

9

MIA

We arrived at the Harris grocery store at the worst time of the week—a Sunday before a predicted storm. The news reported rain coming and dropping temperatures overnight, which meant ice. Lots and lots of ice. "Let's just grab one cart and get what we absolutely need for the next few days," Gus said. In and out. It's only going to get worse, and I still want to make it to the liquor store before it closes.

We walked in and the store was packed.

"They do know it's not Armageddon, right?"

"Chicago may have snow, but," he narrowed his eyes at me, "you know we don't do cold down here very often. Stop ruining our freak-out party."

I held up my hands. "All right, what do we need for the end of the world—besides milk and toilet paper?"

"Carbs and junk food."

"Now you're talking my language." I smiled. "How about some cheese and crackers too? I'm in the mood for a great bottle of wine."

He leaned over the shopping cart and said, "Okay, divide and conquer. Hand me your list." He looked it over and tore it in half. "Head to dairy and get cheese and milk, and then get to the bakery. I'll grab chips, crackers, and whatever else is on this list..." and then he paused. "Except this. You're going to have to get this." He pointed, and his lips clamped shut.

"Tampons," I said, a smile fighting to get through. "They are called tampons, Gus."

"Yes, I know what they're called, and I also know there are like fifty different kinds, and I'm not going to spend time going through and trying to find the right ones when you can probably pick them out by the color of the box from a racetrack length away."

"You're such a guy…"

"Yes, I am, thank you." He literally took a pen and yanked my sheet out of my hand and wrote tampons on my list, crossing it off his. When I stared at him, he shrugged, "You don't want to forget them."

I shook my head and tried to hold off laughing. But, damn, it was hard because there was a tinge of blush on his cheeks, and he was kind of adorable.

We stormed the aisles like a scavenger hunt, meeting back up and tossing our treasures in the cart. "We should get some veggies, you know—"

He waved me off. "Yeah, yeah. Okay. But that's not very fun."

I returned from picking up some cereal with a lollipop in my mouth and handed him a bag with a small hole ripped at the top. I wanted to see if he remembered.

He stared at my mouth as I pulled out the small ball on a stick. It was my favorite—watermelon. He studied the bag and raised an eyebrow at me. "Dum-Dums?"

I shrugged and popped it back in my mouth. When we were in college, and he annoyed me by not showing up or being late to an arranged time, my passive-aggressive self would stick a Dum-Dums in my mouth to stop me from saying things I knew were on the tip of my tongue. When it didn't work, or he really pissed me off, I threw them at him. It was my way of communicating my displeasure.

Eventually, he came to hate the sight of them. Which only fueled my fire. I'd leave them

in his backpack, in his shoes, and on his pillow if we studied in his dorm… It became a challenge to see where I could get them. I even had his professor give him one after he took his final calculus exam—Professor Weber was a good sport, and I was one of his favorite students.

"Figured I'd stock up. I'm sure you'll earn them while I'm here."

He let out a beleaguered sigh, tossed the bag in the car, wagged a finger at me, and shook his head. "You…you're definitely going to keep me on my toes, aren't you?"

I shrugged and popped the lollipop in my mouth. "If you behave, I'll give you a cookie."

"You know you're the one staying at *my* house." He raised his voice so I could hear him as I walked away, turning to the next aisle. "I'm the one doing the favor this time."

My back was to him, and once I was out of sight, I allowed my shoulders to shake with the amusement, the warmth, and the fun I was having with him.

It's like we fell back in step from the camaraderie we had before. And as he jogged to catch up with me, a warmth spread through me. It was easy to get swept back into that easy connection we had.

Until my brain replayed the words that chipped at my heart all those years ago and I slowed my pace down the aisle. I never thought Gus would ever feel more than friendship with me. I never thought he'd be attracted to me—I was okay with it.

Fine, I was a smart girl and proud of it. I was at school for an education—not an "MRS" degree. In other words, I wasn't there to find a husband. I had goals and dreams. Gus's goals and dreams aligned with mine—to be in the racing industry and to work on monster engines.

I didn't need to be friends with someone like Gus—he was Mr. Popular. I was Ms. Smarty-pants. He needed to grow up, and I needed to move on. So, I did. We both did.

I shook off the thought. I was older and wiser, and he was going to be part of my life for the foreseeable future. Racing wasn't just an industry. It was a community, and Gus was helping me out. I could let that one hurtful moment go.

Friends forgave—especially since he had no idea why I never said goodbye. He was clueless as to how he even hurt me.

Once work started and I got my own place, we wouldn't be around each other so much. Now is a good time to re-establish whatever it was we had—see if it could stand the test of adulthood. Once I moved out, we could maintain that level of friendship, hopefully.

For now, it was fun to see how playful he was. He was a great distraction and lifted my mood. This was the Gus I remembered from college—still a young boy at heart. When I turned the corner, he came flying out from four aisles down and yelled, "I scored TP!"

Then he straightened, scratched his head, and came walking toward me, his voice loud enough to be heard from three aisles over. "Hey, babe, are you still baking bread down there? Should we pick up some of that Monistat stuff?"

I sucked on the lollipop, ignoring the stares and a few snickers from some pretty twenty-somethings who'd been eyeing him. Not missing a beat. "No, I'm good," I waved him off, walking toward the cookies. Then, from the other end of the aisle, I turned to him and snapped my fingers, "Oh, wait! Why don't you grab some of the anti-fungal, jock-itch cream…remember you ran out."

He rubbed a hand down his face. Dropped his head and walked away, his fist crumpling his list.

As we stood in line, a beautiful blonde was pulling out all the stops to get his attention—I even saw her pulling her shirt down to show more cleavage. He bent into a cooler to get out a bottle of water, and she bit her lip as she unabashedly stared at his butt. I found it amusing until his cocky smile made its appearance right before he opened the water and began to drink it as if he were posing on a beach.

I mean, what if I was his girlfriend—or his wife?

I turned and, with the biggest, most sincere eyes, said, "They didn't have the condoms I got last time. You know, the smaller ones…I think they're called snug-fit. Maybe we can special order them.

"But I did pick up your Viagra prescription," I patted the white pharmacy bag in my purse, which actually contained my birth control pills.

Gus's face turned beet red, and his chest started to convulse as he choked on the water. I leaned over, hitting his back with all the empathy I could muster, and loudly whispered, "I'm sure it will help this time." Water shot out of his nose and mouth, running down his chin and spraying everywhere—including toward the woman eye-screwing him in the check-out line.

The blonde with boobs stepped aside before it hit her, which was a pity. Because if he'd sprayed her, it would've been epic enough to make me tinkle a bit in my pants.

Although a wet t-shirt was probably something she could work to her advantage.

"I'm so sorry. I—" With watery eyes, he squinted at the people surrounding us, unable to speak while coughing up water. He wiped his face with his sleeve, glaring a shot at me that would've maimed me if it had been loaded. But buried beneath the embarrassment was a hint of amusement. He wiped his hands down his wet t-shirt, now molded to his chest, drawing even more attention. Once he regained his ability to breathe, the corner of his mouth twitched, and his glare held amusement and acceptance of a challenge I unknowingly threw down.

"You go clean up, babe." I waved him off.

He walked backward, not breaking eye contact with me. The intensity of his stare, even with the tight smile that was slowly inching across his face, briefly caused me to rethink the door I may have opened.

After all, how fragile was Gus's ego these days? Ah, screw it. If he couldn't take a joke, then he needed to be taken down a notch or two.

"Don't worry. I got this." I winked at him, putting the items on the check-out belt, and I didn't care what it cost me. You couldn't put a price tag on how priceless that was.

10

MIA

"I called to wish you luck on your first day of school," Shyla's voice was a welcome distraction. The storm wasn't as bad as earlier predicted, but the cold, gray sky, mixed with my best friend's voice, had me considering how far from of Chicago I was as I pulled into the Merlo Motorsports parking lot.

"It really does feel that way," I said quietly.

"But before I give you your pep talk about first-day jitters, how was the party this weekend, and did you meet any cute southern boys?

"I'm not looking for any cute southern boys," I said, pulling into a spot. "I am still dealing with my last mistake. I can't afford to deal with a new one."

Her impatience was laced through the sigh that reverberated from the car speaker. "Bygones. The best way to put him behind you is to put a better man under you."

I smiled at Shyla's boldness and then searched around my car, concerned someone
would've heard her through my windows.

"I don't think I'm quite ready for that either." I gathered my things and checked my purse.

"Okay, you have enough eye candy at home to keep you satisfied, I guess...speaking of Gus—"

"Were we speaking of Gus?" I put in my earbuds and waited for them to connect to my phone, then turned off my car, catching the end of her question.

"—and tell me about his girlfriend."

"Beautiful, of course. Tall, brunette, leggy, fabulous curves. Ambitious and confident—seems perfect for him," I said succinctly and objectively. What I didn't include was how much she rubbed me the wrong way. She was dismissive, snobby, and self-absorbed. What woman would let her man have another woman stay in his house? A woman who didn't think she had any competition—yeah, that didn't sting.

Climbing out of the car, I was aware of a few other employees walking from the parking lot.

Not wanting to discuss Gus's love life anymore and focus on the newer challenge in front of me, I juggled my shoulder bag, my travel mug and surveyed my surroundings. "This is it. I'm going in..."

"You'll be fine."

"God, I've got all those damn first-day-of-school insecurities," I whispered under my breath to her. "Are they going to like me? Am I good enough to be here?" Only to my best friend Shyla would I trust enough to unload these fears.

"These are some of the top people in the industry. You wouldn't be there if they didn't believe you belonged. Remember that. Take in the energy and feed off of it."

I stood by the corporate sign, staring at the building, taking it all in and reminding myself how I got there. If it wasn't for Keith betraying me...I may not have had this opportunity. To work with some of the top people—no—top women in the industry. To be part of something special and maybe even mentor other women who want to make it in this profession.

"Mia?"

"Yeah..." It came out as a breath.

"You've got this."

"Yeah."

"Call me later."

"Okay."

Just as I disconnected and pulled out my earbuds, a voice came up behind me, "You gonna stand out here all day, or actually go inside and get to work?"

Jackson Grove sauntered up to me in jeans and a collared shirt. His white hair was under a Merlo ballcap.

The legendary Jackson Grove was my boss. He came out of retirement just to work with this team. And he wanted me. I wouldn't be here if he hadn't approved. No one worked on his crew without his approval.

That had to mean something.

"Yes, sir. Just taking it in." The large Merlo Motorsports sign stood in front of us, looming glass doors beyond it, drawing your attention to the people milling around inside, already starting their day.

Jacks stood next to me, studying the building. The building wasn't what was impressive.

It was an industrial building with a large glass front that showcased the open, two-story lobby. No—it wasn't an architectural wonder. It was what it housed and what it represented. He stood next to me, slipped his hands in his pockets, gave me about five seconds, then said, "Are you planning to go in anytime soon? It's too cold for these old bones."

I shook myself out of it and said, "Yes, of course. Sorry."

Jacks held the door while I walked in, "Lucia, this is Mia. She's starting today. I'll send her to HR later. Can you let them know she's coming?"

"Yes, Mr. Jacks." The middle-aged receptionist jumped on the phone.

"I've told them to just call me Jacks," he grumbled, throwing up a hand, "but they never listen."

He walked me over to the stairs leading to the second floor. "HR is up those stairs and down the hall to the left. The garage and work-rooms are that way." He pointed to the hallway behind the stairs that led to a large set of double doors. I'll get you set up in an office and such."

I nodded, my eyes darting around.

"Sweetheart, you look like you're about to bolt." He clamped his hand on my shoulder. "You'll be fine. There's nothing to be worried about." Jacks's tone matched the concern on his face. "I mean, you did want to work here, didn't you?"

I held up my hand as if he were going to rescind the offer, and I needed to stop him. "Yes, of course. Yes, yes." I shook my head. "I don't know what I'm going on about. It's just a few weeks ago this wasn't on my radar."

His kind eyes studied me. "Darlin', I know you left your last job, not on the best of terms." He hooked his fingers through his belt loops and rocked back on his heels. "I consider myself a bit of an expert when it comes to being a good judge of character. It's why I dragged my sorry ass out of retirement and came to work for these girls, young enough to be my granddaughters." He shook his head, smiling. "Oh, people thought I was off my rocker when I said I was going to do this. Some people even went to talk with my wife about possible senility— can you imagine?

"But I had a feeling about these girls." He held his hand up to make the pronouncement, "And I'm always right about these things."

He leaned forward and nudged me with his elbow, then whispered, "You belong here. They may think you do. But I know you do." And he winked at me.

As if given a shot of warm adrenaline. This man, who resembled more of an everyday granddad than a motivational life coach, had me straightening my back and realizing that my legs were feeling more solid beneath me.

"Come on, they're waiting for us upstairs, then we can get you sorted with HR and stuff." Without saying much more, he led me up a set of open stairs and down a stark hallway to a conference room where people were milling about and taking their seats.

"Everyone," Jacks said, nodding his head toward Harper, who sat in the middle of the oblong table. "This here is Ms. St. James. She's our new team member and will be our new lead engineer." Jacks, being the old southern gentleman he was, pulled out a chair for me across the table from Harper before taking the one next to me.

There was a chorus of both half-hearted greetings as everyone sat down with their coffee and papers.

Harper started, her posture straight, her voice strong and confident as she took a moment to turn to me. "In season, we like to have a weekly meeting to discuss the previous race and where each team is with their set-ups for the upcoming schedule. Since we are a few weeks out from the beginning of the season, we will also be discussing personnel and logistics."

Each member gave their name and what areas of responsibilities they covered—some were rather long-winded, and Harper would subtly cut them off and move along to the next one.

I would nod and smile at each of them, trying to memorize their name and department. We had the same meetings at my last company. I wasn't included in those meetings, although Keith was. He convinced me I wasn't much of a managerial type but more of a hands-on person and he was more suited for that role. Yeah. That should've been a red flag. Hindsight 20-20, live and learn, and all that.

My shoulders were tensing up to my ears as the thought of Keith was a flashback I didn't need at the moment, and I rolled my head to loosen the tension.

"Mia, why don't you tell the team what you did at Triple R, and also detail your involvement with the Next Generation Car that was just released."

That made some heads turn. There were a few raised eyebrows and even a poorly disguised glare.

"Well, my involvement wasn't—"

Harper turned to the group. "Not only was Mia a senior engineer with Triple R, but she was also asked by the stock car association to consult on the Next Gen Car and make recommendations for improvements."

She ran down my credentials and former position with Rex Richardson Racing—also known as Triple R—and my involvement in the design and development of the series next generation just released —also referred to as the Next Gen Car.

As the term stock car suggested, all teams drove the same car that met strict regulations—making the racing more dependent on the driver's talents and the team's ability to pull out whatever edge it could out of essentially carbon copy machines. It was why stock car racing was so heavily dependent on highly educated engineers—like me. And Gus.

Not comfortable with all the eyes on me, I fell into my habit of downplaying. "It was mostly simulator work. I gathered information from crashes our team experienced and from other teams, and worked with a group to find ways to make the driver safer within the car. Taking information from previous crashes—like the one Grady was lucky to walk away from at Talladega last year—we found ways to move the driver more center to the car and the roll bars on the doors farther away from the driver. It also led to adding the bumpers back on the cars with specialized foam under them to help with shock absorption."

"And this, all while still being a senior engineer? That's impressive," Jacks said. "They must have had some time on their hands?" He smiled at the table.

"Well, it had been information I'd already been compiling, so I was able to apply the same program to other teams who worked with us," I said.

"And she's modest. Not something you usually find in someone in this industry," Harper said, threading a pen through her hands. "Well, regardless, that forward thinking and being on the inside of the Next Gen car design, will definitely benefit us." She shuffled some papers and said under her breath. "Plus, a lack of self-promotion would be refreshing."

11

MIA

After Jacks handed me off to the chief of the car to familiarize myself with the status of their cars, the data they accrued with each of them, and the set-ups they ran in last season, it was time for lunch.

Harper popped in, "Come on, new girl, you're with me today for lunch."

I shot out of my seat, surprised at the offer. "You don't need to do that, Harper—err…" All eyes were on me as I used a familiar tone and Harper's first name. Maybe I should address her as Ms. Merrick? "I mean, Ms. Merrick—"

She gave me her hand. "Don't you dare call me that. Only people I don't like call me Ms. Merrick."

I grinned, more at ease than I had been all day, "Okay, Harper."

"What about people who don't like you?" CJ came up behind me.

"Everyone likes me. It's you they have an issue with," Harper replied, pulling out her phone as it dinged. She glanced at it and turned it off. "But if they don't like me, they usually call me bitch, and I'm okay with that. Because it means I was too much for them," she shrugged. "And that's their hang-up. Not mine."

She turned on her stilettos and power walked out the door.

"Let's go, ladies…I'm starved."

CJ rolled her eyes, then stuck her hands in the pocket of her hoodie. Her stark contrast to Harper's business suit left me feeling less awkward in my boring slacks and blouse as she motioned for me to follow.

We went to a nearby deli, nothing flashy, where the owner knew Harper and CJ enough to wave at them when they came in while he was helping another customer. CJ walked to the cooler and asked, "What can I get you to drink?"

"Water's fine," I said.

She grabbed two waters and a sweet tea that she handed to Harper as we got in line to order. The two of them talked about their latest binge obsession on Netflix while I scanned the board to decide what to eat. Once we ordered, got our food, and sat down, the intention of the meal became known.

Harper took a few bites of her grilled chicken pita sandwich, wiped her mouth daintily, took a sip of her tea, and folded her hands. "One piece of advice I'm going to give you now, and I want you to hear me." Her tone wasn't harsh but gone was the "girlfriend" tone.

I had a mouthful of sub but stopped chewing as she stared me down. She had the same voice she used in the conference room. She tapped the table. "Actually, I have two pieces of advice for making it in this company—in the industry, really."

She held up a finger. "First, don't apologize in that office when you've done nothing wrong." She sat forward and tapped the finger on the table to emphasize her point. "Don't apologize if you're right. Don't apologize if they're wrong. Don't apologize if you need something that will inconvenience someone, and don't apologize if there is a conflict you aren't comfortable with being in."

"That's more than one—" CJ said between bites while digging around in her chef salad.

Not bothering to look up, Harper continued to stare me down but responded to CJ. "It's one—" She again put her finger in the air. "Don't apologize."

She held out two fingers and continued, "And two. Don't downplay your worth. *Don't* downplay your contribution." The vehemence in her voice had me concerned I had angered her. "You sat in a room of engineers and some of the brightest minds in racing—because I only hire the brightest minds—and downplayed being asked to contribute to the creation of the Next Gen car. Something, I remind you, THEY weren't asked to collaborate or even comment on—" she pointed at me. "You were."

She leaned back. Taking a sip of her drink, she gave me a moment to digest what she said. Then she folded her hands in her lap. "As women, we may be making headway into rooms and jobs we weren't in before, but you need to remember, we're there because we deserve it. We weren't always invited. They will take their cue from us as to how they proceed." She pointed at me. "If you downplay your worth. They won't recognize your value if you don't stand up to be recognized."

I opened my mouth but had nothing to say. No back-up. No comeback.

"It's human nature, Mia. People, in general, will treat you the way you allow them. They aren't here to do you favors or to validate you."

Leaving that hanging in the air, she sat back, picked up her pita sandwich, and continued,

"Don't apologize. Own your worth".

And then took a bite as if she hadn't uttered five words I had always needed to hear. Those words would have saved me a lot of heartache if I'd only taken them to heart sooner.

As someone who never missed an opportunity to lighten a serious moment, I waited for a sarcastic quip from CJ, not having the nerve to say something myself. Instead, she glanced at me, shrugged, and pointed at her friend. "She ain't wrong."

12

GUS

I loved my mother dearly, but it had been a long week, and all I wanted was a beer, to prop my feet up on the coffee table, and get lost in some mindless television as I waited for my delivery food to arrive.

As I pulled in front of the garage, turned off the truck, and began gathering my things, I answered the phone as any dutiful son would, "Hey, Ma."

"Can you ask Mia if she got my email? I sent over the referrals she asked for yesterday."

"Well, hi, dear son of mine. How was your day?" I mocked her slight southern sweet voice.

"Yes, of course. Hi, honey—are you home yet? Could you check with Mia?"

Mia.

I should check if she wanted to order something with me. Did she like Thai? I couldn't remember. "Yes, Mom. I will." I cradled my phone in one hand and reached in to gather my jacket, wallet, and reusable water bottle.

"What are you guys doing for dinner tonight?"

"I don't—" I froze. She made it sound like we were a couple. We weren't a couple.

"Maybe you should pick up some steaks or something. Make her dinner for when she gets home. Maybe grab a bottle of wine…I'm sure it's going to have been a stressful week over at Merlo, getting acclimated and everything—"

"Mom." I juggled the things in my arms, managing not to drop the phone as I reached for the storm door.

"What? I'm just saying, as a friend…it would be a nice gesture."

"Would you have suggested it if it were Grady or Davy?"

"No, I may have suggested wings and beer…not wine and dinner. But she's a pretty,

sweet girl, not two-hundred pounds of testosterone."

She was pretty…she could be sweet. I'd give Mom that.

CRASH…boom…

A series of clattering followed from the inside of the house as I walked in the door that led to the mud room and then the kitchen.

"Mom, I've got to go. I will tell sweet, pretty Mia to call you."

"Okay, but Gus—"

"Love you, Ma. Bye."

I hung up, dropped my things, and walked into the kitchen to find Mia's rounded ass perfectly molded in a small set of boy shorts as she bent over, looking under my counter.

"This is the most oddly organized kitchen—" she muttered to herself.

"Looking for something?"

"Oh! Hey!" she stood so quickly she almost tumbled backward. Pushing her hair back out of her eyes and tucking it behind her ear, she stood straight, and I took in her disheveled, but no less adorable, appearance. Scrunched-up socks, striped boy shorts, and a familiar, oversized, well-worn, faded navy UNCC sweatshirt that practically covered her shorts when her ass wasn't in the air.

"Oh, yeah, a stock pot." She put her hand on her hip, turning to look through my small selection of pots. "Something bigger than what you use to make your boxed mac and cheese."

I walked to the pantry, reached to the top shelf to pull it down, and handed it to her. "It didn't fit under the cabinet." She grabbed it from me and began filling it with water, putting it on the burner to continue with her task.

"What are you doing?"

"Making dinner..." she said, as if I were an idiot. "Are you hungry? I was going to make

some spaghetti. My father sent me home with some sauce." She lifted a container of sauce that could probably feed a family of eight. "Turns out he started taking some Italian cooking class and canned a crap ton of tomatoes from his garden this year. His new girlfriend is Italian."

I went to the fridge, pulled out a beer, and motioned to her, silently asking if she wanted one. She wordlessly pointed at her wine glass in response. I popped it open and leaned against the counter, watching her flit around my kitchen, learning where everything was and generally making a mess.

"I stopped and picked up some bread to make garlic bread because you can't have pasta without garlic bread," she said, cutting open the bread and spreading on some butter, pausing only to take a sip.

She froze. "Oh! I didn't even think..." Her hand covered her eyes. "Do you have a date? Did you need me to clear out of here?"

I swallowed my beer, trying not to laugh at her concern and slight embarrassment. I shook my head. "No date, and I'm starving."

Satisfied she didn't make a roommate faux pas, she gave one nod before turning back to the stove and adding some levity to the awkwardness with her tone, asking, "So, how was your day."

I let out a chuckle because this was so damn domestic that it was freaking hilarious. Most bachelors would probably be freaked out by it, having a woman invade and take over his house. But this was Mia. She didn't have any preconceived notions of this being anything romantic or becoming romantic. She never thought of me that way.

No, Mia was seriously the smartest woman—scratch that, person— I'd ever known. She'd always think of me as the guy whom she needed to help limp through his college courses. She was the brain—I was the brawn. Tom and Jerry. Wile E. Coyote and the Road Runner. Bugs Bunny and Elmer Fudd. You get the idea.

I liked cartoons—need I say more? If it was Mia giving the comparison, she'd spout off opposite characters from great classic novels.

Okay, maybe I was the flashy Mustang Shelby GT, but she was a Tesla 3. Both can hit 0-60 in three seconds and hit top speeds of over 160, but the Mustang is easier to identify with a large following. The Tesla, with its sleek, modern, smart technology, was leading the industry into the future. The Mustang's popularity was solely based on nostalgia.

And that was why having Mia around would be good for all of us. We all have a lot to learn from this spitfire currently dancing to the latest Taylor Swift while spilling pasta noodles all over my counter.

I shook my head at her. "You're a mess."

"I'm trying to 'Shake off' my day," she said, cleaning up the noodles and adjusting the temperature on the pot.

"That bad?" I moved around to get a better view of what she was doing.

She shrugged and pulled up a side of her mouth. "Nothing I'm not already used to. I was expecting it in some ways, but it's always difficult being the new kid. Especially someone like me." She glanced up at me and shrugged.

I took a sip of my beer, realizing how young she still looked, not in age, but in a kind of softness. It wasn't weakness, but something I suspected she only showed a few people, and only outside her workplace when she would put away her no-nonsense façade.

"We had a meeting with the engineers, Jacks, and CJ. I gave them more information about the Next Gen car and our testing. Nothing they didn't already know, but I gave some recommendations on things we may want to address in-house. Adjustments we may want to make, and there were a lot of looks tossed around."

"Looks?"

She waved her wooden spoon around, absently splattering small amounts of tomato sauce here and there, "Yeah, you know…as in, who does this chick think she is?"

My hackles rose a bit. "Like who? Not CJ and Jacks?"

She shrugged. "No. Not really. Mostly the lower-level engineers. Especially when Jacks explained the role I'd play and how the changes would be assigned."

I shifted, then crossed my legs in front of me. "What else did CJ and Jacks say?"

"Well, CJ didn't seem too happy to hear I would be working in the sim with her." She didn't look at me but stirred the pasta and then checked the sauce. "You know, with the profile of these tires being lower, tire wear is going to be an issue."

I nodded. It was the biggest change this season—the strategy surrounding tire wear and how to handle pit stops. The new tires were going to have great initial grip but were going to wear fast. More green flag stops meant cars pushing the envelope on tires that were worn.

"CJ is an aggressive driver," I said. "Dialing her back, well, that won't be an easy task." I stared down at my beer, wondering what Jacks was thinking throwing Mia into the deep end with "coaching CJ" on her driving. Lesser men have lost their backbone with that task.

I took another sip, crossing my arms. Mia stared at me, waiting for me to impart additional information. "Best thing to do with CJ is speak logic and don't back down. Let her show you her way, and then ask her to do it your way and let her draw her own conclusion."

She nodded, checking on the bread she'd put in the oven while we'd discussed the rest of her day. "Dinner is almost ready."

"I don't want to give you the impression that CJ is a bully. She may come off that way. But she's fought through so much to get where she is. She doesn't always know when to stop. Don't back down from her. Be just as tenacious. She will respect that, and the next time you tell her something, she may sometimes question you, but she won't fight you as hard."

She nodded with more vehemence. "Okay. Good advice. I know when I'm right, but sometimes, I'm not the best at communicating it to someone who is determined to prove I'm wrong." She glanced over my shoulder, "Does that make sense?"

My insides filled with warmth, and I was tempted to touch her cheek because she was too cute, "Yeah, darlin', it does. Don't worry about CJ—her first response is always to argue with change."

She pulled the bread out of the oven. "Hey, can you go set the table? I think this is almost ready. I just have to check the meatballs."

I took another swig of beer. "Sure." I came up behind her and reached for the plates. My body briefly brushed her back as I grabbed them. Her eyes widened with surprise as a warm shock on contact forced me back a half-step. I smiled down at her, trying to cover up my reaction as I lowered the plates down to her before turning to the table.

As I walked into the other room, she called out, "Hey, would you flip on *Sports Talk*? I haven't had a chance to catch any of it today. You don't mind, do you?"

"No, not at all." Why didn't I think of that? I usually had *Sports Talk* on when I ate dinner. I turned on the television and then laid out the utensils.

She came in carrying the pasta and a plate of garlic bread. My mouth was watering, my stomach was growling. I took my seat next to her so we could both watch the television as we ate.

"Oh, and by the way," she said, twirling her fork in the air and gesturing at the meal. "I made dinner. You're on dish duty."

"Fine." I let out an exaggerated, audible sigh of disappointment.

"What?" she said, annoyance lacing her voice.

"It's just that up until that point when you said I had to do the dishes, I thought you were the perfect woman." I grinned and grabbed a slice of bread.

"Oh yeah, well…" She pointed her fork at me. "I may not be *your* perfect woman, but it doesn't mean I'm not someone else's."

And my grin slipped to a small smile as I realized that she had been someone else's woman in the past…and she would be someone else's in the future, just not mine.

"Touché, darlin'."

13

MIA

I hadn't missed the Chicago wind as it hit my face and played havoc with my hair, temporarily blinding me as I walked out of the airport terminal, searching for my brother's truck at arrivals. I'd only been gone from Chicago a few weeks before the lure of Christmas had me making the journey back home.

His jet-black Chevy Silverado double cab with the 20-inch wheels pulled up among the SUVs and minivans like an NFL football player among mere mortals. Cutting off a minivan trying to pull away from the curb, he lowered the window. "Welcome home, baby sister."

Patrick St. James, my older brother, matched his truck in size in proportion to the minivan mortals. Nicknamed Trick, because Pat was way too generic and Patrick was too strait-laced, he wore a goofy, boyish smile that was at odds with his size and never failed to solicit one from me. "Hey, goober," I said, standing back and surveying his truck. "Compensating much?"

He stared forward, his hand resting on his steering wheel, shaking his head. "Not even in my truck and already busting my balls." He waved his hand to me as the minivan behind him finally seemed to garner the courage to honk. "Get in."

I just barely managed to get my luggage secured in the back of the cab before using the running board along the side of the truck to launch myself into the front of the truck. My brother chuckled as I resembled a toddler trying to get in a chair unassisted. Once I righted myself, I threw him a glare and reached to put on my seatbelt.

"Do I need to get you a booster seat?" He pulled out into traffic, exiting the airport.

"I've seen the women you date. There is no way they can get in this truck in the tight skirts they wear."

He cocked his head my way and waggled his eyebrows. "You'd be surprised."

"Men..." I mumbled. A few quiet, but weighted minutes went by as my brother weaved his way through traffic. I loved my brother and we always spoke freely, except when it came to—

"Speaking of men...or assholes who consider themselves men—"

Except when it came to Keith. "Nope. Not going to talk about it."

My brother bit his bottom lip and tightened his grip on the wheel. "Mia—" he said, softly. "He—"

I put my elbow on the door and leaned my head into my hand, staring out the window at the lights of cars we passed. "Trick, I'm serious. I don't want to discuss it. I should've seen it coming. Live and learn and move on."

The silence was thick in the cab.

"I'm fine, really. Can we just enjoy the holidays without bringing him up?"

He clinched his jaw, and his lips locked tight as if it was taking tremendous restraint. Through gritted teeth, he said, "You're taking away my privilege as your brother to beating the crap out of the guy who hurt you. It's literally one of my God-given rights."

I patted his arm. "You'll survive." God, I loved my big brother.

"Don't expect Dad not to get into it with you."

I took in a deep breath and let it out, "I know." I wouldn't expect any less. "You can be a good big brother and help me divert him, okay?"

He pointed and shook his finger at me while keeping his eyes on the road. "If I see dickhead again, he's fair game." That was the most I could ask for, I guess.

We argued over the music and talked inanely about football and racing. Being raised in an all-man, testosterone-fueled household there were two things I was well-versed in—car mechanics and most major professional sports.

My father raised my brother and me while getting his company, Sweet Rides Car Restoration, off the ground. Now with my brother a partner, they've been able to double the size of the business and really make a reputation for themselves as one of the top restoration and custom car garages in the region.

I grew up in the back of a garage. I was able to install an exhaust system before high school and disassemble and reassemble almost any model of carburetor before I got my driver's permit.

The only thing stopping them from gaining me as a partner was my father's desire to see me go to college.

I was identified as "gifted" when I was in elementary school. The teachers wanted me to skip a grade, but they settled on sending me to a magnet program which eventually led me to a special, accelerated high school program and a scholarship to the same college Gus was attending. I chose Charlotte over other colleges because of its location to the stock car industry. When things didn't pan out there as I'd hoped, I accepted a scholarship to Michigan, eventually settling back in Chicago.

It was dark out when we pulled up outside my childhood home, a modest rancher now in better shape than I'd ever seen it. Raising the two of us and running his own business, he had little time to worry about curb appeal.

"There is a wreath on our door and...candles in the windows, and garland around the posts...I'm kind of confused."

Trick took a moment to study the house as well and let out an amused sigh. "Oh, yeah. By the way. Dad has a girlfriend." My brother dropped this nugget on me just before exiting the cab of the truck.

Wait. What?

In twenty-some years, Dad has never had a "girlfriend." At least not one worth introducing or even mentioning to me.

I scrambled out of the cab, almost falling on my face after forgetting about the six-foot drop. "Jeez, Trick!" My brother stood three feet away, watching me fall, chuckling and flipping his key fob in his hand.

"Yep. That was worth the drive to the airport." He turned to walk from the driveway to the front door.

"Wait. Aren't you going to help me with my suitcases?"

"Wait..." he mocks my voice, "Aren't you Ms. Independent and shit?" he flips the key fob again and gives me jazz hands.

However, of course, before I open the door to the cab, he's there, gently moving me aside and his six-foot-four frame effortlessly grabbing the bags. "Come on, Shorty."

"Well, what I don't have in height, at least I make up for in brains."

"Well, what I may not have in brains, I make up for in good looks," he said, and within two strides he passed me. He stopped dead in his tracks and gave me a side-eye glance. "Wait? That doesn't sound right." He joked, managing to scratch his scruffy chin with a suitcase still in his hand.

"Don't hurt yourself thinking about it." I laughed. "I'm hungry. And I need the 4-1-1 on this woman..."

"You'll see soon enough. She's here." He pointed out the vintage, cherry red Corvette in the driveway.

"Okay, then. At least the pressure will be off me to talk about Keith."

Trick reached the door before me and opened it. "Think again."

He led me to the house I grew up in—brighter than it used to be. Music was playing softly, a fire in the fireplace. My father walked out of the kitchen, towel over his shoulder and a smile on his face before he ever even laid eyes on me. His eyes were lighter, with something that showed a life happier than the one I'd seen before.

"My Mia!" He came barreling toward me. Daniel St. James wore a navy-blue sweater pushed up his strong forearms and well-fitted, dark-rinse jeans. Even with gray appearing at the temples of his black, naturally curly, tight-cropped hair, and a few lines on his face, his eyes were dancing, and he appeared ten years younger than I'd ever seen him.

He scooped me into his arms, crushing me against his chest. "Oh, my baby girl!" He dropped me just as fast, holding me at arm's length, studying me from head to toe, and then pulling me back to him, kissing the top of my head and holding me close. "Oh, my heart is going to burst."

"Hi, Dad." I pushed back to drop my purse and take off my jacket. "Let me come in the door," I said softly.

My father was still staring at me. "Yes, yes. Of course. I have someone for you to meet."

"I heard. Could have mentioned it before—" I whispered with an edge of annoyance.

"Could have come home before—"

"Dad, I was only gone a few weeks!" I threw out my hand. "Are you telling me this

happened just since I was gone?"

He ignored me, waved me off, and turned back to the kitchen, "Fiona! Come meet my Mia."

A woman in her late forties, or early fifties, with dark brown hair, warm brown eyes, and

a curvy figure, walked out wiping her hands with a towel and wearing a beautiful smile that was immediately given to my father.

My breath hitched when I witnessed the way my father looked at her. My mother died when I was young. I barely remember her, let alone how my parents looked at each other. I know he loved her. It's a testament to the fact that he mourned her and didn't marry after all these years. But seeing my father, whom I never really thought of as a man in need of companionship—or love—beyond his kids, find that kind of happiness. I had a wish granted I never realized I wanted.

My father was in love.

An awkward silence descended when I snapped out of it and realized that my father had done the introductions, Fiona was holding out her hand, and I was still staring at the two of them with my mouth mimicking a blowfish.

"I'm so sorry…I'm…" I shook my head. "I'm out of it. Tired."

Fiona's smile didn't waver. "Of course. Come on, let's get you a glass of wine and give you a chance to relax."

Overwhelmed with seeing my father so settled and happy, I leaned toward Fiona and hugged her. Thank God the burning in my eyes didn't lead to any other emotions bursting through.

I cleared my throat. "It's a pleasure to meet you, Fiona. A surprise." I glared at my brother and my father, whose eyes were a bit glassy. "But a happy one."

We ate the delicious dinner Fiona fixed for us with a few bottles of wine. They asked me about living in Charlotte and the new team. Dad was impressed I was working with Jacks. Trick was more interested in hearing about Harper. "She's very involved with Cal, and you couldn't handle her."

He bristled at that and postured some more.

"Is it different…working for them instead of that—"

And so, it began… "Dad, don't."

Dad's lips thinned with the words he was suppressing.

"If I ever see that selfish piece of—. To think he…" he clenched his fists.

"Don't let him do this to our wonderful evening. I am better off where I am. It's a wonderful opportunity. The people I'm working with are amazing, for heaven's sake. The first female race team, a legendary crew chief, the McBane brothers, Gus Quinlan, is my roommate—"

"Yes. About that—" my father leaned back, finding something else to latch his teeth into.

But I diverted him in yet another direction. "And…I am friends with Davy Johnson, who said he was going to introduce me to Dawson Shawfield." Well, I'd met Davy at CJ's engagement party, but I think over time we'd be friends, and he did say he wanted to introduce me to Dawson.

My brother dropped his fork and knife onto the plate with an audible clatter and sat back in dramatic fashion. "Are you…are you fucking kidding me? You spend all that time in the car with me, sit through most of dinner, and now just mention that you are friends with two of the biggest names in football."

"Oh, forget about the racing names I dropped. It's all about football with you."

"Damn right, it is. I can meet those other guys any time I want at the track." Trick used to help out with smaller teams back in the day and knew enough people to make it around Michigan's track or even in Chicago.

"But Davy and Shaw…" A wistful gaze fell over his face. And we've lost him to his childhood dreams of being a pro athlete. "You've got to introduce me."

"That's the enticement it will take to get you to come to visit me."

"Hell, yeah."

I turned to my father, who was staring at his plate. "Dad? What about you?"

"Seeing you happy and knowing there is a group of people down there who appreciate you and are helping you get out from under that…that…" He held up his hand as if to stop himself from another tirade. "It's enough for me." Then, under his breath, he added, "Once you get your own place and stop shacking up with yet another man."

"Dad." I drew out his name with the impatience of a teenage girl. "I told you it's not like that."

"Wait, Gus Quinlan. Isn't that the guy people call Mr. GQ?" Fiona piped up.

I was glad to direct my attention to someone not reeking of male over-protectiveness. "Yeah, that's him."

My father gave me his side-eye look to let me know he ain't buying my "Nothing is going on" reply. And frankly, I was tired of defending myself.

"Well, dang, Mia." Fiona wiped her face and put down her napkin before removing an empty dish from the table. "Why aren't you taking advantage of that forced proximity?" Then she turned to my father to explain. "That's what they call it in my romance books. When a man and woman are forced into living together and discover they can't keep their hands off each other."

My father's side eye turned into a glare. "When did you say your house will be ready? Maybe we can finally find a place for your Mustang to call home."

Come to think of it, that was a good question. I pulled the phone out of my back pocket.

"Not at the table, Mia." My father used a tone he would use when I disappointed him.

"Alright. I'll check on my house later. But, yes. Once I'm settled, we can ship her down. Wait until you see the garage." I placed the phone face down on the table beside me, promising to email Gus's mom when we were done. I should've checked in with her before I left town. But it was the holidays. It could wait.

As I was climbing into bed, my phone alerted me of a new Word Scramble notification. I had Cooper on the run, finally getting the hang of hitting those triple letter and triple word scores. I settled back into my childhood bed, propped myself on the pillow, and opened the app.

Except I had two games now—one from Cooper and one from Gus. A text came through next.

GUS

Hey, hope you made it to the windy city in one piece. Decided to give this game a try so you could have someone to beat and feel better about yourself.

He started off the game with the word "HOT."
Amateur.

MIA

Seriously you can't do more than three out of seven letters?

GUS

I'm just warming up. Get it. I'm "HOT.

I sent him an eye roll emoji and used the T to write "WATCH" picking up a triple letter off the W and the H.

MIA

As in WATCH me kick your butt.

He texted back a face-palm emoji.

We threw back a few more words to each other. His were simplistic. Big, Fine, etc. He was immensely proud when he put a Y on the end of Horny and was able to make the word ONLY HORNY. I'm embarrassed to say that made me shift in my bed. I tried not to think of the word horny and Gus in the same sentence—no, same paragraph—no, same page.

MIA

I think I need to give you some credit for being able to stick with a theme—all things Gus Quinlan.

GUS

How's everything at home? Are they happy to have you there? Giving you a hard time about leaving Chicago?

MIA

Things are good. My brother doesn't like being held back from maiming my ex. My father has a girlfriend and has hearts in his eyes, so I'm off the hook so far with him.

I sighed and snuggled down farther in my bed.

MIA

You got plans with Kellie?

Pause. Dancing dots.

GUS

Nah. We do Christmas Eve at the Merrick's. They have a friends and family party. I'll stay at Mom's tomorrow night and spend the day with her.

He really was a mama's boy.

GUS

That's cool that your father has a girlfriend. Is it serious?

MIA

She seems nice. Glad to see him with someone. He's never introduced us to someone before.

Dancing dots.

GUS

Kinda wish my mom would date someone.

There was a pause, and then...

Don't tell her I said that.

MIA

She doesn't date? Maybe she does and you don't know about it.

GUS

She's never gotten over my father. I'm afraid she won't date. Ever.

MIA

I said that about my father. After my mother died, I thought he was too busy raising us to date. I just thought he never got over her death.

GUS

My father isn't dead. He just didn't love her enough to leave his wife.

Uh. Huh.

I really need to respond. But what do you say to that? Sorry your father cheated and conceived you?

MIA

So your father is still married?

Dumb question. He basically said so.

Dots dancing. Pause.

More dots dancing. Pause.

I was beginning to worry he wasn't going to respond when my phone rang. I stared at it as if a ringing phone was a foreign concept.

"Hey there," I said.

"Hey. Listen. I'm sorry. I don't know why I just text-vomited that information. I— No one knows that except a handful of people. Can you please not tell anyone I told you that?"

"Of course. Gus—"

"Mr. Merrick knows. And Harper...CJ knows I don't have a relationship with my father. But we pretty much never discuss him. Neither does my mother."

"So, you don't ever see him?"

"Nope."

I leaned back against my headboard, unable to stop from prying. "You don't have any contact. He just left you all to fend for yourself?"

"He gave child support until my mom could support us with her own salary, then she told him to screw off." He sighed as if bored already with the subject. "He and Mr. Merrick were old friends. That's how Harper knows. They filtered money for my college education down through Merrick. It was through the company, set up like a scholarship, so no one could trace it back to him."

I held the phone with one hand, running my other hand through my hair, staring at the ceiling, wishing he was in front of me. I wanted to find a way to lighten the weight of that knowledge in some way.

I could hear the hurt in his voice—his father's dirty secret.

"I'm sorry your father is a coward," I said to Gus.

He let out an unamused chuckle. "Coward is an appropriate word. Most people chose asshole, but I think your description also fits." He quickly dropped the topic. "Anyway, what's your father's girlfriend like?"

"She's nice. Pretty. They look adorable together," I chuckled. "Like two lovesick teenagers." I sighed. "Makes me almost envious…but I'm in that jaded, cynical stage of my last break-up where I question my ability to not pick an asshole. Great mindset going into the holiday season. Oh, I meant to ask, what did you get Kellie for Christmas?"

"A necklace from the jewelry store she likes," he said. "She's at her parents and won't be home until New Year's. Reminds me, I forgot to ask before you left, are you staying in Chicago for New Year's?"

"I haven't decided yet. I'm seeing Shyla tomorrow. I'll figure it out." Wait. What if he wants the house to himself for New Year's for him and Kellie? "I could stay in Chicago if you want the place to yourself. It doesn't matter to me. Either way, I doubt I will be doing anything more riveting than watching the ball drop and maybe eating Chinese food with Shyla if she doesn't have plans."

"Don't be ridiculous—"

"No, really, I could do that here. Although, I wonder if my father has plans with Fiona. I'm really starting to feel like a third or fifth wheel," I mumbled while biting my thumbnail. "That reminds me, I need to call your mom to check about my house."

"Seriously, Mia. It's not a big deal. Come home and go to Merrick's New Year's Eve Party with the rest of us. Hell, bring Shyla."

I stayed silent. Trying to gauge his sincerity.

"Come home and go to the party. It will be fun." Was that sincerity in his voice? "Everyone will be there. Even Cooper, I think."

"Why do you say that?"

"Say what?"

"About Cooper?"

"I thought the two of you—"

"No. no. He's just a friend. Jesus, Gus, I've only been in town less than a month. Unlike some guys I know, I don't work that fast," I said with a tease in my voice, but I was still surprised he thought I was jumping into something with someone. "Besides, still dealing with dickweed up here, remember?"

"Alright, well, it will be fun, regardless…"

"We'll see." I let out a long sigh. "I'll let you know. But I better go. I'm beat. Have a great Christmas Eve and tell your Mom I said Merry Christmas! Oh! And see if you can nail her down on a date, I can move into the house I bought. I keep forgetting I own a home."

"Merry Christmas, Mia. The house is quiet without you here."

"Talk…talk with you later." I stumbled over my words. Did he… did he miss me?

"Sounds good…And let me know about coming home for New Year's."

"Alright, bye."

I hung up and put my phone on my nightstand. I turned off the light, smiling as I thought about my conversation with Gus and his jovial voice even after dropping the bomb that he was the product of an affair.

I was closing my eyes when his words played back in my head.

"Come home and go to the New Year's Eve Party."

"Let me know about coming home…"

Come home…

He referred to *his* house as *my* home. Was Charlotte my home now? His house was my temporary home. It was a sense of belonging I needed to anchor myself to after the storm Keith threw me into, and regardless of the context, it was just nice to hear Gus say it.

14

GUS

New Year's Eve. The beginning of a new year.

The time to turn over a new leaf. A fresh start.

I leaned against the bar in a banquet room at the same swanky hotel we've celebrated the past few New Year's Eve with the same people, drinking the same drinks, talking about the upcoming season, and gossiping about who's working with whom.

The only difference was the woman I was with each year. I ran my hand over my face at that realization. No wonder my friends gave me shit.

I glance over at Kellie, dressed to the nines in a shimmering, silver body-hugging dress that looked amazing and undoubtedly cost more than what most people make in a month. Her hair and make-up were professionally done for tonight's event, and she was working the room, not just for my benefit either. She was gorgeous and really was a great woman. Ambitious, smart, and didn't get upset by my schedule. But she really didn't make me laugh, and even after a few months of dating, she was still a stranger to me. I begged off, telling her I was going for a refill of my drink and decided to take a moment to myself. I sipped my drink, trying to relax and find a way to enjoy the evening.

"Hey." Davy startled me by slapping me on the back, almost

sending me into the bar top. Being friends with a running back for the Carolina football team, you sometimes had to brace yourself when he was around. He parked himself on the chair next to me. Since his team was still in the playoffs, a glass of what was probably soda water with lime was in his hand.

"Hey, man." I tip my glass at him.

"How's it going?"

"Good. How's practice going? You guys ready for the playoffs?"

He shrugs. "Guess so. We have some wrinkles to iron out, but I think we'll get there." He took a sip from his glass and then looked down at it. "I'll be happy when the season is over so I can have a real drink—I'll tell you that."

"I hear ya." I only had a few weeks left. Then it would be the proverbial hamster wheel of weekly races and a different city each weekend. It used to be a grueling pace that I looked forward to. I hated all the downtime. By January, I was usually itching to get back out there. Now...eh. I wasn't counting the days like I used to, but that was something to think about on another day.

"Tell Brother Davy what's going on with you." Davy's deep timbre was a trademark of his. And when he really laid it on thick, the ladies were goners. "You're usually in the middle of things at this soiree, instead, you're on the sidelines. What gives? Things good with Kellie?"

I shrugged. Not offering any other explanation because I really didn't have any. "I don't think it's going to work out." I finally voiced what had been bouncing around in my head since I went to pick her up this evening. I hadn't seen her in over two weeks. She met me at her door in her panties and heels. I know for a fact there isn't a bra under that dress she is wearing. And instead of smiling when she lowered to her knees and began undoing my belt, I came up with a lame excuse about the car waiting downstairs.

I stopped a gorgeous woman who was practically naked and on her knees from giving me a blowjob.

I stopped her.

Me.

What man does that? Not this one. Not ever. Not until tonight. It wasn't right.

Davy sat back in his chair and gave me the side-eye. "What's wrong with Kellie? I thought things were going fine with her?"

"They were," I began twirling the scotch around in my glass. "But I...it's just not working out. I don't think she's my type."

Davy's eyes almost popped out of his head in a comical fashion as he swung his head over to Kellie and then back at me. "Excuse me? Not your type? I think Kellie is every man's type. She's smart, classy...not like those other women you used to—"

I pointed at him, my voice laced with annoyance. "You were *dating* those women's friends, so don't give me shit about who I used to date."

He waved me off. "Yeah, yeah. I know." He leaned on the table with all of his weight, and I worried about the table's sturdiness before he said, "A few months ago, you told me how you wanted a change and wanted to see about having more than a bed partner. Since then, you dated Erin and then Kellie. Both professional women with class, both gorgeous and smarter than you and I combined. Both of them you got bored with quickly."

"That's not true."

He gave me his "Bitch, please" face. "You kept Kellie around because I suspect you were either trying to see if things would change, or you just wanted her around for the holidays—"

"I'm not a bastard, man."

"Not saying you are—"

"I think I need to just take a break from women."

Davy jumped out of his chair so fast it almost tipped over. "I think we need to get you seen by a doctor."

I glared at him. "No need to be so dramatic." I finished my drink and began to walk back to the bar, and he followed.

"So, what's prompted this decision?"

"She thinks I'm taking her to Grady and CJ's wedding."

"Well, you did take her to the engagement party. Wouldn't it be a fair assumption?"

I took in a deep breath through my nose, holding up my glass to the bartender to notice. "Wouldn't it be better to ask me or wait for me to ask her before buying outfits and putting in for vacation at work?"

"Hm..." Davy said, pursing his lips. "Well, is that it, then?"

"Yeah. I think so. I take her to a romantic wedding on a beach, and the next thing I know, she's going to have fanciful thoughts of other things that won't be happening. Better to cut it off now."

"Fanciful thoughts, huh? I don't think anyone would use those two words when thinking of you, man."

"Screw you."

"Yeah, I'd bet money Gus didn't even know how to spell fanciful," the sweet voice I'd missed around my house came from the other side of me. I turned and looked down. There she was. Her hair was a brilliant, natural mane of curls, her eyes bright with mischief, and her smile lighting up the room. She leaned against the bar and winked. "Hey, roomie. Miss me?"

My arms moved before I could even think differently, wrapping around her. A ripple of energy shot up my back, lightening my mood.

"You didn't tell me you decided to come back?"

"Well, you made me an offer I couldn't refuse?"

I took her in, and the smile on my face was more genuine than any other I'd given in weeks. We spoke periodically while she was visiting her family in Chicago over Christmas and exchanged a few text messages and things like that. She even got me hooked on that online Word Scramble game.

I asked her if she was going to come back for the New Year's Eve party. Actually, what I'd said was, "Are you coming home for New Year's Eve?"

Home.

I referred to my house as her home.

I held her back and noticed another woman slightly taller and slimmer, wearing a knock-out, eye-catching red dress, and big, assessing eyes. She inserted her hand between us. "Shyla Stern," she said.

"Yes," Mia said, motioning to her friend. "This is my Shyla. Shyla, this is Gus Quinlan, and behind him is Davy Johnson." The judgmental smirk Davy gave me transformed into a captivated audience as she sauntered around Mia and me and put Davy between herself and the bar with her hand on her hip. "Hey, Davy," she held out her small hand, and his much larger paw held hers like glass until she gripped down on his. His polite smile grew to one of interest and an abundance of curiosity. So much so that he barely looked away from Shyla while greeting Mia and leaning down for the peck Mia gave him. Wait. He got a peck. I only got a hug.

Shyla knew what she was about, though, and leaned over Davy to reach the bar. "Hey, bartender, can you get me and my girl two glasses of champagne, please? Thanks, doll." And just like that, I no longer existed in Davy's world, and he was no longer worried about my dating status.

I already loved Shyla.

Shyla warmed up to our group quickly. She was as bold as her red dress, and her quick intelligence made her an interesting person to add to the mix. She was beautiful with a sharp wit that was quick enough to keep all the men in the room on their toes, and Davy couldn't keep his eyes off her, which guaranteed he was halfway in love.

"How long are you in town for, Shyla?" I asked once we found a high-top table that opened up. We pulled two chairs out for the ladies and stood next to them.

"Just until Tuesday. I have to get back to work."

"But she promised to make the trip to Daytona," Mia said.

"We'll see. I didn't promise anything," she said. "But I'll try, it depends on how things are going at work." Shyla went on to tell us about her career as an emergency room doctor and how she and Mia were roommates in college and cut her eyes my way. "So, I've known her almost as long as you have, I guess."

Davy waved over at someone, "Shaw!"

Dawson Shawfield, one of the best tight-ends in professional football, came sauntering over in measured, long strides wearing his custom-made tuxedo and holding lowball glass. His other hand was casually placed in his pocket as if he'd just walked out of a photoshoot, adding to his swagger.

Now I know I carry the name GQ, and I realize sometimes it was said mockingly and with humor. But I also realized the attention I got from women wasn't because I was a crew chief for a successful stock car team.

Dawson Shawfield was a successful tight end for a playoff-bound football team. But the reason women of all ages watched his every move wasn't because of the way he could one-handedly catch and grip a football or that he had the athletic grace of a wide receiver with the strength of an offensive lineman. No, it's because of the way he was walking toward us right now—as if he already owned the room, the conversation...and the women who were sitting with us were already mesmerized.

To top it off, Davy liked him, which meant he was a decent guy.

"Hey, Shaw." Davy held out his hand, giving the guy a backslap or two. "Come meet some friends. Gus, Shyla, and Mia, this is Dawson Shawfield. Tight end for my team and savior of the last game that clinched the playoffs for us."

Shaw held out his hand to me and then to each of the ladies, shaking Mia's last before standing between her and me. "Nice to meet you all. Davy told me about his Charlotte friends. Are you all in racing?"

"No, just Gus and I are. Shyla lives in Chicago and is a doctor."

Shaw nodded, his attention centered on Mia. "I'm afraid to say I don't follow racing as much as I should. I'm a bit of a northerner. Transplant, you could say. Not many tracks where I'm from."

"And where is that?" I asked.

"Central Maryland. About an hour from Baltimore and DC."

"But you went to school in the south," Mia jumped in.

How did she know that?

A blush raced up her cheeks at the same time the corner of Shaw's mouth tilted up. Her enthusiasm gave away her fangirl status. She waved her hand at herself a bit. "My brother follows football and was a big fan of yours—is a big fan of yours. Told me about the Shawfield

Shuffle and how it first happened. He's going to flip when he finds out I met you."

I tried not to roll my eyes. I guess I've become a bit jaded. Being in the sports arena spotlight, I've met a lot of sports figures, and it takes a lot for me to be impressed.

Now I sound like a douche.

Shaw's country-club-boy smile and full set of white teeth gleamed at Mia and reminded me of a shark circling his next meal. "Is that so?"

The pink on Mia's cheeks was pretty and most likely endearing to someone like Shaw.

Shaw put his drink on the table and stepped away for a moment, coming back with a chair to intentionally sit next to Mia. "Tell me what else you've heard about me."

Oh, give me a break. I drained my glass to camouflage my eye roll.

Once again, I was the fifth wheel.

Great.

15

GUS

My date reappeared to remind me I hadn't actually come alone.

"There you are!" Kellie came bounding over, making a dramatic entrance, and wrapping her arms, including one holding an empty champagne flute, around my neck from behind. "I've been looking all over for you." She kissed my cheek and pulled me backward. One look made me realize I should've kept better watch over my date and her alcohol consumption.

"Hey," I said, catching Davy's gaze and inadvertently Shyla and Mia's as well. Davy and Mia were studying me. But Shyla—she was studying Mia.

I was trying to understand the reason for Shyla's focus when Kellie grabbed me by my lapels before wrapping her arms around my neck, practically hanging on me and trying to entice me into a make-out session right there in the middle of the ballroom.

I've never been huge of PDA, especially if I'm not the one initiating it. I pulled back, kissing the tip of her nose to soften the blow of my rejection—especially considering I'd already rejected her and her blowjob once today—and held her hands before wrapping my arm around her waist to hold her steady.

Kellie was working on a slight delay and finally noticed the group staring at us. "Hey, ya'll." Her accent spilled out as if it had been caged up and her alcohol consumption held the key to its freedom.

"Davy, looking good. She batted her eyes, probably in an effort to focus. "Mia, welcome back. It's been, um, quiet without you around." And while the tone wasn't said with jealousy or animosity, it was said as if she wasn't missed. The few times Kellie and Mia had met, they were cordial but not open to more than politeness.

Kellie zeroed in on Shaw as she attempted to stand straighter, her interest piqued. "Who is this fine man standing next to you, Mia?"

"Dawson Shawfield," Davy stepped in with the introductions. It was a testament to Kellie's alcohol consumption that she wasn't registering Shaw was more than eye candy. Because if she did, her business hawk-like instincts would've kicked in, and she would've been calculating how she could use him to further her company's profile.

Instead, Kellie's eyes landed on Shyla and narrowed as her eyes roamed from her

stilettos up to her long shiny, ebony hair. "Who are you?" The question was more of an accusation than curiosity laced with southern hospitality.

Mia stood up, "Kellie, this is Shyla. My friend from Chicago. She's in town for the next day or two."

Kellie slowly moved her gaze from Shyla—who leaned back, crossed her arms over her chest, and cocked her head, a mixture of amused and unimpressed—to Mia, who clasped her hands together, reading the room and the standoff that was coming.

Kellie gripped my waist, whether in displeasure or a need to keep herself upright, as she looked at Mia. "Where are you staying?"

"Excuse me?"

"Where are you sleeping tonight?" She shifted her challenging glare to Mia. "Because it's not at Gus's house. We are staying at Gus's house."

What? Wait. We never stayed at my place.

Mia stared at me with a confused look on her face. "Guess I should've stayed in Chicago instead of coming home."

She called my house home. Not the point. I pull back from Kellie. "What are you talking about—"

Kellie thrashed her head back and forth, making her even more unstable in her heels. "No. I draw the line." She slashed her arm out wide. "You aren't having another woman stay at your house. Nope. No." Another slash. "I don't care whose friend they are."

"Kellie—"

"I mean it, Gus." Kellie's voice rose.

Davy came to stand behind Kellie. Blocking her view of Shyla.

"Come on, Kellie. You know it's not like that—" I said.

"Maybe not with Mia. I'm not worried about Mia." She made a sound like that would be the most ridiculous notion and waved her off to dismiss her. "But with her—" she pointed at Shyla. "That one there —nope. No."

"Hold up." Shyla held up her hand, straightening from her seat and walking toward a clearly inebriated Kellie, who was drawing more and more attention to our group. Shyla walked over to my other side, putting me between the two women.

Mia grabbed her arm, whispering to her. "Don't. Let Gus handle it."

Shyla pulled her arm away, staring at her friend. "What does she mean, she's 'not worried about Mia'?"

"Kellie, come on," I said, trying to get her attention. "She's just Mia's guest."

"No, Mia is your guest in your house. She's not supposed to have other guests."

"I'm staying at the hotel, you insecure—" Shyla began, but Mia cut her off, putting a

hand across her mouth. Shyla pulled down Mia's hand. "Besides, it's Mia you should be—" Mia elbowed her friend hard enough to make her step back into Davy who caught her.

Mia glared at her friend, and they gritted words at each other I couldn't hear because Kellie was whining-slash-bitching, claiming I was "her man" so she had the right to say who would be allowed to stay at my house.

Shyla and Mia stopped arguing, Shyla let out an annoyed breath, pinched the bridge of her nose, and to herself, she said, "Lord, save me from inebriated, insecure women." Then she turned to Kellie, "Girl, I told you I'm not staying there."

She walked up to Kellie, getting within inches of her and placed a calming hand on her arm. "Listen here, honey. I say this to you, woman to woman. I'm more interested in that big teddy bear over there." She pointed at Davy, who suddenly beamed like an idiot. "And I've only just met 'your man,'" she used air quotes to mock Kellie's use of the term.

"Let me tell you something. I'm a pretty good judge of people. And I'm doing you a favor by saying this, though it may not seem like it right now." Shyla tilted her head slightly but still gave Kellie her eyes, "But...your man isn't that into you, and it has zero to do with me."

Kellie bristled, and I held firm waiting for the verbal smack of truth to hit Kellie's pride. Shyla side-eyed me. "You do her no favors by dragging this out. This is what happens when men don't just lay it out," Shyla said to me as if I was the one bringing on the drama, and her annoyance was completely centered on me.

Kellie's eyes begin to well.

"Now, girl. Don't do that here." She patted her arm as if she were a good friend. "But you needed someone to say it. If he were into you, he wouldn't have let you walk around all night without him, allowing you to get this drunk off of drinks other men gave you."

"You're a bitch," Kellie slurred.

"Yes." Shyla nodded, "Yes, at this moment, I really am. But I'm being real with you right now. Go home. Don't cause any more drama for yourself because as fine as that man is, he ain't worth the regret—and the viral videos—tomorrow." Then she stepped back and grabbed her drink off the table while everyone around stared at her —gobsmacked.

What the hell just happened?

Shyla waved her drink at me. "Take this poor woman home before she starts crying, Gus. Jesus. From what I understood, you had this love 'em-and-leave 'em thing down to an art—why did you let this get this far?" She threw a hand in the air in frustration at me as I patted down my pockets for my phone while trying to remember if Kellie had a purse.

"Christ on a cracker. Why am I having to explain this?" Shyla pinched the corner of her eyes before throwing a hand up in frustration.

Shaw whispered to Mia and my stomach clenched at how they leaned into each other.

I leaned forward, "Mia—are you—"

"Don't you worry about Mia." Shyla stepped up and interjected. "You have enough on your hands. Shaw, Davy, and I will take care of Mia. Won't we?"

Davy rubbed his jaw, effectively hiding his taunting smile. Shaw was too busy staring at Mia, and Mia was too busy giggling at Shaw.

"What?" Mia said, finally paying attention to my departure. "Oh, yes." Her attention turned back to Shaw even though she was dismissing me. "We're fine. Go. Don't worry about it."

Yeah, right. Don't worry about it…like that was going to happen.

———

By the time I got Kellie home, everything had sunk in with her and she didn't have anything left to say to me that was worth repeating. As I drove out of her complex, I decided that was it.

I was taking a break. It was going to be me and my hand until I could get my head on straight.

I should apologize to Mia for Kellie's behavior.

At the next light, I texted her.

GUS

I'm so sorry about Kellie. She had too much to drink, but it was no excuse for how rude she was to Shyla. She's welcome to stay here. Kellie is at her place.

> Hey, do you need a ride home tonight? I can come pick you up.

MIA

> No, that's okay. I'm not coming home tonight.

Wait...what? The last line was like a three-thousand-pound car doing a burnout over my chest. Where the hell was she staying then?

Shaw.

She and Shyla were probably still out with Davy and Shaw.

Son of a bitch.

I began pacing my house. I didn't know anything about this Shaw guy. What kind of a name was Shaw, anyway?

So he had a touchdown dance named after him—that was lame. Like really lame.

Where was she? Were the four of them together? Davy...I could text Davy.

And look like the pathetic high school geek that I sounded like. Oh my God. He would crucify me. This would be like when CJ started dating Grady all over again. The girls I'm friends with *are* allowed to date.

Get it together, man. You can't restrict them to being single. They're allowed sex lives.

Mia having sex with a man. With Shaw.

More race cars doing 360-degree donuts over my dead, mutilated body. I sat down. I was having trouble breathing, my hands were clammy, and I ran them down the tuxedo pants that I still had on.

I needed to know... No, I didn't. I didn't need to know a damn thing.

GUS

> Let me know if you need a ride. I'll keep my phone turned on.

> Call me if you need me.

The last text went unanswered, so I went to my room.
I waited and waited to hear a car, a door, or a floorboard creak.
She didn't come home.
And I never fell asleep.

16

MIA

I have officially reached the age when my body has tricked me. "Oh, I can handle another drink."

Yeah. No. You can't. Idiot.

I stole a pair of Shyla's designer sunglasses before leaving her hotel room New Year's Day in desperate need of a Diet Coke, a shower, comfy clothes, and greasy food. Shyla provided the ibuprofen, but she was hogging the shower, and the hotel only sold Diet Pepsi.

What the heck was up with that?

My Uber driver took mercy on me and lowered his radio as my pitiful butt climbed in the back of his car as he kept the conversation to pleasantries and confirmation of the location we were going.

I closed my eyes and leaned my head against the cool door window until we turned into the driveway of Gus's house. I'm home, I thought. No. I was at Gus's home. Jeez. You need to call his mom today and find out the deal with the house. You were supposed to be able to move in last week. Last-minute inspections, painting, and carpet cleaning can't take that long.

After thanking the driver and spilling out of the car, I grabbed my purse, coat, and heels and barefooted it up the driveway, only to see Gus leaning against the post, faded jeans, even more faded Foo

Fighters t-shirt, arms crossed, freshly showered with an amused smirk on his face.

I fought back the smile his smirk was evoking and went for prideful indignation instead, but I didn't seem to pull it off because his smirk turned into a shoulder-shaking chuckle as I walked up the steps and right by him.

"Look what the cat dragged in," he said.

"Shut up," I murmured loud enough for him to hear it but soft enough not to anger the headache just being held at bay with the three ibuprofen swimming in my system.

That made his laugh audible until I nearly tripped on the steps up the porch. His laugh stopped immediately, and he stepped up to catch me. "What the hell? Wait, he sent you home in a car?" His volume was threatening the peace treaty in my head. "I told you to call me, I would've come to get you."

I gave him the universal sign to tone it down, waving one hand and clutching my head with the other. "No, I called the Uber."

I made it to the sofa where I gently settled myself down and assumed the fetal position, not even caring anymore what it was doing to my dress or if it was riding up.

I looked up at Gus, whose jaw was clenched as he laid an afghan over my legs and bottom half—maybe it was riding up more than it should've been.

I pushed my way up to my elbows, "Are you mad at me?"

He turned away, walking back to the kitchen. "What? No." A cabinet door opened and was slammed closed. "Do you want some water?" Opened door. Slammed. "Maybe something to eat?" Opened door. Slammed.

"Um. How about a Diet Coke from the fridge?"

After two heavy steps to the fridge, the door opened and slammed shut enough to make the fridge shake what was inside.

"Gus?"

All I heard in reply was the fizz of the soda pouring into the glass before the can made a noise as if it had been crumpled. A drawer was opened. Can thrown. Drawer slammed. His heavy feet took minimal strides to come back. The Diet Coke precariously sloshed on the side of the glass as he handed it over, then took a step back, not looking at me.

"Gus? What's the matter? If you aren't mad at me, what is it?"

His hands were on his hips, legs spread as if ready for a fight, and his eyes bouncing everywhere except at me.

"Is it Kellie? Here, sit down. Talk to me. What happened?"

"He sent you home in a car?" He gritted out. "Didn't even have the decency to drive you home the next day?" He threw his arm out toward the door. "Seriously? In this condition?"

Clutching my head, trying to open my eyes without my head exploding, I pushed myself up until I was sitting with my feet on the floor. "Gus."

Then he took in air through his nose before he gritted through clenched teeth. "Did he take advantage of you?" His voice, was menacing. "Tell me. So help me God—"

"Gus." I grabbed his hand and tried to pull him down, but he maneuvered away and began to pace, pulling out his phone.

I pushed myself up. "What are you doing?"

"Calling Davy to find out where this fucker lives."

I grabbed the phone. "Gus, I stayed at Shyla's last night with Shyla. At the hotel. Shaw was nothing but a gentleman." He grabbed his phone back but froze and studied me.

"I'm serious. He didn't take advantage of me and isn't responsible for me being hung over—that's all Shyla. If anything, she took advantage of me. She's a terrible friend, obviously." I reached for my Diet Coke.

That caused his brows to rise up into his hairline.

"Get your mind out of the gutter." I took a big sip of the wonderfully cold, bubbly caffeine supply. "Not everything is about sex."

He shrugged as if to say he didn't necessarily agree. But at least the thought seemed to distract him.

"Shyla kept ordering shots as if we were ten years younger and used to that kind of weekly consumption. I'm not," I said, sitting back down and resting my head in my hands. "I didn't go out with her much when I was with Keith, so she was taking advantage of my newfound freedom and that we were out with two hot professional football players."

I peeked up at him. He was back to having his arms crossed, glaring at me like a disapproving authority figure.

I took two big gulps of the soda, wishing I could get the caffeine in my system quicker as he sat on the table in front of me.

"It was fun. So sue me."

He tilted his head, folded his hands in front of him, and silently studied me.

"And why are you all angry anyway? Was the conversation with Kellie so ugly that you have to take it out on the rest of us?"

"Kellie and I broke up."

"I'm sorry, Gus." I reflexively touched his hand. "You probably want to be alone. Not dealing with keeping tabs on me." I got up to leave and get out of his hair. "I'll go take a shower and give you some space."

He reached out and held my hand. "I don't know Shaw very well, and he's a damn good football player. You know...I was...I was just worried about you. It's not like you to—"

"To what? Have fun?" An incredulous chuckle escaped.

"To...be hungover. Hook up with a guy—"

"Jesus. That's right. Plain Jane. Boring Mia. I forgot." My current mood wasn't conducive to being around disapproving people. "It's not like you to be so damn judgmental. And I told you, I didn't go home with him or anyone." I leaned over to grab my shoes and stood a little too quickly, my hand going to my head. "Not that it's any of your business. Because if I did decide to go home and fuck his brains out, it wouldn't be something I would need to share with you or anyone." His eyes widened as if I had slapped him.

"Who the hell are you to judge me? Seriously—" I held up a hand to stop myself before I said something I couldn't take back. I took in a deep, cleansing breath. "Gus..." I sat back down. "I'm sorry you had a bad night, but mine was probably one of the best I had in a while... Please, don't do this." Don't kill my high.

He ran his hand through his hair. "You're right. You're right. I'm being an ass. I'm tired. I didn't sleep much last night. I'm sorry." He put his hand over mine. "I have a tendency to be a bit—"

"Overbearing."

"Overprotective." He squeezed my hand before clasping it in both of his. They were warm, firm, and even calloused and roughened—it was endearing, sweet—as he caught my eyes. "I'm sorry. I'm not used to you being the object of men's attention."

I gaped, dropping my shoes.

"—I mean."

I held up my hand, pulling the other out of his warm embrace. I shook my head. "Just stop. Quit while you're ahead. It hurts to watch you dig yourself deeper."

"You know what I mean. You never had a boyfriend before. I'm not used to it."

"There isn't anything to get used to, Gus. Just because the few months we were friends I wasn't screwing around doesn't mean I was asexual." I laid back and put my hand over my eyes. "I'm too tired to have this discussion with you. I have sex, Gus. I've had sex. Lots of it. There's more to me than just my gorgeous brain. Get over it."

Silence.

"Yes, I…I'm being ridiculous. I—"

Time to switch focus, "I'm sorry things didn't work out with Kellie. I hope it wasn't because of me living—"

He shook his head and cut me off, "Not at all. Things just weren't right with us."

This wasn't going to work out for him and me. We needed to get out from under each other. It was as simple as that. "You know what." I pulled my hand away from his, slapping my thigh before getting up. "Why don't I go take a shower and then call your mom to see what the status is on my house."

He flinched. "What?"

"My house. Maybe I've been underfoot for too long." I shrugged. "I don't want you to think you have to be my big brother. I have one of those back in Chicago. I don't need another one—and you didn't sign up for that job. We could go check on the status of the house and see when I can move in." Yes. This was what needed to happen. "The season is starting in a month. It's probably better if I get settled in my own place."

He stood, striding back into the kitchen. "Good idea. I'll call her while you shower, and then maybe we can get some lunch and go over there."

I yawned. "Okay, something greasy. And then I need a power nap."

I walked by the kitchen on my way to shower and he was braced against the island. He stared down at the counter, his body rigid. Upon hearing me, he grabbed his cell phone and glanced up. His expression was one I wasn't familiar with, but it hit me—maybe Gus and I didn't know each other as well as we thought. Maybe the memories we had of our friendship, of our time together, had been skewed with time or by viewing through our own rosy-colored, youthful lenses. Maybe we had both just changed. Either way, I didn't know him as well as I thought I had.

Because Gus looked...unhappy.

"Sounds good," he said and walked into the other room.

And maybe...maybe, Gus being unhappy was because I was here.

17

GUS

Maybe Mia was right, and I just needed my space. I needed her in her house so I wasn't caught up in her life and could focus on my own. After all, who the hell was I to judge her? I didn't need to be caught up in her love life, her comings and goings, or whom she was dating—or sleeping with.

And I didn't need to think about her having sex with anyone. Resolved to get this moving, I called my mom.

"Hey, honey."

"Hi, Mom."

"How are you? How's Mia?"

"We're fine—"

"Did you two have a good New Year's?" She was implying, without asking, that we were
celebrating together.

"Yes, we all were at the same party with Harper. I was with Kellie, and Mia had a friend in
from out of town."

"Oh." And there was so much disappointment in that one word. Ah. I should've known. I suspected, but yes. That tone proved it.

"So, you're still seeing Kaylie?"

"It was Kellie." Although she knew that and it wasn't worth the effort to correct her. "No. We broke up."

"But I thought you said she went with you to the party," my mom said.

"Yes, but we broke up last night afterward." I walked over to the sliding glass door that

led out to my back patio and studied the garage—wishing this conversation would move along quicker.

"Really?" The word was drawn out before she tacked on, "I'm sorry to hear that."

No, she was *not at all* sorry to hear it.

"What about Mia? Did she and her date have fun?"

I rolled my eyes because without even seeing her face I knew the calculation that was in

her eyes. "Her date was her best friend Shyla from Chicago."

"Oh. Good. Good. And you all had fun?"

"Yes, Mom. Fun was had by all. But Mia wanted me to check in with you to see about

her house. Is the work all finished? I think she's anxious to move in?"

"Why? Why is she anxious?" My mom's voice changed to the tone that made every son bow his head knowing he disappointed his mom. "Have you done something to make her feel unwelcome?"

"No, Mom. Of course not." I drew back a breath for patience. "She bought a new house. She'd like to live in it."

"No reason to get snooty. The previous owners had dogs. I'm trying to get it just right for her, that's all."

I closed my eyes. "Okay, well, we were going to go by and see it and then get some lunch this afternoon."

"OH!" She perked up. "Why?"

"Um..."

"I mean, why don't you get lunch. I'll swing by and check on it. Turn up the heat and everything. Make it perfect so when she comes by it will look so homey and comfy."

What was she up to? "Let me check with Mia about her timing."

"Go ahead. I'll wait. I need to plan my day. See if that works for her."

"She's in the shower."

"Just knock on the door, son. It's no big deal."

I gritted my teeth and walked up the stairs to the bathroom Mia used. "Mia, how about lunch first and then the house? My mom wants to meet us there."

"Sure. Okay. I'm starving."

My mom, overhearing her, said, "Okay. Great...so how is everything else with the two of you? Why is she suddenly so eager to move out? Did Kylie have anything to do with it? Is that why you broke up with her?"

I wasn't going to correct Kellie's name again. "No, Mom."

"Well, you and Kylie break up and suddenly, Mia wants her house right away. Seems suspicious timing to me, that's all." She was relentless.

"Mom...I told you. Mia is a friend."

"Yes. I know." She didn't sound convinced, "Like Harper and CJ—you told me, but—"

"No, Mom. No buts."

"August..." She was pulling out my full name to tell me she meant business. "She's a nice, pretty girl who is also in racing. She has the same schedule as you. She likes cars. Your friends seem to take to her—"

"Come on, Mom...let's not do this."

"You're not getting any younger—"

"You've got to be kidding me? Are you seriously going to give me the 'Your biological clock is ticking' lecture?"

"Well...I'm just saying. She does check all the boxes."

"Mom, I don't have boxes and I don't need relationship help. I realize how old I am."

"It's just you keep dating the wrong girl—"

"I think I want to take a break from dating altogether for a little while."

"What?" My mom's surprise radiated through my phone enough that I had to pull it away from my ear.

I nodded to myself. Seeming to think this was a good idea. "I'm kind of bored with the entire thing."

"You're bored with dating women? Honey, are you feeling okay? Is this about CJ getting married?"

I rolled my eyes. "No. This is about me being older and tired of the same routine. I...well, don't worry about it. No need for me to discuss my dating life with my mom."

"I like it when we talk about your love life."

"I never said love life. I said dating."

Her perky voice became softer. "Yes, dear. And I suspect that's the problem. You've never fallen in love."

The mood I was in prior to calling her and the edge I'd been on since last night had my hackles up already. So when I heard the hint of pity in my mom's voice about never being in love, I snapped. "Well, you fell in love, and from my point of view, it didn't seem like all that much fun."

Silence and immediate dread struck over what came out of my mouth. It was a low blow.

I didn't do that to my mom. I didn't purposely hurt her. "God, Mom, I'm sorry."

A sigh came through the phone. "Text me when you're on your way over, Gus."

"Mom, I—"

Her energy from before was gone. She was quick to sign off. "See you then, honey."

I closed my eyes tightly and put the phone up to my forehead in prayer to take back the last thirty seconds.

We rarely ever discussed my father unless necessary. We certainly didn't talk about how much loving him cost her—her heart, her dignity, her future. In return, she was a single mother with a half-completed college education and a heart of gold who was born to love people but never opened her heart up to another man again.

And me, the son she gave up everything for... Yeah, I'm the asshole who just told her she was the reason I never have, and would never, fall in love.

18

MIA

As Gus drove us to lunch, I texted Keith about Shyla picking up some of the things I left in our storage unit—including my book collection and some off-season clothes.

He hadn't been very responsive about arranging a time with either of us.

> MIA
>
> Happy New Year, Keith.

See, I was attempting to be civil. Take the higher road.

> MIA
>
> I was hoping to arrange a time to have Shyla or my brother pick up the boxes I kept in the storage unit. Please let me know when that can be arranged. Hope all is well.

There. Succinct. Matter of fact. Polite, even.

I moved out without any more drama. I just hoped Keith was happy enough with his life not to cause any more issues at this point.

"Everything okay?" Gus said as we pulled into Belle's BBQ and parked.

"Yeah. Just trying to make arrangements for the rest of my stuff to be shipped down here," I said, getting out of the car.

"I thought you said Shyla had that handled?"

I nodded as we walked to the restaurant. "Yeah, but my ex still has some boxes of mine in storage, which requires me dealing with him."

He opened the door with one hand, and he ushered me into the restaurant with the other on my back. It was nice having that contact. It wasn't possessive, and it wasn't affectionate, it was just a connection, as if protective.

The hostess seated us, and we ordered two sodas, and I scanned the menu.

"Is he being an ass? Your ex."

I ran my hand through my hair, sitting back.

Gus held up a hand, "I only know what I've heard from others. So if you don't want to talk about—"

I flattened the menu and folded my hands over it to spit it all out. "We were living together for over a year. He was promoted over me to lead engineer, and then eventually crew chief, and then I left in a huff when he didn't play favorites and I didn't get my way."

His eyes widened as he took a sip of his soda.

"Or at least that's the story he's telling." I allowed my hands to flatten the menu some more to prevent them from balling up in fists.

Gus coughed a little and said, "What a dick."

I nodded, crossing my arms. "Basically. I did the grunt work, and I smoothed the feathers he ruffled, but when the people who counted were around, he puffed up like a peacock and took the credit. It was subtle at first and took me a while to admit."

Gus held his napkin between his hands, folding it methodically. The waitress returned and we both ordered the Carolina pork sandwiches.

I sat forward. "You know the saying, 'Keep your friends close but your enemies closer'? Well, Keith kept me close—kept me under his thumb with love, flattery, lies…"

I shifted in my seat. "Then Richardson decided to replace the crew chief." I took in a deep breath, letting it out. I hadn't really told this entire story to anyone before. "Keith always thought he'd be the choice. But after I'd been selected to help with the Next Gen car, it put me in the running—gave me some credit Keith couldn't steal." I glanced up. Gus was leaning forward on the table, waiting for the entire story.

I wiped down the sides of my glass with my thumb, focusing on the condensation instead of his attention. "He was livid. Showing his true colors made me admit to myself that he'd been using me. I'd made the decision to move out and had quietly been looking at apartments. Meanwhile, Keith casually mentioned to some of the executives that I wanted to get pregnant. That I'd been hinting about wanting to get married, knowing damn well the owner was a big family man. So that put me on the bench permanently."

Gus shifted in his seat, leaning on his forearms, getting closer. Reaching out his hand, almost catching mine, but stopping just short of them.

I leaned back, placing mine in my lap. "The owner came up to me after the announcement was made about Keith's promotion. He said he was happy for Keith and me and looked forward to our wedding. He let me know I'd always have a job waiting for me after maternity leave." I found a new purpose for my hands, tearing my napkin into small pieces and making a neat pile in front of me.

I couldn't look at Gus. Revisiting how stupid I'd been caused my eyes to begin to burn again, and I was done with those emotions.

"When I tried to explain the breakup, Keith began telling people I was upset for being overlooked, and it was a case of jealousy, and he was devastated by my betrayal. I quit that afternoon and moved in with Shyla." I ran both hands over my face and leaned back in the chair. "He never bothered to come after me. I mean, why would he? He got what he wanted."

Gus had been sitting back in his seat, arms crossed, quiet. But then he leaned forward, his head resting in his hand with his elbow leaning on the table. "Well, honestly, you've upgraded on the roommate situation. You've got an opportunity to grow and are around a hell of a lot better group of people. Plus—" He rubbed his hands down his chest.

"You're having BBQ lunch with me. So, screw Mr. Dickless." The waitress put the plates with the vinegary-goodness sandwiches in front of us just at that moment.

He took a bite and moaned. "If I'm not a good enough reason, isn't this food alone worth moving down here?"

I smiled and took a bite myself. Moaning also and wiping my face.

His beautiful blue eyes turned navy as his knowing grin instantly changed my mood. I swallowed...hard. "Yes..." I said, trying not to choke, "To both."

We continued to eat. Talking about teams and the latest news on each of them. What sponsor had contracts with which teams. We discussed the Next Gen car, and my observations of different drivers according to their stats.

He wiped his mouth, crumpled up his napkin, and smirked. "So, you're driving the SUV,

but I know that's not your car. What are your real wheels?"

I took a sip of my soda. "Well, it's kind of amusing because we both have a Camaro." He gestured as if to tell me to move along with the good information. "I have a 1969 Chevy Camaro SS convertible, in LeMans Blue, because doesn't every girl love a convertible?" I said, and even I could hear there was more to the answer.

"And..." He sat on the edge of his seat—waiting. "You have a smile on your face that hints at a secret."

I gave him my best, most flirtatious, under-the-lashes gaze. The only time I would flash that look at him because when talking muscle cars it was called for. "I also have a 1969 Ford Mustang..." I paused, letting my smile turn feral before adding. "Boss 429."

Gus's eyes went wide. He bit his bottom lip and hit both hands on the table so loud people around us turned. The Mustang Boss was a rare edition—less than 860 were sold in 1969, and they had engines newly developed back then for the stock cars, and were limited to 375 horsepower for insurance purposes, but tricked out, could do 500 horsepower.

He dropped his head back and closed his eyes, then whispered, "What color?"

"Red."

He moaned, a deeper sound than the one he made when he began eating the BBQ, and I felt a slight twitch in a place I chose to ignore. I chose instead to continue to torment him. "Black bucket seats, wood-grain trim—"

"Jesus, Mia, that car's probably almost as expensive as that house you just bought."

I shrugged. He wasn't wrong.

"And you are just now mentioning this piece of art that's in your possession? Where is it?"

"It's in Chicago with my father. He didn't trust it anywhere near Keith," I said. "And now I could kiss him for that foresight. Because if I can't get some books and old clothes back, imagine what he would've done with the keys to that?" Keith never understood my obsession with that car. I bought it with my father's help after a friend of his offered it to him as a private sale. Being in the restoration business, the previous owner knew it would be cared for and restored properly. But being a Boss, it was still a chunk of change. I lived at home, with my first job out of school, and the three of us, Dad, my brother Trick, and I worked on that car together. It was my pride and joy.

"So, my baby stays with her grandpa until I'm more firmly settled with proper security and weatherproofing." I added softly, "Until I find a real home."

Gus rubbed his hand over his face. "I think I'd marry you just for a chance to drive that car."

I laughed. "Wow. Ego. Who'd say I'd ever want to marry you?"

"Well, I'm at least motivated now to get you settled with that beautiful garage to get that
baby down here."

"So now you want me just for my car," I said, crossing my arms. "Men." I shook my head.

"We really are simple creatures."

"No doubt," I said, all worries about Keith and the house disappeared.

Gus got the check from the waitress, and we paid and walked back out to his truck.

"You know, I don't want you to think it's a burden on me to have you around. Honestly, it's not." We got in his car and put on our seat belts. "Truthfully, it's getting old being the third and fifth wheel around here." He stopped at the stop light and smacked my knee playfully. "This is nice. I like having you here."

"Is it nice enough to let me drive your Camaro…" I said, waggling my eyebrows at him.

"Uh, no. No one drives my Camaro," he said, "No matter how nice they are."

"We'll see. Remember, you also want to drive my Boss."

Deep inside, a small voice whispered, *"You'd let him drive anything if given the chance…"*

We drove to the house where Michelle met us with a contractor she hired—how she got anyone to come out on New Year's Day is beyond me. Upon meeting the contractor and his permanent expression of devotion, the reason became clear. Michelle was a beautiful, charming woman.

Bottom line, Michelle somehow talked both Bob and me into refinishing the floors, repainting the entire house, and something to do with replacing the linoleum, and gave Bob a punch list of things she seemed to see, but I was blind to, that needed to be done before I could move in.

"But, Bob, how long will all this take?" I asked, more concerned with that than with the cost.

Michelle literally stepped between us and said, "Don't you worry about it. I'm sure Bob will make it a priority. Won't you, Bob?" She glanced over her shoulder, and all poor Bob could do was nod.

Then she ushered Gus and me out my front door, sending us on our way and wishing us a Happy New Year.

"I swear, sometimes I leave your mother feeling like I just made it through a tornado and I'm not sure what direction I was left in—"

"That's a pretty dead-on description," he said, his lips were thinned, and his annoyance was evident.

"I'm sorry, really. I couldn't have anticipated it would take this long. It's taking longer than planned—"

"It's not your fault." He ushered me to his car, opening the passenger door to let me in. Under his breath he said, "But it's been planned."

19

MIA

Later that week, Jacks and CJ gave me the opportunity to take one of the cars out on the track to get a feel for the modifications that I was suggesting.

I loved to drive fast, but I didn't have the backbone to do it in a field of forty-one other adrenaline-junkie drivers. I didn't care what kind of safety protocols or engineering technology they'd developed. If a three-thousand-pound machine is going two-hundred miles per hour and knocks you into a wall, it's going to hurt.

I didn't do pain very well.

I worked very hard on these brain cells. I spent a lot of money packing them with information, and I didn't want to lose any of them. I admired CJ and Grady for their quick reflexes and skill, but I also admired them for the guts it took to get back into those machines after the wrecks I've seen them have.

There's something to be said about being in that car, alone, and slingshot through those turns with nothing between you and being airborne except for four rubber tires. The g-forces alone remind you how you are bucking the nature of speed.

Later, I stared up at the dusk-lit winter sky and closed my laptop. I was still wired and wasn't getting anything else done. My skin was electrified, and my legs couldn't stay still. I packed up my bag and headed to the garage, opening it to leave and find my car.

"Well, that went over like a lead balloon," CJ said as she and Harper walked toward her motorcycle.

Harper shook her head. "Yeah, I think we managed to get him pretty ticked off at us."

CJ was carrying her helmet and placed it on the bike. She turned and leaned on the seat. "I didn't realize he was getting so upset—"

"I don't know if it's our teasing that tripped him up or us mentioning Mia—"

"What's this?" I said, coming around from behind Harper.

Both women jumped. "Oh, damn, girl," CJ said. "You gave me a heart attack. We thought you left already."

"Sorry. Didn't mean to sneak up on you. But who did you upset by mentioning my name? I haven't been here long enough to make any enemies."

The best friends exchanged the best-friend look that I sometimes shared with Shyla. It was the look that said, "Do you want to take this or should I?"

CJ shrugged and went to open her mouth to speak, but Harper held up a hand and jumped in, "You didn't make anyone angry. We managed to make Gus angry with us."

"About me?"

CJ grimaced. "Yeah, well. Kinda. We told him not to flirt or mess with you."

Um, what?

Harper added, "We don't know what happened to you prior to landing here in Charlotte, but we don't want anything to drive you away. We want you here—with us, with Merlo."

"That's very sweet. But, then why…" I tried to process this. "Why would you—" I searched both women's faces and I smiled as if they'd told me the most naïve thing ever and even let out a small chuckle.

"What's so funny?" CJ asked.

I pointed my finger at both of them. "You two have known Gus as long—actually, longer than I have."

"Yes, since we were in high school."

"Okay, so you know he has a type."

They glanced at each other and shrugged.

"Do you think it's changed in the past ten years?"

They glanced at each other again, this time with a little hesitancy.

"And has his type ever been a woman who resembles me in physical traits, education, background, or personality?"

CJ put her hands on her hips. "No. They resemble Harper, pre-Merlo years, but with

looser morals and no desire for long-term commitments."

"I'm the antithesis of all of those things. I'm nowhere near what Gus would go for," I said, believing every word, even if it kind of stung. No woman wants to know she's not desirable to someone as beautiful, charming, and as playful as Gus.

"Besides the fact that you are also giving the man too much credit," I said, crossing my arms and legs, "Contrary to popular belief, he is resistible."

That was enough to make them smile. "Don't tell him that or he will double down just to prove a point. And whether you're his type or not, Gus doesn't back down from a challenge."

I nodded. "Yes, that I remember."

"Well, he's good and mad at us now," CJ said, "Maybe we should go find him."

Harper shook her head. "Let him cool off. He was right. We've been living in our own cocoon of bliss and have been tugging him along. It wasn't fair for us to be passing judgment on his life."

"But we've been doing that for years, too. Not just since we've been with Grady and Cal," CJ said, "That's what I don't get. Why all of a sudden is he sensitive to it?"

"Give him some space. Do you think he went home? I'll give him a call," I said, reaching for my bag.

"Nah, he's probably at Sugar's," she said, turning to me. "It's the bar down the street from your—his house."

"Alright, well, you ladies have a good night. Today was fun.

Thanks for letting me have that experience, CJ. I think I'll be smiling for days."

She smiled back, "No problem. But if you want to do it again, there will be a commitment involved. You're talented." She began walking away and threw over her shoulder. "See you tomorrow," as if she hadn't just offered to have me drive for a premier race team.

She was kidding...she had to have been kidding. I shook my head and tried to ignore the comment as I slung my backpack over my shoulder and headed out to my car. After starting the engine, I caught CJ and Harper talking to each other and waving at me with a small smirk.

They knew I was going to go find him.

I didn't want him upset. Not because of me.

Sugars was a converted bottling factory changed into a 21st-century type of honky-tonk. It was relatively early for a crowd, so finding Gus was simply a matter of walking down to the end of the bar. He leaned against the bar talking with the ease of being in his second home and speaking to the bartender. Gus wasn't overly muscular or an exceptionally tall man, but he was well-defined, and even t-shirts and jeans set him apart from others. His hair was sandy brown with highlights of blond that would catch the light. It was always a little longer than it should be and gave into a natural curl in the back that always tempted me to thread my fingers through it. Was there a friendly way to do that?

Even with his back to me, I could pick him out of a crowd.

The bartender caught my approach first and nodded my way.

Gus looked over his shoulder, his scruff more defined in the bar room lighting. "Hey, darlin'. How'd you find me here?"

I sidled up to the bar, ignoring his comment.

"One of those, please." I pointed at whatever Gus was drinking, and the bartender walked to the cooler to get me one as Gus signaled for another.

I leaned on both my elbows and turned to Gus. "I heard you and your girls had some words."

"Yeah. Did they send you in as a peacekeeper?" he questioned.

"They hurt your feelings?" I teased.

He side-eyed me. "Don't you start, too."

I shook my head but smiled warmly at him. "Not going to. Just came to check on you." What goes on with you and them isn't my business. I heard the gist of it, though, and told them they were wrong."

"You did?" His tone was surprised.

"Yeah." I shrugged as if this wasn't a big deal. Gus exchanged his empty bottle for the full one. I rested my head in one hand and held my bottle out to him with the other, "Friends." We clinked bottles and took a sip before I surveyed the bar.

"Well, they came at me warning me off of you—as if I would lure you into my lair, ravish you and then chase you out of Charlotte with a broken heart."

I smirked. "They don't know me well," I said. "The hit-it-and-quit-it guys are one of two things. They are usually too pretty for their own good, or they can charm the pants off a nun. You, honey—" I waved my hand at him, "You I'd spot from a mile away."

His head dropped to stare at the table as he spoke low enough, but I heard the blow I'd just struck. "Hit-it and quit-it. That's what you think I am?"

"No." I drew out the word as I threw him a smile to emphasize the tease. "But that's how you flaunted yourself in college. You had a Ph.D. in flirting. It's why I never lost my heart over you as your tutor. It's why we worked so well together. You like to play a broad field, and I'm a serial monogamist."

He let out a low chuckle. "Serial monogamist. What is that?"

"I jump from one relationship to another. I'm nothing, or I'm all in. I think I've only had two single dates that didn't end in a commitment. I had two long-term relationships—not including Keith. Both involved men with whom I had a shared goal. Once the goal was met, we moved on from each other. Sometimes I don't know if it was an actual relationship as much as a partnership that also involved sex."

Gus was leaning back in his chair, arms crossed. "So that's what a relationship got you?"

"Sure, I mean, I knew I loved being in love—being with someone and having that connection fulfilled me. I told you about Keith." I sighed, looking over Gus' shoulder but not focusing on anything in particular, "Keith and I started work at Rex Richardson Racing in the same position as low-level engineers. We were together for a year or so before we even moved in together..." Not wanting to get into that again, I let that sentence just linger in the air.

Thankful he didn't push, I nudged him with my shoulder. "What a pair we make. A burned-out serial monogamist and a reforming womanizer...seems like the start of a beautiful friendship." I held up my bottle in a toast as the piano player began to play.

Looking at me with a strange look on his face, Gus held a tentative smile as he said, "Yeah, a beautiful friendship."

20

MIA

I won't lie. The days leading up to Daytona were always nerve-wracking. It wasn't like I'd never been there before. But this year was different. Different teams, different position, different circumstances.

The weather was mild enough to relax outside the team's trailer before the first event of the season, Daytona Duals—an event that preceded the Daytona 500. I found a foldable chair and took a moment to check my texts and see if Gus had responded to our latest online Word Scrabble game.

Smiling when I saw he used the word "mega" for a measly eleven points.

"Oh, he's going to hate me…" I typed the word "jazzy" for fifty-four points and hit enter with an evil cackle that was meant only for my ears.

A shadow suddenly loomed over me. "That sounds ominous," a very familiar but equally unwelcome voice said.

I closed my eyes, taking in a deep breath. I knew this moment would come. It was inevitable. But damn. I was having such a good day.

The shadow stepped in front of me. "Hello, Mia."

Still holding my phone, I tilted my head, shielding my eyes from the sun to study him, and relaxing my face. He didn't deserve a window into my mood, nor was I going to give him a reaction.

"Oh. Hi." I went back to studying my phone and recrossed my legs. I knew I was supposed to be taking the high road, but if he was here, it wasn't to exchange pleasantries.

He put his hands in his pockets, waiting for further acknowledgment, and then sighed when I continued to ignore him. He glared down at me like a disapproving parent and me, his recalcitrant child. "So, we are going to be like this now? I thought we could be civil and talk for a moment."

I put my phone down and flashed my eyes back to his. He'd been dodging my texts and calls for weeks. "Are you here to tell me when I can get my things from the storage unit?"

"Well, as you can guess, I've been a bit busy with the pre-season work, and since you left so abruptly, I was down an engineer. I haven't had time to go to the storage unit and dig through things."

I stood and gave him a thin, polite smile meant to contain all the words I really wanted to say. Two words, in particular—one rhymed with "duck," and the other was off. "Give me the key for the storage unit, and I'll go get them out myself. You don't have anything down there anyway." I held out my hand. "I'll go this week and leave the key for you when I'm done."

His eyes darted around, as if assessing who was within earshot and what he could get away with saying to me. "I don't have it with me. Again, I've been too busy to worry about this petty—"

"Oh, give me a break..." I said, rolling my eyes and throwing up my hands.

His poorly concealed temper flared. "God, you're such a bitch. A self-centered, entitled bitch." He gritted through his teeth.

Keith thought cussing was beneath him—a sign of a person not in control of their own emotions. It was uncivilized, rude, improper, blah, blah, blah. The times I did cuss, he'd say, "You have a better vocabulary than that."

Well, calling me a "bitch" wasn't exactly polite.

"Wow. That was rude. Keith, I thought you had a better vocabulary than that." I crossed my arms over my chest. His ears pinked up, and it brought me a small measure of satisfaction.

Whatever. I wasn't going to give him any of my words. He surveyed the crowd gathering and closed his eyes, rolled his shoulders, and the fake, public Keith reappeared and spoke clearly and with so much condescension.

"Mia, this is ridiculous. You're being immature—"

I stepped into his space, and he took two steps back, which had to be interesting to watch, given he was almost seven inches taller than me. Some team members around the trailer took notice and began moving toward us.

But I had righteous indignation on my side and a whole lot of pent-up anger.

"Keith, you have no business being over here. As you've stated, your duties as the team's new crew chief have you too busy with preparations to be over here harassing me. I just want my things." I took another step forward. "Since you're flying solo now and no one is around to clean up after you, I'm sure you are very...very busy."

That struck a nerve. Keith's face reddened as he looked around to see if anyone heard me. I held up a hand to stop some of my team members from moving closer to intervene. He gritted out, "I came by today to see you. I heard you were working for Merlo and wanted to see—"

"If it was true?" I cut him off. "If I could function and thrive in a world without you?"

He muttered under his breath. "I wanted to see how you were doing. I—I wanted to check on you—"

I shook my head. "How did I never see this before?"

"What?"

"What a self-righteous, narcissistic bastard you are. People tried to warn me." I threw a hint of condescending pity in my tone. "I told them you were just awkward." I saw the twitch he tried to hide. As someone who spent their lifetime surrounded by men who were usually cast as geeks and nerds, I knew the one word they all hated was awkward. You could take pride in being called a geek or nerd because it came with the understanding that you were also intelligent. But being deemed awkward meant you lacked social skills and maybe even respect. Keith considered himself extremely socially gifted, and he craved respect more than air.

My hands were in fists, and my eyes were burning as I waited for him to lash out at the ultimate insult I handed him. "If it wasn't for me, you wouldn't even have that job, you—"

He glanced over my shoulder, and if I hadn't been so full of rage, I would've appreciated the moment his smarmy, cocky mask slipped into place.

He leaned forward enough to whisper, "You know that's what people think—you know what they say behind your back? Poor, pathetic Mia—what will happen to her now?"

A new, cheerful, calming, and familiar voice lassoed my attention, dragging me back from the brink of losing my mind on Keith. "Mia!" The lifeline reached me through the haze of fury as I held myself back from verbally eviscerating Keith—and giving him more of the reaction he wanted, the reaction that validated his beliefs as to why I left.

Instead, I gritted my teeth. "I should never have—"

"You should never have left." Keith lunged a step forward, his own anger peeking through from the humiliation of my leaving. "Of course, I was going to get the promotion." He held his hands out, shrugged, his arrogance slipped back in place and began to step backward. "You're cute, and you may be smart, but you aren't leadership material, Mia." The cocky son of a bitch turned his back on me as I did give in and lunged for him.

"You are a fraud and a fake!" I needed to get in another jab. I needed to have the last word. A strong hand reached around from behind me, grabbing my own, pulling me into a hard, warm chest, wrapping me in a secure embrace, anchoring me and my anger.

Gus's amber, woodsy scent permeated the other stronger scents of the infield of a racetrack, drugging me.

"And you're delusional," Keith yelled back over his shoulder but did not bother to turn around.

I didn't care. My attention was directed to the breath tickling my ear as Gus whispered, "He's not worth it." Goosebumps raced down my arms, over my breasts and traveled further south. My mind was stunned by the overload of input, the jarring sensations of Gus's body touching mine, and the sudden shift in focus.

Oh, my God. Gus was more of a risk to my mental well-being than Keith.

I struggled against Gus's embrace—not to go after Keith, but step further away from Gus's orbit. Fight or flight. Mentally, I was fighting Keith. But I needed to flee Gus's arms. Right. Now. Because it felt too good. Too perfect.

Screw Keith. Whatever. Gus was my bigger concern.

But Gus didn't let go. "Shh. Just wait a minute," he said. He held me tighter, his jaw ticking, and I followed his gaze to where his eyes were trained on Keith.

Keith stopped. After years of dealing with him, I was familiar with his new expression, the green-eyed monster. Keith didn't share. He thought everything he touched, everything he claimed, was his.

I watched Keith survey Gus's arms around me and the way they roamed carelessly. Keith's back straightened like heckles rising.

A quiet chuckle from Gus clued me into how much Gus enjoyed the role he played.

He turned my back against his front, and we both faced Keith. He adjusted his arms so one was grazing just below my breasts.

Oh, dear Lord...

I glanced up over my shoulder at Gus, who graced me with a smirk and a wink before burying his face in my hair and whispering, "This is going to kill him."

But Keith wasn't going to slink away as I'd hoped. "Gus Quinlan, huh? I knew you were a fast mover, Mia. But I have to say—you really missed the mark with that one?"

I was too distracted by the heat of Gus's body, his forearm stretched under my breasts, his hands touching my body, and his breath traveling down my neck—forget about Keith...Gus was the one twisting me up.

Instinctively, I covered his hands with mine, and to anyone else it looked like a lover's embrace to anyone else. It was actually a case of adrenaline playing havoc with my equilibrium and Gus having to hold me upright. I closed my eyes to try to block at least one sense from being overwhelmed.

"Ignore him. It will make it so much worse." Gus turned me to face him. "Open your eyes, Mia." His voice was soft, and I was mesmerized and willing to do whatever it asked of me. I struggled to focus as he cupped my jaw with his warm hand and ran his thumb down the side of my face, sending tingles where I didn't need them.

He stared at me...as if he treasured me. He cleared his throat. "Pretend you are distracted by my mere presence—that I'm all you see." The hint of a devilish smile played on his lips—lips that were way too close for my comfort.

Pretend he distracted me? He wants me to pretend...the world could crash around me, and I wouldn't notice.

I had to push back. I couldn't do this. I couldn't...pretend. Not with him. Not like this. When his lips parted, my eyes found their latest obsession.

Give me strength, I can't...I can't kiss him.

I shoved away from him with all the willpower left in me. Somehow, I managed not to fall on my backside and managed to get two steps away from Gus, while Keith's back disappeared among a crowd of people and through a path of trailers.

Gus took a half-step closer and slid his hands into his pockets. He leaned in with a small chuckle that wasn't lined with his trademark cockiness, but something less certain, and said, "Hey, darlin', did I make you breathless?"

Hell, yes. It was a monumental miracle I wasn't gasping for air.

I exaggerated an eye roll and shakily pointed in Keith's direction. "You probably just saved that man's testicles. Actually I'm not sure if you did humanity any favors."

Gus rocked back on his feet and stared into the crowd. We both remained silent—which was a bit unusual for Gus. For both of us. Did I just make this weird between us?

Dang it.

While I was good at most sciences, I took the bare minimum in biology—it wasn't as if engineers needed to know much about hormones. What were the sex hormones again? Estrogen, testosterones...? Do humans secrete pheromones? Why was being this close to Gus making me think about biology?

My head was spinning, and I rubbed my forehead as I sat in my chair. Gus came over to stand in front of me.

He was too close. "Are you okay? What did he say?" He dropped down and sat on his haunches, putting his hands on my knees.

I put my hands over his, took in a cleansing breath, and said, "No. I'm fine. He just surprised me." I shook my head a bit. "And he knew exactly what buttons to push to inflict the most damage."

Gus ran his hand over my hair as if to tame it and then caressed the side of my face. The concern on his face was raw...and there went my breathing again.

He took a quick look over his shoulder. "You let me or one of the boys know if that jackass comes back around. I'm going to go to talk to Jacks and the crew—"

I straightened and shook my head. "No. He was just trying to rattle my cage, and I made the mistake of letting him."

I gathered enough brain cells to stand, nudged his shoulder, and threw him a forced but grateful smile. "You. You, my dear Gus, threw it right back at him with that performance. Bravo!"

His eyes narrowed before he gave me his ten-million-dollar smile that would melt the panties off a nun. "That's what friends are for." He straightened and held out his hand to me. "You gonna be okay?"

I waved him off, "I'll be fine." I ran my hands down the front of my pants as if smoothing them out and I tested out the validity of that statement by taking a step or two unassisted. "By the way, why are you over this way? You looking for Grady? Did he sneak off with his fiancée again?" I scanned the area.

Gus rubbed the back of his neck, cringing. "It seems kind of ridiculous now, considering the situation..."

What?

He reached into his pocket and pulled out something small. "Close your eyes and hold out your hand."

I eyed him warily, but his playfulness made me smile as I complied. "Okay."

Something oblong and thin wrapped in plastic landed in my hand. I opened my eyes. "Smarties? You got me Smarties." This was another inside joke of ours. I'd get him Dum-Dums and he'd sweeten me up with Smarties.

His hands were in his back pockets, and he rocked back on his feet. "Yeah," he appeared almost boyish with pride in his gift. "A good luck charm."

I also smiled as I pulled out my tribute to the walk down memory lane from my back pocket. "Dum-Dums," I said.

His smile was amplified with warmth, and a twinkle in his eye did things to me I didn't want to contemplate. He let out a chuckle and wrapped me in a mini headlock, just as if I were one of the guys.

Friends, that's what he kept reminding me we were. It would be good for my heart to remember that, too.

For now, Keith was forgotten. The confusion surrounding our pretend intimacy would hopefully fade. The two pieces of candy made us smile and promised to make the rest of the day sweet.

Gus stuck the lollipop in his pocket, hooked an arm around my shoulder, letting it hang there as if it belonged. I wrapped mine around his waist, leaning my head into the side of him slightly, and said, "Come on, let's go see where your wayward driver is anyway."

"Listen..." He rubbed his hands together, "If we see dickhead again, we really should thank him."

"What? Why?"

"If it weren't for him being such an idiot, you wouldn't be here, ya know...where all the action is. Who cares about Chicago, anyway..." He waved his hand with the lollipop in it around. "The Carolinas are the shit."

I wanted to laugh at him because he wasn't wrong. He broke our connection, stepping away and spreading out his hands. "And you wouldn't be one of my best friends—that alone may be worth it all. You scraped him off, and look what you gained." He gave me the grin that earned him the nickname GQ and waved his hands up and down his body.

He really was adorable. I focused on the lock of hair falling across his forehead and took in a deep breath, blinking fast, trying not to stare at him. I nodded. "You're right."

That was all he wanted—for me to be one of his "best friends."

"Of course I am." He threw me the cheesiest smile and wiggled his eyebrows.

I patted his hard chest, trying very hard not to let my hand linger. "You're a good man, also," I whispered.

He caught my hand, held it to his chest, and his playfulness quieted as the tone of his voice grew serious. "I mean it, honey. You need to let me know if he shows up again. Because, darlin', he's going to realize you didn't just land on your feet," He squeezed my hand with both of his. "You did it with a better view."

I allowed myself to be ensnared by his blue eyes for a brief moment and listened to my traitorous internal voice give a sexy growl, *"Definitely with a better view."*

That's when I found a new target for my aggravation and aggression—it was that damn little voice. Yes, that damn little voice was my new nemesis. It was going to keep reminding me what it was like to have Gus hold me. It was going to bombard me with the memory, whisper the "what ifs" and "maybes" until I convinced myself that the embrace felt like something more than friendship.

That little voice and I were going to have to have a "come to Jesus" moment soon, or this could get complicated…and messy.

For Heaven's sake, I was still cleaning up my last mess, and it was Gus who was helping me. I couldn't risk believing there could be anything more than friendship between us. No matter what that damn little voice tried to tell me.

21

MIA

I had already invited Shaw down for the race in an attempt to get past the confusing feelings I was getting for my roommate. After the run-in with Keith and the subsequent reaction to Gus rescuing me—I wondered if adding Shaw into the mix was the best decision. But it proved to be a great distraction.

Shaw's commanding form was immediately spotted in a dense crowd. He tried to downplay his presence by coming alone, wearing dark shades, and staying away from the more popular spots. However, his overgrown, trademark blond hair peeked out of the bottom of the low-hanging baseball hat, and the shape of his body and his confident stride gave away his status as a professional athlete. For me, he was a welcomed face, and when he smiled at me, it immediately put me at ease.

"You'd think I'd get used to being around sports celebrities, but I guess walking alongside a professional football player is a whole different stratosphere," I said as he was spotted again while we walked by the garages.

Shaw gave me an apologetic smile, "I thought since we were out of the Carolinas it would be easier." He shrugged. "I'm sorry. I didn't think this would be a thing…"

"Not be a thing?" I guffawed at him. "Dude, you're like the most popular tight-end in the league."

His smile was so genuinely warm and almost a bit shy, as he dug his hands into his pockets. I relaxed for the first time since I got down here and, wow, I could see how you could easily fall for this guy.

Then he let out a chuckle and pointed at me, "Oh my God, did you just 'dude' me?"

I stopped walking, and covered my face in embarrassment. "Oh damn, I did. I've been spending too much time with the younger drivers in the Driven Women Program." I peeked out of my hands, and he reached for them, removing them from my face and exposing me to that heart-melting smile again. "That made me feel old just now."

He linked my hand through the crook of his elbow, and we continued to walk as two more women came up for photos and autographs.

The loss of his hand in mine didn't seem to bother me as much as when—

I clenched and unclenched my hand.

Stop it, girl. Dawson Shawfield is available. He's amazing. He's not complicated...unlike others...and look at the way he smiles at you. Sigh. He's gorgeous.

After he finished signing autographs and taking pictures, we went and had an early dinner. It helped get my mind off the fact that the next day I was going to be sitting next to Jacks in the booth for the opening of the season at the freaking Daytona race.

Tomorrow I would be manning the computer, working the magic with the software, and giving him the info he needed to decide on last-minute calls—watching a maestro at work. We had our setup and strategy in place. But that didn't consider white flag pit stops, wrecks, damage, weather, and a million other things that could change in a second. And while Jacks accepted the information the Aries program spit out for us, he also went on instinct and liked to make decisions based on a combination of data and gut.

Thankfully, going out with Shaw the night before my debut in the pit box distracted me from over-analyzing things and was a great way to relax.

When we got back to the hotel, he dropped me off at the entrance. Getting out to open my car door, he said, "Go get some sleep, and I'll catch up with you tomorrow. Davy is meeting me with some of the guys. We scored some great seats, apparently."

"That sounds like more fun than what I'll be dealing with," I said, running my hand through my hair before remembering it was up in a ponytail. God, I was such a dork.

He held my arm, rubbing it reassuringly before pulling me in for a hug. "You'll be fine. I know you will." He kissed the top of my head and continued to hold me, and I put my arms around his solid form, and it felt...well, it felt pretty damn good. He rubbed my back as we held each other right there in the roundabout of the hotel entrance. In plain sight of hotel guests and the fans who were starting to recognize him.

He leaned his head down and whispered in my ear, "What do they say in racing? Good luck? Break a leg?"

The smile that stretched across my face was genuine when I leaned back, his arms still locked around me as I stared up into his face. "There's not really a specific phrase in racing, but I get your meaning," I giggled.

Giggled. I freaking giggled. I don't giggle.

"Man, your smile..." he said, staring at my mouth. "You have a beautiful smile, Mia. It does something to me." He drew in a deep breath, and the devilish lift of the side of his mouth was doing something to me. "I better go because you have a big day tomorrow." He leaned down and kissed me, just shy of my mouth, before walking back to the driver's side of his car. "I'll see you tomorrow."

I waved a ridiculous, coquettish wave before walking inside the hotel lobby. My hand absently found its way to the place where he kissed me. My mind wandered to what would've happened if I'd turned just an inch to the left, when I remembered to watch where I was walking and to look for the elevators.

A pair of blazing blue eyes and a completely blank face had me pulled up short as if I'd been caught sneaking in past curfew.

Gus.

He was on the other side of a decently busy lobby. However, the crowds parted long enough for our gazes to lock—there was no way to claim we hadn't seen each other.

I gave another wave. This time to Gus, except this one was hesitant and weary. He closed his eyes, gave me a half-ass one back, and walked into the hotel restaurant.

Was he mad? I don't think he was mad. Probably just got a lot on his mind. No point in bothering him.

I walked to the elevator and went up to my room.

Besides, for tomorrow, at least, we were rivals. With the racing season starting, we probably needed to start establishing new boundaries.

22

MIA

The morning of the race, I walked to the trailer to pick up my headset and check in with the team. Nerves were getting the better of me, and I second-guessed the extra dose of caffeine I had that morning. I was thinking about my evening with Shaw and how I enjoyed talking with a man again—someone who wasn't always trying to compete or one-up me or prove he knew more than I did. Shaw made me feel special.

Later, after our team meeting, we settled in the pit box, and my phone pinged with a text from Gus. I hadn't heard from him since seeing him in the lobby last night. And I still felt like I had done something wrong.

> GUS
>
> Good luck today.

> MIA
>
> You too.

That's all we'd said to each other since my run-in with Keith.

I was going to ask him what he did last night. It's what I'd ask one of my friends. But it felt invasive and did I even really want to know?

It would have felt as if we were crossing a line that was forming between us.

I was about to put my phone back in my pocket when another text came in.

GUS

Did you have a good night last night?

MIA

Yeah, I did. Thanks. I forgot to mention Shaw was in town.

GUS

You don't owe me an explanation.

Okay, then.

GUS

It was good for you to get out and relax. You've got a good team. Jacks is patient and decisive. Just give him what he asks for. Listen and learn. You'll be fine.

MIA

Alright, thanks. Are you heading back home tonight or tomorrow?

GUS

Tonight.

MIA

Us too. I guess I'll see you later then. Good luck.

GUS

Catch ya later.

I didn't have much experience with CJ on Race Day, but from the tension around the trailer, I'd say she was feeling some stress. She'd bypassed the autograph seekers and beelined to the trailers after meeting with some reporters in the media tent.

There was some buzz from the tent about Grady doing better and heavily favored this season. The commentators were emphasizing how fluidly he moved into the series and gained so much attention and respect. They also hinted that she was, again, benefitting from his popularity, and maybe she really wasn't worth the hype.

"CJ's got some stiff competition to prove who wears the pants in that family."

It was all stuff she'd heard before. But, yeah. It wouldn't make me very happy either.

Harper's smile was that of a shark circling prey as she walked out of the tent.

"That reporter better watch his back because he's not going to see the beat down coming," Jacks said, coming up behind me, adjusting his ever-present trucker's cap on his head as he followed them both. "Harper's got a thing with reporters, and most have learned to play nice, or she teaches them how to be polite and respectful to her people."

I've heard about reporters who've crossed Harper—I wouldn't recommend it.

Grady and CJ usually kept their distance from each other prior to a race. With her temper boiling, they returned CJ to the trailer to focus and cool down prior to driver introductions. Harper walked out of the trailer with her hands together in prayer, and CJ's music cranked up inside.

She spotted Jacks and me and plastered on a smile, "She'll be fine." Just as Eminem blasted through the trailer. "Just fine." She was reassuring herself as well as us. "Let's go get settled." Harper nodded to her assistant, Megan, and bit out, "She has ten minutes to get her shit together, then drag her to the stand."

We walked on with a few people gawking and waving as Harper's long legs had her lengths in front of us. She remembered she was walking with a man way past retirement age, and a woman—me—who had a stride about half the length of hers. "Sorry." She took in a cleansing breath and shook out her hands. "Daytona always has us on edge. Need to shake out the nerves, is all."

We reached the pit stand and checked our equipment, Jacks reviewed the plan for the day, checked in with the crew, and then we just waited. I grabbed my headset from a crew member and stepped up the ladder to my seat at the front of the pit box—ready to be Jacks's data guru. Ready to crunch numbers and do on-the-spot analysis, to be his right hand.

Speaking of hands, mine were shaking, my stomach flipping, and I wished they would just start the damn race, so I had somewhere to focus all this energy. I pulled out the chair I'd be sitting in for the next few hours. A small pink and purple cardboard box laid on top of my laptop. The NERDS candy box had a note under it.

"Time to put that big, beautiful brain to work. Show them how it's done." - Gus

And now the rest of me was shaking with more adrenaline and laughter.

Because at that moment, he was probably finding the bouquet of Dum-Dums I wrapped with a pink ribbon that I paid one of the set-up crew members to tape to his chair.

I shook the NERDS candy box just as a message popped up on my phone. It was a photo of a mouth—a beautiful mouth—with perfectly defined lips and a sexy tilt of the side where a white stick protruded from them. Those beautiful lips were more enticing than any lollipop and I wondered what it would be like to taste them—

Jesus, Mary, and Joseph.

It must be the adrenaline—the anticipation of the Daytona 500—that kicked up my heartbeat at that moment. It had to be what caused the butterflies in my stomach. And not those lips.

I was giggling as I answered his photo with one of me throwing back my head, pouring the overly sweet candy in my mouth. I followed with,

MIA

NERDS rule, jocks drool.

And added a Winky emoji.

I swore I could hear a burst of laughter over all the engines and pit row noise from five stalls down.

Oh my God, I just sent Gus a winky emoji. What was my nerdy problem?

GUS

It's not nice to say things like that about your boyfriend.

MIA

I was talking about you. And Shaw isn't my boyfriend.

GUS

I'm not your boyfriend.

Don't I know it.

MIA

Rolled eyes emoji.

GUS

Kissy-winky-face emoji.

MIA

Face-palm emoji.

GUS

Thanks for the lollipop emoji.

MIA

Smiley face. Four-leaf clover emoji.

There was a smile on my face and warmth inside where worry once resided, as I stuck the half-empty box of candy in my pocket. Jacks joined me in the box, along with Harper and a few important sponsors. It was time to race, and I was ready.

———

Racing was all risk management for the crew chief. He takes in the information from three sources—the driver, the spotter, and me, the engineer—to make quick decisions about when to pit, whether to do a full pit stop with four tires and fuel or a two-tires stop or just a fuel stop.

Then if there is an issue of the car running loose or tight through the turns, or if there was some other anomaly CJ communicates preventing the car from running properly, we have to address it.

"Air pressure isn't right."

"Car's too damn loose—I'm flying all over the place."

"There's a bad vibration."

None of those things are what anyone wants to hear. But you don't just pop the hood in the pit. The team must diagnose the problem prior to the car coming in based on the driver's description, visual observations, and the gauge information I was tracking. The crew has less than fourteen seconds when the car stops to change four tires, fuel up the car, and make any adjustments needed to increase performance to remain competitive.

Fourteen seconds to adjust the wedge (suspension) of the car, or how it grips the track, make any body repairs that mess with the aerodynamics and clean the grill to help with air to the engine.

I studied my laptop—the numbers on the Aries software informing me who's pitted already, who's taken tires, their speed, what their position was, when they would be projected to pit next…almost everything you'd want to follow on each of the forty-plus cars except the color of the driver's underwear. More importantly, nothing can tell us their fuel mileage, like has a driver been doing a decent job conserving, or were they running on fumes hoping for a white flag, or to make it to the finish line?

Conserving fuel isn't something any driver likes to do, but it's all about patience and strategy. Patience wasn't CJ's forte.

Basically, the team was gambling on someone wrecking or another reason for a yellow flag being out, causing all cars to slow to fifty-five miles per hour and all passing to cease. It also is a good time for everyone to come into pit without the repercussion of losing well-fought-for positioning.

Aaron, CJ's spotter who sat in an observation booth above the track, is the voice in CJ's ear while she's on the track. Giving all of us a bird's-eye view from the very top of the track with spotters from all the other teams.

"Sixteen is leading, with thirty-four taking the low line about two lengths behind," Aaron's voice came over the headset.

"Just trying to find some wiggle room around this fifty-six," CJ said. "Crafty son of a—"

"Yeah, Conway's breaking off," Aaron said, talking about the car behind CJ that was drafting her—basically riding her bumper to make both of them more aerodynamic and run more efficiently and faster.

Jacks broke into the conversation. "Yellow flag is out, CJ. Oil on the track."

Half the field of cars came onto pit lane in what looked like an orchestrated dance of machines slowing down from 180 mph to 55 mph onto pit lane to avoid a penalty.

Pit boxes were lined up and the cars must slide into a box twenty-four by nine feet, avoid hitting each other, and stop on a dime while team members from all teams leap the barrier with gas and tires to start their eleven-to-fourteen-second pit stop.

Grady passed by us with his royal blue car, pitting five boxes ahead of us, but I didn't give them a look because CJ's monstrous-sounding engine demanded all our attention. "Who remained out, Mia?" Jacks asked while watching his team go to work.

I rattled off the twenty names out of the thirty remaining drivers who were still in the race after a series of large wrecks.

Jacks stood, legs spread, arms crossed, looking down over his people like a king observing his kingdom. He spoke proficiently and efficiently during a race, focusing everyone on doing the same.

He put his headset closer to his mouth and said to CJ, "Take your time exiting. Don't push getting out of here." His voice was that of a stern father reminding their daughter of her curfew.

"Yeah. Yeah." And CJ's tone was of a teenager who had been reminded numerous times.

Then boom, the moment her car's tires were off the jack, and hitting the pavement, they were spinning out of the pit box. Jacks closed his eyes, his lips moving in silent prayer that she didn't get a penalty for speeding off the exit from pit row that would cost them a lap.

But CJ was a talented professional, and unlike most teens, she did know her limit. She also had an excellent team who gained her a second off some of her competitors.

We were on lap one-hundred seventy out of two-hundred laps when things started to get interesting. Grady had lost position after getting caught up in a scuffle with two rivals and had spent time battling back. He'd caught up to CJ who was running in seventh position but spent the last few laps battling for the sixth position with a veteran.

Aaron came on. "Grady wants to know if you want to dance?"

"Only if he lets me lead," she replied. And the two of them began drafting, taking advantage of the aerodynamics of the two cars together to gain momentum.

Jacks leaned to me, "Give me the rundown for the next stop."

I studied my screen and told him about our position in relation to the other drivers in the top ten. Based on their last stops, we could estimate who probably had enough fuel for the remaining laps, who would have to conserve, sacrifice speed, and hope to pull it out at the end, and who must pit. I told him who was on fresh tires and who wasn't. And which cars were running the best. All from the software crunching the numbers in front of me.

CJ and Grady pulled past the veteran who wasn't drafting with anyone—flying solo was how you lost positioning. For all the jockeying, egos, and rivalries in racing, there were times you needed a partner.

However, in the last few laps, it became every man for himself. As CJ and Grady battled through some traffic, Grady got caught up in another two cars getting loose and lost some traction.

Aaron kept talking in CJ's ear, being her eye in the sky. Jacks was taking it all in and throwing in his instructions. I watched, trying to predict each of his moves. In the end, CJ pulled out a top-five finish, Grady a few cars back.

I was flying high, having finished my first race to the left of a legendary chief and groundbreaking team.

God, I really should thank Keith for being a total asshole...otherwise I would never have felt this alive.

23

MIA

With a few races under our belt, I got into a groove with Jacks, CJ, and the rest of the crew. However, at the Bristol race, tensions ran a bit high. Short tracks weren't Grady's best, and he didn't fare well.

A car tried to pass CJ on the outside, ran up into the wall, blew a tire, and clipped her back end, causing her to fishtail. She did a fantastic job regaining control before heading into the inside wall but lost momentum. A series of bad pit stops followed, and even though she finished the race, she remained a few laps down and never regained good track positioning.

CJ would never take it out on Jacks, but others weren't as fortunate. "How can we expect to win races with twenty-second pit stops? For Christ's sake!" She took off her gloves, tossed them at whoever would catch them, and made a beeline for her trailer with a gaggle of reporters following her, pointing out every mistake she made and even making up a few she didn't.

"I can see why she's...um...abrasive sometimes," I said to Megan, Harper's assistant, as she came over to stand next to me.

"This actually isn't that bad. It's better if she just goes straight to her trailer," she said, searching her phone for something. "It's the adrenaline, and it's stress. It's the expectations and pressure." She looked up at me and shrugged before saying, "It's racing," and walked off.

I stayed clear and hightailed it back to the hotel, where I nursed a beer in the hotel bar while watching some late-night talk show. A disheveled and weary-eyed Gus came up next to me, signaling to the bartender, who seemed to know him well enough to have his favorite beer ready for him as he sat his butt on the stool.

"Hey," he said.

"Hey. You survived?" I said, taking in his weary expression.

He just raised his eyebrows in response. Not much else to say. It was a shitty day. You have them. Most of the time, it was either Merrick or Merlo who had a sucky race. Today it was both teams, so no one was feeling the love tonight.

We sat in companionable silence, sipping our beers and watching a late-night host play a silly game with the newest, up-and-coming starlet.

I side-eyed Gus. Wasn't he in a photo with her in one of those magazines a year or two ago? Maybe before she made her last movie? She was from Tennessee, I think. She may have even been a grand marshal or something at a race.

"Hey, didn't you date her?" I said and pointed with my beer bottle at the television.

"Not exactly," he said, not taking his eyes off the television.

The woman was giggling at the talk show host as they goofed around and bantered effortlessly.

I leaned on my elbow and put my head against my hand. "Do I want to know?"

He put his bottle to his mouth and gave me a "Nope" before taking a sip of his beer.

"Hmm," I said, turning my head to study the woman and then Gus. I let it go. Because truthfully, I didn't want to know.

"It's not what you think," he said, pivoting his chair toward me. "So don't give me shit about it."

"Boy, you're in a mood tonight," I said, mirroring him and crossing my legs.

He ran his hand down his face. "I…" He grimaced, glancing over my shoulder before saying. "I don't want you to think what everyone else does."

"And what's that?"

"That I have a different woman in my bed every weekend. Or that I did—" he said.

"Didn't you? I remember in college—"

"Every guy is like that in college—" he defended.

"Not every guy. Just the ones who look like…" I motioned to him with my bottle. "Well, the ones who are as pretty as you," I said with a twinge of humor.

"Whatever. Speaking of pretty boys. How's yours doing?"

Maybe I should've just gone up to my room. "I don't know what you mean," I mumbled. "But if you're asking how Shaw is doing, he's fine. I guess. We don't have anything serious going on. I'm busy, and he's busy. We're just friends—"

He held up his hand, "You and I are just friends…Shaw doesn't look at you like a friend. He looks at you like he wants to devour you."

"Ha. Don't be ridiculous. Shaw is a perfect gentleman—"

"It doesn't mean he doesn't want in your bed." He stared up at the television, leaned back on the stool, and his arms crossed over his chest.

"Well, I'm not there…and honestly, he hasn't asked."

The slightest lift in his eyebrow was all the reaction I got. As if he didn't believe me or found that information surprising. I didn't care what he thought.

He held up his hand and shrugged, "I'm sorry. I'm being an ass. It's just…I didn't picture you with someone like Shaw."

"Why?"

"Because he's just so…"

"So?"

"Big."

"You have an issue with his size?" I said. "That's kind of ridiculous."

He continued. "I've heard things about him. His reputation."

152

A laugh escaped me. "Seriously?"

"What?"

"You have an issue with Shaw's reputation?" I turned on the stool to face him. "Isn't that

a bit pot meet kettle—whether well-earned or not, don't you suffer from a *reputation*?"

He narrowed his eyes at me. "I'm not talking about me. I'm talking about you. You, who belongs with someone better than that."

I gestured with my thumb over my shoulder. "Even now, there are three women at the table over there waiting for me to leave so they can slip their keys to you. If I weren't here, would you take them up on it? They're all gorgeous."

"Not the point." He pretended to focus on the television.

Holy crap, would he? "So, you would? If I wasn't here, you'd go upstairs with one of

them?"

"Don't be ridiculous." His voice was low, off-putting. But he hadn't answered the question.

"Maybe I should go to the restroom and see which one will approach. Do you feel like a blond, redhead, or the tall leggy one this evening?"

"Why are you being like this? I was just trying to warn you—"

"Gus," I held up my hands, "I'm fine. Shaw and I are friends—"

"He kissed you." He blurted out, "At Daytona."

"You're being ridiculous and an ass." I went to get my money out and tossed it on the bar. "It's been a long day for both of us. May I suggest we end this absurd conversation and go get some rest." I maneuvered around the barstool to leave.

He gently grabbed my arm. "Mia. Wait. Don't."

I pulled my arm away from him. "I'm not going to sit here and be lectured to, Gus." God, I hated that there was a hitch between the words, but I didn't get angry without a few tears breaking through. I was tired, I was coming off a long day of high adrenaline. He was supposed to be my safe harbor, and he was rocking the boat as if it were a hurricane making landfall.

He jumped in front of me, stopping me from walking around the barstool. "Wait, I'm...I'm sorry." He ran his hand through his hair, gripped his neck, and closed his eyes. Once he angled his head down at me, I noticed the dark circles, the wariness, and the paleness of his face. "Please. I'm sorry. I..." He fell back onto his barstool, shoulders sagging and head drooping. Defeat wasn't something I'd ever seen on Gus before.

He turned to the bar and put his head in his hands, dejected. "God, I'm...fucking up."

"Gus," I said softly, before sitting back down beside him. This wasn't about me—or at least not entirely.

"What's going on? Did something happen with the team? Did you get in a fight with Grady? With Bill or...was it Junior?" It must be him...Junior was constantly pushing his buttons.

He shook his head and stared at the TV. I didn't think he was going to say anything else, and then he softly added, "I just haven't slept well the last few days." After a few more minutes, he said, "Tommy's birthday is this week."

"Oh."

He played with his bottle, realized it was empty, and motioned to the bartender. "I think it's messing with me. Normally, CJ, Harper, and I would all go out and have drinks or dinner or do something that would remind us of him, but with things changing...I guess it's bothering me that neither of them has even mentioned him this week."

Now CJ's temper and the general unease with some people around her made more sense.

"I think CJ is feeling it, too," I said. "Actually, it explains a lot—"

He shook his head slowly. "I know between the new team and planning a wedding...but I didn't think Tommy would ever be an afterthought."

Instinctively, I put my hand on his forearm, "I don't think he's an afterthought—"

He shook his head. "No, I don't mean that in a bad way. I get that people move on." He stared at my hand on his forearm as if it were a foreign body—like, who was I to touch him in such a manner? To bring him comfort.

I started to remove it and he put his hand over mine to stop me, "I mean, I thought, well, I thought maybe it would be me or Harper who would need to be reminded or who'd start to bow out. Not CJ."

"She's getting married. Maybe she's not sure how Tommy's memory fits into that part of her life," I said with as much gentleness as I could muster.

I didn't know Tommy or his relationship with CJ besides the one time I met them when Gus took me to a race in college.

He rubbed his forehead as if contemplating that possibility. "I never thought about that. It's just they loved each other so much…"

"What—is that what is bothering you? How could she move on to Grady? Don't you want her to?"

He shook his head, frustrated. "I don't know what I'm saying. I like her with him.

I do—"

Without even pausing to think about it, I blurted, "Gus, do you have feelings for her?" A lump lodged in my throat, and I swear it was because it would make sense—how moody he was being with me and his lack of dating—if he still had mixed-up feelings for CJ. Oh boy, that would be a big, huge cluster—

I winced and tried to hide it before he caught me.

He shook his head without hesitation and reached for the fresh beer the bartender put in front of him. He put his hand back on mine and squeezed. "At one point, I thought I wanted her to move on with me. But that wasn't it. I wanted what they had. That connection, I think. In a way, I was always jealous of it." He took a sip. "I thought it was her. I thought I was jealous because he had her." He took another sip. "Then, after he died, I just wanted to take care of her, the way he'd want me to." He sat back and sighed. "And I realized I'm just not cut out for that kind of relationship."

Hm. Okay. "Why would you say that? I would disagree."

He shrugged. "I don't have a lifestyle that's conducive to that kind of commitment, and I honestly don't think I'd want to deal with…" he waved his arm around, "everything it entails." His eyes flicked over to mine and there was truth in them—sad truth.

I sat waiting for more.

"I watched my mom love a man for decades who claimed to love her just to keep her on his hook." He stared at his bottle, and I sat very, very still. "He made her believe they were soulmates, and he had her so wrapped up she was convinced no one else would be it for her."

He looked at me and said, "That, of course, was my dad. The only thing he gave me was a trust fund for my college education, and even that he hid from everyone. He didn't want anything to tie him to us. It's why I don't have his name because I'm a bastard. A literal bastard in the very sense of the word. My father was a married man when he was with my mom..." He let out a big sigh, put his beer down, and rubbed his hands over his face. "I can't believe I'm even telling you all this. How did we even get on this topic?"

"Gus, hon, you know, I would never say anything," I said, wanting to touch him, but now it seemed too intimate, and I was too unsure.

He patted my knee and left his hand there. "I know, darlin'. You can probably count the number of people who know about this on one hand. Even fewer know who my father is. So please, don't say anything. My mother is very sensitive about it."

"Of course." With no other way to express my sincerity, I gathered his hand in mine. The warmth between them was a promise of silence and an offer of comfort. The fact that he trusted me with this knowledge and that he was opening up to me like this...

He stared at our joined hands and threaded our fingers together, further solidifying the easy connection.

Whatever the moment, he broke it with, "Anyway, enough about my daddy issues, and back to CJ and Tommy. I'm sure you heard I wasn't Grady's biggest fan at first."

I nodded. "I heard you were pretty jealous."

"So, you did hear about some of the drama."

I gave the slightest shrug.

He shook his head. "I thought it was jealousy. But I think I was more confused and hurt. I was still holding Tommy's place with her."

He let go of my hand and reached back for the bottle. His voice deepened and became rougher. "I dream about Tommy occasionally." He cleared his throat. "Usually when I'm stressed or have to make a big decision." He began to peel the label off his beer bottle.

"Sometimes, it was reliving the night he died. Tommy, full of energy Tommy, lying lifeless on an ER bed, people and machines... everyone and everything moving and making noise—except him. He was gone. I knew he was gone. They weren't giving up. They did everything to pull him back. People running around, the beeping machines, all the voices shouting orders—and his lifeless body not responding. I knew..." His voice trailed off before regaining the strength to continue.

I stayed still.

"CJ and Harper running in...the look on CJ's face when she saw the body on the gurney...her collapsing in my arms, sobbing, screaming...falling apart." Gus wasn't with me at that moment or even sitting in this bar. He was inside that memory. "Tommy's mom wailed."

His voice gave out, and he took in a breath. "An intoxicated, distraught Dewey came after CJ as if to kill her there in the hospital ER. Threatening her—throwing accusations and yelling that it was her fault—she killed Tommy."

My poor Gus. Sitting there. Staring at the damn beer bottle... reliving that horrible moment. He continued to peel the label from the bottle, his hand trembling slightly.

"I was supposed to be with him that night, you know...with Tommy. But I wasn't. That night, Tommy and CJ got into a huge fight. Dewey took him out drinking, and I'd had it with all the CJ bashing. I left earlier with a girl—I don't even remember her name." He ran his hand through his hair, yanking on it. "God, I'd give my life to take that night back and do it over. To stop him from getting in that damn car."

That was it. My eyes burned as I suddenly grabbed his hand and held it to my lips, kissing the top of it and forcing eye contact with him. I tucked his hand under my chin, wanting him to know I was still with him. I was always a support for him. My poor Gus. The pain...

"Oh, Gus." I couldn't keep the tears out of my voice. "I...I can't imagine the pain you must carry with you."

He didn't respond but waited for a few heartbeats before continuing.

"Hearing them call 'time of death'..." He blew out a breath. "It haunts me. Knowing that someone that young, someone so alive, could be gone so quickly. It was a revelation."

He squeezed my hand.

"Anyway," he breathed out, his voice seemingly disconnected from the man I knew Gus to be. "Tommy still visits my dreams. Depending on what was going on, sometimes I relive that night. I hear the machines. I hear CJ crying. I feel the numbness, the void, of him being there and then gone. Sometimes the horror is symbolic of some guilt or anxiety in my life. The worst is when he shows up completely alive, smiling and offering advice as my voice of reasoning, my conscious-ness, trying to tell me something. The payment for that gift is to wake up and endure his loss all over again."

He turned to me. "Do you ever feel like that? Your dreams are trying to tell you something?"

I nodded. "My mom," I said, and two tears escaped. "I still see my mom." It was all I could get out.

He nodded too. But then saw my tears, his shoulders dropped, and his face fell further. "I'm so sorry. I didn't mean to make you sad—"

He inched closer to me, but I shook my head. "No. It's okay. It doesn't make me sad. Knowing she's there, seeing her in my dreams... it comforts me, gives me strength, sometimes." I didn't want to steer the conversation away from him. I squeezed his hand, hoping he would continue.

Gus's thumb mindlessly stroked the top of my hand, as if he were the one giving me comfort now. "Tommy was—is—my anchor. Even in death."

He sat up straighter on the stool. "Anyway, one night during the whole Grady-CJ drama, I dreamt about Tommy hanging out on a dock with Grady." He sat back, released my hand, and took a drink. "They were just sitting there on the edge of the dock, their feet in the water, beer in their hands, sun going down. Talking and laughing. I was too far away to hear what they said, so I just watched."

Gus's knee was jumping a mile a minute as he mindlessly stroked his finger up and down the condensation on the beer bottle—his breathing was deep and cleansing. "At one point," he cleared his throat. "Grady'd been telling a story, and Tommy looked over his shoulder at me as if he knew I'd been watching them, and he gave me a small smile."

Gus tilted his head toward me enough to catch me through the side of his eyes, uncertain how I was receiving this. "I think it was Tommy, or my subconscious, telling me that he would've liked Grady. That Grady would've been someone Tommy would've picked for CJ."

"Gus, that's…"

"Ridiculous, I know, but I like to think it's Tommy's blessing."

"I think you're right." I stroked his bicep. I wished we weren't in a public place so I could hug him. Hard. "And I think that's beautiful. That you're blessed to have found comfort in Tommy's memory."

We were in our little bubble right now. One that he needed, and I didn't want it to burst. I also couldn't stop touching him. I wanted to comfort him and for him to know I would always be there to support and care for him. Always.

He was opening up to me. *To me.* I didn't think many people saw this side of Gus.

I lifted my beer to him and quietly said, "Happy birthday to Tommy."

His smile was sad, but his eyes were warm, and he lifted his chin as he clinked his bottle to mine.

"To Tommy." He held my eyes as he took a sip.

24

GUS

We both fell silent for a few minutes, and sports highlights came on the television. She rested her elbow on the bar and cupped her chin in her hand. I mimicked her pose. There was familiarity in our silence, but our moment was over.

They showed highlights from the race on the local news channel, which made us both cringe and side-eye each other simultaneously. That drew a chuckle out of us and broke the ice.

"Tomorrow is another day," she said, finishing the beer and starting to stand. "I better

get going. I'm beat."

"I'll head up also." I signaled the bartender and said, "Put these on my tab and close it out, please." I threw a few bills on the bar for his tip as Mia teased, "Your fan club is stirring." Cocking her head in the direction of the ladies at the table.

"Which is why you are going to pretend you're with me," I said, putting my arm around her waist. "I saved you from Keith, now it's payback time."

She giggled, and it sounded so sweet. She leaned into me close enough that I could smell the fresh water and coconut scent of her shampoo, "Now, I see why you keep me around. You need a break from all the female attention. Is your libido on sabbatical or something?"

"Trust me, there is nothing wrong with my libido or any part of my anatomy." In fact, against my better judgment, things were working, perhaps, too well at this very moment with my arm around her waist. "I just…I'm just taking a breather."

She snaked her arm around my waist as if it was meant to be there.

We walked by the table of women, and someone whispered, "Well, that's a shame…"

Mia flinched ever so slightly, but enough for me to feel it. I pulled her closer and whispered, "Thank you for keeping me company tonight. It helped."

We walked out of the bar and started toward the elevators, but I didn't let go. I was comfortable.

"Tommy liked you, by the way."

We were in the middle of the lobby, and she stood still. "What?"

"The weekend before you left, you hung out at the track with us, he said he thought you were hilarious, a pistol, and kept me on my toes. I think his exact words were, 'She's too smart to be hanging out with the likes of you.' I told him I paid you to hang out with me." I smiled down at her. "He said, 'Oh, that makes sense, then.'"

She elbowed me. "I hung out with you that weekend because you got me into the garages at the track."

"Not for my good looks and charisma."

She huffed. "Please." Her face blanked out a bit. "So you told him I was helping you in school?"

I chuckled. "It was the only way he'd believe someone as smart as you would hang out with someone like me."

She nodded. "He wasn't the first or the last to point out how different we are—probably the reason we're good friends."

Good friends. There was that phrase again.

If that was all it was, then why was I standing behind her to hide the growing "friendship" problem I was having below my belt?

We got off on her floor, and I walked her to her room. I don't know why. I wouldn't escort another friend to their room. She wasn't going to invite me in.

Once she moved out of my house, I'd see less and less of her...and I didn't like that idea one bit.

"Hey, do you think..." I said, my hands in my pockets like a goddamn teenager walking a girl to her door—except I wasn't angling for a kiss or to feel her up before she went in the house.

"What?" She pulled the keycard out of her pocket and then glanced at me.

I ran my hand over the growing scruff of my beard. "Once you move out...do you think we could still get dinner or drinks or something once in a while? You know, like we did tonight? After a weekend like this, it's nice to unwind—to relax—without it being a thing."

She had a small dimple on one of her cheeks that peeked out with her gentle smile. How had I never noticed it? Before I realized what I was doing, my thumb brushed across it and we both froze. That wasn't a friend move. That was a come-on move.

I stepped back. "Sorry. Never realized you had a dimple there?"

"Were you trying to brush it away?" She teased.

"Ha. Ha. I guess I'm loopy from lack of sleep."

"Yeah. You didn't even realize who you were flirting with—better get to your room. No guessing who may fall victim next..."

I narrowed my eyes and was almost tempted to stick out my tongue regardless of how juvenile it seemed.

She chuckled and turned to use the key on her door. "Yes, G. I'd love to have dinner or drinks with you. Maybe at Sugars? Karaoke night could be interesting?"

"Ha. Ha. No," I said, backing away and waving her off. "Good night, darlin'."

"Goodnight, G. Sweet dreams."

Yeah, right. Sweet dreams. Damn, Tommy. And damn my libido. Because both were fucking with my mind and playing havoc with my dreams.

One thing I didn't spill to Mia was that Tommy had been visiting me lately, giving me unsolicited advice—this time about her.

More importantly, I had other dreams about Mia—and they didn't have anything to do with friendship.

And had everything to do with lust.

Later that week, as I was walking through our garage, I was startled by a poke to my back. I jumped back, hand to my chest like an old woman grasping her pearls, "Jesus, CJ. You scared the crap out of me."

She chuckled and smiled—happy with her action and the result I gave her. "Come walk with me." She didn't give me an option, walking out the door and down the walkway leading to a bench area outside our corporate offices, tucked away under some trees. Still holding a rag I was wiping my hands with, I followed her double time, curious about the mid-day visit.

"Is everything okay?"

She straddled the bench and braced her hands in front of her. She tilted her head, "A little birdie reported that you and our new, pretty crew member were seen drinking in the bar last weekend, and you got in the elevator with her—"

Still standing, I threw my hands in the air. "Come on, CJ. I have shit to do today. I don't have time for this again—"

She braced her hands on her thighs, "Well. What was that about?"

My hands on my hips, the back of my neck getting hot. "How about none of your fucking business?" I pivoted to leave.

"Gus, wait." She caught me by the arm, pulling me back to the bench. "That's not why I'm here."

I pulled my arm out of her grip, annoyed, bordering on angry with her. "I don't have time for the CJ Inquisition—"

She deflated back on the bench, her arms falling limp on her knees. "I...I can't help but think of him today," CJ said. There was a slight hitch in her voice, and it hit me from out of nowhere.

Ah, the real reason we were here. "I know." I sat next to her, mimicking her posture. Today was Tommy's actual birthday.

She turned so her back was to the building and parking lot, facing the trees and under cover of anonymity to keep the wetness gathering in her eyes for her first love private. "I promised myself I would stop this…this wallowing." She couldn't help the sniff. "It's not like I think about him all the time—not anymore—and that has its own form of guilt attached."

I put an arm around her, encouraging her to put her head on my shoulder because I didn't really know what to say and needed to find time to come up with something. "It's not wallowing. It's remembering. It's honoring."

I stared at the dirty cloth in my other hand. "You don't have to give him up, CJ. He's always going to be a part of you. He's a piece of who you became."

She nodded and whispered, "I know. But I'm making a vow to Grady that he will own my heart, and he will be the one I love."

My head towered over hers as she leaned against my arm, so I spoke above her. "Darlin', there is plenty of room in your heart to love your husband, and for all other people you love, too." I squeezed. "Talk to Grady about this. I know he'd tell you the same thing."

She sniffed again and turned her head away so I wouldn't see her quickly wipe a finger under her eye. So stubborn to be strong.

"I don't think about him as much anymore, either," I confessed. "Used to be whenever I saw something that reminded me of him or something that made me laugh, I'd have a pang wishing he was there— you know. But now…I don't know." I stared ahead trying to find words to describe what it meant to still carry Tommy with me, but in a different way. "It doesn't happen as much, and if it does, it's not in sadness. It's more of wondering what he'd say? What smartass comment he'd make, or what his take would be on something…"

I debated telling her the next part, but after telling Mia, I didn't feel as ridiculous talking about it.

"One of the reasons I warmed up to Grady wasn't because of his dazzling good looks or charming personality. It was because I know he loves you." I took in a deep breath knowing in my heart this was right and what she needed to hear. Deep inside, it came out as if Tommy himself was encouraging me to say it. "I know Tommy would've loved him. If Tommy couldn't be with you, he'd want someone who would've loved you the way Grady does. That man thinks the sun rises and sets around you."

My eyes burned, and I closed them for a moment, feeling my best friend standing beside us. "Since he died, I've felt the need to watch over you." Heat burned my face when I thought about how I had misunderstood the need to watch over CJ—I thought it was me and her being a couple, being together, that would accomplish that. She was my friend, she needed protecting. Of course, it made sense for us to be together. But, now…God, now…my eyes are so open to how wrong, how different our friendship is. In fact, it's not even as intense as the friendship I have with Mia.

That caused me to stumble for a moment mentally and emotionally, and I had to shake my head to push that thought to the back burner.

"I made a vow, a promise over my best friend's grave. I'd make sure you were…okay." My voice shook. "I wouldn't let you marry any man whom I didn't think would love you the way Grady loves you, darlin'."

CJ's lip quivered. I'd done it.

"Damnit, G," she whispered before slapping my chest and then hugging me. And the tears fell—and not just hers—as we held each other tight.

"Thank you, G." She pulled back, standing to put distance between us before wiping her eyes and regulating her breath, and her emotions. CJ wasn't one to wallow in emotions. "By the way," she took in a deep cleansing breath, "I have another job for you."

I pinched the bridge of my nose to camouflage my own wetness and let out a nervous chuckle at the uncharacteristic moment we just shared and how quickly she shifted gears. "Oh, yeah." I tilted my head, waiting to hear what could possibly come out of her mouth. "What's that?"

She faced me, her eyes downcast, her petite height barely taller than me as I remained seated. She playfully grabbed my hands, swinging them back and forth like a small child asking for a favor. "Would you walk me down the aisle?" She struggled to look up at me.

CJ's father was alive but very much out of her life. I figured she'd have Mr. Merrick or Wild Bill walk her down.

That did it. Fuck being manly. A tear escaped along with a laugh as I stood, pulled her in for a bear hug, and swayed back and forth. I cleared my voice, even as she protested my rough handling of her, then said, "Of course. I'd be honored."

25

MIA

I was packed for the weekend, gathering my things while Gus cleaned up in the garage. We'd planned to spend the afternoon at a car show before we left for Martinsville when my purse began to vibrate.

It was Shyla. Perfect. Keith must have finally agreed to get my stuff out of storage and let Shyla ship it to me.

"Hey!"

"Hey." Her tone was not her usual boisterous self. It was serious, "You got a minute?"

"Uh-oh. That's your serious, adult voice. I don't like that voice," I said, bracing myself.

She was quiet.

"I'm waiting for Gus to pick me up—we're heading over to the track."

She let out a long sigh. "It's Keith."

I dropped my head, and my heart sank. "What did he do?"

"Honey. The weather here has been horrible." Her tone mimicked a doctor delivering

a horrible diagnosis.

"Okay..." And I was the patient who really didn't want to hear it but couldn't bring myself to leave.

"And I had a late shift last night and didn't get home until this morning. Her cadence quickened to get it out. "You know, I told you and Keith both that I wouldn't be around."

"Yes…"

"Honey, Keith left your stuff last night. On the curb. In the rain. Not on my porch. Not near the garage or anywhere under a tarp or plastic. It was in the rain, for hours."

It took me a moment to register the outcome of the news—of what he would've left in the rain that would cause Shyla's sympathetic, tragic tone. Cardboard boxes full of books. My books. My mom's books. Boxes of books.

My breath caught.

"He left the books out in the rain?"

"Yes. They were in a huge puddle at the end of my driveway when I got home last night—"

"That…that…" My mind flashed with the covers of the books I had in those boxes. Signed paperbacks. Some of my mom's favorites. Baby books she read to me…ones I treasured, but Keith claimed we didn't have room for in our condo because it looked tacky to have used, beat-up old books on our shelves in the den.

"The word is narcissistic asshole. Well, two words, maybe."

I sat down, and put my head in my hand. "How bad is it?"

"I pulled them in last night and unpacked them all, I tried to dry them out. A few were salvageable, but…honey. They must have been there all day. We're just lucky it wasn't garbage pick-up day, or they may not have even been there."

"Shy, my mom's books…" and the tears were coming. I couldn't keep them away.

"I know, honey."

My breath was coming quickly, heat flooding from my heart to every inch of my body. I stood up, pulled the phone away from my face, and grabbed the first thing I could find and flung it across the room—luckily, it was a pillow.

It wasn't very satisfying.

Those books were something of my mom's I kept and usually traveled with me. They were more precious to me than any jewelry she could've left. Many of them were old romance paperbacks, the ones with bare-chested men and women clinging to them. Some were even old literature textbooks she enjoyed or nursery rhymes she'd read to me. My dad had always said I got my "smarts" from my mom. She wanted to make sure I developed a love of reading—whether it was a comic book, a historical biography, or an engineering textbook.

I'd wanted to bring them with me but didn't want to clutter Gus's house with any more of my things.

How could anyone who at one time claimed they loved me, who shared my bed and

wanted to be with me, marry me, be so cruel? I screamed expletives and called down a plague on his balls. I never knew it was possible for me to be so angry at someone—someone I thought I loved.

I sat down on my sofa and gripped the top of my hair, yanking on it to feel something besides rage.

Shyla's voice came over the phone. "Mia, honey?"

A hand reached out and took the phone from me.

Gus. "This is Gus. Who is this?"

And that's when my angry sob escaped as he knelt in front of me and stared at me with his navy-colored eyes filled with concern. He stood slowly, focusing on what Shyla was telling him, but reached out and held my hand. His face grew colder as he watched the tears roll down my face. His mouth thinned to the point that his lips disappeared, and his jaw ticked.

He gave a few grunts to assure Shyla he heard every word that she spoke and then said, "I'm with her now. I got her."

Shyla spoke some more.

"We'll handle him. I got it. Thank you for letting me know, Shyla. Here's my phone number..." he rattled off his digits. "If you hear from him, see him...text me."

There was depth in what he said to Shyla that I was afraid to unravel or focus on. He hung up with Shyla and held both of my hands, caressing the outside of them with his palm and breathing audibly.

"Mia—" He breathed my name with such tenderness, and his hand came up to wipe the tears off my cheek. I hated how damsel in distress I seemed. I stood so quickly I almost knocked him over.

I wiped the tears off my cheeks, cursing them for showing whenever I was furious. I was beyond fed up with Keith and everything to do with him.

Gus stood with his hands on his hips, studying me as I paced the room. I was unsure what to do or where to direct the anger inside me. "Say the word and Davy and I are on a plane to Chicago—"

I let out a surprised laugh and combed my hands through my hair trying to fix the damage I'd already caused by pulling on it. "You know what makes me angry—who I'm really angry at—I'm angry at myself. I'm pissed for giving someone the power to hurt me that way."

"Mia…" Gus approached me, pity in his eyes that just drove me to the edge.

"No. Don't." I put up my hand. "Don't look at me that way." I walked to my purse, busying myself with checking its contents and attempting to hide my foolish tears. Don't cry in front of him. Why do I always have to cry when I'm actually mad enough to spit nails?

I took a deep breath in through my nose, both hands wiping my face in an effort to change my expression and not seem so freaking pathetic. "I was the idiot who didn't see him for who he really was."

I glanced over my shoulder, "Maybe I need to be more like you, huh?" I forced some levity but it fell flat on his blank response.

"What do you mean?"

"Be more detached. Stop looking for the romantic, happily-ever-after all the time." I pivoted toward him. "Maybe I should just enjoy life a bit, huh?"

This thought had merit. "I have enough on my plate. I don't need to deal with an insecure man out to prove he's better than me or who just wants something from me." I closed my purse, trying to think of something else to do with the angry energy. I forced another smile and threw out my hands. "Enough."

Gus still hadn't moved or said much. His hands were in his pockets, any pity he wore on his face was gone. He shifted his feet and dropped his head to hide what I thought was irritation. "Just because one man is an asshole doesn't mean—"

"Let's just go." I strode to the door, gathering my things. "Let's go enjoy this beautiful day and not think about this. We both obviously could use the distraction, and then we're leaving for the race this weekend."

Wordlessly, he turned to the door and then held out his hand to me.

I studied it, slightly tan from weekends outside, slightly roughened, but not overly. That hand had sweetly touched my face before, and I really wanted it to hold me now. I reached behind me, grabbed my purse and keys, and when I turned back, it was still there waiting for me—just as he was. Unwavering.

I placed my hand in his, and he led us out the door, letting go to close the door behind us, taking my keys to lock the deadbolt, and leading me with his hand on my lower back over to his Camaro.

"Oh…got your baby out today," I said, running my hand appreciatively down the frame.

"I wasn't going to take the truck to a car show."

I chuckled as he opened the door. "You ever going to let me drive this?"

"You going to let me drive your baby?"

"I don't even drive my baby. She's for eyes only."

He shook his head. "That's like having the most decadent chocolate and never eating it," he said, closing the door and walking around the front of the car. He skimmed his hand over the hood like a man would over the hip of his lover.

I shook my head—I was all over the place. Anger, frustration, sexual fantasies. Sure. They all fit. But staring at the back of his jeans certainly helped my mood.

He sat in the seat, pulled on the seat belt, and said, "Ready?" He started the vehicle, revving the engine, and with his sexy-as-hell aviator sunglasses hiding his disturbingly beautiful blue eyes, he flashed me the sexiest smile.

I side-eyed him. "Yes, of course."

He slung his arm over the back of my seat, put the car in reverse, and began to pull out. He moved his hand to the stick shift and put the car in gear when I impulsively placed my hand over his. "Thank you, Gus." He stared at me, not removing his hand from under mine. "For being here for me. And for not shrugging it off as just a box of books."

He placed the car in neutral, relaxed his arms in his lap, and stared at me. "They aren't just a box of books if they mean something to you. You going to be okay?"

I nodded. "Let's just not talk about it. I'll deal with it—at some point." I took in a resolved breath. "Just not today."

He leaned over, cupped my chin, and kissed the top of my head. "You won't be dealing with it alone," he whispered. "That jackass will get what he's due. Don't worry."

"Gus—"

He held up his hand. It was obnoxious and a bit condescending enough that it made me freeze in place. "We aren't talking about it today, correct?"

"Yes, but..."

His hand went up again. The arrogance that he could stop me from talking with a hand...seriously? "Stop that! This isn't your problem—"

"You're damn straight it's my problem. You're mine—" He quickly shook his head, "—You're one of us, now. He hurt you. That's my problem—it's all of our problems." He drew in a breath through his nose and pivoted to me. "I'm your friend, like Shyla's your friend. You don't think she's planning his murder?"

Oh, she probably was, and I wouldn't know about it until after the fact. Plausible deniability.

"Gus—"

"Not today. Darlin', today we are going to relax and dream about cars." Under his breath, he added, "Tomorrow there will be time for retribution."

26

GUS

Besides being a dreary March day, Atlanta wasn't such a bad race. Both teams did decently, with Grady edging CJ out by a few points so far for the season.

Mia was moving out this week. That was...well...it just was what it was. She spent the last week packing up what she'd accumulated around my house for the last couple of months. Coffee mugs, jackets, shoes...knick-knacks, and other items that were uniquely hers. Like her damn puppy dog slippers, and her damn tempting boy shorts.

The few times I saw her this weekend, though, she hadn't seemed herself. Maybe she didn't like the idea of moving out, either. I'd gotten used to the company. Maybe she had too?

I found my Dum-Dums stick in the pocket of one of my jeans when I got to my hotel in Atlanta. I had trouble getting her Smarties in her bag before she left, so I had to rely on a crew member to hand her an envelope before the race started.

It had become our good luck ritual. I had to come up with something more original, though. Being predictable wasn't my style.

The last time I saw her was walking through the hotel lobby later in the evening the day of the race, and she'd looked...well, she hadn't looked so good.

CJ seemed to wrestle with some issues at the beginning of the race, and from the tension coming from that pit box, there had been some words exchanged. I wondered what was going on over in that camp, but it was a fine line at times like this with friendship being competitors, let alone roommates.

"Mia," I caught her walking toward the elevators. "Hey..." I touched her shoulder to stop her. She pulled out her earbuds, a tissue in her hand.

She lifted her weary eyes up to me, "Oh, hey." Her smile was forced, and the fire was gone from her spirit.

I cupped her shoulder. "You, okay?"

"Just tired. It was a long day." She pinched the bridge of her nose.

"I saw some unhappy faces over there. No one was taking it out on you, were they?"

"No. Everyone is just frustrated. The last two races weren't our best performance. We have room for improvement, and no one quite knows how to get there." Her voice was quiet, as if it was causing her too much effort to speak. She let out a slow breath, coughed, and turned to push the elevator button again. "I need my bed."

"When is your flight?"

"We're leaving at eight in the morning."

I nodded. "Okay, well, then you will get home before me." The elevator dinged, and we both got in. I pushed my floor and hers.

She leaned against the back of the elevator for support, tilting her head back with her eyes closed. God, she really was pale.

"Hey, seriously, are you okay?"

I placed the back of my hand to her cheek. She flinched slightly before leaning against my hand as if seeking support. She was a tad warm, but not enough for me to tell if she had a fever. I caressed my hand against the smoothness of her cheek, and a small sigh escaped her just as the elevator dinged and we arrived at her floor.

Her eyes snapped open, and she stood, shaking her head, trying to focus. She stared up at me, giving me a brief look into the eyes of a softer, more vulnerable Mia. A side I hadn't known she possessed. I blinked and she was inching out of the elevator.

"Let me walk with you," I said as I followed out of the elevator.

She adjusted the bag on her shoulder. "I'm fine." She crooked her head over her shoulder, "Just tired." She reached her door, fished out her card, and waved me off. "Good night, Gus. I'll see you back at home."

She disappeared into her room. I stepped back into the elevator.

Home.

This time when she said it, it kind of clenched my insides. It wouldn't be her home for much longer. I both appreciated and cursed my mother's machinations in the delay she caused with Mia's house. While I enjoyed the time Mia and I had together in the house, I wasn't expecting to be so down about her moving out.

I'll be fine. I just enjoyed the company. That's all.

I got off the elevator and headed for my own room. Entering, I pulled out what was in my pockets and tossed them on the nightstand.

These feelings must be surfacing because it's all this wedding business—this couple business—and me being so damn single. I peeled off my jacket and shirt. Toed off my shoes.

I caught myself in the mirror. Maybe I'm having a mid-life crisis? I wasn't even close to forty. Too young for a mid-life crisis? I stared at my reflection. That's ridiculous.

I ran my hand over my five o'clock shadow and then my hair.

Not a gray hair in sight.

Later that evening, lying in bed, my mind wandered, and I decided after CJ and Grady's wedding, I was going to shake myself out of this and get back on the horse, so to speak. This self-reflection was obviously messing with my head.

Relationships like CJ and Grady's, like Harper and Cal's—I didn't get them. That level of commitment. That intimacy. The minute a girl said anything close to the L word, I ran.

Well, I didn't run. I just cut things off before it got any more complicated. I didn't want that responsibility—I couldn't be responsible for someone's heart like that. Having that power over someone's life was too much for me to consider.

No. I couldn't do to a woman what my dad did to my mom. I wouldn't. The sins of the father would not be duplicated by the son.

But I also know I couldn't keep latching onto Mia for company, holding her back from her own future.

The next day, after arriving back in Charlotte, I was driving down the highway nearing my exit when my phone display popped up with "Harper."

"What's up?"

"Hey, are you home yet?" She clipped with no other greeting.

"No, why?"

"Cal says I'm acting like a mother hen, but...I'm worried about Mia. She didn't look great on the plane this morning. I tried to insist that I drive her home, but she wanted to take a car service. She said she wasn't feeling great. She said it was a cold and didn't want to expose me any more than she already had."

"Great," I muttered. I knew she wasn't feeling well.

"Be nice, Gus. It's not her fault she's sick."

"I'm not sayin'—"

"I just tried to call her, and no one was answering. I'm worried. I haven't heard from her since she left the airport, and I was getting ready to drive over to check on her—"

"I'm almost home. What's wrong with her?"

"Headache, sore throat. She looks like hell. Flushed. Chills, I think by the time we landed, so probably fever."

I simultaneously gritted my teeth and pushed my right foot down on the pedal a bit more.

"Gus, should I come over?"

"No. No. I'll take care of her," I said, and I damn well meant it. "I knew last night she wasn't feeling well. But she said she was just tired. I'm almost home," I repeated to both of us.

"Okay. Call me when you get there and let me know how she is," Harper said.

"Okay."

"I mean it, Gus. Otherwise, I'm going to worry she never made it home and will come over to check for myself."

"I'll call you," I gritted out, not sure if she caught the end of that because I jammed my finger on my phone, disconnected the phone from the car, and broke records to reach home. I was worried about Mia and frustrated with myself for not checking on her this morning.

I practically ran in from the garage. "Mia!" I announced myself, already beginning to search the house for her. She wasn't in the kitchen, on the sofa in the living room, either. Her bedroom door was closed, so I knocked lightly before cracking the door open slowly and found her in bed, curled up like a small kitten under her blankets, with just enough of her showing for her to breathe.

I softly said her name, "Mia?" and took a step in the door. "Mia, honey?"

Nothing. I walked over and sat on the bed, putting my hand on her forehead like my mother used to do.

Yep, fever.

I pulled the blanket back enough to run my hand over her hair. She didn't stir. "Poor thing," I said while stroking her head.

She stirred, and with great effort, she pried her eyes open. A raspy "Gus?" came out with her lifting her head an inch off the pillow.

"Lie down, sweetheart, it's okay," I said, rubbing her back. "Have you taken anything? Tylenol, Motrin?"

She grunted before shaking her head.

"Okay, let me go find you some and some water. You have a fever." The phone in my back pocket buzzed. I stood, pulled out my phone, and answered Harper. "She's here and she definitely has a fever."

"Do you want me to come over?" Harper asked.

"No." The word was firmer than I intended. My sudden need to take care of her, to make her feel better, was…surprising. "I got her."

"O-kay," Harper said. It was the lack of other words that spoke volumes—she noticed my tone as well.

"Alright, well, I have to go find her some medicine to bring the fever down."

"Do you need anything?"

"No, I'm good. I just got home. I just need to get everything together."

"Call me if you need help. Or if she needs to go to the doctor or something."

"We'll be fine."

And there it was again. Me referring to us as a "we."

I pushed that to the back of my mind and got to work taking care of her. Hating that she was sick but did not mind the job.

27

MIA

I must be dead.

No, if I were dead, I wouldn't feel like death. I would feel...well, not sure what I would feel—I'm guessing nothing because you don't feel things when you're dead, right?

What the hell was wrong with me? It hurt to think, but I persevered, trying to remember if I chugged down a bottle of vodka, swallowed the shards of glass from the bottle, chased it with tequila before being hit by a Mack truck, and then dropped in the sauna—because I felt horrible.

I moaned and rolled onto my side, prying my eyes open to get a clue as to what the hell was going on and whom I could blame for my condition.

In the chair on the other side of the room, closest to the door, Gus sat up, completely asleep. He didn't look great either. His five o'clock shadow was more of an eleven o'clock, his hair had seen better days, he wore cut-off sweatpants and a wrinkled Green Day t-shirt, and his bare feet were crossed at the ankles, which was kind of endearing. His elbow was propped on the armrest, his head resting on his hand, but with his mouth just slightly agape, there was no doubt he was asleep.

I shifted to sit and tried to clear my throat, which was a major mistake only second to the original idea of even trying to move. My head swam, and I almost passed out just trying to sit up.

"Ugh. What the hell…"

Gus's eyes flew open, and he was immediately at attention. "What? Where?" He stood unsteady. "Mia." He surveyed me, stepping forward and laying a hand on my forehead, grasping the back of my head with his other hand. "Oh, thank God. Your fever is down." He sighed with relief, dropped his shoulders, and slumped back in his seat.

My hand fell to my throat as I tried to speak. He reached for the bottle with a straw sitting sentry on my nightstand and moved to the bed, sitting next to me and poking my mouth with the straw.

"Drink."

My mouth obeyed as if my body and Gus were in a routine that my conscious mind was not aware of yet.

As I drank the cold Gatorade, my eyes focused on him. He had circles under his weary eyes. I pulled back and after a few attempts, was able to croak, "What's going on?" My voice sounded foreign to me.

"You've been sick. Pretty damn sick. I think the flu," he said, putting the bottle back on the table. "Didn't you get your flu shot this year?"

"I thought flu season was over with?"

"Not the point. Didn't you get your flu shot?"

I attempted to sit up straighter. "No, I guess I didn't. I kind of had a lot on my plate." I attempted a glare at being scolded, but it fell short since moving my eyeballs hurt.

"You've had me scared to death. I swore to my mom and Harper I'd take you to the hospital if you didn't get better by tonight. They insisted you probably needed an IV or something.

"I'm sorry if I caused you any inconvenience—wait, an IV. Come on, I just laid down for a nap—"

"A nap?" The tone hinted that he questioned my intelligence. "You laid down for a nap three days ago, Mia."

I laid back down slowly, staring at him. "Seriously?" I whispered.

My mind was racing with all that was implied. I whispered, afraid of the truth. "So, you've had to take care of me...this whole time?"

He nodded, moving over to sit on my bed next to me.

I tried to push him off the bed. Dizziness reminded me that I didn't have the energy to sit vertically, forget about attempting to move a hundred-and-eighty-five-pound man. "I'm so sorry. Jeez, Gus. I was supposed to be out of your hair. Not causing you this much grief." My eyes began to burn. Why the hell was I going to cry? Because I was sick, and when I was sick, I freaking cried.

I hated being sick.

But what I hated more was someone having to take care of me.

Crap.

He stood. "Do you have to use the bathroom?" He went to help me up, supporting me under my arm.

I pulled away, pushing to stand on my own. "No. I..." Oh my God. Had he...had he helped me to the bathroom? Had he—

I swayed.

"Whoa. Easy, killer. Sit back down. You aren't going anywhere."

"Gus—"

"Seriously. You're going to hurt yourself." His tone brooked no argument.

I fell back onto the bed and put my head in my hands to keep the room from spinning and to hide my face. "I can't be sick," I mumbled, and my emotions were a mess.

He sat next to me and put his arm gently around me. "Mia, honey. It's fine. You're going to be fine. You just need to rest."

"I can't be sick. I have a new job. I have the race this week. I have to move. I have to give you your life back..."

Stupid, freaking tears came regardless of how hard I tried to rail against them. I tried to punch my covers but didn't have the strength for that either. "God, I can't imagine how pathetic I must look..." I mumbled.

He pulled me closer to him, wrapping his other arm around me in a true hug. "Mia, darlin'. You're fine. Even the smartest, most clever women get sick." He kissed the top of my head.

"Don't hug me. Don't kiss me."

He pulled back as hurt splashed across his face as he peered down at me. My hand was on his hard chest, and the softness of his old concert shirt beckoned me to lay my head down on it. But instead, I whispered my concern, "You'll get sick, too." I watched my hand trace a path over his chest to his shoulder. "I couldn't bear the thought of giving this to you."

"You won't." A side of his mouth tilted up.

"Why? Because you're such a tough guy?" I teased, almost wishing he would get sick so he could look as pathetic as I felt right now.

"No, because I was smart enough to get my flu shot." He smirked and gently kissed my forehead. "Besides, I've been exposed to you already... and it wouldn't have stopped me from taking care of you, anyway." He pulled me closer. "Or for listening to you and all you had to say to me." He leaned back against the headboard of the bed, adjusting the pillows with his free hand that wasn't holding me.

It took me a few moments to let the last line process through my foggy brain. One, I was still a bit feverish. Two, Gus was lying me down on his chest. His hard, inviting chest that I couldn't help but luxuriate in and rub my hand over as if it belonged to me. A sound reverberated from him that I didn't have the capacity to analyze because it was at that point that his comment hit home.

"Wait. What?" I pulled back so fast I broke his hold. My brain worked frantically to retrieve whatever I could from my cloudy, nonfunctioning memory banks. "What do you mean? All I had to say to you? I don't remember saying a thing to you. I remember falling asleep when I got home from the race Sunday night, and I remember waking up three minutes ago."

Okay, yes, I remember him coming in when he got home. Giving me medicine. Something to drink. Being sweet...there were glimpses of him putting cold clothes on my head and neck. Almost yelling at me to drink. Rubbing my back and whispering, *"It'll be okay, darlin'."*

Oh, God. And yes...I closed my eyes and cringed. He did help me to the bathroom once when I actually had enough fluid in me to need to use the bathroom. He left it up to me to handle things. I almost collapsed but was able to cover myself before he carried me...carried me...back to bed. "I vaguely remember you being around. I don't remember talking to you."

"Yes, I know," he said, slowly reaching over, almost as if he were afraid to spook me. He tucked a piece of hair behind my ear. "Your fever spiked pretty high Monday night, and nothing I was doing was bringing it down. You were scaring me."

"I considered stripping you down and putting you in the bathtub just to bring down the fever."

I slapped his chest—however weakly—and he waggled his eyebrows. He schooled his features as if imparting important information saying, "Seriously, though. Turns out, when you get a fever, you get chatty."

Oh, hell. What the hell did I say to him?

He bit his bottom lip before flashing me a replica of the flirtatious smile he used to mask other emotions.

"Now, I really hope you do get sick."

His laughter was genuine but showed equal fatigue and relief. "There she is. Now I know you are feeling better."

But, seriously, what the hell did I say?

28

GUS

I was never going to tell her everything about the Monday evening confession session.

That night I'd changed into some running shorts and a t-shirt, grabbed some water for both of us, a cold compress for her head, and some extra blankets. I climbed into the bed and began plumping the pillows against the headboard and flipping on the television before I wrapped her up like a burrito and pulled her into my arms. She immediately fell onto my chest, burrowed into it as if it were her pillow, and I put my arms around her very warm body.

It's how we were lying now and why it seemed so natural. Over the last few days, we laid like this whenever she got restless. Not that she may remember much of it because she slept through the majority of it. But I would. I'd remember it. Just like I'd remember what she said to me.

That night, I tried not to worry as I gently rubbed my hand up and down her arm and back, stroked her damp hair away from her face, and listened to her fast-paced breathing.

But now, she stiffened and pushed away, employing the frown I found so endearing as I delayed in offering an explanation.

"Around midnight, I got you to take a few ibuprofen and some more fluids. We'd been up off and on all night."

"And...when did this chattiness occur?"

I debated what to tell her. She was scooting further away from me, putting distance between us as if ready to bolt.

How much truth was in what she told me, and how much more was there that I didn't know. I studied her, wondering if I could find out now that she was coherent.

I ran through the conversation again in my head, leaning across the bed, putting my head in my hand.

"Why are you being so nice to me?" she said, her eyes not even open.

"You're sick, honey."

"No, no. You're not usually this nice. I don't understand." She laid her head back down. "Well, sometimes you're nice. And I start to like you, and then you hurt my feelings and I don't like you anymore," she said, nuzzling in to my chest again. "I just don't understand you, Gus."

"I don't know what you mean," I said, because I didn't. "When have I hurt you—"

She tried to push herself up. "I mean, you know you're sooo handsome." She didn't get far and fell back on my chest. If I didn't know better, her slurring could be mistaken for being drunk. "And I get that I'm not...handsome." Her brow furrowed as she seemed to be struggling with what to say. "I mean...and I guess you are kind of smart, at least smart enough—" She pushed her head up a bit and stared off into space, seeming to forget her train of thought. "But I think you're my friend..."

"Of course, I'm your friend," I said, holding both of her hands to my chest.

"Then why do you hurt my feelings. I get it. I do—" She stared down at my chest, absently stroking it. I was torn between the ache her words caused my chest and what her hand was doing to the ache farther down.

"Mia—when have I—"

She wasn't listening to me. Her head began to droop, whether with emotion or just lack of energy. "I know I don't look like your girl-friends. But why do you always—always—have to remind everyone…" Her voice kept trailing off, soft and vulnerable. She shifted as if she were going to lie back down. "What's wrong with me?"

I didn't have an answer because there wasn't anything wrong with her. I lifted her head gently to see her naturally thick lashes brushing over her flushed cheeks, hiding those beautiful tawny eyes but still needing to see them.

"Mia, honey, open your eyes for me."

And there, I found too many things that were too damn perfect.

There wasn't anything wrong with her, but what was wrong with me? So much. So much was wrong with me.

A tear fell from those eyes, and it broke through my revelation. Tears. From her eyes. I would never be the cause of tears from those beautiful tawny eyes.

Like my mother's eyes whenever my faithless father's name was mentioned… No. I would not be that man.

"There's nothing wrong with you, honey." I pulled her into me, cradling her—so clearly out of my depth, not knowing how to comfort her. "You're just not feeling well right now, and everything seems confusing."

"You're being a condescending shit right now, but you're comfy. So, I'm going to lie here…maybe pretend…" She shifted, then pushed her head up with so much effort I thought it cost her all the energy she had left. "You know, maybe you're not my type either…think about that." But she said it while staring at my lips. "Even if you're beautiful and I'm smart…we just aren't compatible."

She fell back on my chest, threw a leg over mine and mumbled something about Shyla saying she was "So intelligent but stupid with men."

I gently held her hand that had rubbed my stomach a little too low for my comfort. "Mia, why did you stop talking to me after college?"

She moved her head in what I think was a slight nod, and that was all the fevered confession I was getting.

"Gus!" Mia waved her hand in front of me to get my attention.

I blinked, shook my head, and decided to leave the details of the conversation to myself.

One thing I discovered over the past few days, I loved to play mindlessly with her curls. That night, I spent the rest of the time trying not to think about what she told me, or what it could've meant. I just played with her curls. Just feverish ramblings. Mia never had feelings for me, but maybe I had hurt her in some way. Why hadn't she ever told me? If I pissed her off, she would've told me—wouldn't she? She ghosted me all those years ago intentionally—and this confession had something to do with it.

Mia pulled her hair back with her hand. "God, I feel gross. I really need a shower," she said.

I pushed up to stand. "No shower until you try to eat something. You can't go standing in the shower without food in your system. Let me go get you something."

"I'm fine—" She tried to push me away, and it was like a little kitten batting at me.

"Get back in bed, Mia." I barely held back my amusement at her furrowed brow as she tried to swing her feet out of bed. I knew how much she hated that I was helping her.

"I can get my own damn food, Gus."

"No." I bent over, picked up her little feet before they hit the ground and plopped them back in the bed, covering them and sitting on the comforter before she could get them back out. "I didn't nurse you for the past few days," I tucked the blanket around her waist, "just to have you faint and get a concussion." My face was level with hers and I winked.

She crossed her arms over her chest, and her bottom lip curled out before she let out an exaggerated sound of frustration. "Gus. I'm fine. You're relieved of duty."

"Sit here, smarty-pants. I'll get you some soup. Maybe some toast." I got up to leave but turned and pointed at her, "Stay in that bed, St. James, or you won't be happy with the repercussions."

"You're not the boss of me." She leaned forward to get in my face. Her bottom lip jutted out in adorable defiance.

187

Oh, that bottom lip gave me ideas that I shouldn't be having. Ever. So, I deflected. "At least when you were feverish, you were more sweet than sour." We stubbornly stared at each other. "Alright, well. Give me a few minutes to make you something. Then you can take some more medicine and shower, okay?"

"Whatever..." She fell back against her pillow.

I leaned over and pulled on a curl—our eyes connected, and her face softened. I patted her leg and got up to leave.

Just as I walked out her door, she raised her voice, "Gus!"

I popped my head back in, "What? Are you okay?" She was leaning forward to stand, and within two strides I was in front of her. "Get...back..."

She waved me off, "Yes, yes. I'll stay in bed. I...I just wanted to say..."

She took my hand in hers and stared at them. The difference in our size and texture didn't seem to matter. She ran her finger over my knuckles, and I shivered a bit.

"Thank you. Thank you for taking care of me," she said softly with her eyes as much as with her words. "For looking after me. Only my father has ever done that. I was so scared when I got home Sunday night because I knew I was sick and I..."

I sat back on my heels so I was below her. "Sweetheart, I wouldn't leave you to fend for yourself—"

She shook her head. "No, I know. You're a good person, August Quinlan." Tears welled in her eyes. "But still...thank you for being here with me. You could've just thrown some Tylenol and Gatorade at me a few times a day." Her voice caught, the rest of her words coming out with a labored breath, "I won't forget it."

My eyes tracked my thumb wiping tears off her face.

"Always." I wanted to say. *"I'll always be here for you. I want to take care of you."*

But something stopped me from saying it. Something held my tongue, and stopped me from making such a promise, such a declaration. It was the way she looked at me the other night that did it.

Instead, I stood, resting a hand on her head. "Dar—" I stopped, removing my hand. Something stopped me from calling her darling. That suddenly felt wrong, and I didn't know why. I placed my finger under her chin, gently tilting it up so I could see her eyes. "It was my pleasure. Let me see about feeding you now." I kissed her forehead as I had done many times before and went to focus on the task that I could control. Not the emotions that I didn't understand.

29

MIA

Gus brought me some food and kept me company while I ate.

"I'm going to miss this...you know," he said, leaning on an elbow, hand propped in his hand as I sat with my back against the headboard as I sipped the broth he brought me.

"What? Having a needy girl living with you?"

"No, having you living with me."

I looked down into the mug of clear broth as if it held the answers to my life, "Yeah, me too." I paused before adding, "But it's for the best."

He cupped his head in his hand and asked, "Why would you keep saying that?" His brows fell over his blue eyes—they always managed to cause my brain to short-circuit.

I blinked to recover my thoughts, "Because..." my voice made a scratchy noise, "Be...cause," I cleared my throat, my hand flying to my neck, remembering my throat was still angry at me. "Because we need to get on with our lives without getting in each other's way."

He flinched. "I didn't realize I was in your way."

I shook my head. "No, I'm in your way. I mean, come on, I've kind of put a cramp in your dating life living here." I waved around at the room.

"Not really—"

"And living with you, along with working, of course…hasn't exactly encouraged me to go out and meet new people, either." I stared down at my clear broth again. "I don't want it to seem like I've latched myself onto you or become so dependent on you—"

"Wait…" he held up his hand to stop me and began to sit up.

"Really, I think we could both use a social life. I've definitely gotten over asshole. The girls have been pushing me to get out more. Maybe start seeing Shaw more."

"Shaw?" He straightened some and looked like he smelled something bad—I really needed that shower.

"I think we kind of put a cramp on each of our personal lives. I know Kellie didn't seem to be bothered by the idea because she didn't think I was any kind of competition—"

"Wait? What?"

"But I don't think other men would be too crazy about me living with you. They

wouldn't get us."

"Why would—"

I was verbally vomiting everything in my head, and he wasn't keeping up. "Because clearly, how could a woman live with you and not want to—you know—" I gestured with rapid hands all around his body.

Seriously, after catching glimpses of his naked chest, or that dip in his lower back right before his butt flares out into a perfect bubble of muscle…a bubble I wanted to squeeze…I mean, what woman wouldn't want to squeeze that…Any woman—but me, of course.

He held up his hand to stop me from going further.

"Wait. Back up. Why wouldn't Kellie find you a threat? You mean she wasn't jealous of you?" He tilted his head, his brow furrowed, and his mouth motioned as if he were trying to find the words.

"No."

"Why would she be jealous?" Okay, the fact that he agreed did kind of hurt.

"Exactly."

"I'm confused." He put his hand to his forehead.

I took in a deep breath to explain. He stared at me blankly. He couldn't be this dense. "Gus, she didn't think I was attractive enough to detour your attention away from her. I wasn't competition for her."

"Oh, come on—that's ridiculous. I told her we were just friends. That's why she didn't think you were a threat."

"Yes, a friend who works on cars, is in the industry, and whom you knew in college—ya know, one of the guys."

"Well, yeah. But I never said you weren't attractive."

"You didn't have to. You never have to. You don't look at me the way you look at other women. You don't flirt with me the way you do other women. They don't see me as competition because I don't get your attention—not in that way. She was just stating the obvious."

He scratched his head. "I don't understand the problem then."

And that admission, the one I always knew was true, still kind of hurt. He wasn't attracted to me. Sitting in bed, caring for me—I was like a little sister to him. The extended family he never had.

I swallowed. "There isn't one." I pushed myself up to readjust the covers and said, "However, if a man sees me living with a guy like you...they won't want that kind of competition or complication."

"If he was a decent guy—"

I pushed back the covers. "Anyway, my point is, that's why it's better for both our lives that we get on with this move." I didn't want to sit next to him anymore. Without realizing it, I added, "I need to start dating. I want to start dating. It's time."

"Why did you ghost me a decade ago? What happened?"

I started toward the hook on the door where I kept my robe.

"I think I'm feeling lightheaded."

His tone was firm as he said, "Well, then sit your ass down. But what I really want to know is why," he patted the side of the bed.

I sat back down. The memory of being sick and telling him how I felt started to come back into focus. It was cringe-worthy—like the morning after a bender when you remember all the stupid crap you did and said, but just want to hide your head and hope everyone else was drunker than you, so they can't remember.

God, I was such a baby when I was sick.

"You know what, fine." It seemed stupid to keep it a secret any longer. Perspective. Rip off the Band-Aid. I needed to stop being so attached to this man. Maybe a little humiliation of being a simpering little girl would help. I climbed under the blanket again, needing another layer between us.

"A few days after our weekend at the speedway, when I met Tommy and all your friends, I came to your dorm building. I wanted to give you some cookies and thank you again for taking me around and introducing me to everyone. It had been one of the best things that had happened to me at that point—the tours of the garages, being on the frontline, the contacts I made, you were treating me like one of your people. It gave me a lot of bragging rights, you know." I tried a half-hearted smile as I pulled the blanket over my legs.

"It was a gorgeous, sunny day on campus, and there were a ton of people outside. I came from around the side of the building and there you were, sitting on the steps with a girl...I don't even remember her name...sitting in your lap. This was not a new occurrence. Hell, I had to run interference a few times to keep you on task while we were studying."

I licked my lips and paused, tried to clear my throat, and winced because my throat was still dry. Gus leaned over and handed me my Gatorade. "Thanks." I gave him a hesitant smile as I took a sip. I was unsure what he was thinking, but he remained silent as I handed it back to him to place back on the nightstand. "It was just that, well, I guess after that weekend, I thought...well, my delusional young mind thought we were getting close—that I was a friend to you—like your friends from home."

He opened his mouth to say something, and I quickly held up my hand to clarify. "Not like you were making moves on me or anything, but that we were close and more than just a tutor and student thing. But then this girl started grilling you about where you were all weekend and why you disappeared with the weird, nerdy girl who was always around."

I couldn't retell this story without reliving it. Me bopping over with my jean shorts, sneakers, t-shirt, and ponytail just to hear this sorority chick call me a puppy dog who liked to follow him around and to have Gus laugh at it. Not at her. The comment—as the comparison amused him. And then she joined in and giggled at it while she rubbed up against him.

"You didn't rebuff her." I smoothed the blanket over my legs. Even now, I could hear the hurt in my voice, dammit. "You didn't tell her to fuck off or even correct her. You smiled at her assessment of me."

He didn't claim to forget it.

"She asked you if you were hooking up with me. If we were a thing?" My chin was at my chest, trying to bury my face, but I would get this out because it was already feeling cathartic. I took in a deep breath, and then I found the courage to look him right in those big, dark, beautiful eyes that always caught me. "And you laughed. You laughed at the possibility, Gus." I didn't break eye contact. "As if that idea couldn't be any more hilarious. Anymore absurd. The thought of hooking up with the nerdy tutor. The puppy dog whom everyone saw following you around."

He closed his eyes. Tight. "Mia."

I shook my head for him not to interrupt me because I wasn't done.

"You shook your head so vehemently and said, 'No. No. Of course not. There's nothing between me and the pipsqueak. She's just helping me pass calculus and physics—that's why she's around so much. It's not like we're BFFs or anything.' And you continued to find it all so amusing, and then you began kissing her and walked her into your dorm, the denial of us even being friends still hanging in the air."

"Mia...darlin'."

"Please don't call me darlin'. It's so patronizing when you do it at a time like this." I burrowed down into my covers. "Anyway, that's why I left without saying goodbye. It may sound immature, but I was much younger then. I hadn't had a lot of experience with men—friends or lovers—and well, it hurt because...I did begin to think of you as a best friend. Not boyfriend material, because I knew I was...I knew who you were. But I certainly considered you one of my best friends. And you saw me as a pipsqueak who was tagging along and hanging around too much. It was embarrassing. I knew my worth—even if you didn't. You knew I was leaving after the semester ended. I had the scholarship to Michigan. I just left early…eager to move on with my new life. I didn't want to be anyone's obligation."

"Mia, really. I'm so sorry. I didn't know you were there. I didn't think—"

I flipped onto my side and sighed. "I've gotten over it, obviously, or I would never have come here, let alone agreed to move in with you." I looked over my shoulder. "It's fine. Really. I've grown past it. You wanted to know what happened. Now you do. And I'm glad we got it out there, so there's nothing left unsaid." I let out a deep breath and coughed a bit. "I really should go back to sleep. I'm still exhausted…could you turn off that lamp for a bit?" He turned off the lamp but continued to sit next to me quietly.

"It was Melinda Carmichael. She was a gossip and vicious toward other girls. If she had even an inkling of a suspicion that you, that we…"

"No one would've believed her. But it doesn't matter. It's over."

"I could've told you. You stopped talking to me because of that whole thing?"

"I left for Michigan a few days later."

"Without saying goodbye." His tone was harsh, hurting.

I flipped over, my own tone becoming hard. "I wasn't going to drag myself over there for a tearful farewell that I assumed you didn't care about."

He crossed his arms over his chest, his jaw ticking from clenching his teeth.

I flipped back over. "Let it go. There's no crying over spilled milk. We're friends now. And screw Melinda Carmichael."

He sat quietly for a few minutes, and I began to drift off—now emotionally and physically drained. My body reminded me I was still recovering. But, I don't think I imagined it when he sighed. The bed shifted as he got up. Then there was a kiss on my forehead. "You've always been beautiful." As he walked out the door, even softer, I swore I heard him say, "I did know your worth. I knew you were too good for me."

30

MIA

After a few days of recovery, I walked into Merlo to check on things. Harper tried to talk me out of going to this weekend's race, but that didn't take.

Mother Hen Gus had delayed my move out until after we returned from the weekend, so really, I might as well go do my job.

Things between Gus and me had been…different. Not good, not bad. Different. I almost felt as if he'd seen me emotionally naked.

I walked into my office, checked the messages, and skimmed the paperwork on my desk before heading toward Jacks's office. I overheard CJ's voice booming from inside a small conference room, figuring it was Jacks she was talking with. I headed in that direction to check in with both of them.

"She's doing better."

It was Gus.

"Harper told me you were a nursemaid to her for three days," CJ said, a tease in her tone. "Can't seem to picture it."

"I'm compassionate," he said. "She had the flu. Why wouldn't I take care of her? I'd do it for you, or Harper or any one of ya'll."

"Uh-huh," CJ said, her chair squeaking as if she were getting up.

"What does that mean?"

"Nothing." A pause as a soda can was opened. "Just thought it was nice of you to devote three days to her. Even called in sick, from what I heard."

"Let it go," Gus said.

"What?" Innocence personified in her tone. "I just thought it was sweet." The squeak from the chair sounded when she sat back down. "But let's get something straight, Gus Quinlan. Don't mess around with her—"

"CJ, we've been through this." His voice tightened.

"No, I'm serious. You've been going through a dry spell or something, having her in your house. I don't know if anything has been going on and frankly, I don't want to know, but don't break that girl's heart and have her hightailing it out of here. Harper may lock your balls in a vise grip if things go sideways."

Exasperation was evident in his tone. "I was taking care of a sick friend who didn't have anyone else around to help her. For Christ's sake, when are you going to give me some credit." There was a loud noise that sounded like a chair being pushed into a table.

My hands were shaking, and I jammed them in my pockets. Why was I shaking?

Because of his aggravation, it sounded like he pitied me. Again.

"Was that why you called me in here? For another lecture about my morals and where I stick my dick?" He wasn't messing around anymore with her.

"Gus—" CJ's tone softened, turning conciliatory. "Gus, wait." There was a pause. She must have gotten him to stop. I tried to find a place to hide, but I couldn't move yet. "Listen, if I've overstepped—if Harper and I are misreading this and you have feelings for Mia—"

"No!" His voice was on the verge of a growl. "I don't have feelings for Mia."

Gut Punch #1.

"Why would I?"

Gut Punch #2.

Again. Why did it hit me so damn hard—each time. How do I stop giving his words the power to damage me?

I turned on a dime and beelined it out of there. Finding my way down to the garage, feeling a bit dizzy again. Maybe I was pushing it too soon.

Just like he said…I didn't have feelings for him.

Why would I?

Because I did…and there wasn't a damn thing I could do to get rid of them.

31

GUS

"Easy, killer," CJ said, approaching me as if she'd been thrown in a cage with a pissed-off tiger—me.

Yeah, well, she's the one who had been poking at me.

I ran my hand through my hair. "I gotta go. I got shit to do." She was right about one thing—I missed a lot of work while caring for Mia. Junior was having a fit and I was behind on a ton of things. We had a less-than-stellar race last week, and except for a few Zoom meetings, I was M.I.A.—Missing in Action because of M-I-A.

Ha! I just made a joke. Whatever.

"Don't be pissed," CJ said, pacing a bit. "I'm sorry, alright? It's just...I don't usually see you spend this much time with a woman. Both Harper and I are just, well, confused." She shrugged.

Yeah, well, they weren't the only ones.

She held up her hand. "Fine. I get it. We just...I don't know. If you like her...I mean...like her-like her—that would be great." Her face actually brightened with hope for a fraction of a minute. "But if you were screwing around with her, that ain't cool, and you're just too hard to read sometimes." She plopped back in her seat and kicked her feet up on the table.

"Like her-like her? As opposed to just liking her? Do we have a junior high handbook to break down the definition of these labels?"

God, I was even sounding like a woman. I needed to hang out with the guys more.

CJ rolled her eyes like I was ridiculous, waving a hand at me, but the atmosphere eased up as I began to joke again. She asked, "So, do we get our race engineer back now?"

"Yeah. She should be around here." I went to look out the conference room door. "She was leaving right after me."

CJ watched as she ran her finger over the seam on the armrest of her chair.

"Now that that subject is out of the way, let's talk wedding." She switched topics so fast my head spun. "You haven't said whether you're bringing a date?"

"Yes, I did. I said I wasn't. I thought most of us who weren't dating anyone were going solo?"

"Well, I think Davy is bringing someone. Actually, I think he's bringing Shyla. I have to double-check—"

That treacherous traitor.

"And now that I am clear about you and Mia not being together, I guess I should check with her to see if she's bringing anyone. Maybe she'll ask Dawson Shawfield. He's in the off-season." She was getting too excited by this idea. "That would be a great guy for her to bring—especially since he's friends with Davy."

Nope. Nope. Nope. Wait...was I actually shaking my head?

"Why are you shaking your head, Gus?" she asked with more innocence than CJ could ever possibly possess. "Do you know something I don't? Is Mia dating someone else?"

Shit, was she? No. I would've known.

Why did I care?

I didn't. Did I?

"I don't know what her plans are." I pulled out my phone and tried very hard not to react.

CJ was fishing—damn her. I loved my friend, but she was ruthless when she felt she was onto something and not getting a straight answer.

Hell, I didn't even know the question, let alone the answer to give her.

But I sure as hell didn't want Dawson Shawfield coming to a romantic beach wedding with all of us.

And that thought made me a monstrous asshole.

The way CJ smirked at me—she damn well knew what she was doing.

And she was poking at me. All indications were that she would continue to poke, too, until I got my head out of my ass and decided what the answer was. Because in my heart I knew damn well what the question was…

I glared at my best friend, who just stared me down without an ounce of remorse.

Did I like-like Mia St. James?

I didn't break eye contact as I grabbed my things. CJ's smirk grew into a full grin as I turned and walked out.

When I was further down the hall, CJ yelled out, "Let me know about those plus-ones, Gus."

"Fuck off, CJ," I yelled back—screw it, it wasn't my place of work, I didn't give a damn who heard me.

32

MIA

I pulled up to my house. My house. Not my father's or Keith's or Gus's —mine.

There was so much sweetness to that revelation it made me smile. Because even if I may find myself lonely in this house, in this town, on my own…this house was mine—bought with my money. I could decorate it however I wanted. I could work on my car in the middle of the night or dance to 1990's hip-hop naked.

Gus liked old-school grunge and 2000's rock when he worked on his car. Would he walk around naked in his house?

While I didn't have proof of that, I had glimpsed his abs enough to store data in my memory bank.

Stop, Mia.

I pulled into the garage, got out, grabbed my bags, walked into the house, toed off my shoes, and flipped on the light. Thanks to Michelle, my kitchen was completely unpacked, and my fridge was relatively well stocked. I grabbed the beer from out of my fridge. It was one of Gus's favorites. I'd grown accustomed to his brand while living with him.

Bypassing the "to-do" list of projects on my counter, I put the bags by the stairs that led up to my bedroom and flung myself on the couch.

I opened the beer and took a sip, realizing how pathetic it was that I even bought his favorite beer now. It was as if I were indoctrinated into the GQ fan club like any other pit lizard—just a regular racing groupie.

Ugh.

My head flung back onto the sectional I recently bought, and with a pathetic groan realized how similar the sofa was to Gus's. I closed my eyes. My house was quiet. Too quiet. Maybe I needed to get a dog. Or a cat.

Because it may have only been a few days, but this living-alone crap...it was for the birds.

The next morning, I found myself not in my bed but curled up on my "Gus" sofa with an afghan Michelle gave me as a housewarming present that—geez, Louise—was the same as Gus's, just different colors. Surely that wasn't intentional from his mom.

If the conversation I overheard between him and CJ was any indication, I needed to de-Gus my house...my life.

I rubbed my eyes, determined to break this cycle, and padded my way into the kitchen. I would have tea this morning...Gus hates tea.

As I sat at the counter—my counter—sipping my tea, my phone dinged. A new Word Scramble came in. One from Shaw and one from Gus. I was easily beating Shaw by about seventy-five points. God bless the man. He always kept himself vulnerable to those triple-word scores.

Gus, well, he was a little more creative. He just played to see how many suggestive or ridiculous words he could fit in.

Today was "melons." Clearly innocuous—unless you knew Gus's mindset.

I stared at my phone as if it had the ability to electrocute me. Trying to forget his kindness, his comfort that was overshadowing those words I heard him say to CJ. *"No! I don't have feelings for Mia. Why would I?"*

Nope. Nothing was drowning out those words. They were screaming in volume over all the sweet memories of him holding me.

But I'll be damned if he thinks I have feelings for him.

So, I threw down words they'd both have to look up the definition for. For Gus, today was "zaftig."

GUS

There is no such word.

MIA

Good morning, sunshine. Look it up.

A few moments went by and then…

GUS

Hello. Smart ass. I picked up something you're going to want to see. Come by. I swear it will be worth it.

I paused. I needed to say no. I should say no. Cut it off.

MIA

I have some things I have to take care of around here.

Pause. Dots dancing. Pause.

GUS

What do you have to do?

MIA

Just errands and stuff. I'm going to buy a lawn mower.

GUS

What? You mow your own lawn. Hire a service. Blow it off.

Be strong, girl.

MIA

Let me see how the day goes. ;-)

Then, I added,

MIA

My zaftig figure could use the exercise of mowing the lawn.

GUS

Fine. But your figure is perfect. Don't you change a damn thing. I'll pay for the lawn service myself.

Hmm. Was that him being kind or was that him being...Nope. It was Gus.

Besides, I didn't need to get distracted by Gus today. I was supposed to have dinner with Shaw tonight. CJ and Harper had been on me about asking him to go to the wedding.

Shaw and I had just been talking the last few months, exchanging texts and game messages, seeing each other out when the group was together. Depending on how things went tonight, maybe I would suggest spending more time together? Maybe I would ask him to be my date for CJ and Grady's wedding weekend?

If I could have impure, unfriendly nighttime thoughts about my roommate, it was probably proof that my body was ready for me to date, at least.

The rest of me needed something else to fixate on—and Dawson Shawfield was one fine man to fixate on. Spending time with him on a beach shirtless...yes, I think that could distract me pretty darn well.

It was actually perfect since Shaw was friends with Davy, who had begun seeing Shyla. He even flew to Chicago last weekend to visit her, and asked her to go with him.

Gus will probably have a date—a thought that sat in my stomach like sour milk.

I couldn't be the only single person there. It would be fun if I asked Shaw. We were all friends. He'd fit right in with the group.

It was quite a perfect scenario, and I was warming to the idea even more.

I could go by and see Gus for a little while after my errands. I didn't want him to think anything was different between us—our friendship was fine with me. Then I'd have time to get ready for my date with Shaw.

What do you know…I may actually be getting a social life.

Go me.

Later in the afternoon, I grabbed one of Gus's favorite coffee drinks and headed over to his place to see his surprise.

"What the…" I pulled into his driveway and around to the back where his garage doors were up, displaying the back end of his covered Camaro—that I still hadn't driven. His everyday SUV was parked off to the side like a forgotten relative, but what had all of my attention was the Carolina blue Bronco, top off, parked diagonal to the garage— a beautiful, refurbished classic.

No, it wasn't fast or flashy, but it screamed fun.

Gus came out of his back door, dressed in cargo shorts, a well-worn Linkin Park concert shirt, and a pair of slides. It was only the end of April, but it was Carolina, and it was beautiful enough to have everyone believing summer was on its way.

I got out of my SUV without taking my eye off his new, flashy toy and didn't give him more than a cursory glance. I walked around the truck close enough to stroke my hand down the frame, just barely touching it. "Oh my God, Gus. What did you do?"

When I got to the other side of the truck, I could barely see over the hood but asked, "Did you buy this? This is what you wanted to show me?"

I glanced up to see the biggest shit-eating grin on his face. Pride beamed off him as he nodded his head. There was more teenage boy in him than any bravado in his head nod and glint in his eye.

My hand went to my chest to still my heart. Whether it was from the endearing expression on his face or the excitement of the truck, I'm not sure and won't ever analyze.

I finished my promenade around the truck and stopped in front of him. He'd been watching me survey the truck with his hands in his pockets and his legs splayed, but the smile was still in place.

I stopped inches from him, putting myself between him and the truck. "I can't believe... What made you decide to do that?"

I was nearly jumping out of my skin. I had always wanted a truck like that. It was what I had told him while we were at the car show last month. We'd been touring the shows and auctions in our downtime and came across a car like this one. I fawned over it.

This truck was beautiful. Iconic.

He scratched his scruff under his chin, pulled the keys out from his pocket, and went to open his mouth. I went to grab them. "I want to drive!"

He held them above my head. "Hello to you, too, darlin'. Do you realize you never even gave me a proper greeting?"

I stared him down. "Hi, Gus." I put my hands together in a prayer-slash-begging clasp under my chin, giving him what I hoped were my biggest puppy dog eyes. "Can I drive it?"

He purposefully held them higher and jingled them. The truck actually had keys that jingled, not just a key fob, like the newer models.

I loved it. He opened the door of the driver's side with the hand not teasing me with the keys, and I was entranced with the retro dashboard, the saddle leather bucket seats, and kicked out with surround sound speakers, which obviously weren't original.

This was not an inexpensive purchase.

I managed to lift myself into the car which was jacked up on huge thirty-five-inch wheels with almost a foot clearance. I sat in the seat as if I were a small child pretending to drive my father's truck.

As he walked around the vehicle, Gus's grin was full of pride and satisfaction. He climbed in, saying, "Go ahead and turn it on. We can go try her out."

I buckled myself in before he could change his mind.

It really was the perfect day to enjoy a vehicle like that one. I pulled a hair tie from my pocket and yanked my hair back. We drove off. First, just through the neighborhood, then venturing down some back roads. We sat quietly, just enjoying the outdoors and each other's presence before coming back to the edge of town.

"Want to stop and pick up some barbecue?" he said, pointing at our favorite take-out place.

Wait, do "we" have a favorite take-out place?

Um.

"Actually, I need to head home."

"Ah. Hot date?" he teased, but there was a hint of something else in his tone.

I shrugged. "I wouldn't say hot, but...well. Okay, I mean, he *is* hot." I winced. "But, I mean, we're just going out to eat—"

He put up his hand. "Say no more. You may hurt yourself trying to explain." He chuckled but it sounded flat.

"Ha. Yeah."

There was an awkward pause. Then we both tried to fill the silence.

"I assume it's Shaw?"

"Um-hmm." I nodded a little too enthusiastically.

"I wasn't aware you two were seeing each other."

"Well, we weren't. Not really. An occasional lunch or something, but now that things are starting to get in a groove with me at work, and his life has settled down after the postseason, we have started spending time together."

We were driving through some traffic, and I couldn't take my eyes off the road to gauge his expression. A more awkward silence took over before we both asked questions at the same time.

"So, are you going to take this baby down for the wedding?"

"Is Shaw going to the wedding?"

We pulled up to a stop light and I glanced over at him as he motioned for me to go first. "Are you planning to take this down to the Outer Banks?" Grady and CJ's wedding was at a huge mansion-slash-private hotel in what is considered the 4x4 beach properties north of the Outer Banks. You can only access the house with a four-wheel drive vehicle. Perfect for this kind of truck. "It would be awesome on the beach."

"Yep. That's the plan." He forced a smile. With the soft top off and the huge wheels on this Bronco, it would be a blast.

Yes, for him and his date. I'm sure it will be romantic as hell, putting the seats back, star gazing on the beach...finding a private cove...

"So is Shaw going to the wedding?"

I shrugged, "Not sure yet. I was going to ask him this evening if he'd be interested."

I nodded, focusing harder on my driving than I thought I had since I was sixteen.

"So, things are good with you two?" He was studying the stitching on the upholstery and wasn't looking at me when he was asking the questions.

"Like I said, we don't see a lot of each other. We try to when we can make our schedules work. You know how it is..."

He nodded.

"What about you? Are you inviting Kellie...or anyone?" My body clenched, I gripped the wheel tighter, but pushed through it.

He shrugged and flashed a small smile, just as we pulled back up to his house, ending the unreasonably uncomfortable conversation. I parked the truck, and we sat quietly for a moment as I tapped the steering wheel with my fingers. "Well, I think you're really going to fall in love with this." I turned to smile at him. He had his elbow resting against his door and his head resting against his hand, studying me with an unreadable expression.

He briefly closed his eyes and reached for the door handle. "Yes, I think..." he opened it and began to step out. Looking over his shoulder, but not at me directly, he said, "I think I may."

I stepped out of the truck. I had to hop out because there was a bit of a drop. Gus anticipated my predicament and was standing there with a hand out to help me down. I got caught in the seat belt, and he ended up catching me, his hands resting on my waist.

He held me up for a moment as if he knew my knees needed a

moment to stabilize. "Thank you for coming by and seeing it. I promise you can have a turn with it down on the sand."

My t-shirt had risen just enough for me to feel his hands on my midriff. Just the barest movement of his thumb on my abdomen and I was frozen.

It burned me.

It branded me.

Son of a bitch. I had a date...ugh. I didn't need to leave thinking about this skin-on-skin

contact.

His hands were still on my hips, and I couldn't look up at him. Because if I did...I knew he was staring at me, and he'd see everything.

Don't be ridiculous.

I wasn't going to let my farfetched imagination get away from me.

I stepped back as if it were nothing. I tucked a piece of wayward hair behind my ear, then shoved my hands into my jeans pockets, thereby guarding any exposed midriff skin against further contact. Why were there butterflies dancing around inside me? Damnit.

"Okay, well, the truck is amazing." I pointed at him. "I'm sure you will enjoy it." As I stepped backward toward my car, I said, "Have a good evening."

"Hey, Mia..." Gus said.

One-liner declarations of love and lust, pivotal romantic moments, heart-melting scenes of first kisses—all the things my romance novels were full of—flew through my mind as I turned to him and studied the face I tried so hard to keep out of my dreams.

He ran his hand over his neck, pulling on it, and then down over his face, grimacing slightly. "Have fun..."

That was it. Of course, it was it. He's not into you. Get it through your head, idiot. Friends. Not even friends with benefits. Just friends.

"Um. Okay..." I stared into his navy-blue eyes.

Those damn butterflies. I wonder if there was some kind of organic butterflies-in-the-stomach repellant you could take to get rid of them.

Could you imagine the billions you could make if there was a cure to ward off the butterflies the wrong people gave you?

I'd sell my soul to stop crushing on him when he looked at me that way.

"But call me if you need anything."

"Why would I need anything? I'm just going to dinner?" I didn't think it sounded snarky, but he immediately waved me off.

"I don't know. Just...whatever." He turned and walked into his house, and I swear the door slammed behind him.

33

GUS

The Charlotte race was the prelude to a two-week break that would be filled with CJ and Grady's destination wedding. Since Charlotte was CJ's home track, the team had hoped for a win to slide them into the playoffs, but the season was still young, and a top-five finish was enough.

As far as Grady was concerned, he could've wrecked the car on the first lap because nothing was going to bring him down. Well, except maybe one thing…

"I want to know who put the idea in her head that being celibate two weeks before the wedding was a good idea?" We were all kicked back on the dock of CJ's and Grady's lake house late in the morning, the picture of men of leisure. Grady stood over all of us, board shorts, t-shirt, sunglasses, and a Bloody Mary in hand.

We all glanced around at each other, chuckling. Grady studied us, and he settled on me.

I held up a hand. "Do you really think I'd talk to CJ about your sex life? Seriously?" I said, "She's my best friend, but I draw the line, man."

"My money is on Sadie or Amara," Cooper said. "Just to watch you squirm."

There were some general comments about blue balls and Grady taking things "in hand" that kept laughter flowing for a while.

Generally, these guys didn't have much sympathy for a man who never had much of an abstinence streak, except for the season he was competing against CJ, and they were dancing around each other.

"Well, it's not funny." Grady's bottom pout was amusing enough that I considered reaching for my phone to capture it for the bride to see.

"It's good for you...consider it a trial to show your worthiness for the bride," his brother said, rising to answer his cell phone and walk down the dock.

Grady shook his head and murmured something that sounded like, "Fuck that." He replaced his sunglasses, settled on a chaise, and laid his head back down, broody as hell. "Laugh now, assholes. Just wait until it's your turn. I'll return the favor."

"Not even the least bit of nerves. Really?" Davy's brow quirked up.

"Nope." The word was accompanied by a grin and no other movement. "Just want that part done so we can have a hell of a party."

Cal, Grady, Cooper, Davy, and I were going to enjoy a day on the lake. The plan was dinner downtown in a private room with cigars and poker at an exclusive club this evening before driving out the next day to the Outer Banks for the wedding.

Yes, we had planned on a weekend in Vegas, but we were tight on time, and Grady's done it all before—he had no interest. Plus, between him and Davy, it was hard to go anywhere and not be recognized, especially in Vegas. We didn't need anything resembling a rumor getting back to CJ or ending up in an online tabloid.

So, we went for the more subdued bachelor party. One that sounded like it matched the girls' spa weekend—a day on the lake, dinner, a whisky bar, and poker. Perfection.

"Girls are hanging on the beach. Pampered and relaxed, as well. Your girl is good, brother." Cal walked back down to where we sat.

Grady shaded his eyes toward his brother who dropped into the chaise next to him. "No doubt. She's gone radio silent for the last day, and I'm not happy about it." He sat up and pointed at all of us.

Once it began raining, we decided to head downtown for a late lunch-early dinner. We popped into the bar where Grady first met CJ. Cooper's eyes rolled heavenward when Grady decided to walk down memory lane and into the bar, detouring us even more from our planned evening.

"We've got 'sentimental and all-in-his-feels' Grady to deal with this evening…" Cooper groaned. "Wonderful."

Having a string of professional athletes and very wealthy businessmen with you did have its perks, and we were quickly given VIP service—seats at the bar and a cocktail—or in Grady's case, a few to add to the ones we'd already consumed.

"…and…this (hic…hic…) is where my bride stumbled and fell into my arms. Isn't that right, Coop?"

A defeated Cooper's shoulders dropped, "Yes, Grady."

Grady's drunken enthusiasm overflowed, as did his drinks as he ran between the tables, "And this…(hic…) was where she had toilet paper on her heel…remember!" He laughed as if he were at a stand-up comedy bar.

"I'm getting a drink. What can I get you, Coop?" I asked, clapping him on the shoulder.

"How about something laced with a sleeping pill for Mr. Nostalgia over here?" He jerked his thumb at Grady who was weaving between tables.

I gave him a sympathetic shrug. "Ah…I'm responsible while he's in the race car. This falls under the realm of best friend duties, I'm afraid."

Cooper searched the bar, impatience grating on him. "What happened to his brother? Why can't he relieve me, at least? Damn, this is going to be a long night."

"I'll grab you a beer and see if Cal can come direct him to a chair. Right now, you better go grab him." I pointed to the ladies' room where Grady was heading.

"Son of a b—" Cooper took off, pushing chairs aside to catch up to his charge.

I walked up to Cal who was standing at the bar, "Hey, Cooper

215

wants a beer for himself and a leash for your brother."

Cal craned his neck, spotted the two men dodging chairs around the back of the bar, and chuckled. "Mom punished me for trying to put a leash on him when we were younger. Cooper can deal, but I'll buy him a beer for his trouble." He held his hand out for the bartender's attention and we ordered a round of drinks.

I took a sip of my beer, sat up in a chair at the bar, and surveyed the growing crowd as Cal pulled out his phone.

"Any word from the women lately?" I asked.

"Not since I left a message earlier. Harper said they were on the beach, which was why they probably didn't get the call. Coverage is spotty out by the water."

"Did she say how everyone was doing?" What I really wanted to know was if Mia was having fun? Why was this concerning me? I had thought about her a few times today as we were out and about. Little things that were reminding me of her—making me miss her.

I thought about texting her myself. But what would I say? "Hey, how's the bachelorette party going?" Sounds kind of like something a boyfriend would do. I wondered if Shaw was texting her. I couldn't ask him—that would be weird. But...I wanted to know.

I didn't like how this felt.

She had a date for the weekend. Shaw would be with her, and my third-wheel status would be activated once again. Yay.

I was analyzing this way too much.

We were going to see our friends get married. We were going to spend a few great days relaxing, by a pool, on a beach, with drinks and friends and shorts, flip flops, sand, and bathing suits.

Oh. Goddammit.

She was going to be wearing a bathing suit. I'd never seen her in one. Actually, while she was living with me, I never even caught an "Oops!" of her in anything less than an oversized t-shirt and boy shorts. She managed to only be braless around me a handful of times—not that I always noticed...alright, fine. I'm a man. I did. They were always under very big sweatshirts, so I didn't see much. Alright, there was an occasional tight tank top.

They were round with the slightest bit of a drop that would fit in my hands perfectly—Stop! God, man...

It was enough to fuel my imagination. Geez, I sounded like a perv. She was an attractive

woman. Any man would think that way.

I wonder if she was a bikini girl? Or a one piece. I could see her being a one piece. Which was fine, too—it was all good—very, very...good.

I shook my head, dispelling the images of Mia in different kinds of bathing suits...her beautiful hair down and pulled back with a pair of designer sunglasses propped on her head as she gave me a sexy side-eye wink.

Jesus Christ. I shook my head again. I wonder if it was too late to call up one of my ex-pseudo-girlfriends and see if they wanted to go at the last minute? I needed the distraction. I needed to think of someone else's breasts, someone else's bikini-clad body...someone else... Fuck, what I needed was to get laid. On the other hand, I didn't want to deal with the complications of entertaining a woman and having her tag along. But I really didn't want to watch Mia and Shaw enjoy the romantic setting all weekend together.

Would they be staying in the same room? Same bed? Had they slept together already? Fuck. My. Life.

I downed the drink in my hand, not aware what it was.

I wouldn't know. She lived on her own now. They could be fucking all over her house and—

Stop! Stop.

That's not an image I needed to set up residence in my mind. Friend or not—I didn't need to think of Mia being...touched...by anyone. I had my eyes shut tight as if that would keep my imagination from torturing me.

Nope. Wasn't working—in fact, making it worse. I opened them just to beeline my attention to Shaw, at a high-top table with Davy, having joined us shortly after getting to this bar. My enthusiasm couldn't be contained when Davy told me he would meet us—same with my sarcasm.

His boy-next-door good looks were only altered by his well-toned, athletic frame and the confidence that came with the entire package. Yet, as much as I wanted to pigeon-hole him into a cocky-bastard personality, and find numerous faults with him, he really was a pretty good guy.

It made me want to hate him.

And I wasn't that kind of guy. I wasn't petty. I wasn't envious. I never compared myself to other men. I never felt the need for it. But I'd also never felt threatened by someone being in my face with Mia.

Cal waved his hand in my face again. "Gus!"

My attention snapped back to Cal.

"Gus—hello." Cal waved his hand in front of my face. "I'm going to step outside." He motioned to outside the bar. "Harper just tried calling and I can't hear anything. I'm going to check in on things."

"Yeah. Okay. Good. I'll go give Cooper his beer."

Cal glanced over his shoulder, noticing who I was shooting eye daggers at, and then nodded back at me, a ghost of a smirk on his face. He nodded before leaning over to his other side to tell Davy to watch his beer. To both of us he said, "I'll be right back."

Before disappearing into the gathering crowd, I spontaneously shouted, "Hey, ask him how Mia's doing." Because I wasn't making a big enough fool of myself as it was.

Cal froze. I froze. More embarrassingly Davy pivoted his stool my direction at the same time Shaw stopped his conversation and gave me his attention.

A grin danced over Cal's face, and he mouthed. "I knew it."

"What? I hadn't spoken to her in a while. Just ask Harper to, you know, keep an eye on her." I tried to dig myself out and just dug myself deeper in it.

He narrowed his eyes, pursed his lips, and gave me a nod with mock seriousness, "I'll take care of it." Then he winked at me as if it was a code between us with a different meaning.

I turned my back on all of them as I felt heat rise over my neck and face. *Don't you blush, asshole—if the guys see you blush after...*

I walked the beer over to Cooper, who'd managed to corner Grady,

218

and thrust it into his hands before walking back, motioning for the bartender.

Play it cool, Quinlan. And have another drink because obviously, you have such a clear head the more drinks you consume.

What did I just do? Who cared? I just wanted to know how she was doing. It wasn't a declaration of anything. And the women she was with...it was good to have someone watch out and make sure she didn't drink too much or do anything crazy—

I turned back to the bar, rubbing my hand over my face. "Shit."

"And why haven't you spoken to the woman?" Davy asked.

"No reason. Just busy." Where was that damn bartender?

"Busy, huh?" Davy said, sipping his own drink, eyeing me like his weakened prey. "Doesn't have anything to do with her dating status?"

I turned my back on him.

"Tell Davy the truth." He grabbed me by my shoulder, turning me around and leaning over me, and I forgot how much bigger he was until he did shit like this. "Are you going to get off your ass and admit that that girl means something to you?" Davy asked. "And don't give me that 'we're just friends' bullshit."

I leaned against the bar. A denial was on my lips. The one I gave whenever questioned about any girl, sometimes with a "fuck off" tone in my voice if the interrogator was persistent. I opened my mouth. I closed it. I stared ahead at the wall of liquor bottles that were lined up against the bar back. Energy was radiating over my skin—like a tangible thing inside me that was looking for a way out. My leg was bouncing a mile a minute, and I couldn't clear my mind.

My confusing thoughts about Mia were zinging through my body like electrical impulses and the alcohol were upping the wattage.

The inhibition that went hand in hand with alcohol consumption was also the gatekeeper to secrets...and my feelings for Mia, previously locked safely inside my walls, was rattling the cage to come out.

Truth was, I hadn't spoken to her in a few days, since her date with Shaw. I couldn't. I couldn't bear to hear if she was happy. And, oh my God, if she started to talk about him—even if she started to gush about what a great guy he was, I may have lost it. Because I didn't care if the guy was a Nobel-prize-winning, SEAL Team member and Boy Scout, no one was good enough for her. I knew that sounded so damn cliché. I also knew how ridiculous it sounded.

I don't know how long I stared at the bottles, but I heard Davy mutter, "Damn. I was just messing with you, man. Gus?" I dropped my head in my hands, but from the corner of my vision I saw my muscular friend wave down a bartender and order something. A minute later a shot was stuck under my nose. "Drink up, my man."

I stared down at the liquid in the shot glass. "Drink," Davy said, again.

I threw back the shot and turned over the glass. The liquid burning my chest somehow managed to be the final key that opened me up. "She's more," I rasped out. "She's more," I repeated and braced myself on the bar and stared down at the upside down shot glass. "Fuck me, she's more," I said, with the low growl of an animal walking into the sunlight after being in the dark for ages.

It was out in the world. It was out of my subconscious, and it was now real. Now what the hell was I going to do about it?

Davy clamped his big paw on my shoulder, grounding me.

"Just breathe. It'll be okay." He reassured me, clapping me on the back. "Just because you said it doesn't mean you have to do anything about it…" Then he stared over his shoulder, remembering Shaw. "Well, I guess you probably need to decide if you *want* to do something before *something* else happens." He leaned forward onto the bar, mimicking my stance. "Because you've got my man over there looking forward to spending a romantic weekend with her starting in a few hours."

"For Christ's sake." Incredulously, I stared at my friend who had basically just met me at the end of a marathon and asked if I wanted to go for a run with him. "Do you know how long it took me to say those words? Now you want to know if I'm going to do anything in the next hour. Give me a minute for all this to process." I ran my hand through my hair and turned to walk away, without any knowledge of where I'd go. Maybe brood in the corner like a drunken moody ass. Maybe drunk text her if that shot proves to have too much of an effect. Fuck no. In a moment of clarity, I handed my phone to Davy and said, "Don't let me text her."

"I got you." He gave me a sympathetic pat on my shoulder as he pocketed my phone and turned around toward the rest of the bar. He leaned over with regret in his voice. "Unfortunately, I think you're going to have to decide pretty damn quick."

Tracking Davy's focus and tone of voice, I knew Shaw was coming up behind me and braced myself because I didn't know what to do —or say.

"I think now is a good time to find the bathroom, or somewhere else to be but here," Davy said and high-tailed it out of there, passing between Shaw and me as if I just handed him a football, and the back of the bar was the end zone.

I slammed down the second shot the bartender had just given me, eyeing the hulk behind me.

"Hey, Gus—"

"Hey, Shaw…wanna drink?" And yes, my voice was too enthusiastic, too loud and too

stupid for words to describe.

Shaw leaned into the space Davy had vacated but hadn't sat down. I focused on waving down the bartender, refusing to make eye contact. "I think I'm going to have another one."

He held up a hand that could palm a football, and probably a large portion of my skull, before shaking his head. He leaned toward my ear, shouting over the din of people. "I'd like to speak with you for a moment, before you have another drink."

"Okay?"

"Can you come outside so we can have this conversation without yelling?" We made eye contact, and I managed not to flinch.

"Yeah. Okay." I signaled to the bartender that I'd be back and followed Shaw as he worked his way through the bar, the crowd parting like the Red Sea.

Let's hope he wasn't planning on parting my skull in the same manner.

34

GUS

The muggy twilight night met us with relative silence compared to the noise from within the bar, which made the focus of the conversation even more daunting. Shaw walked a few feet past the bar and waited for me to catch up. He turned, taking a stance with his legs spread, hand in one pocket as he palmed something in his other hand. Fidgeting with it and focusing on what his hand was doing, rather than watching me, had me on edge.

He held up what appeared to be a flat stone. Nothing remarkable. Just a gray flat stone, slightly bigger than a quarter, smooth from being tumbled over time in probably a riverbed.

"This stone here is my talisman," he said, his voice was so soft, and after being in the noisy bar I had to step closer to hear him. "A real good friend of mine from home gave me this stone. I carry it every-where with me."

Okay.

"It's a good luck charm, but also a constant reminder of things I missed out on because I didn't have the guts to be honest with myself. I missed opportunities..." He studied it, even though it was clear he knew it as well as his own hand.

"I carry it with me to remind myself not to make the same mistakes," he said, stepping closer, he held up the unremarkable stone. "You see, instead of holding someone's heart... instead of having someone to care for, to cherish...I'm holding a goddam rock."

Our eyes locked and his jaw was tight, but there wasn't anger on his face, although he was serious. He pocketed the rock. "I like Mia. I do. I enjoy spending time with her. I find her adorable, charming, intelligent, and sexy as hell," he said, his body easing as my body stiffened at his declaration.

"Your point?" I tried, but failed, not to grit out.

"My point is that if I go to the beach this weekend with her, I am going to try to make her something more to me than just a lunch date. Because, frankly I want to kiss her, and I really want to do more."

My fists clenched and my arms moved as if I wanted to take a swing at him. He didn't flinch. A knowing, smug expression spread over his face. "Thought so...the idea of me touching her... It doesn't sit well, does it?"

I stared up but didn't meet his eyes, unable to speak because a red filter of rage had covered my gaze. A need to squeeze the life out of his beefy neck was overwhelming even though I knew I'd be on the losing end of that decision.

"I didn't think so." Shaw took a step back, tossing his river stone in the air, catching it, and stepping toward me, pointing at the ground. "Gus. Man, you tell me right now...that she belongs with you. That you've been a fool. If you tell me right now, I'll politely back out and you can go tell her. But, man, if you fuck this up..." he shook his head, "Man, I'll give you one shot because I was once in your place, and I didn't have the balls to go for it. I let one incredible woman get away already...and I won't do it again."

I took a step back for fear that I was going to step up into this man's face and it wouldn't end well.

Breathing slowly in and out of my nose, I ran my hands over my face.

I could say it was the alcohol that gave me the courage, I could say it was the idea of him touching her that drove me insane, but it was the regret he blatantly held, like a weight around his neck, that made me honest.

I drew in a deep breath, and firmly and with absolute conviction, said, "She belongs with me."

Shaw nodded. Studied his rock again, rolling it around in his hand, and then flipped it up in the air again. "Alright, then."

He led us back to the bar and grabbing for the door, he turned to me and said, "Good luck, man. I do mean it. Because something has been holding her back, and I don't think it was her twat-head ex." He pointed at me, "I think it was you."

He turned to walk in the bar, and I stopped him. Thankful for this man's honesty and straightforwardness. "Hey, about that other woman —the one you missed out on—"

He had a regretful, sad smile on his face, but sharing time was over. "Don't fuck this up with Mia. I won't step aside a second time."

I followed him back into the bar, wanting Mia to magically appear. All the information, all the revelations...and the alcohol-fueled courage I had to confront this challenge head-on, I wanted to do so right now. It made me want her to appear in front of me now. I could take her in my arms, smell the scent of her hair, feel her tucked in under my chin, her breasts against me, her breath on my neck, and I'd whisper to her...what? What would I say?

I probably needed some time to let this sit.

Shaw was sidelined by a group when we walked back in, but I beelined it to where Cal had returned and was talking with Davy, who stared at me expectantly. Before Davy could pry, Cal said, "Well, the girls are having a blast from what I can tell—including Mia." He emphasized, and if I wasn't still reeling, I would've rolled my eyes. "They're relaxed, pampered, and well taken care of."

"Are they okay out in the middle of nowhere? Are they bored?" Davy asked.

"Certainly didn't sound like it. Music was blaring and there was a lot of laughing going on. Harper didn't say much, actually. Said she'd talk to me later and jumped off. Sadie was yelling out 'sisters before misters' or something. And then reminded me to stop and get a bunch of batteries."

"Batteries? Doesn't the place we're staying at have a generator?" I asked.

He shrugged. "She insisted. She said not everything runs off the generator."

Grady comes over and chimes in, "I've got a wild idea!"

He pulls out his phone and tries dialing...talking nonsense about chartering a jet and flying out to the house tonight. Cooper tried to grab the phone from him, and they played capture the phone.

"Davy, a little help over here," Cooper asked while dodging Grady's sloppy attempts at tackling him. "Doesn't this fall in your wheelhouse?"

"For one thing, I get paid a shit-ton of money, and the guys I chase aren't drunken idiots," Davy says. "Besides, I'm off duty."

Cal laughed. "Did anyone slip something in his drink?"

"He told the bartender about his blue balls, and the bartender thought he said Blue Bull ...as in the cocktail. And well...he liked them. A lot," I said, searching my pockets for my phone and then remembering I gave it to Davy.

"Someone should be recording this for posterity," I said, but then noticed a few patrons had that covered and it was probably being live streamed.

"Okay. Well, shouldn't all that alcohol have calmed his ass down?" Davy said.

"They had Blue Curaçao, vodka, rum, sweet and sour mix...and each had a can of Red Bull in them. Hence the name," I said.

"Who the hell thought it was a good idea to give Grady Red Bull?" Cooper fell into a chair. "That's like giving espresso to a five-year-old. Thank God he's marrying her. I'm too old for this shit anymore."

"Man, you're barely thirty."

"He ages you."

"Hold up." Davy was peering over Cal's shoulder of the video recording from earlier in the day he just received of the girls dancing, drinking by the pool with very young, good-looking bartenders. I grabbed the phone out of Cal's hand to see Shyla handing Mia suntan lotion, and a kid who was probably barely old enough to drink take the lotion from her hands and offering to put it on her back. Shyla went for the camera as another bartender handed Mia a drink and a wink.

A shot of adrenaline raced through me as if Grady were on the last lap of the Daytona 500, only half a length in front of his competition. I've never become so sober, so quickly.

"Oh, hell no," I said, handing his phone back to Cal. The crew chief in me took over as I stood on the chair next to me and began shooting out orders. "Everyone in the McBane Party, I hope you're packed," I called out to people. "Davy, pay the bill. Cal, pull your strings and get us a ride." I jumped, okay, fell, off the chair and went to Grady, slapping him on the shoulder, "Grady, my man. We're going to go see CJ."

"Yes!" He pumped his fist like he just scored a touchdown, did a victory dance, and then sped around the bar as if he were in his car, doing donuts on the track—complete with sound effects.

"Alright, people, let's go!" I clapped my hands together and the men actually listened and began to scurry. It wasn't from their desire to follow my instructions, more likely they wanted to see the women also. Everyone began gathering things to leave except Shaw.

He stood still, a glass of what I think was scotch in his hand, his other in his pocket, watching everyone move. I stepped over to him.

"I texted her and said a family matter came up and I had to fly home," Shaw said.

I nodded.

"Come to think of it, I may just do that this weekend." He stared into his drink before taking a sip.

"It seems weird to say 'thank you'," I said, holding out my hand.

Shaw stared at it for a moment before pulling his hand out of his pocket and offering it to me. We shook. "Don't make me regret this," he said, but there was a hint of warmth on his face.

"All I can do is give it a shot."

He nodded, finished his drink, placed the empty glass on the nearest table, gave me a wave, and wordlessly parted the crowd as he walked out.

35

GUS

We had a few guys who hadn't been drinking drive us down to the Outer Banks in trucks able to access the 4x4 beach area—including my Bronco. It was after midnight, before we pulled into town, the moonlight, along with the headlights of our trucks, guided us down the seemingly deserted beach.

Grady and CJ wanted a private location for their wedding. They found a brown clapboard, historic Nags Head-style house that split into two wings for guests with twenty-four bedrooms and twenty-six bathrooms.

Once we turned off our engines, the heavy beat of music battled the melodic sounds of the waves, and the laughter caught up to us as we walked through the gates. The party was in full swing in the center courtyard. It held a deck and bar strewn with white lights and a huge pool that, when covered, became a dance floor.

We walked up the stairs to the deck alongside the massive, covered pavilion that would later be the center of the reception and went unnoticed by the partygoers.

"It looks like we arrived just when things were getting interesting." Cal's dry tone was not appreciated, as my attention was caught by Mia being helped up onto the bar top by two young bartenders. With their sun-kissed, shaggy hair, board shorts, and perfectly faded t-shirts, they were almost too much of a cliché to be believed—but the women surrounding the bar were clearly big fans.

Mia moved her hips to the rhythm of the seductive, heavy beat music. With her eyes downcast to her subjects below her, her expression was blissful as she was lost in the music. She ran her hands down her sides, accentuating her curves and then pivoted to the other side of the bar where more of her friends were whooping and encouraging her out-of-character behavior.

My legs moved before the rest of the guys. While I shortened the distance between me and Mia, she bent down to get something from CJ. I got a full view of her perfectly rounded ass—so did one of the bartenders. When he pulled up a stool to sit and enjoy the show, I yanked it out from under him, letting him fall on his pretty-boy ass.

"Hey—" he yelled loud enough for the women to notice our entrance, and the party came to a full halt. After a half a second of shaking off their surprise, the women rushed from the bar and to my companions, leaving the pretty boys to lurk behind the bar knowing their monopoly on the women's attention had ended.

That's right, bastards. Pack it up.

My eyes were glued to Mia. She was a bit dazed and maybe more relaxed than I'd ever seen her. She wore a halter top, her hair was pulled up exposing her beautiful neck with little tendrils of curls framing her face.

Seeing how gorgeous she was, taking the time to admire her sun-kissed beauty...I tried very hard not to glare at my girl—yes, I said *my girl,* because for the first time I was looking at her with a new understanding. She was standing on a bar top strutting around for men to appreciate. But she was my girl.

Mia stood, open-mouthed, her eyes darting between me and the other men as I walked toward the bar. She squinted, scanned, and studied the guys as they walked farther into the lighted courtyard, closer to the bar.

Dammit. She was looking to see if Shaw was here.

Okay. Yeah. That stung.

I schooled my disappointment and held up my hand. "Mia, I think it's time to get down, sweetheart."

She tracked my new position under her and my outstretched hands…and didn't seem in a hurry to comply. She shook her head with a devilish smile and a playfulness I'd never seen before. It fueled the need to have her in my arms. "I don't want you to fall. Come on, honey."

She put a straw up to her lips and sipped while her eyes were fixed on me. "I like it up here."

I dropped my head so she couldn't see my eye roll.

"Harper…" I growled for my best friend, my tone low and aggravated before surveying the melee around us. She was hanging on Cal's back, straddled, like a chimpanzee.

"Yes, Gus, dear…" she yelled back, kissing her man's neck and giggling.

I gestured with both hands toward the now gyrating Mia. "What the hell—"

She stopped kissing Cal and was a bit confused at my tone of voice. She studied me, then studied her, and it clicked, and she grinned knowingly, wrapping her arm around Cal more tightly and said, "Aw, Gus. Look how happy she is…and she's not with anyone." She kicked Cal like a pony and told him to move closer to me, then leaned over, trying to whisper, "At least not yet. Although, I have to tell you that took some serious work because my man, JD, over there," she nodded her head in the direction of the pretty boy, "wasn't making it easy."

I glared at the pup.

"JD. He's so hot," Mia piped in from above.

"He is—but look who's here…" Harper volleyed back, waving her hand at me like a drunk Vanna White.

It took her a few moments to process that Harper was offering me as an alternative and she didn't think it was a fair exchange. "That's just Gus—" Her face twisted, and she sighed.

I climbed in a chair to get in position to scoop her up as Harper's friend, Amara, came to their defense. "Seriously, Gus, it was shots or skinny-dipping. Considering the wild streak your girl has, it wasn't an easy task."

"I'm not his girl," Mia said, her brows creasing was endearing. I couldn't even explain that she was—with her level of intoxication it would be pointless. "I was supposed to be Shaw's girl, but he stood me up. When you all showed, I'd hoped he changed his mind and would surprise me. But, no. I'm all alone. So I have to find someone else to keep me company." She winked at the pretty boy.

"Mia, honey." I motioned to her. "Come on, let's get down..." I tried to keep my voice reasonable.

"Gus doesn't think of me that way. He certainly doesn't look at me the way JD is..." She waved her fingers at the man-child and tried to capture the very strange-shaped straw from her drink with her mouth and seemed to miss it each time she lunged for it. Focusing her complete attention on trying to capture the straw, she began to sway to one side, and I'd had enough. In moves too quick for her to track, I took the drink out of her hand, grabbed her in a fireman's hold, and pulled her off the bar. She was in my arms, sliding down my chest while still protesting the loss of her drink.

She slapped my chest. "What the hell, Gus?"

"You shouldn't be dancing on a bar when you are that inebriated."

"You mean tipsy," she said, "I'm tipsy. Not drunk...not ineb... ineb-neb-ibiated...not yet," she giggled.

This wasn't going the way I planned it. The entire time it took to get here, all I thought about was kissing her...not that she'd be this drunk. She reclaimed her drink, and my eyes went to her lips. All I could do was stare at her dark pink lips, as they finally caught the straw. A strangely shaped straw. The straw was a penis. A gold penis. She was tonguing a gold shaped-penis straw.

What the fuck?

And she was tonguing it and staring at me from under her lashes.

She was killing me.

If I didn't know better, I'd think she was trying to seduce me in her drunken state.

My Mia. My little, innocent Mia—had she always been a temptress, or was it just now because I was open to seeing it.

My hands were still on her hips, noticeably tightened, and tugged her until she was flush against me. She let out a little "Oh..." and stared down at the hardness pressed against her abdomen. Confusion masked her face as she tried to pull away.

"Drinks!" a female voice called from somewhere behind me.

"Woo Woo!" burst out of Mia so loud it jarred me into releasing her.

A chorus of "Woo Woo!" responded, and the women stampeded back to the bar where there was a list of drinks on a chalkboard titled, "CJ's Night of Flights."

The list included samples of Woo Woo, Tie Me to the Bedpost, Panty-Dropper Punch, You Sexy Dog You, Sex of the Beach, Dirty Sadie Slush and Dick Sucker.

The women lined up like little birds to be fed, and the bartenders with their sinful smiles, mixed drinks and basked at having the attention back on them.

Davy stepped up to me. "Clearly, we should've gotten here a few hours earlier."

I nodded as my hand rubbed my forehead. "Yeah. I'd like to know who the hell booked the bartenders."

Harper's Aunt Sadie, whom I normally adore, but I suspected was behind hiring Dumb and Dumber Bartenders, chose that moment to come up to Cal. "Did you bring the batteries?"

Cal nodded his head toward the matriarch of the group while politely answering, "Yes, ma'am. They're in the car."

Her eyes grew. "Well, then go get them!" Then she turned to the women, "Ladies, we have batteries! Although now that some of the guys have arrived, I'll assume some of you won't need them. Just remember they don't have to be used solo."

She turned to Cal, "Come on, dear boy, Go! Most of my presents were rechargeable, but some take hours to charge and, well, I'd like the ladies to have options." The most devilish half-smile tilted up the woman's carefully maintained features. And then her brows wagged beneath her almost magenta-colored hair.

Cal shook his head and turned to walk back outside. Grady made a beeline for CJ who held out a bag to him. "Wait until you see what Aunt Sadie gave me!"

He scooped her up, stopping long enough for her to grab her rather large gift bag, and ran off with her.

"Hey, what happened to not having sex until the wedding night—" Davy reminded him.

"Shut the hell up...don't remind CJ. Let the man have sex. He will be much more tolerable," Cooper said, falling into a chaise like a beleaguered parent who just got their toddler to sleep.

"There are several things in that bag they can play with and still keep their vow of no intercourse until the wedding night. Trust me, they'll be completely satisfied," Sadie said, and turned on her heel.

The men stared at her as she walked off, and then practically ran to the women, asking for a peek. Some indulged, and some refused. But we all got the idea.

Sadie's outspoken belief of women's pleasure being of utmost importance was well-represented.

Some of the women unashamedly brandished what they received and compared length, girth, rotation, vibrations, and other options, as if they were about to try on shoes. Male cheeks pinked up at times, and more beers and shots were ordered to stave off staring at the presents and contributing juvenile comments to distract from their blush.

I walked over behind Mia. She was digging through her own bag, and I couldn't help but wonder, "So, what's in your bag?"

She slammed her drink, "Do you really want to know?"

I leaned my elbows on the bar closer to her. "I do," I whispered to her, deep, and even I could hear the need in my tone.

Mia didn't acknowledge my tone. She was either too inebriated to pick up on it, or too excited to show me her new treasure. With a flourish, she pulled her hand out of the bag, "Ta Da!" presenting me with a red, ball-shaped object." It was a red, rubber nose...no, wait, it was a red rose. Not what I was expecting. "I'd wanted one of these for a while." Her eyes twinkled with the white string lights above us, and she looked like she just unveiled her Christmas present. She pointed at the top of the flower and said, "This is going to be my new best friend this weekend." She threw her head back and laughed. "See it has this little suction thing right here between the petals—"

I held up my hand because I didn't need that image in my head. "I get the idea of what it does—"

"And you just put it—

"Yes, honey. I get the idea. You can put it away." For now. My new goal was to be there

when she unveiled that for the first time.

She put it back in her bag. "I hope Cal brought the right batteries for it." She dug around in the bag. "Oh, good. It comes with a charging cord." She yanked out the cord like it was a prize.

Her challenging yet adorably awkward smile was waiting for my reaction to the idea of her having a "toy". She wanted to shock me.

Quite the opposite, I was so incredibly turned on. I wanted to go find the damn batteries and mimic Grady with the caveman performance of carrying her out of here and finding the closest private space for us to try her new present out together.

Given that we haven't even kissed yet, we'd be jumping a few steps. I'd had six long hours to think about us. Okay, fine. I'd been dreaming of doing things to her for a while. But nothing that involved using that toy. That was new imagery I wanted to explore.

"You're staring at me funny." Her expression waffled between interested and confused. She giggled, "I adore your blush." She rubbed my arm as if reassuring me my blush wasn't anything to be embarrassed by. "I never knew there was anything I could ever to do shock you or leave you speechless."

"I'm not blushing..." I leaned forward and my voice deepened as I said, "It's not what's in that bag that's making me feel hot. It's the idea of you using it..." I cupped my hand around her cheek, whispering directly into her ear, "While I watch."

I stepped back slowly, as her breath caught and one of her soft curls brushed my cheek. The hint of coconut lotion, how she stared at my lips before making eye contact, her brows arching with surprise. I could imagine her replaying my comment, wondering if she heard me correctly. I tucked another curl behind her ear and said, "Yeah, you heard me."

She closed her eyes and shook her head, confusion etched on her face. I wasn't being fair. She'd been drinking and I shouldn't be saying these things... Not like this. She didn't have the capacity to filter out what it all meant.

But damnit. What I always thought was just a warm affection of friendship between us was unbanked desire, and now that I felt the heat...I wanted the burn, and she stared at me like she was going to go find a hose.

Breaking the connection, she shifted things in her bag. "I guess I better keep the rest of these contents to myself."

She snatched the bag, and stepping back, tripped over the foot of the stool.

I caught her offering an apology. "I didn't mean to embarrass you. I meant to tell you it's hot—"

"La-La-La." She tried to stick her fingers in her ears, and when she couldn't manage that and hold the bag, she just put her hands up. "No, stop. Don't. You need to get laid...worse than I do, evidently."

She began to hiccup. "I get that it may have been a while for you (hiccup)...but seriously. Don't mess with me and embarrass me like that...(hiccup)...it's just not (hiccup)...cool."

I leaned back against the bar. "You're so damn adorable. Beautiful. But so damn enticing and adorable."

"What is wrong with you?" she yelled at me, as if I'd just told her I purposely wrecked her vintage muscle car.

She turned to stare and scowl at her drink glass, and at the bartenders, and then at the women around her. "What the hell have they put in these drinks?" she yelled in exasperation.

Amara leaned back around Cooper "What's wrong, hon?"

Mia pointed at her empty drink and at the buffoon bartenders. "They spiked the drinks...(hiccup)...with something!"

Amara and Cooper stared at her like she was three sheets to the wind...well, because she was.

She pointed at her empty glass—her mouth open and closing, hiccuping each time she tried to start speaking. I crossed my arms over my chest, the way men do when they want their biceps to bulge. I gave her my best smirk because she was staring at them. She was really, really staring at them, and the hiccups were almost on top of each other at this point.

I grabbed her, hugged her tightly, picking her up off the ground, twirling her around, and kissing her cheek. "God, I missed you!"

She screamed in protest. The hiccups stopped.

"What the hell?" She pointed at me. "See! That's what I mean. Either they spiked my drink and I'm imagining Gus is flirting with me, or Gus is on something and he really is flirting with me."

My smirk turned into a full grin. Because God, she really was delectable when she was thrown off kilter, and all I wanted to do was kiss her. Anticipation. She needed to be fully sober for our first true kiss.

She pointed an accusing finger my way, "Either way (hiccup) something is very wrong with our world—"

I captured her finger, pulled her until she fell into my arms, bent and flung her over my shoulder in a fireman's hold, twirling her around. "Gus!" she yelped, hiccuped, burped, and struck me on the ass to put her down. But that only turned me on more.

"Mia, you are adorable...even when you're drunk." I barely resisted the urge to smack her ass.

"Gus! Put me down!"

Davy's voice yelled from the other side of the bar. "Gus, man. This isn't exactly what I meant by sweeping her off her feet."

Mia kept slapping me with her uncoordinated fists on my backside. "Put. Me. Down. You Dum-Dum!"

The nickname pulled complete joy from me even more because of all the imagery and symbolism of her calling me a lollipop. Oh...the comments I wanted to make about giving her something to suck on. The innuendos that were flying around in my head begging to be laid at her feet. I needed to stop.

I set her back down, making sure both feet were steady before backing up.

"What has gotten into you?" Her hand went to her forehead as she stumbled into a chair, her body slumping, her color draining. "I think I'm done with the Woo Woos tonight."

Hmm...she was more than a bit pale. She closed her eyes and started to breathe through her nose.

Maybe twirling a drunk woman around wasn't such a great idea. I'll admit I may have let my enthusiasm get away from me.

Shyla knelt down beside her, "Honey, are you okay?"

Crap. Guess I really needed to work on my timing.

I bent down beside them. "Mia? I'm sorry. I was just—"

"I don't feel very good..." She ran for the nearest plant, Shyla followed, falling into the role of BFF and the practice of being there to hold back her hair just in time.

Davy walked over, slung his arm over my shoulder, and dropped his head while slowly shaking it. "Clearly you're a little rusty at this..."

I ignored Davy's condescending comment. "This wasn't supposed to happen. I thought Cal would tell Harper my intentions and she'd watch out for her until I got here." At that moment, Harper's giggling from the other side of the pool made me realize my miscalculation. "Of course, me spinning her around wasn't my finest moment."

Davy replied, "Ya think, dumbass?"

36

GUS

The next day, in the late afternoon, the wedding party went through rehearsal down on the beach, going over final details with the planners, while Mrs. Merrick was suitably distracted with newly arriving guests. CJ didn't want any last-minute changes, additions, or even "just a small tweak or suggestion."

After being instructed of my duties for the next day, playing double duty of father of the bride, and bridesdude—instead of bridesmaid—I set off for my real purpose of the evening, to find Mia.

I'd left her alone all day—hadn't sought her out. I spotted her on the beach earlier with the girls but decided to wait until later this evening to speak with her. There was too much commotion with people arriving and preparations.

She should be sober, recovered, and probably piecing last night together. It was time to clear up my intentions now that she was coherent enough to understand.

After the rehearsal, I searched the gathering area inside the house and was stopped by some people, eager to catch up as they sipped cocktails and grazed at a buffet.

"My goodness, this is such a beautiful, romantic place...Gus, honey...where is Mia?" My mother eyed me with purpose while standing next to a sympathetic Wild Bill, my and CJ's mentor. My mother was as subtle as a brick.

Wild Bill intervened for me, "Come on, Michelle, let's go see what they have for dessert."

I escaped my mom's machinations this time and went to seek out Mia. I found her outside talking with Mrs. Merrick and Harper. Great. Just who I needed to approach. Vaguely feeling like a boy asking a girl to dance for the first time, I walked up to the three of them as they were laughing about something Harper said.

Stepping behind Mia, I caught a whiff of her scent—something new, different. Maybe because we were at the beach, but it was so enticing. Coconut and something floral. I had to stop myself from leaning over and sniffing her. She had her hair pulled up off her face but cascading down her back. I wanted to run my hands through her curls and bury my face in her neck. Okay, yes, I know—I was walking the line of borderline creepy since I hadn't even spoken to her about my intentions.

"Do I even want to know what has the three of you laughing?" I said, as I stepped beside Mia, my eyes dropping to her chest. Because, damn. That rich, Kelly green dress accentuated her breasts with a deep-cut-V neckline, the thin spaghetti straps had me contemplating how much effort it would take to remove them.

Mia had gotten enough sun to turn her skin a beautiful warm honey, a sweetness I was craving. There was a lack of tan line on her shoulders which had me contemplating her bathing suit preference again.

My God, her breasts were glorious—perfectly round—

"Gus?" Harper said as if she'd already repeated my name. Her tone shook me out of my stupor because I had been caught staring at Mia's chest like a damn creep.

"My God, Mia, you…are…" I put my hand over my heart, and I wasn't faking my lack of speech. She was leaving me speechless. The light evening wind pulled some of her wispy curls into a slow dance. Her skin glowed in the soft evening light, and her eyes were soft, her smile relaxed.

Until she caught my eyes on her chest.

"Mia, sweetheart. You're breathtaking." I turned to Harper, startled, and wiped my hand through my hair while pulling on the back of my neck. "You are all stunning tonight, of course." I pulled out my most charming smile. "Please forgive me, I'm a bit out of it. Guess the festivities are catching up to me."

"If that's the excuse you're going to go with..." Mrs. Merrick said from behind the martini glass in her hand before she took a sip.

Mia stared at me, tilting her head slightly as if I were a stranger she didn't know how to act around. "Were you seriously staring at my boobs?"

I shrugged, with an unapologetic, flirtatious grin.

Her sweet mouth dropped open in surprise.

"On that note...Mom, I think it's time to refresh our drinks?" Harper pulled on her mom's arm since she didn't seem to be inclined to leave.

"Wait. I want to hear how he gets himself out of this—" her mom said as Harper stepped between all of us, essentially cutting off her view.

I pivoted back to Mia, slowly slipping my hands in my pockets, trying for my best apologetic-but-not-ashamed expression.

She stood with her hands across her chest, not realizing it just plumped them up more...glorious...and again, I couldn't look away. "Up here, buddy." She dropped her arms, waving one of her hands in my face and motioning to her own face. "What has gotten into you?"

I smirked, keeping my hands in the pocket of my shorts, trying to camouflage the bulge the ogling was producing in my pants. "Sorry..." I shrugged again, shifting on my feet. "Well, not really. You're beautiful." I locked eyes with her, "All of you." Staring at her, my eyes were open to her—it had a greater effect than anything ever had.

It was liberating—allowing myself to have these thoughts about her. Allowing myself to react the way my body wanted to—for once.

She broke the contact, shaking her head. "You know, Gus, if you wanted a date for this weekend, you should've just brought one. You don't have to keep flirting with me because you're one of the only ones here who are stag."

Metaphorical cold water was thrown on me.

Whoa. What? "Excuse me?"

"Fine, you want me to say it, I'm going to say it." She practically stomped over in the

direction of the pavilion being used tomorrow for the reception, but tonight it was far enough away from the smaller gathering where we wouldn't be overheard. She walked a few feet from me, turned around and motioned for me to follow her, scowling. I was still frozen in place.

Had I really misread this…messed this up that badly?

When I followed her back to the pavilion closest to the dunes, with enough moonlight

for me to see her many expressions as they fleeted across her face the closer I got, I saw hurt, frustration, betrayal…yet she settled on anger.

"I'm not a possibility." Her words were clip and succinct. "Why would you wreck the friendship we have because you decided not to bring a date and now regret it." She waved her hand at me. "Why not bring one of the many women in your contacts this weekend?" Her anger ramped up, as did her volume, and she caught herself.

The moment she took to catch her breath, I tried to interrupt, "Mia, it's not like that—"

"Don't." She threw her hand down to stop me from defending myself. "I don't know what has gotten into you, but you know I don't do one-night stands. I don't do casual. So you're wasting your time." She refused to look at me. "Jesus, Gus. I thought—" Her hands going to her hips, she turned from me.

"I don't want a one-night stand with you."

"Then what is with all the comments? Staring at my boobs? The sexy eyes, looking at me

like you never have before."

I leaned closer. "How am I looking at you?"

"The way you look at other women."

"You're not other women—"

"I know, so why are you looking at me like you want to—"

"I want to kiss you."

She stared at me. Within a three-second period her expression morphed from confusion to appalled and then disappointment with a touch of anger. "W-w-why?" She stuttered.

"Because it's all I think about. It's all I've been thinking about."

She stepped around me, her hand going to her forehead. "Since when, Gus?" She pivoted abruptly, her tone turning to straight sass. "Since you realized I didn't have a date and you didn't have a date, and wouldn't that be cute—it would be perfect, right? Everyone would have a match and you wouldn't be left out. And I'm a perfect match for your friends. Except I'm not a perfect match for you, Gus. Because if I were, you would've been attracted to me any of the times I lived with you for the last several months." Her anger seeped through as the volume of her voice increased. "Or, I don't know," the sarcasm was laced in her words like venom, "all the time we spent together. You never once made a move on me, never once indicated you even found me attractive, barely even touched me—"

"Honey, I always thought you were beautiful—"

"Stop. You're you, Gus. If you wanted me, you would've done something about it." She stepped around me, her voice dropped in tone and volume. "You're lonely and full of it." She walked away.

I watched her walk away. Damn. I was in uncharted waters and didn't know where to even find a boat.

37

MIA

What the hell has gotten into that man?

I walked away from Gus, just to walk away but not really knowing where to walk to—I just needed to move away from him.

I didn't want to talk to anyone. I didn't want to explain why my hands were shaking or my mind was racing.

My face was probably flashing through a barrage of expressions because I knew my mind was racing with a series of emotions. I walked over to the walkway that led to the gazebo and started to pace. Luckily, the party was at the other end of the courtyard, and I had some privacy to freak out.

Without a better alternative of what to do with the emotional energy coursing through me, I began to pace back and forth.

When that didn't quiet my emotions, I walked toward the gazebo and leaned against the railing overlooking the dunes, listening to the waves crash just beyond. I replayed what he said, and it still didn't make any sense.

Then again, he hadn't been making sense for a while now. It got weirder once I moved out, after I was sick, and then after he heard I was asking Shaw to the wedding—

"Mia..."

I whirled around, startled and a bit ticked he wouldn't leave me alone to puzzle this together.

"What?"

He held out his hand. "Listen, I know I didn't come at this the right way—"

I turned my back on him, staring back at the dunes. "Go away, Gus."

He stepped up behind me. "Just give me a minute—"

"Gus—" His name was accented with a plea—to leave it. To not go there.

He touched my shoulder, and it was…different. It was a soft caress. Just the fingertips, as if asking for permission to connect further. "Honey…" His voice also sought permission and he tried to turn me around.

"If you think of me as one of your women…" I said over my shoulder as he turned me around. I caught his eyes and held them, "Our friendship is ruined." I didn't need to define how. He knew. It was his pattern. It was what made me different.

He trailed his hand down my bare arm until he held my hand and squeezed it gently. "You could never be one of them—"

I must have flinched slightly because he brought my hand up to his lips, kissing first the top of it, and then the inside of my wrist. "You are so much more than any woman I've ever known."

I closed my eyes. Taking a moment to savor his words. To try to believe in the romance of the moment. Then I opened them and stared at his beautiful eyes and at what our reality was. "Gus, this wouldn't be happening if Shaw had come. If you had brought a date. It's the beach. It's the wedding—"

His lips thinned in frustration just before he cradled my face in his hands and whispered, "Mia, honey. Tell me honestly…have you ever thought what it would be like—the two of us? Because I can't stop thinking about tasting your lips." He stared down at my lips as he licked the bottom of his own. "I think about running my hands over your curves and—"

I held up my hand, tried to shake my head, and closed my eyes because I didn't—I couldn't—hear anymore.

"Do you, though—think about what it would be like if we kissed?" He stepped me back against the railing. "Aren't you curious?" His hand trailed up under my hair. "Because I think you'd be an amazing kisser. I think you'd bring me to my knees in the sweetest possible way." He leaned forward until his mouth was by my ear. His breath on my neck sent tingles all over me. "And, honey, while I was on my knees, I'd let my hands roam up that beautiful dress and worship you until you cried my name." His last words were growled and weakened my resolve, "So, so many times."

He ran the pad of his thumb over my now over-sensitized bottom lip. His forehead against mine, his hand playing with my hair, "I think of this beautiful mane of hair laying across my chest as we sleep."

A breath of air escaped me that could be considered a moan. "Gus...but we're friends..."

He pulled back, but our lips were close enough, so we were breathing each other's air. "It's safe to say my dreams about you took us well out of the stratosphere of friendship many months ago—but right now, I'd give up my soul just to kiss you. Tell me, Mia. Aren't you curious?"

"Well, yeah," Of course, I was. Duh. "I've thought about it—"

And, I guess, that was permission enough. He went for it.

And hell yeah. So did I.

The kiss...Before I go on, let me take a moment to breathe and contemplate the wonder that was kissing Gus.

Dear God in Heaven. Had I wondered what it would be like to be kissed by Gus Quinlan? Hell yes. Anyone who laid eyes on him probably had. His lips were pillow soft but moved with such purpose. Nothing prepared me for the skill he wielded with those weapons, and they were just a part of what made me melt.

His mouth brushed mine a few times, and his tongue teased enough to entice. His lips were so seductively indulgent, even when surrounded by his permanent scruff that added an edge to the sensation. After the initial contact, we both paused. We pulled back and stared at each other, mouths slightly open, dazed, drugged.

The reins came off—the shackles of friendship were broken.

It wasn't safe or patient. It wasn't polite or tempered. He was on me—both hands raked through my hair, his mouth on mine, stealing the very breath from my body. He pushed me farther against the railing, his hardness against my abdomen was exhilarating—it was because of me, for me—I had that effect on him. Every cell in my body that wasn't already awake was electrified by that realization.

And when he moaned, my knees gave out. I grabbed his shoulders and held on for the ride.

This...was more. More than I ever even imagined. I was lost to him. I gripped him, climbed him, and cursed the dress I wore because I couldn't lift my leg properly.

He broke our connection, loosened my grip, and was lowered to my feet—coming back to Earth. Our foreheads together and our breathing in tandem as he whispered to me, "Mia, honey. Let's...we need to go somewhere—"

The balmy ocean air tickled my sensitized skin, awakening me as the sound of the waves behind us further pulled me out of my fantasy.

This wasn't going to be a happily-ever-after ending.

No. No. My head was spinning as I pushed him back. More air. I needed more of my own air. The breeze intensified enough to further wake me from my Gus-induced fog as if whispering *"Get with it, girl."*

Just friends. I'd rather keep our friendship than risk it on his sudden whim of curiosity.

Because if I allowed myself to believe we could be more...if I allowed myself to feel more...and then he walked away...because he would eventually walk away. It would never mean the same to him.

Wait. Just wait. I needed to not be touching him.

"Mia? Honey?"

I needed to find a way out of this without him knowing...without him knowing how much that kiss meant—how badly I already craved it.

I hid my trembling hand by trying to smooth my hair, erasing the memory of his hands threading through it. I conjured enough bravery and mojo to force a half-smile and said, "Well, that was, um, interesting?"

I skirted around him, careful not to touch any part of him. The evening breeze off the ocean emphasized the cold void left between us. My body already craved the connection, the warmth.

He pivoted, dumbfounded. "Interesting?"

I ran my hand down my dress, readjusting it and taking a small step farther from him. I went for casual. "Clearly, you're a very good kisser. Talented. Exceptional, I'd even say."

His brows rose, he tilted his head, trying to make sure he was on the same frequency as me.

Stay cool, Mia. Breathe. I made enough eye contact with him to try to make it believable, but was having difficulty with the expressions of confusion, arousal, and possibly hurt flashing over his face.

"What are you talking about?"

I held out a hand. "We were curious what it would be like to kiss each other." I held out my other hand. "Now we know." I extended my arms and clapped my hands together, going for all coolness, coming off way-awkward, "Er, I mean, we know...now we know. We know what it's like to kiss...each other." *Smooth, girl.*

Now, step back toward the party, my ego coached me, *but don't run.*

The slightest burn started in my eyes, threatening to draw tears. "Probably better that we leave it there." I fumbled for where to put my hands. "Don't want to further complicate matters," I shrugged slightly. "It would definitely change things if we actually saw each other naked." A nervous laugh escaped, saying the word "naked", as if I were a preteen. Oh geez. I didn't need to put that thought, or imagery, in either of our heads.

Time to go.

He stared at me, his mouth moving, his eyes darkening. There was a touch of frustration edging his mood.

"I'm just gonna..." I gestured over my shoulder to the rest of the party. I walked backward and said, "I'm going to go get a fresh drink."

I thought I was clear of him, but then I heard, "Mia—" as a hand gently reached for me. "Wait—"

"Gus. Don't. Okay. It's CJ's wedding." I gestured to the beauty around us. "It's fairy lights, moonlight, ocean breezes, and a gorgeous man who just gave me an amazing kiss—it's the most romantic moment of my life." The tears were burning my eyes, taking another step back. "And it's you." I put my hand over my heart, dropping my gaze, as even I heard my voice hitch. "My best friend—who doesn't do relationships, doesn't cross the lines."

I took another step back and looked him in the eyes to make my point. "I won't sleep with you tonight just to lose you tomorrow."

He stepped toward me, "Mia, honey, it's not—"

"If you feel anything for me..." I swallowed. "Gus, respect what we've meant to each other up to this point to not follow me."

Because, so help me God, I don't have the strength to walk away from you twice.

38

MIA

I beat the sun the next morning, sitting in a chaise, my knees pulled up to my chest, drinking my tea on the main front porch overlooking the dunes with the moon on the horizon. I listened to the waves crashing, only able to make them out by the fading moonlight as it set. I enjoyed the silence of a sleeping house since I was the only one crazy enough to be awake after an evening of late-night revelry.

Truth be told, I barely slept.

After that amazingly stupid, mind-numbing kiss, I practically ran back to my room and locked my door—ignoring any texts except the one from Shyla, to which I replied, "Headache. Probably too much sun, I've gone to bed. See you tomorrow."

I closed my eyes, my body replaying its response to that damn kiss. The intensity of his arms around me. His grip on my hips, in my hair, the reverence in his touch.

My body drifted off, my mind looped through the kiss on repeat until someone was tucking a tendril of hair behind my ear, Gus's warm, inviting breath, whispered, "I've been looking for you. Thought you may have run back to Chicago."

Damn. I peeked through my lashes, turning to my side to face him and break the physical connection he had with my hair. "I considered it."

The softness in his eyes changed what was usually a bright blue, to one softer and more suited for an early morning by the sea. A moment caught on the page of a romance cover—seductive, tender, mesmerizing. He sat on his knees beside the chaise. He'd changed into cargo shorts and a faded blue, long-sleeve shirt. His sandy hair was a wild mess, whether from the sea hair or from a night as restless as mine.

"What are you doing here, G?" I pushed a hand under my head, tilting my face up more to meet his gaze.

He pillowed his own head next to mine, as if he would climb next to me if invited to share the intimacy. "I couldn't sleep." His eyes flicked down to my lips. "You asked me not to follow you last night. Well, I figured this doesn't count since it's the next day."

I watched him, studied him. God, it would be so easy to fall in love with this man. Hell, truth be told, I was at risk already.

He sat back and nodded to himself as if he'd decided, "Okay, then…let's go." He stood and held out his hand to me. "Come on, lazy bones. Let's go have some fun." I stared up at him, "Isn't that what this weekend was supposed to be about. Enough of this heavy talk." He reached in his pocket, pulling his keys out and jingling them. His expression back to the boyish, playful one he reserved for me and a select few.

I watched him toss his keys in the air, then catching them, his smirk was captivating. He knew he got me. "Want to go for a ride?"

"How did you get it down here? I thought you all had been drinking before you drove down?"

"We had been. I let Cal drive it down."

He tossed the keys in the air again.

He stepped back, allowing me to stand as he slipped his hands into the pockets of his cargo shorts. He eyed my boy shorts and then the braless sweatshirt under the blanket that slipped off my shoulder. "Go grab some shoes and…" he rubbed his hands over his eyes, "For the sake of my sanity, put on a bra and let's go." He waved me forward. "I'll meet you outside."

I ignored the blush climbing up my neck and skirted past him into the house. Once I changed, I ran out under the house to the carport with my ponytail refreshed, a shelf-bra tank under the sweatshirt— refusing to completely comply out of spite—and flip flops. There he was leaning against the blue Bronco, as if he'd been just sitting there waiting for me to appear.

I practically skipped toward him. The closer I got, the more flirtatious his smile. I mindfully kept my distance when I held out my hand for the keys.

"Where shall we go?"

"To watch the sunrise," he said, skirting the truck to the other side where the doors had been removed, along with the soft-top roof. He pulled himself up in one smooth motion, leaving me to fend for myself as I tried to find the arm strap and leverage myself in the jacked-up machine.

We buckled up, turning on the fog lights until we backed away from the house, so we didn't wake anyone. Once we reached the end of the sand-packed street, the real fun began. My hesitant smile switched to a full-grown grin as we passed the dunes, driving right onto the beach down to the shoreline.

The Bronco's engine battled with the sound of the waves, challenging our senses with the salty brine off the ocean breeze and the grayness of the pre-dawn atmosphere.

He directed me to drive a few miles north of the house. "I heard some of the wild ponies were spotted back here yesterday. Here, turn down this way," he said, and I navigated the Bronco over a bumpy offroad area through a few desolate homes. "I heard there was a foal with one of the herds. I thought we could find together."

We drove around, seemingly in circles, the night sky seeming to turn grayer and the stars dimming with the dawning sky.

"I'm sorry, I thought they'd be easier to spot," Gus said, as he looked over his shoulder, still searching for the ponies.

"It's fine." I was more focused on the road and not getting his new truck stuck in a sandhill. "I'm still having fun with this new toy of yours."

"As much as your new toy," he teased.

"I don't know, I haven't tried it out, yet," I responded. Damn. That was more flirtaeous than friendly. I squirmed.

Damn. Damn. Damn. This was what I was worried about. This. It was already weird.

He threw his hand over the back of my seat in what I would've thought was a companionable, casual posture. But with everything in my head, the gesture seemed more possessive...more couplish—as if he were touching me.

I wanted him to touch me. Heat creeped up my face. Was there enough light from the dashboard for him to see my blush or to see my awkward expression?

"Let's go back to the beach and catch the sunrise," he suggested, gesturing back to the dunes and the dawning horizon, bordered with a pink glow, that led us back to the water.

I focused on getting the Bronco over the dune and settled in the perfect spot to watch the rising sun. Turning off the engine, we were left with just the crashing waves and the sounds of the different birds greeting the new day. Some skimmed the waves for fish, some were dashing across the beach, diving for sand crabs who scurried into the numerous holes peppering the area.

"This is so beautiful. So peaceful. I could just stay like this...sit with this peace," I said, burrowing into the driver's seat, adjusting the seat to move away from the steering wheel.

"I'm sorry," he said.

"What?"

"I'm sorry if I scared you off, if I handled this the wrong way." He didn't look at me, instead staring off at the ocean.

I burrowed farther, wrapping my hands into my sweatshirt.

"And I guess you're going to be pretty pissed off when you hear that I was the one who told Shaw not to come," he said, getting out of the truck before I could even react.

"You what?" I followed, marching in the uneven, cold sand, right up to him. "You told him not to come? Why?"

He turned on me, pointing at his chest, and said, "I told him you were mine. I told him you couldn't be his because you were supposed to be with me."

His hands opened and closed as he moved, radiating with energy, and unable to stay still.

"He asked if there was anything between us. He said he felt something was holding you back. He picked up on how I was acting around him."

"How were you acting?" This was not computing. None of this was making sense.

"Like a jealous idiot." He bit out.

Huh? I stood there dumbstruck at Gus' statement.

"Oh. You were jealous I was spending time with him."

"No. I was jealous because I didn't want him to put his hands on you. I didn't want him kissing lips that I hadn't kissed. I didn't want you smiling at him. Talking to him. Holding him—"

He stood still. Then wiped his hand over his mouth as if going further left a bad taste there.

Rationalizations kept spewing out of my mouth. "You are just being overprotective...you did the same thing with—"

He was in my space in a blink before I could finish the sentence. "Don't. Don't you say it." Gus's frustration was tinged with a piece of his anger. "This is nothing like CJ or anyone. The way I feel about you..." His arms were at his sides as if he wanted to touch me but was afraid to. "It's nothing like anything or anyone. I don't know how to— dammit, Mia. I don't know how to feel about it, let alone explain it."

He took in a breath and took a back step. "Shaw asked me if I wanted to be with you and then he told me to get my head out of my ass and do something about it."

That woke me up from my stupor that was this confession. "So you and Shaw discussed who was going to be with me..."

He nodded.

"Without me. Without my input." He saw the error of his statement and opened his mouth. I held up my hand and said, "I think I'd have some say in the matter."

"It wasn't like that—" he began to say.

"You had no right..." I bit out. The damn air off the sea was making my eyes burn—not the intensity of the moment, or what it could mean—and I shut them tight.

He stepped closer, "I know. I didn't, but I swear to God, you weren't going to be with that man until I had a chance to tell you how I felt. Until I had a chance to—"

Interrupting him, I said, "You know, I'm the one who will pay the price for this experiment."

"Why would you say that?"

I held on to his hands, "Fine. You were curious. You saw Shaw gaining ground and wanted a shot with me first. But you will make me fall for you and then you will leave. I'll be invested and you'll be ready to move on." I hardened my heart even as I said it, ready for him to agree on my logic.

"Mia, honey..." He stepped forward, cupping my face in both his hands. His lips so close I could feel his warm breath kissing my face through the cool air.

"Please don't lie. Don't say you wouldn't do it." I pulled from his embrace. "Because I know you would have the best of intentions, but I wouldn't be enough for you, Gus. I know you well enough to know that."

39

GUS

She broke away from me and climbed back in the truck but didn't turn it on. The area of the beach we were tucked into was a bit more deserted, with high dunes behind us and curving to the north. The Atlantic Ocean was in front of us and the sun had not completely risen. It gave the illusion of privacy and the world standing still.

I kept my back to her and stared at the horizon of the rising sun. It was layers of pinks and peaches falling into the darkness of the ocean with a small scattering of clouds just off to the south giving the colors some perspective. It really was going to be a beautiful day.

I pinched the bridge of my nose. What was I going to do now? This was so outside my wheelhouse. Women I'd been with never had an issue with my past. Sure, they wanted more than what I'd offered sometimes, but I was always straightforward, and it was usually only after they thought they could change my mind.

Not Mia. She knew me better than most people. It's why it hurt so much to have her throw it all in my face.

All I could do is lay it all out.

I turned to walk back to the truck. She was still in the driver's seat —literally and figuratively. And I was well-aware she had the power to wreck me. Once I climbed in, she reached to turn on the truck, but I stilled her hand. Staring at it, pulling it away from the ignition, settling it on her lap.

"You think you know me. And you do. But you don't know my heart. You don't know what I'm feeling. And frankly, it hurts that you can't see past the surface of me—that you can't believe there's more to me."

Without even looking up, I felt her open her mouth to respond, but I held up a finger. "It's my turn," I said.

I turned her hand over in her lap, studying how petite her hand was, I don't think I ever noticed. "It's funny how much we thought we knew each other, but there was still so much to learn. Like you have this small scar on your right hand right over your thumb." I stroked it. "I've always wanted to know how you got it, but never asked."

She didn't respond but watched as I stroked her hand.

"And since you never asked, I'll tell you. I haven't dated anyone, haven't slept with, kissed, or even looked at anyone since you moved here. Once I broke up with Kellie, that was it. Hell, I didn't even touch her once you came to town."

I grasped her hand, turning it over and spreading her fingers wide, threading my fingers in between.

"You said you were taking a break," her whisper was feeble.

I nodded. "But didn't you wonder why?"

"You said you didn't have a lot of time...and..."

"And, sweetheart," I said, resting my head against the headrest, pivoting my face to stare into her gorgeous tawny-colored eyes, the tendrils of her hair dancing a hypnotic dance from the breeze. "The free time I had, I wanted to spend with you."

The pupils in her eyes grew.

"I assumed you were seeing someone or at least were..."

"Getting laid on the side."

She shrugged, looking past me to the sunrise, "I tried not to think about it, honestly."

With one finger, I coaxed her face back toward me. "I took a lot of cold showers. Because of you." I stared at one beautiful tawny eye and then the other, the gold in them beginning to glow with the change on the horizon. "I berated myself when you crept into my mind while in the shower. I blame my wayward thoughts on the fact that I know the toy Sadie gave you isn't your first..."

She gasped.

I took pleasure in that gasp, and the side of my mouth ticked up a bit. "And the thought that toy you keep in your nightstand, of you using it..." I groaned and closed my eyes.

"How did you—"

"Not the time for that." I cleared my throat and peeked over at her. She was biting her lip—I was getting somewhere.

"But I also blame the damn tiny boy shorts of yours, and all the times you walked around without a bra—because yes, I could tell, and yes, I noticed. I couldn't wear sweatpants around you because of it."

A small smile was contrasting with the wetness in her eyes. With the smallest whisper she said, "Don't hurt me. Please..."

I shook my head. "I would never intentionally hurt you. That's not to say I won't screw up." My hand behind her neck, I gently drew her closer to me, our foreheads touching again, but still giving her a chance to pull away. "But you hold my heart, Mia. I will prove to you it's not about this weekend. It's not about you moving on without me. It's about me getting my head out of my ass and finding the courage to..."

She cupped both her hands around my face and kissed me. It was a meeting of lips. It wasn't as eager as last night's, it was slow and soft, hesitant, longing, and full of feeling. I let her lead but poured my desire for her in the touch of my tongue, in the gentle way I wrapped my arms around her. She gave this to me—she was giving herself to me and it was precious.

My mouth roamed down her neck and back up to whisper in her ear how badly I wanted her naked. As the sun rose over the beach, it blessed the Earth with a soft pastel palette and haloed her in its light. I knew until the day I died, this would go down as one of the most memorable moments of my life.

She climbed over the gear box and into my lap—straddling me, her knees falling alongside my thighs as she settled on the bulge that was impossible to restrain in a pair of cargo shorts.

I reached for the reclining lever on my seat to give us more room and further our privacy as I leaned us back.

She ran her hands up under my shirt and raked her nails back down sending shivers all over my body. She stretched over me to reach under my neck, kissing below my ear. Jesus, she was going to kill me—a sweet death.

Her body shifted farther up, rubbing her center over my shaft. A small sound escaped her, that was an aphrodisiac to my ears. I repeated the movement and was awarded with a clearer moan.

My hands traveled up and found a camisole under the sweatshirt instead of a bra. She hadn't listened to me—there wasn't any further barrier to those globes of temptation. With a small tug, I pulled the front of the tank down, low enough to cup a naked breast in my hand. I was still hampered by the sweatshirt but fell back on my sense of touch to squeeze and flick the nipple with my finger. Swearing to her, I said, "As the sea is my witness," I pulled the other side of the camisole, cupping the other breast, flicking that nipple and caressing both in tandem. "I will see these, lick these, suck these, nip at these. Do you understand?"

"Definitely," she said with need, gyrating on my lap some more.

I stilled while watching her face, her hair curtaining around us was a sexy mess, "But I'm not going to explore your body for the first time in this truck."

"Gus…" Her hands traveled up my chest and we moved against each other while she trailed one finger delicately over my bottom lip as if to silence me.

"I'm serious, Mia," I said, stifling a groan, my hand grabbing a head full of hair, gently but firmly. "You will know I'm sincere about how I feel before this weekend is over." Because while I was going to do everything in my power to make her weak in the knees and satisfied, I would not be inside her. Not now. Not yet. She must believe in me first—believe in the possibility of us.

Her rocking against me had my cock rebelling against my plan of waiting to be inside her. I found myself thrusting up into her—even fully clothed—as I caused the truck to move and creak from our activities

"Gus, oh my...Gus. Maybe we should rethink that idea—"

"I know, honey," I said, nipping at her earlobe. Pinching a nipple as I thrust against her again, "We can get creative, but I'm not going to—"

"What the hell?" The Earth moved. Not like if-the-truck-is-a-rocking-don't-bother-knocking kind of way. It did it again, the truck shook from side to side, and Mia was screaming and grabbing at her hair, jettisoning off me so fast she hit the gear shift and let out an "Ouch!" Once she was off me, the source of the interruption made itself known.

Big brown eyes, and a long, equine nose with a white star on it and black mane was sticking his or her head in the truck, checking us out.

We found the horses.

Or they found us.

And it didn't seem that they were too happy with us impeding on their morning stroll. A horse followed Mia to the other side of the truck, seemingly interested in her dancing hair that probably looked like something yummy to him.

Mia shooed him. He kept bobbing his head as if arguing with her. I popped my seat back to the upright position, listening to her delighted laughter. I sat up straight and eyed the determined horses, promising myself this would seem funny later in the day when we told the story.

As if satisfied that they successfully stopped any further inappropriate displays of affections, they began to slowly saunter off, the larger of the two ponies shaking its mane and neighing for the foal to follow.

Both Mia and I sat watching for a minute or two, and then turned to each other. "Who would've thought 'equine interruptus' was a thing?" I said, and we both laughed, breaking the moment. Her smile was infectious, her eyes dancing. I grabbed her hand, kissing it, enjoying the laughter we always did as close friends—only now we were so, so much more.

40

MIA

We were filled with anticipation and joy as we walked down the pathway leading to the beach. As we drew closer, the voices of the guests became more reverent, as if we were entering the sanctity of a church. It was a beautiful, peaceful contrast to the afternoon of primping and girl time we'd shared getting ready.

Behind us, the sun was on the horizon and in front of us the clouds over the ocean were scattered—offering a perfect canvas of purples, peaches, and pinks. The early evening sun had set the perfect ambient lighting for the flower-draped archway and small stage set up for the ceremony. The stretch of beach between the shore and the dunes was wide, and the ceremony was set up far enough away for the crashing waves to provide the beautiful natural music, but not drown out conversation.

Shyla, Davy, and I found spots in the second row as everyone milled around, greeting each other and passing along good wishes for the couple. Shy did my hair in an updo with small tendrils loose on my neck. Soft pink makeup complemented the lace-up back, off-the-shoulder blush pink dress that was stunning, but definitely more daring than I would've worn before. Shyla, in a pale peach strapless dress that hugged her figure and complemented her rich brown skin so beautifully it didn't need any adornment, turned to speak to someone behind us. Davy couldn't take his eyes off her. I took a seat wanting a moment to just relax and soak in the beauty of everything.

I agreed with CJ. This was the way to do it. Strip away all the glitz, glamour, protocol, and headaches, and get married on a beach with those who matter in a memorable scene. It was better than any fairytale I could imagine.

Soft music began to mingle with the natural sounds around us as a signal for everyone needed to find their seats.

Grady, with the smile of a man with the world at his feet, came walking down the pathway from the house, followed his brother Cal and Cooper. All three were in natural-colored linen pants and vests with white shirts, the top buttons open for a beachy-casual vibe.

Grady shook out his hands at the end of the aisle runner, before taking his place beside the officiant under the awning.

Mr. and Mrs. McBane next down the aisle toward the front of the chairs, followed by CJ's pseudo-parents Mr. and Mrs. Merrick. Both wearing soft, subdued natural colors. Mr. McBane, still managing to seem formidable, but at ease in a full summer suit, and Mrs. McBane in a dusty blue, Grecian-style dress that made her smile even more brilliant. Mr. Merrick wore a linen suit, Mrs. Merrick a dusty mauve tea-length dress, all feminine and beautiful.

Next came Harper dressed in the boho-style dress with the tiniest hint of blush to it, and a flowing skirt that the slight wind had fun dancing around her bare feet.

Cal's face at seeing Harper...his face lit up so brightly, you'd think he was the man at the altar. I suspected, the only thing holding this man back was waiting until CJ and Grady were off on their honeymoon before they'd be next.

I don't think I'd ever seen Harper in anything but heels. I let out a small humph because I knew the lack of shoes was CJ's order. It was CJ's wedding...besides, how did you wear heels on a beach?

The opening chords of a piano began playing, beautifully capturing everyone's attention as we pivoted with anticipation.

Over the dunes, approaching the stairs, Gus's tousled hair appeared

261

first as he had CJ's arm linked in his. My heart skipped a beat as he scanned the scene, his eyes settling on mine, and for a moment we lingered on each other.

CJ had always been a gorgeous woman with a tough, invisible exterior.

Today she was Grady's Charlotte Jean. Her hair was pulled up in a loose updo, with the breeze picking up the tendrils that had broken loose, speaking to her free spirit. The dress had a dramatic, plunging neckline and thin straps. A soft almond/pink color underneath showcased the vine-like lace covering the entire dress. Light boning narrowed at her waist—defining her petite shape—but then hugged her hips before dropping into an A-line as it teased her toes.

CJ paused at the top, she stared down at the stairs. Gus readjusted her arm in his and focused on steadying her.

The music transitioned into a piano instrumental of John Legend's "All of Me."

Gus leaned over, squeezed her arm as he said something to her, causing her to lift her head toward him, and even from this distance her anxiety was evident. He wrapped his hand around her arm, leaned in closer to say something in her ear, and pointed toward the front of the group. She searched the landscape spread out beneath her.

My attention followed her gaze as she zeroed in on her strength. Her lodestone—her true north—what centered her. Her face relaxed the moment she found what she needed—who she needed.

Gus wrapped one arm around her back, his other holding the arm with the bouquet as she navigated the stairs, holding her dress with the other one.

He wore the same natural linen vest and pants, the color of the white shirt opened at the top showing the tan he'd enhanced that afternoon. There was such joy in his eyes for his friend. Such pride and support.

The lyrics to the song, even though absent, wove through my mind, gaining new meaning.

Don't watch the bride walking down the aisle, always watch the groom's reaction. Because the naked adoration on Grady's face—it took my breath away. One only had to watch him watch his bride to understand what love looked like.

To have anyone look at me that way—just once in my lifetime—would be a dream fulfilled. Between that and the lyrics haunting me, my eyes began to burn as I watched CJ practically drag Gus down the aisle to get to Grady—a stifled chuckle here and there at Gus's dramatic eye roll was caught by those near him.

Grady shifted his stance, rolled his shoulders, but we all saw the wetness in his eyes because he refused to take his gaze off CJ to hide them.

She was a far cry from her ponytail and fire-retardant race suit, or her Chuck Taylor's and cut-off shorts. The dramatic back of her dress, her bare feet, and the twinkle of hidden crystals woven throughout, all contributed to her romantic glow and beauty. It was like looking an entirely different woman.

Harper joined Gus and CJ and all three smiled as they exchanged a few soft-spoken words. Taking on the role of her absent parents, Harper and Gus both kissed her cheek before they moved to walk together behind her.

The trio continued with CJ walking herself toward her future—with her two best friends a step behind her, always having her back.

After a few steps, she gave up on being patient and double timed it to Grady, leaving Gus and Harper several steps behind her. Gus shrugged his shoulders to Harper as if to say, "Did you think this would go differently?"

Grady held open his arms, and she ran into them just as the chorus of the song ramped up. A series of "awws" and chuckles traveled through the crowd, leaving hearts melting until they started kissing. Gus and Cooper rolled their collective eyes while trying to subtly tell them it wasn't the time. His brother just shook his head as if it were a hopeless cause.

With his task of delivering CJ complete, Gus took his position beside Harper and let his gaze float around the crowd. He did a double take, landing back on me.

Heat spread over my face, and I tried to hide my face, glancing away briefly from the intensity in his stare.

"Dear friends and family who have gathered to witness this joyous occasion—" the officiant began, but a porpoise could've walked out on the sand and nothing was cutting the burning connection I had with Gus.

41

MIA

The officiant asked us to be seated, but all it did was make Gus's attention on me more noticeable. His face slowly lit up as his eyes narrowed on me. He licked his bottom lip before biting it. I would've sold my soul to know what he was thinking, but I would've bet my precious Mustang, given the moment, it wasn't appropriate. Thank God I was sitting, or my knees would've given out.

As the cool breeze blew against my heated cheeks, I unconsciously laid my palm against them to confirm they were burning. My cheeks weren't the only things getting hot, even with the sun behind us and the temperature mild, there were areas of my body that were hotter than I could find words to describe.

Harper nudged him in the ribs and gave him a side-eye stare down, like a mom scolding a child in church to pay attention.

We both tried to refocus on the couple. I shifted in my seat, but it just made the ache worse. Tightening my thighs—nope, made it worse. Sitting up straighter, nope. No relief.

The wedding party all sat except the bride and groom, and I was out of his line of sight gaining some relief. Then he looked over his shoulder—at me—in what I could only describe as a smolder.

August Quinlan just smoldered at me in the middle of CJ's wedding, and I was melting.

"Goddamn," Shyla leaned over my shoulder and mumbled. "If I took a peek in that man's head right now…I guarantee he has plans for you, girl." She gave a satisfied, soft giggle. "And from the looks of it, it's a good thing you read those smut-books because you're going to need that education."

I elbowed her and dropped my head to avoid anyone seeing my flush. There was no way my face could become any redder. "They aren't smut—they're spicy…" I said, for lack of any other response.

"Regardless, girl…" she left her words hanging, her tone conveyed her thoughts about where her imagination was heading.

Harper's Aunt Sadie stood and walked in front of the group. A collective intake of breath occurred, wondering what the woman would say. She wasn't exactly known for her decorum. At least she wasn't handing out her party favors today.

"I was asked to give a reading today. Since these two are unconventional, I didn't want to do something sappy like, 'How do I love thee…' or some sh— um, something more traditional." She unfolded the paper she brought up with her. "I came across this excerpt from Captain Corelli's *Mandolin* and thought it really fit these two and the advice I would give them. It spoke of love not being like a volcano of emotion but the intertwining of roots that could never be untangled and furthers the depths of passion.

I glanced over at Gus, amazed at how much this spoke to me.

I lusted for Gus. The anticipation of laying my hands on him…it did things to me without even a touch from him.

But when all was said and done. I liked Gus. I liked being with him. I liked listening to him. I wanted his opinion, and I wanted his quiet approval.

Sadie continued, talking about love being what is left when the romance of love—the glory and fever of it—has disappeared.

I clasped my hands in my lap so tight they turned white and stared down at them. I couldn't look up now because I knew any hope of a poker face was gone.

The rest of the ceremony took place with relative efficiency and beauty, with the culmination being the inevitable kiss.

"I now pronounce you man and wife. You may—"

They were on each other. Grady had little regard for her professional updo, running his hand straight into her hair to consume her.

The officiant cleared his throat. "Well, I can see you have that part figured out."

Applause erupted, along with Gus throwing in a piercing whistle with his thumb and forefinger. When the kiss was never-ending someone shouted out, "Alright. Enough! How about taking a breather so we can hit the open bar?"

They broke apart and CJ used her thumb to clear the lipstick off Grady's face with loving preciseness.

The officiant held out his hands over the two of them and announced, "Ladies and gentlemen...Mr. Grady McBane and Mrs. Charlotte Jean Lomax-McBane."

Everyone cheered as they walked back down the aisle as man and wife and lead the party from the beach to the reception in the pavilion by the house.

"Well, I have to say, that was just about the best wedding I've ever seen," Shyla said. "It got me in my feels, and that's not an easy thing to do. I usually hate these things."

"Must be the ocean air," I said.

A hand wrapped around me from behind. As I was backed up against a firm chest, his breath was on my neck and was having a magical effect on my nipples. "You are beyond...everything," Gus' scruff was tickling the ridge of my ear as his hand began to fist the material around my waist. He flattened his hand on my abdomen under my breasts, his thumb barely caressing the underside of one, before flattening and stilling a bit lower to appear as if it were accidental and not indecent.

My hands gripped the wayward hand to anchor it and make sure he behaves.

But then, I tilted my head to give him more access, telling him without words that I was accepting this—accepting us—in front of others. He nuzzled my neck, his scruff just scraping my ear and his breath hitched.

I turned slightly, to try to face him and regain my composure.

"Hey." My voice was subdued trying to act casual and relaxed—I was not relaxed.

We were an inch apart from each other, but I was never more aware of our height difference.

"Hey." His eyes were dancing, the sides of them crinkled with amusement. He played with my fingers, and I just watched as they intertwined. We'd held hands before, innocently, friendly, but this wasn't either of those things.

His thumb found the underside of my hand and stroked it. Wow. When did my palm become an erogenous zone? Sigh.

"I don't have the right words, but sweetheart, I'm having trouble breathing right now…you are literally leaving me breathless."

And now the words were lost.

No words.

"No, I take that back. I have lots of words, but not ones we can share in public."

"Well, well. You two finally got your shit together," Davy said.

I felt Gus' smile against the side of my neck.

"Yeah and someone has been tight-lipped on the details." Shyla playfully glared at me.

"It's not like that. We just—

She held up her hand. "I need a drink. I know I'm going to need a few drinks to listen to this…enough lovey-dovey stuff. Let's go." And she grabbed Davy, leading us all off to the stairs that climbed over the dunes.

He threaded our fingers tighter together, his smile connected with so much mutual happiness between us I was floating. The sun had set while the ceremony finished. Tiki torches on the beach led us to the stairs back to the house. We followed everyone as they made their way up the stairs to the house.

The pressure inside me became worse when we climbed the stairs up to the gazebo and walkway, his hand on my back leading me forward to protect me from falling. Of course, all I could think of was how close his hand was to my backside, and how badly I wanted it all over my body.

We reached the top and he threaded my hand in his again. Walking a half-step behind me, he said, "Wine?"

I nodded, not trusting my voice. Throughout the day the catering staff had busily transformed the courtyard of the house into a magical, romantic garden for the reception. The pool had been covered with a parquet dance floor, the string lights had doubled along with decorative lanterns to add light and beauty to the area, while the perfume from the arrangements of calla lilies, roses, and orchids peppered throughout the path to the pavilion fought to enhance the fantasy.

We got to the nearest bar and greeted a few people who stared at our linked fingers but didn't say anything. A few smiles turned up a notch or two, and glances were exchanged, but it was as if no one was fazed by it.

He handed me a chardonnay, and then we caught up with a few more people he knew from

Merrick and other parts of his life. He introduced me, I nodded and immediately forgot their names. I wanted to have him to myself and making small talk with people wasn't on my agenda for the night.

We walked around the reception, always touching, always connected as if it were the most natural thing.

At dinner, we sat next to each other, and while talking with a guest sitting across from us, with my legs crossed, he slipped his hand under the table, laying his palm softly, possessively, just above my knee— never breaking his conversation with Davy and the man next to him about Carolina's rookies.

His hand became restless and began to caress. My legs were already crossed, but at his touch they tightened even more. I became increasingly afraid of what he intended to do…here…with that hand.

I reached for my wine, readjusting the napkin on my lap, and using that opportunity to make sure no one could see what I could clearly feel. Of course, all they had to do was pay attention to the blush from the heat spreading through my body.

With my glass to my lips, I darted my eyes to him, and he never even cracked a smile. He just kept talking with the guys about football. I kept the glass in front of my face, trying to disguise my growing desire as his hand fell to the inside of my leg before his thumb began slowly stroking back and forth. Back and forth. But his fingers, especially his damn pinky, were completely still.

"I was surprised they traded for him instead of taking Victor from Clemson as a tight-end."

His hand squeezed my leg at the mention of Shaw's name, his hand traveling closer, the hem of my dress moving up maybe an inch more, but the napkin still in place.

"Oh, I don't know…" Davy said. "The man has earned his reputation. He has the stats."

"He's injury prone. He's getting up there in years," the guy said, I think his name was Thomas or something.

He called Shaw old. Really?

"Shaw's in great shape—" I said, taking another sip of my wine and shifting in my chair, trying to figure a way to move Gus's hand down out of my danger zone without making it obvious.

Gus's pinky came alive and took advantage of the movement, wedging itself between my legs, making me jump as I sipped on the wine. Slight choking and unladylike snarfing on chardonnay, then coughing ensued. Gus removed his hand and took the offending appendage and rubbed my back as I tried to muffle my cough with a napkin. I glanced up to see Shyla stifling her laugh, and Davy discreetly hiding his chuckles behind his napkin before saying, "That's right. I forgot what a fan of Dawson Shawfield's you are, Mia."

My eyes were watering, but I caught the glare Gus shot at Davy, and the shit-eating grin he got in return.

I continued to cough and stood, knowing how much attention I was drawing to us. I waved off Shyla, finally clearing my throat as I weaved around some other chairs to excuse myself to the house and recover my dignity.

Just as I approached the door to the house, a familiar hand reached out, opening it for me. My glare was in place as I pivoted on him, clearing my throat again. "Do you know how uncomfortable it is to snarf chardonnay?"

Unrepentant, he shrugged. "I didn't like to hear his name on your lips, let alone how much you like his body—"

I walked three steps into the house and down the hallway to the bathroom. "Oh, my God. I said he was in great shape. Anyone with a set of eyes could see he was in great shape—"

He pulled me into a darkened hallway and had me up against the wall in one move that I wasn't sure my feet were even part of the action. My cough was history. His hands on my hips, his knee wedged between my legs, and his head tilted down so close to my cheek I could hear his breath as he whispered, "I'm very much into taking things slow. The anticipation...just touching your knee, I wanted to push your dress up and..." He tightened his hands on my hips. I clung to his shoulders waiting for him to finish that sentence. "But, sweetheart, don't tempt me into showing you how jealous I can be." His breath was heavy, his tone deepened. "It's new to me, and I'm still trying to get used to how to rein it in."

"Gus—"

He me off by rocking into me as he kissed me. The possessiveness coming through in how he devoured my mouth. His cock rocked against my leg, his leg against my center, and a small gasp escaped from both of us as we broke apart to breathe.

"We have to go back in there. Because I said we'd take things slow—"

"Kiss me," the words, a mixture of a command and a plea, came out before I could even consider them.

He lightly traced my face with his, skimming his scruff deliciously over my cheek, inspiring thoughts of it on my inner thighs. He traced his nose over mine, his lips so, so close. He pressed his chest into my own, there was hardly a part of us not touching. "No. I think I'll make you wait. You can think of *my* body and *my* shape."

I pouted—my hands traveled down his chest.

"Anticipation, sweetheart. I'm anticipating—"

We both froze at the sound of the door opening and closing, and the voices coming down the adjacent hall.

He took a step back, turning from me and the hallway, running his hand through his hair and then adjusting the tent in his pants with a quiet, "Fuck."

I covered my face with my hands, attempting to regain my composure, straightening my dress and smoothing my hair.

"Go back to the table and I'll meet you there," he said, leaning over and giving me a quick peck on the cheek, gone before I could even grab him to give him one of my own.

42

GUS

She was in my arms. We were dancing with our friends and family all watching. We were fully on display, and I was fine. I was more than fine—I felt fantastic as if this was the most natural thing. As if this was exactly the way it was supposed to be.

I don't think I'd ever been so grounded, so…happy. The way she held me, the way I saw her guard come down and the new kind of smile she was giving me. It was a new connection being formed between us. One I wasn't familiar with, but I needed it like air to breathe. I wanted it more than adrenaline and was becoming addicted to it.

I held her closer as "Can I Be Him" by James Arthur wove its lyrics around us.

I couldn't wait. I needed to be with her in ways you couldn't be in public.

I had her hand in mine, kissing it before pulling her across the dance floor, already having

scoped out a nice, darkened niche tucked behind the pavilion beyond where they had outdoor showers. I could at least take her there for a quick grope session because I needed to get my hands on her in some of the most inappropriate ways.

From her giggles, she knew what I was up to and wasn't against the idea.

"Where're you off to in such a hurry?" Grady asked, as he and CJ walked toward the dance floor.

"If you have to ask, you aren't as smart as I thought you were," CJ answered.

Deciding it wasn't right to be dragging her behind me, I resisted the urge to scoop her into my arms, and gently nudged her in front of me instead—my hand on the small of her back. Tapping her sweet backside discreetly, I said, "Get moving. I want you to myself."

She mocked offense and tried to stomp off until we reached the spot I had in mind, a small deck area off the side of the house, lit only by moonlight. "If I take you back to a room, we won't come out, and it's probably too early for that without it being noticed."

I pulled her around, pushing her against the building, fencing her in with my arms, and devouring her mouth. Not messing with small kisses to tease her mouth open, I dove right in. She'd been teasing me all evening with the lip-biting. She'd always done that, bit her lip when thinking, when contemplating. I always found it endearing, and it had always drove me insane. Now, I nipped at it, tasted it, then licked it to soothe the sting. Her hands ran up my back, pulling my shirt up so she could get—yes, sweet God—her hands on my skin as she scraped her nails up my back.

Her kisses became more forceful, taking the leash off as she tested how much I was willing to take.

My girl was more of a hellcat than I could've hoped for.

My girl. I liked that. My hands gripped her waist and then traveled up the sides.

Her nails dug into my back as she began to climb me, rubbing her breasts against my chest. I cupped a breast, my mouth taking a moment to lick the top swell of it.

They were perfect. Not even seeing them yet, just the feel of them. They fit my hands perfectly. Not too big, not to small. They were made for my hands. I needed to keep exploring her. I needed more hands.

I ran my hands down her side, pulling her against me so I could wedge my hands behind her and grip her adorable backside. I'd admired its curves clad in different kinds of clothing, bent over cars, tables, and in many different positions.

The ass that always fascinated me. Confused me. Teased me. I never even hoped to get a chance to feel it. Squeeze it.

My mouth found its way back to her neck, as her hands raked through my hair, her nails scraping my scalp.

Hitching one leg up to my waist, I held my hand under her thigh and found it perilously close to her center.

"Gus, I...I need you to touch me." The voice that came out of this seductress was one made for the most erotic dreams. My mouth traveled down her chest. I yanked the top of her dress down hoping to expose more skin, and instead getting the entire beauty of her breast to feast on.

With just enough moonlight to illuminate her anticipation, I locked onto her gaze as I teased the tip of her nipple. She bit her lip, closing her eyes.

"Oh, no, love. You need to watch."

I sucked her nipple into my mouth as my finger found her panties and brushed the silk against her center.

She thrust forward and gasped before I released her breast, putting my hand over her mouth.

"Shhh," I said, her erotic response running through me as if we were joined. Her cheeks were flushed a pretty pink, and she panted as she shoved my face back down onto her breast.

She wanted more.

"You know anyone could walk around that corner at any time."

She nodded.

I loved how daring she was being, so I obliged. She struggled to stay quiet as I continued to stroke her center through her panties. I latched back onto her other breast, synchronizing the sucking, licking, and stroking until she began to rock against my hand, lost in the movement. I couldn't wait until we got home where we could be as loud as we wanted, and I would tease her until she cried out my name several times—every night.

I pulled my groin away from her body. Her moans, the carnal way she looked at me and the friction caused by her leg rocking against my cock was all it was going to take at this rate—and, yeah, that wasn't going to happen.

"Hush. I've got you." I stared down at her, her flushed face, desire-filled eyes on the brink. I ran my hand reverently over her cheek that was bathed in moonlight.

Against her mouth, as I kissed her cheek, her jaw, and her ear... "You are so everything..." I went back to her mouth and my hand kept stroking her through her panties.

"Let go, baby," I said.

She broke apart in my hand, and so help me I had to focus on not joining her like a pimple-faced teen. I had to bury my face in her hair and put my other hand over her mouth softly. "You are so damn beautiful, honey."

I slowly removed my hand, teasing one more caress, and being gifted with a moan then a weak giggle. "Enough...you're killing me..."

"Dying of orgasms isn't a bad thing...but hold off until I'm inside you and we can go together," I said.

"And when will that be?"

"When you believe in us."

She kissed me and threw her arms around my neck, holding me so tightly I thought she was going to wrap her legs around me. If she did that, my resolve would crumble, and I'd be ripping those panties off—screw the consequences.

She buried her head in my chest, with my arms tightly around her, and we stood there quietly as both of our breathing slowed.

"Gus—"

I pulled her back, bent slightly so we were eye to eye. "Honey, Mia...we have time. We are going to take it slow, and we are going to do this right." I gave her a quick chaste kiss.

She laid her head against my chest. "You've scrambled my brain and made my knees weak."

I couldn't hold back the energy coursing through me—fueled by unbridled happiness, need, and anticipation—all warring for domination inside my body, my heart…my very soul. "My Mia…all the things I want to do with you—all I want us to share…Sweetheart, I haven't even started."

43

MIA

I'm not sure how I managed to put one leg in front of the other walking back into the reception. One thing was certain, I should've checked myself out in the mirror before returning to a room full of friends and co-workers. They all had their mouths and their opinions properly liberated with libations.

Harper and Shyla's smug faces—as they slowed from dancing with their men to properly assess my new, slightly ravished, thoroughly well-kissed, post orgasmic appearance—said it all. Their knowing laughter might as well have broadcasted that Gus just did wondrous things to my body.

Gus never broke contact with me, his hand stayed on the small of my back as I nervously tugged on the hem of my dress, unconsciously straightening the neckline.

I could feel my face heat with all seven shades of red as each set of eyes turned and Gus's chuckle grew deeper.

"Relax."

"I need a drink," I growled. "I'm not good at this."

"At what?" Amusement laced his voice as we stepped up to the bar, and he flagged down a bartender, ordering us a beer and a glass of wine.

"At sneaking away for a…a…a hook up."

He pulled up a barstool for me, stood at my side, never losing touch with me.

"You enjoyed it." His whisper sent shivers over my body, contrasting with the heat already there.

Even though it wasn't a question, I nodded. We hadn't even lost any clothing. Lord, help me when I got to see him, touch him. I mean, I'd seen him without a shirt, I'd seen him in gym shorts and even caught a glimpse of that glorious ass in his boxer briefs before.

Now, I would get to touch all of him. A thrill went through me, right down to my center, and I shifted in my seat, crossing my legs to put pressure on the area that ached for more of his attention.

I touched his chest, just because I could. Feeling the hardness of it and wanting so badly to slip my hand inside and touch his skin.

He handed me my drink and I gulped it, which wasn't a fun thing to do with wine. I needed a drink with ice.

Ice, and Gus's body. Ice on Gus's body. Gus's body. I needed to get my hands on his body.

I took another long sip of the wine. Sip is a conservative term. I gulped again.

"Mia?"

I stared at the small triangle of chest teasing me at the top of his shirt. I reached to touch the exposed, tanned, skin. I focused on my hand as I trailed it down the buttons on the front of his shirt, restraining myself from popping them off.

I stood, pushed him up against the bar, and shifted to position myself in front of him, hiding his growing interest.

I glanced up into Gus's entertained expression, an eyebrow raised as if to challenge me, *Where are you going with this?*

I made it to his belt buckle and pulled him by the pants closer to me, the sudden movement surprising him, and he let out a gasp before I kissed him.

"Dayum…" Grady said next to us as he and some others sidled up to the bar.

Gus's hand cradled the back of my head, and he licked my top lip before he drew back, his eyes dancing.

"I guess it's safe to say you won her over," Cooper added.

Gus's focus never wavered from me as he replied, "I'm still working on it."

"But it's looking good so far," I whispered, not caring if only Gus heard me.

Later that evening we tumbled into my room, our hands groping each other. "I'm not going to sleep with you, Mia."

"I never said anything about sleep, Gus."

He laughed, albeit a bit nervously, as I grabbed at his belt buckle, pulling him into the middle of the room as the door shut behind us. He stilled my hand.

"Mia, honey. I'm not going to have sex with you this evening," he said, kissing me to soften the words. "I told you. I want you to—"

I gave up on the buckle for the moment, going to his shirt instead, practically tearing through the buttons. "Yes, I heard you," I said, not losing focus.

He acquiesced after the first few buttons were undone, pulling it slowly over his head and unveiling his tight abs, like a curtain being raised on opening night.

I couldn't wait and followed the progress with my hands, starting at his waistband, traveling up through the sparse golden-brown hair, and over his nipples that peaked with the contact. His head popped through the shirt, and my fingers combed through his hair, pulling him down into my kiss.

His hands immediately went to my ass, cupping each cheek and lifting me to straddle his waist, turning me against the nearest wall and pushing his length against my center.

"Oh, Gus…"

He ran his kisses down my neck, behind my ear, to my collar bone.

"Bed. Please take me to the bed," I said.

As if remembering his vow not to have sex with me, he dropped me softly to my feet, leaning away. Staring with such dark desire, his bottom lip was swollen and begging for me to bite it. I reached for his belt again, and again he pushed my hand away gently before pulling on my dress.

"The back." I hinted.

He pivoted me around, shifting my hair to lay on my shoulder and traced a finger down my backbone to the corset-like laces that held my dress around my waist. A kiss turned into nips at the base of my neck and over to my shoulders, accompanied by a small growl.

"You smell incredible. Always. I missed your scent in my house. It doesn't feel the same."

I closed my eyes.

"I missed you, too." The words poured out of my mouth without thought.

A tug came from my back as he pulled loose the strings. His kisses traveling up and down my neck and shoulders as he pulled me up against him, his hands wrapping around me, cupping my breasts and brushing my nipples through the material.

My knees gave out a bit and I wrapped an arm behind me to anchor myself to him.

"I love how sensitive your nipples are."

With a few more tugs on the dress, it fell to the ground. My strapless bra was discarded, and he peered over my shoulder, watching as he brought both hands around to continue playing with my breasts. I squirmed and leaned farther into his chest, my hand sliding around the back of his head, pulling on his hair to steady myself. He shifted, and now it was my turn to watch as he slid a hand down my abdomen and into my lacy panties.

Our heavy breathing was broken by the sound of his growl as he found me.

"Oh...Gus. Not yet." I turned on him, breaking the connection because I couldn't take more from him without exploring and having a bit of fun with him first. I dropped to my knees, facing what awaited me.

He tried to push my hands away, but not this time.

"Please, let me," I said, determination had my hands working fast and furious on the belt and pants, unfastening and pulling them off before he could take back control. I pushed him back on the bed, pulling off the legs of his pants, his shoes, and socks. He was left with only his briefs, and an erection no longer being restrained.

I repositioned myself between his legs and glanced up at him to make sure he was still on board with what I was doing. His eyes were hooded, his jaw slackened as his breathing increased. Oh yeah. He was all in. My hands traveled up to inside his muscular thighs. He trembled slightly and he closed his eyes as I cradled his balls with one hand and ran my hand up his erection with the other one.

He tried to speak. "Mia. Honey." His breath hitched, and he cleared his throat, running his hands over mine and then caressing my head. "This wasn't what I wanted to do."

The tenderness in his touch, but the tension in his expression—those two juxtaposing responses—it empowered me like nothing ever had. My lips turned up into the most satisfied smile and I said, "But, Gus, it's what I wanted to do," before I took him into my mouth. He hissed out unintelligible words as he fell back on the bed, supporting himself with one hand and grasping my hair with the other, watching me with such intensity, it had me clenching my thighs.

The power in seeing what I could do to him—for him. It was heady. The hissing of his breath leaving his body, the myriad of euphoric expressions, his hand threading through my hair—gripping and caressing—it was an aphrodisiac that I had never experienced with anyone.

His breath became fast and ragged, the intensity showed in his gaze when he locked eyes with me right before I took him over the edge. Falling back onto the bed, he gasped, "Mia—" My name was a prayer on his lips.

Once he caught his breath, he pulled me to my feet, wrapping his arms around me and burying his face in my middle. He held me as if the world stopped.

I wordlessly stroked his hair and caught us in the mirror on the wall

—holding each other—our lives entwining right before me, and it scared me to death.

The intensity of his gaze was the sexiest warning of pleasure as pulled me down on the bed, rolling me to my back. His straddled me, his hands skimming down my body. When he reached his destination, I was begging for him to continue.

His scruff intensified the light sensation on the inside and apex of my thighs. He watched me from under his lashes, the blue so vibrant even in the dimly lit room as he pulled off my panties. But it was the quirk of his lips that nearly drove me over the edge as his tongue licked his bottom lip and then me. His attention became focused on the center of me. He softly closed his mouth, zeroing in on the pleasure, intensifying it until my body bowed off the bed. With one hand he gripped my ass firmly, with the other he ran it over my abdomen gently, guiding me back down.

He held me there in a state of continuous bliss as I muttered incoherently. He'd slow down if I got too close to the edge, only to drive me back up to it. It was all too much.

Then he moaned, the reverberation better than anything with batteries could ever accomplish.

I gripped his hair and moaned louder as he quickened his ministrations. The next time I bowed up, he chased me with pleasure until I detonated.

My body was a quivering mess. My emotions were chaos.

Then he arranged us for maximum comfort and cuddle, moving me around like a limp doll and cradling me to his chest, so every possible inch of us was touching.

The room was still, almost peaceful—further emphasizing the miracle that had just occurred to my body. His hand stroked my back as our breath fell into a companionable cadence, the only sound and movement in the room. I promised to save freaking out for the next day as I began to drift off.

"Mia, honey." Gus's voice was as soft as a caress.

"Hm?" I snuggled into his chest more.

"Are you okay? Are we..."

That cost him. Showing his uncertainty, his insecurity—it cost him. There was vulnerability in the tone of his voice, in the tilt of his brows, the downturn of his mouth. I stared up at him and put my hand on his beautiful lips. "I'm good. Good God. I'm more than good." I folded my hands on his chest and stared up at him. "How about you?"

He played with my hair, and it felt so good—so intimate. And wasn't that a funny thing to think given what we just did to each other. There was an indiscernible expression on his face, watching his fingers loop around my curls. "I've never been better."

I reached up and kissed his lips, long, slowly. I put my forehead to his and touched his cheek. "We'll be okay. I'll talk if I get scared. But you need to promise to do the same."

He squeezed me tight, burying his face in my shoulder. "I will. I promise."

44

MIA

Back to life, back to reality. It meant driving back to Charlotte and diving right back into the season. I had my own car parked farther inland, and Gus drove his mom back in the Bronco. I could only imagine how that long drive went with Michelle grilling him about us.

Once home, I flipped through the stack of mail Michelle picked up earlier in the week for me, before she headed down to meet us, and I almost tripped over the box on the floor. It was heavy enough that when I bumped into it, it barely moved.

On the counter under miscellaneous fliers and envelopes, was a yellow, pillow-packed manila envelope that also caught my interest.

After changing clothes and settling in further, I went back to the kitchen. I grabbed a pair of scissors from the drawer and plopped on the floor by the box. It was like Christmas morning tearing into the box, but too curious at the contents to check who sent it.

Inside, under some brown filler paper, was a book lover's vision of happiness. A variety of familiar titles were stacked in two neat piles— twelve altogether, and all of which I already owned. Or, wait. I had owned. I pulled them out, enjoying the feel and scent of new books as I studied them closer. They were twelve of the ones that were destroyed by asshole Keith leaving them out in the rain.

I flipped through them, the scent of newly printed books increasing the level of happiness at seeing such beautiful unmarred covers. A pang of pain hit knowing they weren't the original, dog-eared with love.

But how…

I covered my mouth just as my mind short-circuited between a laugh and a cry, letting out a small gasp instead that no one else would hear but me.

Shyla. That girl. I went to find my phone, searching the floor and realizing I must have left it in my room. I pulled myself up, the yellow envelope was glaring at me like a neon sign that read, "Open me now!"

I grabbed the envelope, walking back to my room to retrieve my phone and call that girl—although she was probably in the air right now back to Chicago.

I ripped open the envelope, discarding the strip in the trash without breaking stride into my room, with another book sliding out.

The Splendor in Tomorrow…a hardback edition, with a shiny new cover, almost fell out of my hands. It was my favorite author, Addison Wood's novel. One that always struck a chord. The kind of book that you reread over and over, and it still gave you "the feels."

I dropped onto the bed, tossing the envelope aside and staring at the book.

I opened the beautiful cover, running my hand over the title page as the book binding creaked, letting out the only sound in the room. There on the title page were bold strokes of handwriting:

"Mia—I'm so sorry to hear about what happened to your collection. Your "friend" seems determined to help you restock it. Those are the ones you keep. Sincerely, Addison."

Holy cow, a signed copy with a personalized note. I have to call Shyla. I reached for my phone, dialing her number, and it went unanswered. She was already in the air.

Going to close the book, I caught the postscript, *"Please let me know how this story ends. I love a good HEA, and he's adorable."*

"What?"

Just then my doorbell rang.

And it clicked. There were only two people who knew what those books meant to me and what happened to them.

I flew to the door and never felt my feet even hit the floor.

The door opened and I was in his arms. Thank God it was him and not a pizza delivery man.

He had to take a step or two back to brace for my impact as I also accidentally bashed him in the head with the hardback book. I buried my face in the crook of his neck, breathing him in.

"What did I do wrong? We've only been in town for less than an hour? Not even I could've screwed this up that fast?" he said, returning my embrace.

I squeezed him tight, climbing him like a tree monkey as he walked us further in the house, closing the door behind him. "I know I was holding out on you until we got home, but I thought you'd at least feed me dinner before you jumped me?" His hands came up and cupped both thighs, holding me closer to him.

He stumbled briefly and we both glanced down to see the box at our feet. "Oh, the books came..."

"Yes. They did." Tears pooled in my eyes. Too many emotions for me to sift through why my hormones were also causing havoc on me. "I can't...I don't know if anyone has ever done something so thoughtful for me. Thank you, Gus."

I cupped his face and kissed him. Because Ms. Addison Woods was correct, he was the one you keep. "No more waiting." I kissed him thoroughly to punctuate my exuberance. "No more talking about it." I threaded my fingers through his hair, tugging on it to emphasize my meaning.

I slipped down out of his arms and walked him up the stairs, looking over my shoulder at him, a thrill going through me knowing he was mine. I wouldn't doubt this man's intentions again. What we had was solely ours.

We entered my bedroom, the sun peeking through my closed shades was just enough to soften the light. I looped a hand in his pants, tugging him over to my bed. I pulled his head down to mine, "I believe you. I believe in us." I kissed him softly, tenderly, to convey how precious he was to me.

His hand on my waist tightened as if ready to unleash on me. I wasn't any different. We'd both had the appetizer at the beach—all it did was tempt us more.

First, I wanted access to his chest. His glorious chest that I'd been teased with and haven't had enough time to enjoy. "Lose the shirt," I ordered. He raised one eyebrow, a small smirk appearing before his head disappeared under the shirt, reemerging with heat in his eyes.

I slid a hand inside his shorts, surprising him. His gasp was a lightning bolt giving me the same level of exhilaration as my hand was giving him.

"Mia...Jesus."

"Nope, just Mia." I smiled, as I stepped back, locked eyes on him and tried to slide down to my knees. His eyes on me, he didn't seem to notice as I took his shorts and boxers with me...until I had him in my hand.

Once his brain caught up with what I was intending to do, he grabbed me by the elbows and said, "Oh, no. Not this time." He walked me toward the bed. "Now I know what you can do with that mouth and it's counterproductive to what I want to do to you right now.

I let out a devilish giggle that I didn't know I had in me as I caught him in my hand and stroked.

He allowed that exploration and we settled on my bed. Learning what he liked, and what drove him to utter more expletives.

"That's it. I'm done playing around," he growled.

When he was done wrestling my clothes off me, he left me in a bra and panties. He leaned over me, his shorts and boxers no longer tangled around his feet. He was gloriously naked.

His eyes were full of all the warmth and desire I needed to see. I unfastened the front clasp on my bra and removed it. "Have I told you how breathtaking you are?"

"Not today." I said, "And thank you—that's sweet. But, Gus, I think we can skip the foreplay. I'm ready to move on to the main event."

Ignition. His eyes went deep, dark navy. He licked, nipped, and then sucked one of my nipples into his mouth while tearing off my panties. Distracting me with kisses, his hand worked between my legs while he whispered how glorious I was, how much he loved the way my body responded to him.

"God, I love the feel of you. I love that this is what I can do to you." He pleasured me and his voice, deeper than I've ever heard it, said, "My name on your lips. I want to hear it, honey."

"Gus," I breathed. "Stop talking." I threw my head back so he could kiss my neck.

He let out a quick laugh and kissed me. "Yes, ma'am."

"No more waiting," This time I moaned it.

His smile was blinding. "I love hearing you bossy."

"Shut the hell up and—"

"If I hear you utter the words, 'Fuck me,' right now in the state I'm in—I may embarrass myself, so save those words for another time," he said, shifting over me.

I giggled.

"You think I'm joking." He leaned down to nip at my nipple.

"Gus…" I reached between us, wrapped my hand around him as I lined him up and got his full attention. "Shut up and…"

He thrust in me. Once and then again…and my mind went blank. No words. No thoughts. Even the momentary tightness of him entering me for the first time was pleasure. Unending pleasure as we adjusted to each other for the first time. Finding ourselves together. Deep inside me, he paused and leaned down to kiss me. Then three other words came to me. "Please…Gus, more." I wrapped a leg around him.

"Mia." Was all he got out before he moved. And we moved. We were together in all ways. I never wanted to be apart from this man— from this moment. He threaded his fingers in mine and held them to the bed above my head. I used my body to reach up and meet his—to deepen his movements. Our breaths mingled and grew in sync with each other's. His hand found its way to cradle my face, and my eyes opened to see him studying me—my lips, my hair, my eyes, the curve of my cheek. "You. Are. Everything." And with those words on his lips, we both fell headlong into oblivion.

———

We laid in bed, molded into one being. Draped across his chest, my hand lazily stroking and exploring, I admitted to myself how much I'd always wanted this. All the times I'd seen him without a shirt, how often I'd wondered about the smoothness of his skin, the coarseness of his sandy blond chest hair, and how it darkened as it made its way past his navel.

His kiss, on the top of my head, was accompanied by a squeeze around my waist and a hum of contentment. All that was missing was the quiet tapping of raindrops on the window to make it the idyllic evening.

"If I would've known getting you a few books would've brought this kind of response, I would've bought you a library long ago."

I tugged at a few pieces of chest hair, enough to get a yelp out of him, and that morphed into a soft chuckle as he rolled onto me and lifted one of my breasts to his mouth. Bending his head to place a soft kiss at the top of the swell, he traced the outside of the dusty pink areola, avoiding the nipple and causing shivers to awaken many parts of me I thought had been content.

I grabbed his hand, and slowly lifted it up to my lips. I watched his eyes dilate more before I flicked my tongue over it and slipped it in my mouth, sucking gently.

"Now you're playing dirty," he said.

"I'm learning fast," I said with so much vixen in my voice, I surprised myself.

I held his gaze as his hand traveled down quickly, cupping me between my legs. "I have more to teach you."

I let out a squeal when his finger slipped over my sensitive center, but my body couldn't decide if it wanted to buck and welcome the invasion or beg for mercy.

He withdrew from me, leaving me whimpering, and rolled out of bed, giving me a glorious view of all of him. "Maybe my next lesson would be in denial..." he said as he walked his fine ass out of the bedroom.

I sat straight up in bed. Where the hell was he going? Naked. He wouldn't actually leave...

"Gus? Get back here. What are you doing?"

A minute passed and I thought I heard him in the kitchen, and then he strolled back in giving a frontal, unabashed view of all of him. I had to stop from doing grabby-hands and saying "Gimme."

Standing in front of the bed, with a book and two bottles of water, wearing nothing but a seductive grin, he teased, "See something you want?"

I snapped out of it, realizing I was biting my lip and possibly drooling. "All of you. I want all of you."

He laughed, and it was so genuine, from his very core, it made me the happiest I'd ever been.

He tossed me the book, put the waters on the nightstand and crawled in the bed to lay down beside me.

"So...what is it about these books? I went to get this signed by the author and the women there were lined up out the door and down the street."

"Wait, you stood in line to get this signed?"

"Oh, no. I knew her publicist—well, my agent does. When we were in Richmond, she

was nearby doing a signing and I was able to swing by." He shrugged, like it was no big deal. He was Gus Quinlan and, because of his "minor" celebrity status, probably one of the only crew chiefs who had an agent.

"So, what is so special about this book that you kept it?"

I blushed, holding it close to my chest. Imagine. I'm in bed with a man I've lusted after for a decade, after having made love to him for the first time...but now I blushed.

Because of a book.

And, of course, he noticed.

He pushed the book aside, lightly skimming his hand up from my chest, over my neck, and to my cheeks. "You kill me…" His voice was almost a whisper. The tone was softer than it had ever been before. It was a tone used between lovers. He tucked a wayward curl gently behind my ear. "The things that make you blush. Now I must know. Even after watching you orgasm—multiple times—" He tipped my chin to meet his eyes. His trademark cockiness was in the raise of a brow. "Now I mention this book and it makes you blush like a whore in church."

He leaned back, throwing an arm behind his head, the picture of a beautiful man in repose waiting to be painted by a master from the Renaissance. His hair was perfectly rumpled, his lips were swollen, his eyes were throwing me serious smolder. "Explain, please."

I hesitated, and he was fast as a whip, reaching over me, grabbing the book. Using the space between us to prop open the book and flip through some pages, he wasn't giving up. "Is it the sex scenes?" he said, flipping through fast. "Is there a sex fantasy in here I need to know about—"

"Stop…" I pleaded, bordering on whining as I tried to close the book, but failing. "Please, Gus." I reached for the book again.

He playfully batted away my hand. "Because if there is, I could fulfill it for you. I'm game."

"Are you hungry, let's order some food." I rolled to get up.

"Stop changing the subject." He sat up, pulling the book into his lap and flipping through the pages even faster.

It wasn't the sex scenes that made me uncomfortable. Yes, they were hot, but it was the premise of the story. Old friends, who'd never dated before. They leave town to find their way in the world, only to realize they may have lost their opportunity to be happy together. They find solace in each other, and so on and so on.

It was a little too close to home. Shyla must have told him it was a favorite—cringe. It was like the popular boy in school finding your diary.

I forced him to shut the book, "I'm hungry—feed me."

He tilted his head and smirked at me. "Fine. I will do some research later when you're not around."

With all seriousness, I said, "Gus, there's nothing in a book that you haven't already surpassed for me."

That worked. Maybe too well. The book went sailing over his shoulder and I once again, became the center of all his attention.

45

MIA

After we shared some Thai, me in my robe, him in his boxers, we found ourselves back in bed, working out all the pent-up sexual energy we'd been restraining for what seemed like years. I dozed off in his arms to the sound of his rhythmic breathing, only to wake up the next morning to him still next to me, and the sound of ripping paper. I rolled over to see him sitting cross-legged on the bed next to me, a book in his lap, tearing strips off the yellow pad I kept by the phone in the kitchen.

"What are you doing?" I wiped my eyes, an attempt to focus, trying to make out the book he had in his lap that he was so fixated on.

He grabbed a pen by his side, jotting down a note on the scrap of paper, then tucking it in the seam of the book before turning the page. "Oh, good morning, beautiful."

I sat up with effort, my body still languid and depleted from last night's activities as I pointed at the study session he had going on in my bed.

"Oh." He flipped the cover of the book over to show me it was *The Splendor in Tomorrow...* "I woke up early, so rather than wake you, I decided to do some light reading. Maybe take a few notes."

I pushed myself to a seated position next to him, the sheet pooling at my waist to reveal my bare breasts, immediately catching his attention.

"But study time is over, I can put to practice some of what I learned —" he shoved the book aside, the pen and pad making a clattering sound as they hit the floor as Gus pulled me under him.

Through my laughter, I asked, "Were you inspired by what you read—"

"No, honey, I was inspired by watching you sleep. I read so I would keep my hands off you and instead fantasize about what to do to you once you woke up." He turned me over, spooning me from behind, pulling my body flush against him so not one part of him wasn't connected to me. He breathed in my ear. "Since this was a favorite of yours, I could imagine you liked some of the steamier parts of it—I particularly like what happened on page 126.

I let out a squeak as he pinched my nipple. "How much reading did you get done?"

"You like to rub against me and moan in your sleep. Do you have any idea how confusing that is to parts of my body? I was "up" for a while." He nuzzled my neck. "Plus, I may have skipped around to the good parts."

Good. He didn't get the underlying reason why that story meant something to me. I rubbed my backside against him in response.

"Jesus, you're playing with fire, sweetheart."

He moved his very hard cock against my ass before lifting a leg and pulling it back over his, positioning himself against the apex, but not invading farther, but leaving it there to tease us both.

His fingers began to play between my legs, slowly, teasingly exploring.

I arched my back, causing my breasts to lift farther.

"God, I wish I were a writer...so I could put what you do to me in words." The whisper tickled the sensitive part of my ear he'd been kissing before he nipped at it.

His fingers continued to tease, stroking everywhere except the pressure point I was desperate for him to touch. He adjusted himself behind me but didn't enter me. He just thrust between my legs, a dance

LARALYN DORAN

of foreplay in the most tortuous way. He was on the cusp of entering
the ultimate pleasure, but lingered to build the anticipation.

"Gus...I want you to—"

"Oh, I know..."

I stopped, then rolled over. "But do you?" I kissed him thoroughly,
all the while climbing over him, straddling his hips, and without any
other preamble, took him inside me.

His kisses stopped and his eyes closed in benediction as I lowered
myself onto him. "Oh, fuck, Mia." His hands dropped to my hips,
tightening, as I adjusted myself completely, and then pushed up to my
thighs as I began to move.

"Yes, that's the idea," I said, a brash smile on my face and immense
pride in my body to bring this pleasure, joy—dare I say, euphoria, to
this man's face.

I grabbed his arms and pinned them over his head, his mouth was
slack, gasping for air, as I began to move, up and down, gyrating when
I was rooted down on him. His pleasure came out in a burst of laughter.
"Fuck. That's it, you rule. I'm yours. Do whatever you want with me."

I gyrated again and then paused, knowing the pause would drive
him insane. I leaned down and whispered, "Was there any question?"
Where did this new Mia come from? I'd never been so confident—so
dominating. It was because of him—he made me feel that way.

"Never." He panted and pulled up enough to watch where our
bodies met for a couple of strokes before glancing up at me with
such awe.

Pants and gasps and inhales and exhales. The cords in his neck
strained as he held up his head, wanting to continue to watch how he
would enter and disappear into me. Animalistic growls from him as he
would sporadically kiss me in between. Our fingers entwined, I used
his hands as leverage and picked up the pace.

With him thrusting up to meet me, the angle he was hitting inside
wasn't something I'd felt before. It was cataclysmic, and it came so
fast I didn't even have time to prepare for it. My eyes flew open, then
squeezed shut, my body went taut, and he threw his arms around me as

if to tether me to this earth and stop me from shattering into a million pieces. What air was in me escaped as his name. "Gus."

I felt his arms tighten around me and his body shake. I fell on top of him, his body fell back onto the pillows, taking me with him. I tried to shift off to the side, but he kept me flush on top of him, his arms were belts around me. And in that moment, while we were still joined, and almost every part of me was touching every part of him, I felt whole.

Our breathing leveled. "You have wrecked me," he said, squeezing me, kissing my nest of hair even as he smoothed it out of his face. "Truly wrecked me."

I wanted to say, "Can we stay like this forever?" But I was too afraid to utter the words. Too afraid that even in jest it would be too much of a request.

Too afraid that I wouldn't get a chance at forever with this man.

46

MIA

The honeymoon was over for our favorite newlyweds, and the screws were beginning to tighten on CJ. She came back from the wedding ceremony weekend to find out they had some bad press about her early season performance, and the gossip rags started "baby watch"—because once a woman was married, that was her job—to produce an heir.

Maintaining sponsorships—the bread and butter of our operations—was a concern. "It's the same for a woman in a corporate position. Do they give the promotion to her or a married man who may be more likely to work the extra hours without a possible maternity leave to get in the way?" Harper whispered to me after a meeting.

"Preaching to the choir," I said.

We all knew the score—she needed to win a race, not just place well.

The weekend's race in Atlanta was a flashback to reality for me and Gus as well. We had a newly defined relationship and were reminded of the challenge of working for different teams.

We spent the remainder of the week going through the pre-race setup, addressing concerns about the tire wear and pit stop strategy. CJ,

Jacks, and I went over to Merrick's shop where we had an agreement to use their simulator as we tried to figure out our tire strategy.

The Next Gen car's tires were different from what we were used to, and while they allowed for more grip, they also wore out faster. Great for restarts, hard for CJ to deal with when she was aggressive going into turns on tires that needed to be replaced. A blown tire while you're driving at a hundred-eighty-five miles per hour into a twenty-eight-degree bank turn with forty other cars surrounding you...it was reckless to put yourself in that position. Those are the kind of wrecks that take out half the field.

I was making notes on the latest data as CJ finished in the simulator. I said to Jacks, "I know it goes against her grain, but she's going to have to ease up on those turns if it's going to work."

He stood looking at the screen, then watching her, his arms crossed, a thoughtful look on his face before turning toward the door that led to the simulator room, "Yeah, I know. I'll talk to her. Let me handle it."

A minute later CJ led them out. "Tell them to get the set-up right and it won't be a problem." Her tone was a bit snippy, and my head popped up to meet her. I gave her a tense smile before she brushed by me. Jacks followed her, his head down, adjusting his trucker's cap as was his habit when he was thinking.

I busied myself with gathering my things, deciding it was better to stay out of it.

"She'll be fine. She doesn't take constructive suggestions well when it comes to her driving. Even from me, but she knows we're right. The sim showed her she can't drive the way she wants to on these new wheels. She'll need to adjust like all the other drivers." He held his head high. "Give her time."

Still, I'm glad it was him having to deal with it and not me. Conflict wasn't something I dealt with very well—it was the reason I let my ex get away with things for too long.

As we were walking out into the parking lot, I got a text from Gus.

GUS
Hey, gorgeous, your place or mine?

My smile was instant. Body on high alert. Shivers up the spine just from a text. God, I had it bad.

> **GUS**
>
> Cute smile. It does wonderful things to my ego and other parts of me.

I snapped my head up, scanning the area until I spotted him leaning casually, that gorgeous seductive smile in place as he winked at me from the second floor, in a glass conference room full of people, over-looking the lobby.

"Oh, good Lord. Here we go again," Jacks muttered as he turned to walk to his car, motioning to me, and then pointing at Gus. "I swear it's like one of my wife's soap operas around here."

"See you later, Jacks," I said, smiling ear to ear, my giddiness over-riding any concern or apprehension left back in the simulator.

> **MIA**
>
> Your choice. I'll bring dinner.

> **GUS**
>
> My place. I'll bring dinner. You just bring you.

> **MIA**
>
> ;-)

> **GUS**
>
> Just get your ass over there. Been thinking about you all day.

I put on my best flirtatious smile as I glanced up, but he had already turned away, rejoining the discussion inside the room. Inwardly, I swooned, locked my knees momentarily to stop them from giving out, and tightened my hold on my phone to focus on myself. He was such a distraction.

A happy, glorious distraction I would revel in for as long as I could.

47

GUS

My personal life had never been so solid. Over the next few weeks, Mia and I spent every evening together. We found time on the road to be together—in and out of bed. She was mine.

Professionally, she was going through some growing pains. Merlo went through a string of bad luck starting with Nashville. A massive collision happened toward the end of the race when many cars were due to pit for tires. The number eighty-six blew a tire, taking out almost half the field of drivers—including CJ.

The season was proving that tire strategy was a challenge for all teams.

Next came the road course at Road America. Road courses were in Grady's wheelhouse since that was where he originally raced and was an Indy champion.

Nonetheless, CJ still wanted to be competitive at a track that wasn't just four left-hand turns. Grady took the win, CJ finished a respectful top fifteen, but she still didn't have a win that would qualify her for the playoffs.

I honestly didn't know how they kept that out of their relationship. Mia and I were lucky Jacks was the man in charge and we didn't have the additional pressure in our relationship of being competing crew chiefs.

When we went to the Poconos, we rented a property, and it almost seemed like we were on vacation, except for the fact that we'd be gone most of the day. We came up early Thursday, spending the evening lounging and enjoying the hot tub at the Tuscan-style house surrounded by woods with a view of Lake Harmony. It was easy to pretend it was a vacation, with each other's undivided attention, until Friday afternoon, when we had to separate and make an appearance at our separate garages to check on things before practice the next day.

Poconos was called the Tricky Triangle because it was tricky for a crew to set the car up to run fast through the straight section and still handle well through the three different kinds of turns.

It made for good racing.

Given how mellow and relaxed I was, it was amazing I was able to focus at all.

"What are you smiling about?" Junior's tone was back to the obnoxious level it took when he was annoyed that someone was happy around him. He strolled into the garage, reading his phone and only glancing up to make sure no one ran into him.

"If you were dating a woman like Mia, you'd be smiling like that too," one of the crew members said, continuing to walk by.

"How's the love nest?" Grady said, stepping into the garage to check on the adjustments we were making.

"Fuck off," I said, as I went over to read through some notes.

Wild Bill strolled in. "So, our boy Gus has a legitimate girlfriend now."

"What is it with you people?" I said, finally looking up at the smirks that were all around me. "I've had girlfriends before."

But I'd admit the term didn't readily roll off my lips.

"No," Junior chimed in, but still hadn't committed his attention fully to the conversation. "You've had women."

Wild Bill pointed at me, "And you've had 'friends.'"

"Lots of 'em," Junior mumbled.

"Yeah. Well, you got to grow up some time," I said, walking out, a trail of chuckles and comments following me.

Grady caught up to me, his race suit on but unzipped and tied around his waist. "Don't let them get to you. They're like old, gossipy women. It's just hard to see a legend fall." He clapped me on the shoulder. "Suck it up, buttercup. I told you one day it would be your turn, when you gave me the same shit with CJ."

I side-eyed him. "You're ridiculous. We just started dating."

Grady jumped in front of me, walking backward and pointing at me with a know-it-all smirk that turned into the tone of a sage, old married man, "You have to start somewhere, my man."

48

MIA

"I've been thinking," I said to Gus the morning after we got home from our latest race. We were cozied up in his bed as he ran a finger down my naked hip, causing goose bumps to arise all over my body and awakening my senses. "We know the grip on these new wheels is better than the previous model. But they've proven to have quicker wear. Logically, it doesn't make sense to use the same strategy as before. Adjustments need to be made to the timing of pit stop and tire strategy."

"Hmmm." He kissed my shoulder.

I said, "I need to do an analysis to see if there would be any benefit to changing the strategy of when to pit."

"It wouldn't be worth the loss of track position," he murmured, continuing his ministrations as the other hand dipped toward my lower abdomen. I arched back into his embrace.

"I'm not so sure. It's worth further study—" my words ended in a moan as he dipped his hand down farther, cutting off all analytical thought.

"Hmm. Always studying…" his voice was deep, seductive, and his breath was erotic on my skin. He caressed, teased, and devoured me as I tried to string a few words together.

His proud smile was glorious. He had me so undone.

Between kisses, he mumbled, "God, I love…"

Then it was a full stop. His kisses stopped, his body froze for less than a moment and then he continued. "I love when you talk cars…" he said. "But now I'd rather think of other things I'd like to hear out of your mouth."

Was he about to say…

I clung to him and dove deeper into our pleasure, with just the possibility—the possibility that he may love me.

At Merlo a few days later, we met to discuss the set-up for the Richmond race. I presented my idea to Jacks.

"What's this?" CJ said, legs kicked back on the table as she read over the graph and report I gave out.

"I laid out a new strategy I'm recommending."

"What has Gus been putting in your morning coffee?" CJ said, immediately taking her feet off the table and planting them firmly on the ground.

I pointed at the report and then clicked on the presentation that flicked on the wall next to me. "You hired me to help you find an edge." I nodded to the data on the screen. "That's where we find the edge."

"Hm…" was all Jacks said, his hand stroking his day-old scruff, then adjusting his cap.

I took the lack of immediate argument as a signal to continue. "With teams getting only a certain number of tires each race, it's up to the crew to make sure they are utilized at the right times. I think the benefits outweigh the lost time involved—" I said, the boldness in my voice surprised even me.

"There's no way…" CJ stood, she was ready to argue, putting her hand down on the table, "if I'm running in the front—"

"CJ, just wait." Jacks held up a hand. "Let's look—"

"It doesn't make any sense." She gestured to the screen.

"If you look at the report. This graph shows—"

Jacks put a hand on CJ's forearm. "Let's just take a moment." He scanned the room and the faces of the other engineers in there. "There are no bad ideas in this room. Let's talk it out. There's no point in shooting it down right off the start."

CJ sat down, side-eying Jacks and me. "Fine. I'll keep an open mind." But her body and tone conveyed a different attitude.

You would've thought I was defending a thesis or fighting for my sanity—maybe something in between.

As we left, Harper pulled me aside. "Mia, this is really good work. Keep it up."

"Thanks."

As she gathered her things, she said, "Question. What did Gus think about your idea?"

I gestured toward CJ who was still talking to Jacks, aggressively pointing at the figures on the wall. "Pretty much that. We didn't get into it too much. But he didn't think the idea held much weight."

"Good." She hitched her bag on her shoulder, and a half-smile broke out over her face. "That's what we want."

It turned out Richmond was the perfect track to test my approach.

Typically, when a crash or something occurs during a race, a caution flag is thrown up, and cars can't pass each other while maintaining the same speed. Many drivers take the opportunity to come into pit rather than during regular racing because they don't lose as much track position.

At Richmond, a short track, there weren't quite as many caution flags for cars to take advantage of to change tires.

Jacks implemented my plan...and it paid off.

In fact, it was more talked about it than the race itself.

When a caution came out in the last stage of the race, most contenders came in for new tires. CJ stayed out, gaining the best track position she had that day. Taking her last set later while under green gave her better wheels to finish the race when others were on worn treads. She cut through the traffic like a knife through butter, missing the leader by a second—her best finish yet.

The crew was shocked. Probably just as much as the commentators.

Later that evening, back in my hotel room, I watched *Race Center* give a wrap-up on the day. There was a replay of the driver in the winner's circle holding up his big trophy and then a cut to CJ climbing out of her car and hugging Jacks and then me. I watched her pull me to her and whisper in my ear. "So, you may have a point..." and then me smiling at her concession.

"I don't know what's gotten into Jacks and his team, trying something so—"

"Oh. Something tells me that's his new engineer who came over from Triple R...bet they are regretting letting her walk away."

"Bet Merrick is regretting not snatching her up. Gus Quinlan can't seem to decide if he wants to smile or not. He's just over in his box shaking his head."

"Well, one thing is for sure. These crew chiefs need to stop resting on their laurels. Next Gen car means Next Gen ideas..."

"Yep, back to the drawing board, boys...er, um...people."

Later, there was a knock at my hotel door.

I was nervous—in a different way—to answer the door. It wasn't like I kept the idea from him. I told him. In fact, I probably shouldn't have said anything.

Besides, I didn't owe him any explanation. He was on the opposing team—no matter how friendly we were.

I swung open the door, and my *GQ* man was leaning against the doorjamb holding a bottle of wine in one hand, and two glasses in the other. "I ordered room service," he said as a way of greeting.

"Okay..."

He stepped by me, putting the wine and glasses down carefully, purposefully. "You surprised me today."

"It wasn't intentional. It wasn't like I kept it a secret—"

He held up a hand. A move I found condescending as hell, and my hands went to my hips, my mouth open to tell him so.

"Tell me, was it all your idea?"

"Well, yeah. I told you—"

In one move, he pivoted, wrapping an arm around my waist, burying his hand in my hair, and cutting off any possibility of me arguing.

His kiss was deep, thorough, and claiming. His grip on me was the same.

Just when I thought he'd take me directly to the bed, he stopped, pulled back, and leaned his head against my forehead. "You pulled one over on all of us. My mistake for underestimating you. I think you have bewitched me so thoroughly you've made me stupid. Regardless, I'm so fucking proud of you."

Warmness started in my chest and spread through my body, reaching my fingertips as I gripped the chest of his shirt.

"Let me open this bottle of wine, so I have something else to do with my hands besides maul you, and we can actually get to eat some dinner before I admire you some more." He reached into his back pocket and pulled out an opener.

A coy smile played on his lips as he went to work opening the wine, pouring both of us a glass and gesturing to the seats on the balcony.

He waited for me to sit down, handing me a glass, and kissing me lightly before taking his seat, a soft smile on his face.

"I wasn't sure how you were going to react to this. The way the reporters were questioning Jacks, it sounded like I kept the nuclear codes from you guys."

His shoulders shook a bit before he sipped. "Nah. Oh, Junior is going to tear into me, no doubt, but it's going to be about why I haven't seduced you over to Merrick yet with my magic cock."

I almost spit out the wine I was trying to swallow.

"Please tell me you're joking," I said, thankful I didn't just snarf pinot. That would hurt as much as the chardonnay did.

"Well, maybe not in those terms, but he tried to convince me months ago, before we even got together. Now that we are actually sleeping together and my cock is playing a part in your life already," he slumped back in the chair, kicking his feet up on the railing, "he's going to be relentless."

"Well, at least he's not attempting to do it himself."

Gus glared at me. "Don't even joke about that. He comes at you and there will be words—more than words—and I want to keep my job...at least, for now."

"It's fine. He's harmless."

We both took sips of our drinks.

"I'm so proud of you, honey. Really. You and CJ both did amazing today. This is going to really get some people talking, and CJ really needed the confidence boost and the points for the season."

"Yeah, well, she didn't make it easy on me," I half-joked.

"What do you mean?"

"Well, it's like she was all supportive until it didn't work for her. I mean, I have these ideas. That's why they hired me to give them fresh new ideas, insight with the new design. I have the background, the data, and knowledge to back up my reasonings, and some still resisted changing anything." I took another sip, trying not to work myself up or sound arrogant.

But something small and petty inside me wanted to tell him how much CJ fought me about this. Because it wasn't just the one time in the simulator—she was passively resistant up until race time. After the gamble gave her the best finish the team had all season, she admitted I was right. I guess I earned my stripes, and we are officially a team now. It was a team who got us those points today. But we also needed to work as a team to get a win.

"At least Jacks was a bit open to the ideas—" I said, shifting in my seat.

"Yeah, well, it's going to take some time teaching the old dog some new tricks. Maybe I should start listening closer to your pillow talk, too," he grabbed my hand, kissing it.

The breeze and moonlight were doing funny things to my insides, and damn if I wasn't falling harder for this man.

"Speaking of pillows…" he said, stretching up to stand in front of me, purposefully eye level with a new inspiration. "Before room service gets here, how about I inspire some new ideas while you make use of a pillow." He kissed me, his tongue languidly seducing my mouth. "If I'm successful, words won't be possible, it will just be intelligible sounds."

"Show me what you have in mind."

And did he ever. He made this celebration all about me. Except for me insisting on him taking off his shirt—because damn, I loved that man's chest—his pants never came off, he just touched, kissed, and caressed me within an inch of oblivion. I wasn't reciting numbers or stringing together words, I used my pillow to muffle the moans of pleasure he drove out of me with his mouth and fingers.

With an extremely satisfied grin, peering down at my languid body, he stood and left to receive and sign for our dinners.

His eyes were full of warmth as he put a knee on the bed and climbed over me to kiss me softly. The moment was the closest I've ever felt to anyone. Not because of the intimate act we'd just performed because we'd done it before. He made me feel like he respected me for what I brought to the racing industry. I didn't get that with my ex.

"We need to eat…" He paused and leaned over me before he said, "actual food. And you, my dear, need to stay naked so I can stare at your breasts." He twirled a finger around one of them.

I rolled my eyes at him. "You've seen plenty of breasts, Gus."

"Not yours." He bent over, sucking on one of them and causing me to squirm beneath him, laughing.

Intelligible words were gone from my brain except for four. "God, I love you."

He froze for a moment as we both registered what came out of me. Actually, we both froze as all playfulness disappeared. He was so worried he'd screw something up, but it seemed I beat him to the punch.

I tried to backpedal, but now nothing was coming out. "I...I…"

Surprisingly, instead of running, he caged me in with his arms, lowered himself onto my body and kissed me slowly. And even though he never responded with the words, I felt him respond with his body.

I tried desperately to believe it was the response I wanted, and I prayed that with those four words I hadn't destroyed how far we'd come.

49

MIA

The next few races were a string of more bad luck, and really, that was racing. It didn't matter how freaking fantastic your race plan was, or how foolproof. Your car could be at top performance, but if the idiot you were behind tried to tag the guy in front of him, and that ricocheted into you. Oh, well—that was racing.

But when you are falling behind in the points and the playoffs were looming, and you're a small, young team that needs the position, the pressure mounts. Especially, if you are currently the only woman driver and a highly publicized, woman-dominated team.

"We'll get our groove back at Daytona. Daytona is a good track for her," Harper said, more to herself than to her staff back in the office conference room for our Monday meeting, before CJ arrived.

"Um…didn't she get a concussion at Daytona a few years ago?" someone from the back piped up and then was quickly shushed as CJ walked in, pumped, smacking her hands together.

"Okay, folks. Superspeedway. I feel the need for speed!" CJ said, summoning enthusiasm.

"Isn't *Top Gun* a little before your time?" Her spotter, Aaron turned to her.

"Aw, come on…that quote is timeless," she said, pulling out a chair and sitting next to him.

Jacks walked in behind her, a little pale, his years showing on him like never before.

"Harper…" I said, under my breath to her.

"Yeah, I see it too." She stood, walked over to him before he sat down, and whispered to him.

He waved her off. "Alright, let's keep this brief. The wife wants me home early tonight." He sat down slowly and gestured to me. "Mia, give the rundown."

I paused, thrown by him handing the meeting over to me. This was his territory. I just sat back and took notes as to what still had to be accomplished. The hauler with the equipment, the car racing, and our back-up car, was scheduled to leave that evening. The rest of us were leaving tomorrow.

My eyes shot over the other department heads, CJ, and settled on Harper.

She nodded at me and gestured for me to stand and take over.

Pushing up on wobbly legs, I tried to remember the order Jacks ran these meetings and emulated his tone the first few minutes, then started discussing the things as I thought they needed addressing. Before I knew it, we were done. Harper's assistant Megan had taken notes for me and handed them over, efficient, and concise.

Jacks took out a cloth, wiping his forehead. "Good job," he said. "I gotta go now."

"Okay." I watched him head out the door and gingerly walk down the hallway, holding his side. "Jacks…do you need any help?"

He waved me off without turning around, "Don't be ridiculous. I'm fine. If you want to be useful, go make sure the hauler has everything and that the boys have double-checked it."

The next morning, Jacks wasn't on the plane.

Harper, however, was the last one to climb on. The minute she walked on the plane and scanned the area, I knew we were in trouble. It was more than her "focused, no BS face." It was a restrained panic. Like she was trying to keep it together as a leader would for the sake of the team.

I stood, working my way past the other team members who hadn't noticed, my voice low. "Harper, where's Jacks?"

She pulled me aside to two empty seats and pulled me in to sit down. "He can't make it."

"I'm sorry, what?" I stayed standing.

She held onto her ever-present phone and put her carry-on and purse under the seat in front of her. "It's fine. It'll be fine," she said, using her hands to pretend to tamp down my panic. "Things are under control."

My mouth moved, but it was all I could do to breathe as I processed this. My hands grew clammy, and my heartbeat accelerated as I came to the same conclusion as she uttered the words. "You are going to have to run the pit." She shifted around, looking for the seat belt and buckling it. The jet engines fired up, and as our ears adjusted to the noise, I shook my head vehemently—like a dog shaking off water.

She motioned for me to sit and snap on my seat belt also. But I was frozen in place. "No. No. That's not possible. Harper, don't do this to me." I fell into my seat. "When will Jacks be back? What's wrong with him?"

"He's going into surgery."

"Surgery? What?" My concern overrode my own panic. "Why? Is he okay?" Of course, he wasn't okay, he needed surgery. It didn't seem like this was a voluntary procedure. I closed my eyes, trying to slow my thoughts. "What is wrong?"

"Gallbladder. He went to the hospital last night. His wife called me this morning and told me. I talked to him briefly, but he was in a lot of pain. He said you could handle it. You knew what had to be done, the strategy was sound and just to roll with it."

I gulped—or at least tried to—and cleared my throat, not looking at her. "So, to get this straight. Jacks isn't coming to Daytona, at all."

"Correct."

"And I'm responsible for the team."

"Also correct."

"And the only advice he left for me was to just 'roll with it'."

"Yep. You got it."

I nodded my head, then dropped head into my hand as my vision blurred. "And you are

telling everyone when?"

"As soon as you have a moment to digest this and allow the circulation back into my hand." I looked down and saw her hand in mine, turning reddish purple.

"The plan for the race has already been laid out. Just adhere to it, make adjustments as needed, and we will be fine. This is one of her stronger courses," Harper said. "You've got this."

I nodded to reassure her more than anything. Fake it 'til you make it. I straightened and took in a deep breath. Resolve. Resolute. I opened my mouth to thank her.

She held up her hand. "You wouldn't have made it this far if we didn't believe you could be in this position and kick ass." Her eyes grew hard. "Remember what I told you about being unapologetic."

I nodded. "Got it." I didn't get it. I was just an engineer.

I sat back while she announced to the crew the change in plans. I wanted to talk to Gus. One of the biggest races of the season, and easily the biggest challenge of my life.

I was ashamed to admit I needed to hear his reassurance in telling me I was capable. That I was going to kick some ass… I needed him now more than I cared to admit.

50

GUS

It's been years since I'd been this nervous before a race—and it wasn't even about me.

Once we were in Daytona, Mia's mood had been unpredictable and edgy—with good reason.

Harper, their PR person, and other support staff maintained a perimeter around her, allowing her to focus just on the race and handling all the other details that came along with the position—meet and greets with reporters, sponsor events, commentators, etc.

It was all the buzz of the weekend.

There was more than a little concern about Jacks, but even more interest in how Mia St. James, a new addition and a virtual unknown, outside the engineering community, would be able to lead the team.

The fact that her ex had come crawling out of the woodwork within the hour of the announcement, flinging lies about her, even ramped up the frenzy. The only thing stopping me from castrating that man was the knowledge that he had well-deserved payback heading his way. I was going to have to bump up the timing, though, because I was impatient in seeing that settled.

On my way to track down Mia to check on her, I stopped by CJ's trailer. Mia and I had been missing each other for the last day or two, and prior to that we were busy at home. The elephant dangling from a high wire was the fact that she told me she loved me, and I said nothing. I never responded—at least not verbally.

But it wasn't what either of us needed to be focused on right now.

A muffled "come in," came from within CJ's trailer.

Surprisingly, her trailer empty except for the woman herself walking out from the back of it. "Well, I can't say I'm surprised by this visit…is this the conversation where you tell me to take it easy on your girlfriend? Is it my turn to be told not to run her out of town."

"Of course not. Mia can take care of herself. You aren't that scary." I slid onto the bench used as a kitchen table. "But I am looking for her…and wanted to wish you good luck."

She blatantly stared me down, calling bullshit, before ducking her head in the fridge to grab two bottles of water, tossing one to me.

"I'm not the ogre you all make me out to be," she said, slipping onto the bench across from me. "And I know Mia can handle herself. I was only joking with you."

I left that alone, both to annoy her, but also not to get in the middle of things with her and Mia. "Any word on the ol' man?"

"Last I heard he's recovering and is sending notes to Mia about our practice runs—which he's monitored from his hospital bed to his wife's dismay." She took a sip of the water, slumping down in the booth and playing with the cap.

"How are you holding up? I know this must have thrown you."

She didn't look up, but there was a small frown on her lips, before she said, "You know we need this race to go well, if we have any hope of making the playoffs. You guys are locked in with that win, but—"

"Yeah, I know," I said.

We talked shop a bit about how everyone did at practice, and she told me Grady was on his way back from some interviews.

I stood, wanting to find Mia and see if she'd eaten.

"Don't worry, I won't run her out of town," she stood. "I know you have it bad for her."

I ran my hand over my jaw, my initial instinct was to tell her to shove it. I was used to pushing back from her jabs. I turned to her.

"You and Harper claimed to have known this for months. Everyone seems to have it all figured out."

"I just wanted to hear you say it, that's all," she said, a grin on her face, warmth in her eyes. "It's cute. I'm happy for you, G."

The eye roll I threw at her could've rivaled a teenage girl's. I left the trailer to the sounds of her laughter.

An arm grabbed me from behind. "Hey, man, what was so funny to get my wife laughing like that."

I turned to glare at Grady. "My love life."

"Ah." He crossed his arms across his chest, adjusted his stance, his grin peeked out as he tried to keep a straight face. "Yeah, well, we both warned you, Karma."

"What is it with everyone's need to label someone as being in love? I mean, can't two people just enjoy each other's company, be in a monogamous relationship and care for each other without it being labeled as being 'in love'?" I used the sarcastic air quotes gesture, my frustration of wanting to be left alone to figure out my relationship without others pushing me toward coupledom so damn fast.

Grady's face fell, his eye grew concerned. "Dude, what's going on with you?"

I waved him off. "Nothing. I just need everyone to stop trying to make my life into the next great romance novel. There isn't a meet-cute or a HEA—"

Grady's brows furrowed in confusion. "A meet-what? What's a HEA—"

"Forget it." I shook my head, my frustration had me spitting out nonsense. "They're terms Mia told me—not important. Never mind. I'm just...I just don't want to talk about it. Yes, I'm in a relationship. No big deal. Yes, I like her. No big deal. It doesn't mean I'm the next big romance story like you and Cal have with your women, okay? I'm not the romantic hero-type." I threw my hands up in the air.

Grady held up his hands in defense. "Message received. I'll talk with CJ, bro. It's fine, I get it." His tone was pacifying, trying to calm the bear he poked too much.

"I gotta go," I said, shoving my hands in my pockets and stalking off, realizing now I didn't have it in me to be around Mia without feeling uncomfortable. Damnit. How did they do that to me?

The minute she said the words...those four words, *"Gus, I love you."* Things just got weird. Why did she have to say them?

My father told my mom he loved her.

But he also loved his wife.

I heard the begging. I heard the crying. It was a dramatic cycle of it. Not only did he break her heart. He derailed her life by saddling her with being a single mother, making promises he never intended to fulfill.

All by saying he loved her. The minute she'd get her feet under her...he'd say those words and she was hooked again. He used it as a weapon to control her. To hold her in place.

Why did she have to say those words? We were fine.

I answered my own question. Because *she's Mia—she's passionate and fearless and... she loves...she loves me.*

Well, today wasn't the time or the place to figure this mess out— besides, she needed to concentrate on the race, and for that matter, so did I. We could deal with love another day.

51

MIA

I really wish I hadn't overheard that. It was like a flash back from college.

Why the hell did I always find myself in the wrong place to hear the wrong thing from Gus's mouth?

We were in Harper's RV after qualifying on Friday, and I tried very hard to stay focused on what would be one of the biggest races of my career—not replaying my boyfriend's indignation when people tried to define our relationship as serious.

I realized I never should've said that I loved him, but it was spontaneous. I felt it. It came out. Granted, he never said it back. He never even acknowledged hearing it from me. But I tried to believe he was beginning to feel something. I wanted to believe it.

Now I was in purgatory. I was in that stage in the relationship when you've pretty much laid it out and you're left hanging—analyzing everything, criticizing yourself to see if the person you are in love with reciprocates, or if you're going to be left dangling in the wind, alone.

So the words were laid out before us, like the elephant in the room. And we were going about our lives as if I never said a thing. We made love in hotel rooms, in my house, his house, in his backyard, in his garage. But I swore, each time it wasn't just sex. It just felt like more.

I didn't think I was imagining it. But after hearing his frustration, maybe—God, maybe I was. Maybe it was one-sided.

"I'd like to go on record again as stating, I don't think this is a good idea," Brett, one of the veteran engineers said, refocusing me on the important discussion I was missing. "With Jacks not being here, and everything that is on the line, I really think CJ is better off going with our normal strategy. The one we laid out earlier in the season." He stood with legs spread and his arms crossed over his chest with the slightest lift of his chin to give him a pseudo air of authority—one he didn't have.

With Jacks missing, and him with seniority, it probably rubbed him the wrong way that he wasn't the one calling the shots. I was left in charge.

Harper, CJ, Brett, Aaron, a few other crew members, and I sat in Harper's RV versus the garage or hauler because we were discussing how we were going to handle not having Jacks at the race. Well, it had already been decided, but clearly a few people felt the need to open it up for discussion again.

"So noted," Harper said, leaning back against a captain's chair. She stood, cast a glance at me and began to pace the length of the RV, walking past each person there. "Based off the data and Jacks's recommendation, the plan is as stands. We are going with Mia's format."

I glanced over at CJ to get her reaction. She sat at a table, her leg bouncing with excess energy, and she stared at the water bottle she held, turning it around and around and not contributing or even looking up at Harper or me.

"CJ?" Harper said, stopping in front of her. "Anything to contribute?"

She shrugged. "I already told you what I thought." She glanced up at Harper. "I'm the driver. These guys are the brains. I just sit in the seat and push the pedal."

Harper gave her a side-eye glance and then her back as she turned to the rest of us. She crossed her arms over her chest and zeroed in on me, prompting me with a nod to say something.

Leadership. That's what Gus and Jacks had told me I needed to work on—backbone and leadership. Don't undersell yourself—that's what Harper and CJ told me. The team was doubting me—that was on me. I hadn't given them anything to follow.

I stepped forward. "We're in the eleventh hour. Regardless of who developed the format, Jacks chose it and is counting on us to follow it through. I'm not going to sit and justify it any longer. We're a team—we need to act like it and get on the same page. We have one of our biggest races tomorrow and can't be doubting ourselves—or each other."

I began pacing the small space, but purposefully made eye contact with each of them as I moved, waving the folder at them.

"Merlo was formed because you wanted to be bold, innovative, badasses who shook things up. Can't you feel the quake? Can't you hear the shift?"

I pointed at CJ. "Let's continue to be unpredictable, uncompromising."

She studied me, biting her thumb nail and then giving me a half-smile and nodded. "And unapologetic."

I nodded back.

There was a general murmur of assent. CJ gave an affirming nod. "Now, I need to find my husband and get to bed. Catch you all later." CJ got up to leave but then caught my arm. "Mia, can you walk out with me for a moment."

I followed her out and around to the side of the motorhome. "What's up?"

"We need this." She held up her hand. "Like really need this. It's not just my ego. I need you to understand, The Driven program, the girls coming up behind me..." She tightened her ponytail. "They need to see that we aren't just shouting into the wind—do you get what I mean?" She put her hand on her hip, but the other hand was flying around as if it didn't have something to hold onto. "We have to make it to the Chase. We have to show something for this season—it's put up or shut up time. The novelty of us is gone."

I found the confidence to put my hand on her shoulder and say, "You drive the car, I'll steer the team."

I squeezed her shoulder, and she smirked up at me. "Cute tag line, you been working on that?"

"Maybe." I lifted a shoulder with a cocky shrug.

Half-smile still in place, she walked backward and said, "See you tomorrow, boss."

"Don't let Harper catch you saying that," I shouted to her as she walked away.

She waved me off and disappeared behind some other RVs.

I didn't care that it was a 7 PM start. I stood in the pit box sweating through all my clothes. I think my earlobes were sweating. After all, it was Daytona, Florida, in August. Are you kidding me? I know most of these people are from the Carolinas, but what the hell? "They shouldn't have races schedule below the Carolina line in July and August," I said to the team.

Wearing a short-sleeve shirt while saying that didn't earn me any respect from those who were stuck in the heavy fire-retardant suits. I tried my most sympathetic smile, but I'm pretty sure it fell flat.

Somehow Harper managed to still look stunning while standing behind me with her hands in her linen pants—cool, in command, and ready to take on the world.

"Everyone ready?" she said, grabbing her headphones and receiving a chorus of varying confirmations.

It was then that I realized…I didn't get my candy.

I searched my pockets, my seat, looked under where I was sitting.

"Anything wrong?" Harper asked.

"Have you seen Gus lately? Did he give you anything?"

"I saw him at the media tent earlier, but he didn't say anything or give me anything." She put her hands in her pockets as if to double check.

I checked my phone. There was a text from him.

GUS

I'm a Dum-Dum.

Ran out of time to get my good luck piece to you. Give it you in the winner's circle.

My shoulders dropped and I restrained myself from tossing the phone on the table in front of me, pocketing it instead. This wasn't a sign. It wasn't about him.

It was about me, this team, and my career.

CJ was strapped in her car, the net was up and the rest of us took our places as the announcer said the famous words, "Drivers, start your engines."

Harper put her hands on my shoulders, squeezing them with silent support as she said into the headset to the entire team, "You know Jacks is watching, so let's make him proud.

"Alright, y'all, let's do this," I added. "CJ—go kick some ass."

"That's my job and that's our new motto."

"You got it," I said, smiling and deciding I was going to enjoy today.

Forty beasts came alive.

I didn't care how many times I was present when that roar went down Pit Road, there was nothing like it. For a gearhead, it went through your chest and embedded itself into your soul.

The race was going according to plan—well, as much as a race like Daytona could. You could never predict what other teams were going to do or how they were going to perform. You didn't know if someone was going to get loose, causing a seven-car mess and an unfortunate flag that worked against us.

Grady was taken out in the end of the second stage. He was caught up when another car caught the corner panel of the next to him and ended up with irreversible damage to his back right wheel, sending him to the garage, finished for the night.

It was a tough night for Gus and Grady, but neither CJ nor I had time to feel sorry for them. Afterall, with Grady's win earlier this season, they were already locked in for the playoffs.

We were still sweating to earn ours.

CJ came sliding in for our next stop, four tires, and fuel. "Get me out of here before Moyer," she said, and even through the netting I could see her gloved hands gripping the wheel, anxious for the fourteen-second pit time to be over.

"You're fine," Aaron said.

"Watch your speed!" I said, mimicking my mentor and what he always said to her after ever pit stop.

The last thing we needed was a speeding penalty off pit road because she was overzealous—that would've sent us back through pit lane for the penalty then to the back of the pack. The most restraint a driver has to show is staying at sixty miles per hour while exiting the pit road, especially when their rival is beating them off pit lane.

Too anxious to sit, I stood watching the monitors and the track. I wasn't sure I had any feeling left in my fingers from gripping the chair in front of me. I had to lock my knees to stop them from trembling as I listened to the back and forth from Aaron and CJ. Taking in what they were telling me, what my crew was telling me. Making assessments, processing, and trying not to think, "What would Jacks do?" Because Jacks wasn't here, it was all on me.

CJ had contact with one of the drivers battling it out for the front, scraping up her side but otherwise, holding on. She fell back slightly, before fighting her way back up to the front again.

"How are things holding up?" I asked.

She responded, "I'm good, it's all good?"

"Aaron?"

Our spotter cut in the headset with his assessment from up in the booth above the raceway, "I can't see anything from here except maybe some panel damage."

I turned to my engineer who nodded that everything still looked fine. So, CJ dove back into the fight in the last stage of the race. We were a few laps from a scheduled stop, and her tires had to be getting bad, especially with the abuse they were taking. I gripped the chair so hard my fingers weren't numb—they hurt.

CJ was quiet. She and Aaron had a flowing conversation throughout the race. I picked up enough over the season to know that CJ being quiet meant she didn't want to reveal something over the line.

I pressed down on my comm. "Say hi, Jacks." That was our code for this race to come in for a strategic stop. I was more convinced with her silence, we needed it.

"I'm good." She wasn't. There was something wrong with the car. I felt it. I knew it. She was trying to wring out a better lead. She was waiting to see if someone would do something stupid. If there was a wreck, a yellow flag would be thrown eliminating the need for her sacrifice track position to come in for new tires while everyone else continued to race. But if she didn't come in at this point which was their scheduled time—while the green was still out—she would lose momentum on bad tires—or even wreck.

That was what made tire strategy a gamble.

"CJ, come in."

"Give me a minute." CJ passed Smith, who was losing ground on Diaz and Moyer.

Instead, she passed the pit road entrance and continued to trail after the leaders.

"CJ," I said, gritting my teeth. She was going to throw the entire plan out the window.

The lead pack was coming around turn three, and CJ made a move on the inside. Her car

got loose, a tire blew apart, and she slid up at an awkward angle into both Diaz and then Moyer, sending all three cars spinning. CJ's car went into the outside wall, sending it airborne, spinning to land on its side, perpendicular to the track just as Smith's car came through, hitting the back end. It was knocked around like a pinball, pieces of the car flying off in all directions before the main chunk of it finally came to a stop at the infield wall—the remnants resembling a crushed beer can more than a car.

The images on the monitor and the horrific sound we could hear from even the other side of the track didn't register but froze us all in place. Her engine wasn't even in the car—it was about ten yards away from where the car stopped rolling. The tires, and miscellaneous pieces of debris, were a trail of breadcrumbs from where she started to where she landed.

I couldn't even make out enough of the car to see if the net on her window was down—indicating she was okay.

The air left my lungs, my knees buckled, and I would've fallen to the ground had the person next to me not caught me.

"Oh my God," I whispered.

And then the world began to move again at breakneck speed.

Headsets were dropped.

Harper was gone. Her long legs eating up pavement and jumping into a cart her assistant had ready for her.

The team was either stunned still, unable to process what to do, or they were in a full sprint.

What was I going to do? What should I do?

Pray. All I could think to do was pray.

52

GUS

"Moyer and Lomax, down on the inside, making their move up on Diaz and Smith who are going...yes, we have three wide. Moyer, Diaz, and Smith with Lomax looking for her opening. Smith falls behind, giving her a space, and she takes it. But not before Diaz tries to block, giving her contact with her right side.

"That's my girl!" Grady said, the pride emphasized with a fist in the air. "Come on...come on..."

I sat on the edge of my seat because if we weren't going to win, we sure as hell wanted our girls to win.

"If I didn't know better, I'd think you two were glad you were done for the day and could watch the rest of the race from here?" Junior quipped. "All that's missing is a beer in your hand."

"Hey, that's not a bad idea. Want to hook us up with a few?" Grady said, waving his hand in the air but not taking his eye off his wife's car.

But I was studying CJ's car with the eye of a crew chief. I didn't like how she was coming out of those turns. The car looked loose...a little roughed up from the battle it had just been through to get its hard-won position.

"Hey, when's the last time she came in?" Grady asked.

I looked on the screen with all our data on each team.

Grady quietly said to me, "I don't think I like the way it looks."

"Neither do I," I said, my mind racing. I was about as familiar with CJ's driving as anyone else. I knew how she drove, and how the car should be responding. This car didn't look right.

She passed pit row's entrance again, but the positioning she was gaining—

And then it happened. My brain wasn't registering what my eyes were seeing until I was able to comprehend that CJ's car was a shredded heap already on its side, and Grady launched himself out of the booth.

I followed him—tossing my headset on the ground. "Whoa. Hold up, we need a cart. We won't make it over there running."

He searched frantically over the heads of the crowd milling around, people staring at him, and the press closing in. "Grady, Grady? Did you see—"

I pushed a reporter out of the way, shielding Grady with my body, saying to Grady, "She's fine. You know she's fine." Trying to convince myself as much as him as I turned in circles searching for a way to get him out of there.

A crowd was pushing in when Harper and her assistant, Megan, pulled up, and we wordlessly jumped in back. "Is her net down?" I shouted over the group trying to close in on us.

"I—I don't know," Harper said, with her phone to her ear. "I don't think so."

Megan swerved through the traffic, yelling at people like a New York city cabbie.

"They are still working on getting her out of the car," Harper had to raise her voice over the noise around us.

We were just about to pull into the Care Center when Harper stopped us, grabbing an EMT who seemed to be waiting for us. "Grady, go with this EMT. Go! He'll take you to CJ."

Grady didn't need to hear anything else. He leapt out of the cart and took off.

"Wait? Where's he going?" I asked.

The minute he left, Harper closed her eyes before pulling the phone away from her ear, saying, "They pulled CJ from the car and loaded her in the ambulance—" her voice broke.

They pulled CJ from the car. Not that she got out of the car on her own. "They're loading her in an ambulance to take her straight to the hospital." She let out a shaky breath, her hands trembling, as she fought to hang on to her composure.

They were bypassing the Care Center and taking her straight to the hospital. They pulled her out of the car…This was not good.

I opened my mouth to say something, but nothing came out. No. Not CJ.

Harper grabbed my hands, and I squeezed tight. No words were exchanged. We were both shaking. Harper managed to yell, "Megan, we need a car. Now." I wrapped my arm around her and we climbed back in the cart.

Megan got us back to the Merlo hauler, jumped out of the cart and sprang into action.

"How is she?" Junior came up behind us. "No one is saying anything?"

I put my hands over my face. Trying so hard to keep myself together. But hearing Junior's voice. His panic and concern…that almost did me in. Junior and CJ's rivalry was legendary.

I couldn't look at him. I searched for Megan and instead saw a sea of pale, concerned faces surrounding us. I don't think in all my life I'd ever heard such stillness and solemnity at a track.

Fuck them and their sad faces.

I focused on following Harper. We'd get to the hospital and see everything was fine.

I was not going to relive this nightmare.

"Gus?" Junior put a hand on my shoulder. "How's CJ? What's going on?"

It was like drowning and hearing his voice through water.

CJ had been in accidents before. Hell, at this very racetrack. She's always okay. She's too small and too tough for anything major to happen to her.

There was some conversation between Megan, Junior, and Harper before we all piled into Megan's rental SUV.

The last time someone pushed me bodily into a car was when I went to the hospital to see ... Tommy.

I shook my head. No.

But as I stared blankly out the window, my leg bouncing by the door and Junior on his phone shouting out questions and demands, I couldn't stop the flashbacks.

Unbidden, they crept from the locked drawer inside me. *Someone handing me a phone. A girl draped over me. Junior yelling in my ear. "Tommy was in an accident." It was bad. Get my ass to the hospital.*

I sat up. Sobered up. Pushed the girl off me. Stood, and swayed a bit. Searching for my keys. "What about CJ? Where was CJ?" Because she had to be with him. She was always with him.

Then Dewey was on the phone yelling at me. "Fuck CJ. Fuck that little slut. It's all her fault. All of this—" he was crying.

"What are you talking about?"

"Don't bring that bitch here, G.—don't need her here. Tommy..." his voice hitched. "He doesn't need her."

Not sure how I got to the hospital the night of Tommy's accident. But it was in the backseat of a large truck that felt like it was going twenty miles under the speed limit.

The hospital was conveniently located near the track, so it took longer to get out of the infield, than for Megan to pull the SUV up to the emergency room, where Harper, Junior, and I all jumped out and raced into the waiting area.

Harper led me and Junior to the desk. "I'm Harper Merrick We'd like an update on CJ Lomax. We were told she was brought in here."

"Miss. Only relatives are—"

"We're her family," I said. My first words since understanding the severity of things and the ferocity in my voice stunned even me.

Junior's hand rested on my shoulder as he attempted to smooth the waves I caused. "Please tell her husband, Grady McBane, that we're here."

A second nurse who recognized us said, "I'll go check on both of them."

Harper grabbed our arms and pulled us both back to some chairs.

I had too much emotion…too much energy to sit or stand still. I began to pace the room, walking toward the doors that led back to the emergency bay.

Doors from the triage area opened and we caught a glimpse as they wheeled her by. "Take her to curtain two. And when are we getting that CT? I need to know what we're dealing with." They must have cut off her race suit because her arms were bare, an IV was attached to a very limp, pale, lifeless hand.

Lifeless.

And my thoughts were no longer under my control.

Running in through the trauma entrance to the area where they were working on Tommy, I only caught a glimpse of his face, distorted, injured, and waxen.

All that was visible was a pale lifeless hand that seemed to be left out of all the attention being paid to his body.

With his ever-present energy missing, I had trouble believing it was even him. A man was pumping oxygen into him while another was doing compressions.

I held onto the wall for balance.

Another man in scrubs barged in, demanding an update and answers to questions. He pushed past others at the bedside and pulled up Tommy's eyelids. "Stop compressions."

"Both pupils are dilated and unresponsive," he informed the room.

"Where's the family?

"The brother is in the waiting room."

"Such a shame…so damn young."

And like that, my best friend…my brother in all but name…was gone.

I was transfixed on CJ's very still, bare hand—how small and delicate it seemed.

But it was Tommy's larger one I saw.

All my senses were haywire and tangling with my memories and spitting out and unbalanced reality—It was the harsh fluorescent lights, the unforgiving plastic chairs, the sterile rooms, the smell of ammonia, bad coffee and fear.

I braced my hand against the wall and struggled to breathe—the memories being feed and betting stronger.

No. This wasn't happening. Not again.

53

GUS

A nurse came from around the desk, asking Harper to follow her. Harper turned and said something to Junior and I before disappearing behind the bay doors as they closed, also cutting off my view of CJ as they moved her out of sight. I made my way to a chair, dropped my head in my hands and tried desperately to separate the past from the present.

I felt someone settle beside me but didn't look up. Junior tried to engage me. "I heard from Sam. She wasn't conscious when they pulled her out," he said, his hands were on his thighs, and he leaned his head back against the wall and stared up at the ceiling.

Interestingly, it's what I did when I was trying to control my emotions. I'd look toward the sky as if answers to my problems would magically appear. I wonder if Junior was doing it for the same reason. It reminded me how Junior was once a close friend—before Tommy died.

"She wasn't..." Junior's voice hitched. "She wasn't moving." He stared at me—years disappeared—all the anger, resentment, painful words were gone, and my old friend's eyes were filled with fear. As much as he seemed to resent her—even loathe her at times—he was afraid. He stared down at his feet and said softly, "I never imagined CJ could be still."

Crew and teammates, and even other drivers were coming into the ER. I knew I should do something, but I was frozen to my seat. Waiting. Head in my hands trying to block out the world. Where was Grady?

Why hadn't he come out to tell us what was going on?

Where was Mia?

Then, as if I conjured her out of thin air…she arrived. The sliding doors opened, and she practically ran in, surveying the area until her eyes landed on mine. Her face was pale, her eyes rimmed red and her nose pink from crying. She dodged a slew of crew members, pushing through them, before she fell to her knees in front my chair, her arms going around me. "How is she? Where is she?"

I didn't respond to her hug, and she pulled back, surveying my face. She wiped the tears that fell down her cheeks with one hand, grabbing for my hand with the other. "Gus, honey. What's going on? You're scaring me." Fear. I saw blatant fear in her eyes. Not remorse, sadness, or concern. Fear.

It was all I could take. I couldn't take any more.

"Where have you been?" I said, standing so quickly, she fell back.

"I told Harper to go, that I'd cover—" She scrambled to stand up.

"You'd cover what? What the hell happened?" I threw my hands out. My adrenaline was spiking. My past and my present were tangled. My voice was harsh. I'd been struggling to maintain control, to stay still and quiet, since we got here, and I couldn't contain it anymore.

Dewey yelled in my head. People were crying. Crashes and best friends on gurneys not moving. And beeping machines and—

"Well, I'm not sure. I spoke to Aaron, but I think she—"

"You're not sure? How can you not know? You're her crew chief." I pointed my finger at her chest. "You were responsible for keeping her safe?" I leaned toward her and pointed at myself, disdain lacing my voice.

"Gus, what the hell?" She struggled to stand while taking two steps from me, her eyes wide.

335

"We saw there was something wrong with the car—we all saw it." My hands flew out to the waiting room full of stock car professionals. "Why didn't you do something about it? Was this one of your new 'plans'?" I bit the words out with as much venom as I could muster.

She shifted her eyes from me to the crowd of onlookers. She shook her head vehemently. "Gus, no—" she said.

"Another way to show everyone how smart you are. With Jacks gone—was that your chance to prove how much you deserved to be in his chair—to win the big race?"

"Gus, man..." a male voice tried to interrupt us, putting their hand on my arm before I shrugged them off. "You need to cool it. It's not like that. You—"

But all my attention was on Mia—who was frozen in front of me—her eyes wide.

"You think I'd do that?" her hand went over her heart, as her body shrunk in on itself.

"Is my best friend—" My voice shook as I pointed to the door between me and the emergency bay. "Is she going to pay the price—"

My voice broke, and a man's hand was on my back, a hand trying to pull me away. I faintly heard them try to speak to me and I shrugged them off again. But this time they didn't let go, their grip got firm and the voice deepened into a tone that wasn't going to back down. "Gus, son. You need cut this shit out, right now."

I turned to see Wild Bill's determined eyes staring at me and I said, "She hasn't fucking woken up." My breathing was heavy, and my mind was racing.

His gruff voice was sympathetic but firm. "I know, son. But this isn't the way to—"

I turned back to Mia, Junior was standing with her now, trying to pull her away in the other direction. Something about that stirred me up again. "You know, these people aren't data you collect or analyze," I said to her, not registering the tears spilling down her face as she shot me a lethal glare before she turned her back, allowing Junior to lead her away...away from me.

"Enough!" Bill yelled.

Choking on my tears I motioned to those around us as if trying to explain. "These people are my family, Mia. They're all I have."

Two sets of hands dragged me away from her, and Wild Bill said, his deep, gravelly voice. "Get him outside and don't let him back in until he can keep his mouth shut."

I was kept outside for a while. They didn't trust me not to pick a fight with someone else.

Eventually Harper came out from the crowded Emergency Room. She was as tall as I was in her heels and zeroed in on me. She grabbed me by the arm and dragged me back in the ER and over to the seats where she and Cal had been camped out.

Practically tossing me in a chair next to Cal she bit out, "Boy, G, you know how to take an already messed up situation to a whole new level of drama." My adrenaline had slowly dissipated. I had a better idea of the level of drama I'd previously caused by the stares I was receiving from everyone around us.

Standing over me, Harper glared. "Sit here and don't talk to anyone. No one needs your shit right now—especially not Mia. I have enough to deal with without you taking a wrecking ball to your life."

"I think that horse is already out of the barn," Bill said, giving me the warning glare of a parent whose patience has reached its limit.

As soon as Harper marched off, her heels angrily walking back to the reception desk, I caught Junior and Mia walking back in the waiting room together. He positioned them as far away from me as possible. She was ghostly white. Her hand on her stomach—probably from being verbally gut punched by my words and then stabbed in the heart by me. Junior eased her down into a chair and sat next to her, putting a protective arm around her shoulder, and shielding her from me because I'd been the one to verbally eviscerate her.

"You okay, man?" Cal said quietly.

I held up a hand. I wasn't going to talk to anyone—it was safer that way.

Finally, the doors opened, and everyone stood, gathering toward Grady like a magnet. His race suit was gone, and he wore a set of scrubs as he dragged himself farther into the waiting area, searching for and finding Harper. He stepped up to her and said, "Go back, she wants to talk with you."

He ran his hands over his face as he addressed all of us. "She's going to be okay."

There were collective gasps and cries of relief. Crew members shifted, hugging each other, and clearing my line of sight.

Mia's knees were bent to her chest with her head resting in her hands and her body shaking. Junior stood over her as he listened to Grady.

"She took a hard hit to the head and was unconscious for a while—which gave everyone a scare. But she's awake, a little groggy—" his voice drowned out as I sat back down. Mia was wiping her eyes as she stood. Her eyes met mine and went blank.

"They just came back from the CT scan. They are going to watch her closely, run some more tests to make sure there isn't any swelling."

A chorus of variations of "Thank God" went around the room, with the tears everyone had been holding back beginning to flow out of relief as they crowded in on Grady. Mr. Merrick and Mrs. Merrick grabbed Grady in a parental hug, offering him comfort as I approached and gripped his shoulder.

He turned to me and surprisingly grabbed me in a huge hug. "I know we all skirt the edge of these kind of dangers, but today..." he said as I held him and felt his breath catch. "I wouldn't survive without her."

"Yeah," I said, involuntarily my eyes roamed for Mia. "I know, man."

I wanted to offer a comment about CJ's hard head being good for something or some other levity, but it was lodged in my throat.

Today was different. Today's accident—there wasn't anything left of that car except a cage with metal wrapped around it.

"When his car hit the roof of hers—" He couldn't finish.

"But she's here and she's okay." It was my job to reassure him—I was his friend. Her friend. It was what I was supposed to do—be here for them. Not be stuck in my head. I pulled back from him as I held him by the shoulders. I managed to get out, "And now you get to give her shit as being the driver in the family with the worst accident record. Screw her getting on you about 'Dega. I think this trumps that clusterfuck."

He let out a surprised chuckle. "I'm going to tell her you said that."

I shrugged. "So be it."

Harper's clicking heels were heard over all the commotion of relief the group was generating. She searched the area. When she couldn't find what or who she wanted, she came to us. "Where's Mia? CJ wants to see her?"

Mr. and Mrs. Merrick pulled Grady aside, hugging him and asking him what they could do.

Harper demanded my attention, "Gus, where is Mia? They aren't allowing CJ many visitors and she really wants to see her."

I turned back to where she was last, and the space was empty. I clenched my jaw shut and my back straightened. She'd taken off.

"She was here," I said, I think Junior took her home.

"Goddammit, Gus," Harper cursed at me.

"They must have left after Grady said CJ was going to be okay—"

Harper shook her head, glaring at me like I was an idiot. "And you didn't stop her?" She shifted on her feet. Digging in her purse for her phone, she bit out, "You really screwed the pooch on this."

Junior stepped into our circle. "I think he may have surpassed my level of asshole this evening." He put his hands on his hips. "At least I'm upfront about who I am. I don't sweet talk someone into falling in love with them and then turn on them like a viper."

I stepped into Junior's space, but this time he didn't flinch, and he didn't back up. "What the hell does that mean? And where is Mia?"

He gritted his teeth and stepped until our chests bumped. Usually, Junior was mostly swagger. He rarely followed through on his taunts, insults, or threats. The look on his face, the set of his shoulders, he had every intention of following through with the anger racing through him now. "You heard me. You think you were the only one reliving a nightmare this evening? You self-involved, selfish piece of—"

Harper shoved her brother out of my grasp while a few crew

members grabbed my arms and Wild Bill replaced the space Junior previously held in front of me—up in my face.

"What did I tell you?" Bill growled, and for a man his age, Bill could be very intimidating, a shadow of who he was from his past.

But Junior continued. "—that doesn't give you the right to just go off on people. You think you win the blue ribbon in the number of scars you carry or burdens you bear—" Junior yelled at me, pointing his finger accusatorially.

"Fuck you," I said. "It was the only comeback I had.

"That woman loves you—everyone can see it. And the first time you're tested, this is what you do? This is where she ranks with you? Just another woman—just another outlier trying to penetrate your exclusive circle." He waved his hand over the room. "Great show of loyalty and trust, asshole."

He stepped back from his sister, his hands going up as if to regain composure. He slicked his hair back with his hand and straightened his posture, taking a deep breath and looking at all the faces who were staring open-mouthed at him. He turned his attention to Grady. "I'm glad CJ is going to be okay." He took a step toward him and lowered his voice to be personal and intimate, but the room was silent enough that everyone heard, "I am sorry for my outburst—this shouldn't be about me or about Gus." He held up his hand, his eyes skipping around them once again…around the room full of people fixed on the drama unfolding. "I'll just go. I'm leaving to take Mia home, anyway."

Harper stepped up to him, as if to say something. He held up a hand to her and began to walk toward the exit. Then he turned back through the crowd and stared down Gus. "Maybe once you take the time to find out what really happened—that CJ was being CJ—no disrespect, Grady," he glanced to Grady. Grady nodded.

The minute Junior's eyes hit mine his coldness was back. "You're going to realize how badly you just fucked up and there's no one else to blame. This time, jackass, you're the bad guy."

Then he stormed out of the room, leaving a trail of shock and confusion behind.

54

GUS

I knew I was wrong even when I was doing it. I knew I was being unfair and irrational even when I was spewing all that I did.

Later, I was thoroughly chewed out by Harper and CJ, and given the whole story. I knew I needed to find Mia. I needed to find a way to attempt to undo my damage. Not only was my treatment of Mia cruel, but it was also unfounded, and no apology could take back what I said to her—the verbal public lashing I gave her. Junior was right. I was the asshole.

Reliving Tommy's death in real time while dealing with CJ's accident...but it was more than that. I didn't know who that person was who said those things to Mia. I didn't know how I became that person at that moment.

I waited until we were back in Charlotte to drive my sorry ass over to her house to apologize. It was cowardly, but truthfully, I didn't want the conversation or any further confrontation in a hotel room. And I wasn't sure what to say—how to explain how I was capable of being so cruel...how I could purposefully inflict so much pain on someone who had told me they loved me.

How did I apologize for that?

Would we ever recover?

I'd tried calling and texting her and got no response.

I grew a set of a balls and went to her house. No one answered at first, and there was a moment I thought she'd refuse to see me. But not my Mia. She opened the door, just enough to ask, "What do you want?"

"To talk to you, to apologize." I leaned a hand on the doorframe and tried to soften my tone with remorse and sincerity. "Can I come in?"

"I don't think that's a good idea," she straightened. "I don't feel like talking to you, Gus, not now—"

"I want to apologize—"

Her face grew hard—harder than I'd ever seen it. "Well, I don't care much for what you want." The tenor of her voice dropped, and her eyes surveyed me and found me lacking. "I said I don't want to talk to you. I don't want to see you and I sure as hell don't want to hear anything else you have to say to me. I think you've said enough."

I gaped. I hadn't practiced for this reaction.

"In fact," she flung open the door and stepped out on the porch so fast, I instinctively backed up. "How about we go to a crowded building surrounded by a group of friends, professional colleagues, media, and complete strangers with camera phones who can record every moment I yell about how inept you are, and what an opportunist you are at the expense of your friend's safety and wellbeing. They can capture the look of pain you have when you realize the person you are in a relationship with thinks you are lower than the shit they stepped in. Then once they upload it to social media it's there for all time. Very convenient in case you missed special clips you want to relive.

"Mia—" I ran my hand over my face.

"Don't you dare tell me you're sorry." She held up a finger and pointed at me, eyes narrowed, challenging me.

My hands on my hips, I shifted position and tried to open my mouth.

She stepped back toward her door. "Because people who care about each other—hell, even those who are *just friends*—" She took in a hitched breath. "You don't even treat a friend that way, let alone someone who... You know what, forget it. I can see I've run my course—"

"Mia—that's not—" I tried to step up to her, and the hurt etched on her face turned to full-on coldness with her hand separating us.

"I know you well enough, Gus Quinlan, to know you would never have publicly torn apart anyone you truly cared about—not like you did me—like I was nothing."

If hearing me tell you I loved you caused your brain to melt down, you should've had the balls to just break up with me. Then you wouldn't have been so primed to lose your shit on me.

Dropping her voice, she gritted out, "We're done here."

I dropped my head as she stepped inside her house, the door slammed so hard the potted plants we had bought together on the front porch shook.

And something inside me broke.

55

MIA

The last two weeks had seemed like two years. Without breaks in the weekly races, we had to bring in a substitute driver to run the car while CJ was recovering. Besides the concussion, she also broke a few bones in her left foot that would require her to be out for the remainder of the season.

Yeah. That didn't go over well.

Mel was still trying to get Harper to let her sub in for CJ, but with only a few Energy Blast races under her belt, Harper said that was a no-go. She wasn't ready for the big dogs, yet.

We rotated drivers, depending on the track, from Energy Blast and those who had recently retired but wanted to moonlight a bit. It was nerve-wracking and challenging. Having to adjust the cars for each driver's size and weight, not to mention inserting someone new into the team each week.

Once Harper had tracked me down, CJ and I had a heart-to-heart, where she actually apologized for not listening to me the way she should've. Water under the bridge, and I think if anything, living through the experience could make us more formidable if we ever raced together again.

If.

Jacks was on the mend, but his wife was formidable, and her patience was thin. She was done with his "comeback" tour. The couple were in "negotiations," but it sounded like he was being sidelined and regulated to expert consultant with limited time spent in the garage or on the track.

I didn't blame her.

It would've been a gracious and easier exit for me if he'd returned. I promised Harper I wouldn't make a rash decision, "Just because Gus was being an idiot." Even though, I was done letting a man dictate my life, I was considering leaving. The whole experience of being in Charlotte had soured with the drama between me and Gus. It put everyone in a bad position.

As much as I had come to think of Harper and CJ as friends, Junior had been right when he said, "You will never be able to crack that shell they've built up around their clubhouse. There is only so far you're allowed in." His expression was weary more than angry, like he'd lived it for so long, he'd just given up.

And as much as I'd hate to admit it, he had a point.

I wasn't going to run off and leave them in the lurch. I was going to finish the season. What I refused to do was deal with Gus—it felt good venting at him the day he came over to apologize. Because even before the altercation at the hospital, I felt him pulling away. Sure, Gus had some issues with emotional commitment, everyone had known that. I knew I wasn't going to get a declaration of love anytime soon.

Before the accident, I'd planned on talking to him about my L-word declaration and telling him it was no big deal when we got back. I could just kick myself for saying it. I was going to tell him things were perfect how they were. I didn't want more because I was still working through my own issues, and the declaration had come too early for me, too.

But it was safe to say we put the nails in the coffin. He kept his distance, and I kept mine.

I was in a hotel room the night before the Kansas race, on the phone with Shyla, waiting for room service.

"So what are you going to do?"

345

"I don't know. I'm still so angry. Hurt. Like I have all these negative emotions and nowhere to unload them," I said, flopping on the bed without dislodging my earbuds. "I still feel unsatisfied. As if there doesn't seem to be closure, and I really wish there was."

"I know. I get it." And she did. "Have you seen him...from a distance, I mean."

I let out a sigh. "No. I think he's avoiding me, which is just pissing me off more. Like what the hell. Am I supposed to go to his house and collect my stuff—give him back his key?" Tears started to well up in my eyes. "Jesus, Shy. I don't even know."

"Why don't you swing through Chicago on your way home. Tell Harper you are going to see your father for a day or two and come stay with me. You can fly home Tuesday. Just take a detour and come here?"

"I can't this weekend, but we are going to Chicagoland in two weeks, I'll come stay with you instead of a hotel."

"What about your father's?

"I don't want to talk about Gus, and it will be all him and my brother want to talk about."

"Okay, you've got a deal," Shyla said. "I'll find something fun for us to do."

My heart lightened for the first time in weeks, and I even cracked a true smile.

"Give me something new to talk about, tell me how things are with you and Davy?" I said, wanting to get my mind on something else.

Knock-knock

"Hold on, I think my dinner is here."

I grabbed my phone off the bed as I went to the door, looked through the peephole and whispered, "Well, that's strange...Shy, I've got to go."

"Is it Gus?"

"No. It's Robby from Rex Richardson."

"What? Really? At your hotel room door—"

"Gotta go."

"Call me—"

I hung up, pulled the earbuds out and opened the door. "Robby? What a pleasant surprise." Was I supposed to invite him in?

"Hey, Mia." He scanned the hotel floor for anyone in the hallway. "Can we talk?"

"Um, sure," I said, opening the door farther, wishing I hadn't just messed up the bed.

I skirted around him to casually straighten it as he awkwardly searched for a place to stand or sit. "How are things going with the team? I heard CJ is on the mend."

He settled on a desk chair and straddled it, facing me. I sat on the bed, tucking a leg under me. "She is. Watching each race from home and driving me and Harper crazy with her 'notes'," I smiled.

He gave a half-hearted smile back. "How are you doing with everything? Losing CJ and Jacks within the same week, that's a lot of pressure?"

I shrugged, "It hasn't been a joyride. But I'm managing."

He tilted his head back, assessing. "I'd say you're doing more than managing. I think you're doing an amazing job." His eyes narrowed to make a point, "Rex thinks so, too."

I stumbled over my words for a second. Not sure if I was hearing him correctly. "That's very kind of him."

He tapped the back of the chair. "In fact, that's why he asked for me to come see you."

I pulled up my other leg and shifted on the bed. "O-kay."

Robby stared down as his hands traced the back of the chair, "Well, it turns out we may have let the wrong person go."

"Ah." What else was I supposed to say?

Duh.

"This is about the penalties you've been getting," I guessed. This was about Keith.

He nodded once. "And the cheating scandal he's gotten us roped into and was suspended for…not to mention the employee turnover." He looked up at me, "Also, the guy is a Grade-A dickhead. Triple R takes their reputation very seriously, and this isn't the way we want to be seen."

I let out a huff of agreement.

"How the hell did you ever deal with him?" His tone was incredulous, and then he put up his hand to stop himself. "I'm sorry. That was completely out of place. I'm sorry. It's just that I think everyone sees how much you covered for him or corralled him—"

"Well, he is a smart man, he's also a very competitive and insecure man. It didn't do his ego any good to see me get another job over here."

Robby nodded. "Merlo is a great team. Young, but very in the forefront."

I nodded.

"I know this is a fool's errand, but I promised Rex I'd ask." He slowly winced, tilting his head again as if afraid to utter the next words, "Is there any way I could lure you back to Chicago? Back home?"

Home.

"You mean to work for Keith—hell, no. Nothing could get me to work for him or with him. You don't know what he's put me through —" I shook my head, pushing myself off the bed.

"No. You misunderstand." He stopped me. "We should've given it to you—the crew chief spot—it would be yours." He also stood from the chair, and in front of me, his eyes wide, he continued, "We were wrong—we'll admit it." His words sped up, excited energy lacing them. "And we'll match whatever Merlo is paying or give you what we're paying Keith plus fifteen percent. Whatever is greater—" His face was lit up at the prospect, and the fact that I hadn't said no—yet.

"But I bought a house and moved and—"

His eyes seemed to get brighter as he realized I hadn't shut him down...yet. "We will help with relocation expenses."

I stepped around him.

Chicago. Shyla. My dad and brother. My old life. Not feeling like I had to try to fit in. Not being reminded where I rank in Gus's life.

I stood, quiet, as I contemplated both options.

Because damn, I didn't want the discomfort of being around Gus to drive me back to Chicago. I wasn't going to let any man dictate my career again.

I came to love these people, but would I ever truly fit in down here?

Home. Where was my home?

I looked up and realized I was looking out my hotel window, into the dark night. Hell, I even forgot what city I was in.

"Mia, what would it take to get you to come back to Triple R?"

"I'm not sure. Let me think about it."

"Okay. Okay, fair enough." He started toward the door, and with his hand on the knob he turned. "But, to be clear, so I can tell Rex, it's not a no?"

I glanced over my shoulder and was able to muster up a small smile for delivering his proposal, because Robby had always been kind and fair to me. This may be a way out of my heartache and yet, another new start. "It's a let me think about it."

But I was tired of looking for new starts.

And I was really tired of letting men hurt me.

56

GUS

A few weeks went by, and I spent that time trying to get my head straight. She was right about all of it.

Of course, she was. In many ways, Mia knew me better than I knew myself and it scared the hell out of me.

I was working on it.

But now, I had to speak to her. I had to go see her again, and at the very least attempt to find a way to make it up to her with or without an actual apologize. I went by her house a few times and she wasn't there. I didn't want to try the office and deal with Harper, or God forbid, CJ's wrath.

I broke down and called Harper, who said she flew straight to Chicago after Daytona. That didn't surprise me. Davy confirmed she was at Shyla's, but that was all the information he'd give, and that was communicated with a mixture of censure and pity.

"Is she...what is going to happen with Merlo?" I asked Harper.

"What do you mean?"

"Is she still CJ's crew chief?"

There was silence. Heavy silence. "Harper, you wouldn't—"

"Gus," her tone was laced with disappointment, and I could almost picture the stern expression. "What happens at Merlo isn't any of your business."

At home, I paced around my garage, randomly picking up tools, cleaning them with a cloth and placing them back down. I'd already ran my legs into the ground. Even taken a shower, and it was too early to drink—plus, there was the pesky problem of having to leave for the next race tomorrow.

How else did you handle your life when you fucked up so majorly but were still so screwed up you didn't even know if you were worthy enough to put it back together?

It took a lot of strength not to hurl the socket wrench at the wall.

I mean, how do you hurt someone you love? Love. I fucking love that woman and I lashed out at her so harshly. So thoroughly.

I wasn't just a bastard. I was the lowest scum ever to walk the—

"I didn't take you as the sulking, broody type." Junior strolled in my garage, hands in his jeans pockets, and the fact that Junior was wearing jeans was enough to make me pause what I was doing.

"I'm off work until tomorrow," I said, keeping my back to him, not wanting any company, especially from someone who made it his mission to poke at me.

"Just wanted to let you know I heard from my contact at Triple R. Turns out they are getting a new crew chief."

The sound of my freshly clean socket wrench falling to the ground registered before I even realized I dropped it.

"Okay. Good to know."

"Well, since your tips to the officials were what finally got Keith, the asshat, fired for cheating, I thought you'd like to know."

"He deserved it."

"No doubt. However, I'm not sure you're going to be happy with the outcome of your maneuverings." He crossed his arms over his chest, staring me down.

I slowly pivoted to him. "What do you mean?"

"Spoke to Rex himself. Turns out they offered Mia the job." He walked over to my Camaro and glided his fingers over the hood.

"What?" Hold up. That got my full attention. "She's leaving?"

I caught Junior's shrug. "He didn't say."

He slow-walked around the Camaro, as if giving me time to digest what he was saying—time to respond.

I bent over to pick up the wrench, giving him my back, not allowing him to see my pain. I tossed it on my work bench to prevent me from launching it at his head or anywhere nearby it.

"Anyway, thought you should know."

He continued the same pace, slipping his hand back in his jeans pocket, and walked right back out as if he were simply taking a Sunday stroll and delivering the latest track news—not sticking a nail in the coffin of my relationship.

It was true…some things you didn't come back from, after all.

After making sure Junior was gone, I ran into the house, grabbed the keys to the Bronco and drove to Mia's house. My heart sank as I spotted two unexpected and unwelcome sights. My mom with a "For Sale" sign she was shoving into Mia's front lawn.

"Son of a—"

I cut off my words, realizing I was pulling up to greet my mom. She didn't deserve my anger, but I knew I was going to catch hers. I took a deep breath and let it out.

For a moment I considered making a U-turn, but she spotted me. There were no other cars in Mia's driveway except my mom's SUV.

My mother walked over to meet me before I was even out of the truck. Her hands folded in front of her, but her face unreadable as she came alongside the driver's door. I lowered the window. "Is this for real?" I nodded at the For Sale sign.

She nodded. I stared at the house both my mother and I helped Mia pick out less than a year ago. Lost in the memory of that fateful day. "What did you expect?" she said softly.

I ran my hand over my face. My eye had been twitching since Junior left—it was just another aggravation to go with all the rest. I pressed my fingers into my eyes to blur out the world.

"I don't know how to undo this."

"You apologize."

I dropped my hands. "I can't get ahold of her. I tried."

"Try harder." My mother leaned her back against my car, as if she were a priest in a confessional, making it easier to spill my heart. "Do you love her?"

Silence.

My mother's voice grew stern. "Gus, do you love her?"

"I hurt her."

"Yes, you did, quite spectacularly, too. Can't say it was my proudest moment as your

mother."

She studied me, and I hung my head. Waiting for my answer, she continued, "I haven't exactly given you the best examples of what real love—romantic love—is supposed to resemble." She took in a cleansing breath, studying her feet as she shifted. "But not claiming to know what real love is, son, it's a cop out. You love me. You love your friends. You know love. It doesn't stop someone from falling in love, it gives you an excuse not to take a chance on it. And I didn't raise you to be a coward."

She turned, put her hand on the window, and patted it. "I know I pushed this. Maybe I was wrong to do so. I'm sorry, honey."

She bent down, her hand on my arm. "I know you don't like to talk about it, but..." she paused. "You know I loved your father. In his own way I think he loved me and you—just not the way we deserved to be loved. I don't regret being in love with him." She sniffed, but I couldn't look at her. Talking about him always did this to her. "I have very fond memories that aren't diminished by the outcome. Plus, I have you. You were made from love. You are my love."

She rubbed my arm. "What makes me sadder than anything that your father could've ever done to me—to my heart—is watch you lose the potential you have with her, with Mia, because we were such bad role models."

My eyes were burning. I needed to blink. But I was afraid if I did the wetness that resided there now would fall.

353

Mom stepped back from the car. Straightening, she smoothed down her skirt and shirt. "Anyway, enough of my romantic ramblings. I have to get going." She leaned in, giving me a kiss on the cheek. "I love you so much," she whispered in my ear, then dabbed at her eyes the way ladies did when they were trying to protect their makeup from running. "Good luck this weekend, honey." She walked toward her car down by the curb, and threw over her shoulder, "With everything."

57

GUS

To satisfy Merlo's sponsors and the fans, a retired Merrick driver, Trent Lawrence agreed to finish out the season for them.

What remained a mystery was who would be the crew chief for the Talladega race. At the pre-race meeting, when drivers and crew chiefs are given the rundown for the race, Trent showed up, walking in with one of the Merlo engineers who had always given Mia a hard time with her new race strategy. I was waylaid by reporters and members from other teams before I was able to make it over to anyone from Merlo to find out what was going on with them and with Mia.

Finally making it over to the Merlo trailer, I was greeted by Grady as he walked out. "Hey, Gus—"

Not in the mood for small talk, I said, "Is Harper in there?"

"No, actually, I think she's down at the garage."

I was heading that direction before he finished the sentence. I couldn't believe Mia

wasn't at least finishing the season.

She was gone.

That was it. She was gone. I raked my hand through my hair, yanking on it as I tore through the crowd milling around infield. Well, if she wasn't with Merlo, I'd head over to Triple R's pit and see if she was there.

Junior intercepted me before I stepped into the Merlo garage, "Hey, hey…where do you think you're going?"

I pushed him aside, not sparing a moment or a breath to communicate with anyone until I spoke to Harper.

He stepped in front of me. "Hey, man, we have a race to get ready for—"

I pushed past him, not trusting myself to lay a hand on him—determined, he stepped in front of me.

I wasn't dealing with him shit today. "Get out of my way, or I swear to God I'll quit right here, right now." If I could sling daggers out of my eyes, he'd be a dead man.

Instead of throwing a tantrum, as I imagined he would, he took two steps back and motioned for me to walk by. I started to walk farther into Merlo's garage, and he shouted out, "Mia isn't in there, but half-a-dozen reporters are. They want an update on the team's situa—"

I stopped listening, pushing my way into the crowded garage where Harper was answering questions and Trent was leaning against the car showcasing his name instead of CJ's.

I stepped up to Harper, who seemed to be wrapping up her interview. A reporter from the group was asking, "So Talladega seems to be a big track for Merlo and Merrick personnel—"

Harper bobbed her head back and forth. "We've always enjoyed this track, yes."

Another reporter jumped in, "But now you're running with a back-up driver and a back-up crew chief." A grin spread over Harper's face as she made eye contact with both reporters, turning on her southern charm. I found it odd considering the circumstances. It was her Cheshire Cat grin—her casual, playful attitude was grating on me, considering my world was falling apart. I wasn't feeling particularly playful.

Megan ushered the reporters away as I guided Harper to the side. However, my appearance caused the reporters to dig in and stand their ground. While it wasn't unusual to see me around Merlo's garage, it was very close to start time, and given the situation with CJ, my melt-down in the ER, and the disappearance of their crew chief...there was blood in the water.

They smelled the drama about to unfold and they weren't going to budge.

I tried to block their view with my back, but I wasn't delaying this any longer. I wanted answers.

I wanted Mia.

"Where is she?"

"Excuse me?"

"Don't play with me, Harper. I'm really not in the mood. Where's Mia? Why isn't
she here?"

Harper was completely unfazed by my barely restrained emotion, increasing my level of frustration. "She's not here, she's—" She began to gesture, but I stopped her, my impatience at an intolerable level.

"I know she's not here. Why? What's going on? Did you replace her?"

Harper's eyes widened, and her patience waned as her voice rose, "Why would I replace her?" The entire garage was silent. She glanced over my shoulder, nodded, and then her attention was zeroed in on me. "Don't you look at me like that, August Quinlan—don't you dare." Harper's voice rose to new levels. "I'm not the reason she's not here." She pointed at herself. "And you..." she poked me in the chest, "Damn well know it."

"Is this where you say, 'I told you so?'" I shifted, leaning into her. "Is this where you threaten me again and remind me of all those times you told me not to get involved with her?" I threw my hands up in the air.

Harper cocked a hip and crossed her arms over her chest.

"All those times you predicted I'd fuck this up—that I'd hurt her. That I wasn't good for her. That I...that we would lose her. Yes, I know." I stepped back, tried to catch my breath, and pointed at myself. "I am a selfish bastard, and I didn't listen."

One perfectly sculpted eyebrow arched on Harper's face.

The volume of my voice ratcheted up. "Okay. Satisfied. Now I want to—" my voice leveled off and then cut off. "I need to see her... speak with her."

There was a pause between us as a reporter began broadcasting from just a few feet away. Running a commentary as if narrating a play and bringing the audience up to speed with the soap opera occurring in the garages. *"This is Cara Bristow, I'm down at the Merlo garage checking on the Merlo team, already strapped with a string of bad luck, this team's resilience is being tested further..."*

"Gus, I love you like a brother, you know that." Harper held out a placating hand. "And I did warn you about messing with Mia." She shook her head, staring down at her shoes as she shifted weight to her other hip. "So why—"

"—with the arrival of Gus Quinlan, the crew chief for Grady McBane. He seems to have had a fallout with his girlfriend, the absent chief for Merlo, Mia St. James."

Another reporter joining in the commentary. *"Yes, these two teams seem to have more drama than the daytime soap operas my mom used to watch. And I'm here for it."*

The reporter's words were background banter for the tragedy of my life that was playing out in front of me. "Please—Harper, I need to know what's going on."

"What do you really think seeing her will do at this point?"

My shoulders slumped, "I don't know...at least it will give me a chance to apologize—"

"Send an email," Harper quipped, she glanced up at the reporters, gauging the audience we'd acquired, and scanned the crowd.

"It will give me a chance to convince her to stay in Charlotte and not go to Chicago."

She doubled down as she braced herself to poke me. "Why? Why should she stay? You don't want to be with her. You made that clear."

"You don't know that." My anger tipped over and I was definitely yelling. "You don't know what I want. You warned me not to mess with her because you didn't think I deserved her. You know what— screw you and your 'I told you so'."

"Gus—I didn't say that…I haven't said that." She softened her voice.

"You didn't need to say the words." I glared. "Don't you think I knew that…that I didn't deserve her—didn't deserve a chance to be with her. I knew it was a train wreck waiting to happen the minute the thought of being with her entered my mind." I pinched the bridge of my nose. "But you know what you and CJ did—you gave me fucking hope."

I stepped back, agony ripped through me at the word. "Hope that I could have what you two have—that happiness you guys have —that I could have that with her. With the most beautiful—" I held up my hand, then clenching it into a fist, as I shut my mouth tight to stop verbal vomiting that I was spewing in front of these growing group of reporters who were silently live streaming all of it.

Harper's eyes grew glassy. That was pity I saw in them. Goddamn it. Where the hell were my balls? I straightened and took in a loud audible breath. Fuck it.

With resolve I asked Harper, "Do you want her to stay?"

"Yes, of course—" she said.

"Fine. If you can get her to stay at Merlo and not move to Chicago…I'll leave her alone. I won't step foot in this garage. She deserves to be here—she wants to be with Merlo, and she is meant to be here."

"Yes, but—"

The first reporter said, *"Rumor has it that Mia St. James was offered Keith Thompson's position after he was let go following allegations of cheating. Mia had previously worked with Triple R prior to Merlo and left when Keith assumed the crew chief position."*

Harper crossed her arms over her chest and narrowed her eyes at me. "Why should she stay?"

"Because she loves working with you—even with CJ—all she's ever talked about was being part of this team and further women in the sport. So, if it means staying away from Merlo—I want her to have it. I don't want to be the reason—"

Quick enough to startle even the badass I was trying to channel, Harper stepped up to me, in my face. "Why do you want her to stay?"

"Because—" I said, defensively.

"Because why?" She shot back.

"Because I love her."

58

MIA

I was walking over to the pit when Junior caught up to me, and insisted I return to the garage with him.

"Come on, I really need to go. If this is some crazy tactic to keep Merlo from performing well at Talladega, I have to say I thought you were better than that," I said, with a bit of tease in my voice.

"I swear, I'm not being underhanded." His phone buzzed and he glanced at the display, "Give me one minute. Please don't leave. I'll explain everything. I promise, Harper asked me to get you."

He put the phone to his ear and mumbled for a moment. He handed the phone to me and said, "Here, CJ wants to talk to you."

CJ? On Junior's phone. Was the world on fire? "Hey. What's going on—why are you calling Junior?"

"Eh, well. Mutual goals make good peacemakers," she said.

Junior, meanwhile, was taking my backpack and putting it on his shoulder as I

asked CJ, "What is going on?"

"Well, I was watching the pre-race show, and lo and behold, one of my oldest friends is making an ass of himself—not that it's unusual— but he seems to be taking it to a new level. And I need you to intervene."

"What?"

"Go with Junior. Now. Good luck today…and by the way, tell Trent not to get too comfortable in my car."

Junior took the phone with one hand as he grabbed me by my elbow with the other and ushered me through the crowd, "Let's go."

"This is about Gus, isn't it—"

He kept pushing me forward.

"Junior, I don't have time or energy for any more of his drama."

He pushed me through the crowd with forward momentum and without offering any further explanation.

"Wait—" I dug my heels in, but he refused to stop. "I hope the car is okay—is the car okay?"

He let out a chuckle, nudging me forward still with his body. "It's fine."

I stared at him, not following anything that was happening. "What does this have to do

with me?

"Everything, my dear." He put his hand behind my back, in order to steer me into the garage area and Merlo's bay. "Come on, there is something you need to see."

I couldn't see anything through the throng of reporters with their cameras pointed inside, but questions weren't being tossed around. There was a cacophony of noises from the garage area—familiar voices laced with emotion yelling above the reporters.

"Because she loves working with you—even with CJ—" Gus's voice, his breathing, was harsh. I needed to see his face, to see his expression. I just need to lay eyes on him. God, I was so pathetic. I pushed through, with Junior backing me.

"—All she's ever talked about was being part of this team and further women in the sport. So, if it means staying away from Merlo—I want her to have it. I don't want to be the reason—"

I pushed through one last person, so I was standing to Gus' side, but out of his direct line of sight.

Harper was in his face—I'd never seen her so harsh—so cold and she snapped. "Why do you want her to stay?"

"Because—" He wasn't backing down.

"Because why?"

"Because I love her." The rawness in his voice had my knees weaken and I held onto Junior's arm, just as I had the last time I heard it—when he broke us.

But his words. Those damn words...they echoed through the garage...through my head and into the broken pieces of my heart.

The gasps and whispers were drowned out by those words. I looked between Gus and Harper, trying to better understand the situation. Harper directed her attention to me and smiled her Cheshire Cat smile. Satisfied with her task being successful, she stepped back, gesturing to me.

Gus turned his head, his body following until he was in front of me. "Mia."

He slowly reached for my hand and cradled it in his own. As he took another hesitant step into my personal space, the background noise of the gathering crowd fell away, and all I heard...the only thing that spun around me were the whispered words, "Because I love you, so much...so damn much. I would lay my world at your feet. Please, don't leave. You don't have to forgive me, just don't leave."

"If I left, it wouldn't be because of you, don't be so arrogant."

"Okay." He stood still, his eyes wide.

"If I left it would be because I would be happier somewhere else or because an opportunity was better...not because of you."

He nodded slowly.

"But I can be happy in Charlotte with or without you, because being with Merlo is what makes me happy. Being surrounded by these people—people who appreciate and trust me—makes me happy." I dropped his hand.

"Good." He nodded and took a step back, his head dropping, his shoulders slumping, a bit defeated. I was not warming to his confession. I wasn't returning my feelings because I didn't know what they were.

Oh, screw that. I knew what they were. I just didn't want to let him off the hook that easy.

We stood there, glancing up at each other. Neither knowing what to do and with an audience watching our every move.

"I love you," he said. He held out his arms as if embracing the world with the three words.

"I love you, Mia and all I want is for you to be happy. If that means staying away, I will do that. If that means giving you space, I'll do that. Just tell me what to do."

Murmurings began to ramp up around us and I was done with public confessions and the reality TV moment we were giving them.

We didn't touch or do more than stare at each other. The chasm was still there, but we could still see each other over it. It was a start. Harper walked over to the two reporters and whispered something about wrapping things up.

"And with that, ladies and gentlemen, the bachelorhood of another one of the most eligible men in racing is wrecked. Hey, Skip, what's happening back where you are? Whatever it is, I bet it's not half as exciting." The reporter signed off, dropped her microphone down by her side and turned to the woman next to her and said with barely restrained enthusiasm, "God, I love my job."

Reality began to creep in as Harper and Junior emptied the garage, and then stood like guards outside it. What next? I broke our connection, taking a step back, and hooked a thumb in my belt loop. Then motioned to the bay door leading out, "Um, we both have actual races to oversee—"

He shook his head. "It can wait. Both of our bosses are right there. No one is going to fire us."

"They will if we miss the race—"

"One more minute." He held out his hand, as if he was going to try to pull me

back into the moment.

"But—"

"I love you. Christ, Mia...you are it...absolutely everything to me."

"Gus."

"I know I don't deserve your forgiveness, and I don't deserve your trust. But please, God, give me a chance—give me time—to work through my shit. To get to the point where I deserve your trust, win back your friendship—"

"Gus—" My knees were weak, and I leaned against the car we set up for today. I hadn't been prepared for this. I hadn't steeled myself for this possibility.

He leaned down to be eye level with me, his hand to his chest. "I haven't been able to breathe right since then…I don't know why I lashed out at you. I don't know how to make it up to you—but please. Let me try."

I studied him. The words from the hospital replaying in my head and the pain renewing. "You hurt me." My voice gave only the facts, holding back the emotion that still coiled inside. "Again."

He closed his eyes. "I know."

"I had nothing to do with CJ or with Tommy or with any other pain you have felt from before. All I've ever wanted was to be happy with you—"

"I know. And you are what makes me happy. You are—"

I stared away from him and firmed my mouth to stop myself from diving into this in the middle of a garage surrounded by people.

He held my hand and then brought it slowly to his lips as I watched his fingers stroking the spot he kissed. In a husky voice he whispered to me, "I realize—"

I closed my eyes. "I'm not your damn doormat, Gus. I'm done being anyone's

doormat. Anyone's crutch or anything else. I deserve better than that. I deserve someone who is willing to tell me how he feels about me…instead of running. I deserve to have a man who doesn't unload on me because I'm convenient and he's hurting."

I was talking myself out of giving him a second chance and he saw it.

His eyes widened, and he held my hand tighter, tucking it close to his heart. "I'll see someone—talk to someone. Get my head on straight about it. Anything."

His eyes traveled up to my face, pleading in his eyes with the slightest glimmer of hope.

I'd never seen him so vulnerable. So exposed. He meant it.

I stepped up into his chest and bent my head back to stare up at him. "You love me?

He nodded emphatically. "I didn't know what love was until you showed me.

It was always different with us—I was just too ignorant to understand what it was. I wasn't exactly a quick study—it just took me a bit longer to learn. Just like in college, I needed you to teach me."

Harper and Junior came back into the garage. Harper clapped her hands together,

"Alright, you love birds all made up—we have a race to run."

"Harper, did you tell Gus—"

"Yes. Yes, I did. I told him it was his fault you were moving to Chicago. He was responsible for getting their former crew chief fired, and that almost led to me losing you. So, I let him sweat it a little," she shrugged, completely unapologetic. "We even got his mom to put a "For Sale" sign up in your yard, to really push him over the edge."

"Wait, my mom was in on this?" he said.

"You got Keith fired?" I had a hard time keeping up.

Harper started shooing us out of the garage. "I think we've covered enough for now. You gave the reporters and bloggers more than enough material and may have even inspired a new stock car reality show." She pulled out her phone. "We need a golf cart—actually two." She shoved the phone back into her bag.

Junior added, "Now go do your jobs and you can gaze into each other's eyes all you want after one of you wins. Preferably you." He pointed at Gus.

"Let's go!" Harper's voice jarred both of us to break apart as she held my elbow, ushering me away.

"Wait," I said, pulling out of her reach. "Just one minute." I walked slowly over to Gus.

"We aren't done with this," I held out a hand.

He nodded. "I know. I will do whatever it takes. Whatever you need. I'll go to counseling to deal with Tommy's death. If we have to start over—I can. I will work through that."

I lifted up on my toes and kissed his cheek, then dropped his hand. He stayed still, but I felt the energy flowing off him. I pivoted and began walking back to a cart.

Looking over my shoulder, I caught him staring at me, his hand on the cheek I kissed him on. Reporters were gathering around him again, swallowing him up.

He raised his head and yelled. "I will make it up to you." His eyes were glassy, and he ignored everyone else around him. Determination and maybe a touch of loneliness were still etched on his face.

I couldn't. I couldn't leave him this way.

I stepped out of the cart and ran into his arms. He held me and hugged me, and a familiar comfort that had been missing washed over me. His body relaxed, and a breath escaped him in a hitch—he felt it, too—our connection was still there. "God, I missed holding you." I squeezed him tighter.

On a sudden burst of excitement, he lifted me up, spinning me around—the reporters forming a circle around us again. "I fucking love this woman," he yelled.

I laughed. "I'm going to kiss you, and then you're going to put me down—" I didn't finish because his lips were on mine—kissing me sweetly, not taking more than I was willing to give. I wrapped my arms around him, pulling him close before breaking the kiss.

He lowered me to my feet and saw Megan driving her golf cart around us to chase off the reporters and fans closing in on our perimeter.

I cupped his cheek one more time before jumping in the cart and taking off for the pit box, lighter knowing what was waiting for me after the race.

The road wasn't going to be easy for us—two leaders on two rival teams. I may be clever enough to see we were supposed to be together, but Gus was stubborn enough never to let me go. After all, there was more to life than just racing...and leave it to the women to educate the men on how to have it all.

367

EPILOGUE

Gus

The season didn't ease up on us just because we sorted ourselves out. It got crazier—in a good way.

Grady clenched the win at Daytona and eventually won the Championship as well—being the only driver ever to secure a championship in both series.

We were all battered and bruised, but we had enough gas left to celebrate at Lake Norman for several days. CJ led the celebration, promising she was next.

After much discussion, we decided to put my house on the market and move into Mia's. She had a kick-ass garage, and it had just been recently renovated.

I walked out to her garage one evening with a glass of wine for my Mia and a beer for me. She was leaning up against her work bench, staring at the cars in the garage bays.

"What are you doing out here?"

She took a sip from her glass and gestured to the garage. "It's too small."

"Too small?"

She nodded, taking another sip.

I stared at her draped Camaro, her everyday SUV, and my truck parked there.

"Once you bring your toys over here, we won't have enough room to move."

I shrugged. "I don't need the Bronco and the Denali—"

"I don't want you to get rid of the Bronco..."

Yeah, I didn't, either. I had plans for it.

We went back and forth on how to downsize our collection and decided to sell the Denali or her SUV—not being able to part with one of our fun toys.

She put her wine down on the table behind us and stepped over to take a better look at the space as if it would be bigger from a different angle.

I took another sip of my beer, watching her.

She tapped her finger on her mouth—that adorable crease between her brows that I had become so enamored with showed up with whatever was whirling through her mind. "We may need a bigger garage..."

I let out a chuckle. "Most women would be more concerned about closet space or even bedrooms—" I wrapped my arm around her shoulder, pulling her into me, her hand resting on my chest.

"I'm not most women—"

I kissed the top of her head, "Yes, sweetheart, it's why I love you. They broke the mold after you."

"Damn, straight." She reached for her wine and took another sip before looking up out of the side of her eyes at me with mischief. "Let's get ready to go to the Merrick's."

I looked up at the clock on the wall. "It's early."

She finished off her wine. "Yeah, but you never know what distractions may pop up."

I agreed, faithfully, following her back into the house, hoping to be one of those distractions.

We got dressed—even though I tried to undress us a few times.

"Not not. We don't have time for that."

"There's always time—"

"Move it, G."

My girl put her foot down and was running around, stressed about being on time. She was done before me and began walking around the house, fidgeting with things—seeming nervous…

"Mia, honey. What's going on?"

She plumped up a cushion, then walked into the kitchen. "What? Oh, nothing. I'm fine." She looked at the clock on the stove. "Want another drink?"

"No, I have to drive out to the lake."

She walked around me, not making eye contact.

"Mia, what's wrong—"

A baritone horn blared from outside, and her face lit up as she ran for the door, throwing it open before I could catch up.

A massive, black, jacked-up pickup truck pulled up out front of the house, towing a car trailer with a man in dark sunglasses and a beard waving out the window. Mia was down the driveway like, well, a race car.

"Yay! You made it!" She ran to the truck, jumping up and down like a small child on Christmas morning to the amusement, and slight annoyance, of the man lumbering out in faded jeans, a Carhartt jacket, and heavy boots. He was proportionate to the size of the truck. But when Mia got to him and went on tiptoes to reach up to hug him, it gave perspective of his true size.

I meandered outside, hands in my pockets, and stood on her front step, taking in the scene. Mia laughed while the beast of a man practically dropped her on her ass. She swatted at him and said a few words, but his eyes shifted to me, and his expression changed, hardened.

He began to walk, "So this is him, huh?"

One of his steps was equal to three of Mia's, so she was jogging to keep up with him. "Trick, we talked about this—" She tried to employ a firm tone, but his pace didn't slow.

"It's about time I met the man you're shacking up with this time." I tried not to bristle at the "this time."

"He managed to break your heart once and you took him back already. Time for him and me to have a chat." He reached me, and I was two steps above him, but maybe only a few inches higher in height. "Let's get something straight. My sister hates me interfering in her life, so I promised her I'd stay out of her business…until I can't. So any guy she dates get one pass from me." He held up his hand to me with one finger up. "You've used your one pass. You get me? The next time you're a dipshit, I'll be here."

I rocked back on my heels, respecting the fact that he loved his sister. I loved his sister.

"I love your sister."

He didn't move. He didn't put down that one finger. His eyes were daggers pinning me to a promise. Those words didn't sway him.

"And yes, I get you." I held out my hand. "Hi, my name is August Quinlan, call me Gus."

He paused for a moment. He looked at my hand, and then the hope he saw in his sister's eyes. "Trick St. James," I swear his voice had a natural growl to it. "I'll call you Dipshit while you're on probation."

Mia groaned. "Trick—"

The guy was funny. I let out a snort. "Fair enough."

He shook my hand, doing the manly thing of squeezing it—but not being an asshole and

trying to overcompensate. No, Trick St. James had nothing to prove.

But he made his point with his dark eyes and heavy brow narrowed on me. "I'm not amusing, nor am I amused."

I threw up my hands.

Mia batted at him like a mouse flicks an elephant with its tail. "Cut it out, you, moose." The energy in her body switched from nervous to anticipatory. "Did you bring my baby?"

He nodded and motioned to the car trailer without taking his eyes off me.

She took off. He followed her.

It could only be one thing. I walked slowly out to meet up with her, but she was already releasing the latches. Trick wordlessly began to help, and so did I, unveiling the beauty.

It was her Mustang.

She had him bring her Mustang.

The one she never moved from her father's garage. The one she never felt settled enough to bring with her.

She brought it here—to our home.

She was home.

Trick tossed her the keys, and the barest, indulging smile peeked through the gruff. His eyes caught mine, and he straightened to his full height, masking himself again as the big, bad brother.

She shot him the look of an aggrieved little sister, "Cut it out, Trick, you've had your say." Trick helped her unload the Mustang, and she pulled it into the driveway.

"Trick, get your stuff out of the truck, and let's get you settled."

Oh, great, he's staying. Of course, he is. He just drove from Chicago.

As he walked by with his duffle, he shot another glare. "Where should I put my things, Dipshit?"

I went to answer, but Mia beat me to it. Wrapping her arm around my waist, pulling me close, she said to her brother, "Put it in the room upstairs to the right. And drag a brush through your hair, and make sure you don't have food in your beard. Try to look like you can string more than two words together."

He grunted and walked inside.

"Listen," she whispered to me. "Trick is just playing with you. He's not that bad."

I gave her a loaded look.

"Once we get to the Merrick's he will settle. I didn't tell him Davy was going to be there. He has a man crush on anyone on that Carolina team."

"Of course, he does."

"Just ask Harper to have him seated next to Davy at dinner and we'll be fine."

We got Trick settled, then grabbed our things. "Trick, go unhitch the car trailer. You're driving separately."

A grunt was his response.

As we walked out of the house, it dawned on me—we never put

her car in the garage. "Oh, do you want to put your baby to bed," I said, motioning to the Mustang. "We can move some cars around before we leave."

She held up her hand with the keys and dangled them in front of me. "Let's take her for a spin."

"Cool." I began walking to the passenger side. "Is this why you wanted Trick to drive—"

"Hey, Dipshit," she giggled, clearly enjoying the new nickname for me, "I meant you could drive."

"Drive. Your. Mustang?"

She graced me with her sweetest, most trusting, earnest smile and nodded. Her eyes became glassy.

I stepped to her until we were nose to nose. "Are you sure?"

She nodded again.

I cupped her face gently in my hands, once again realizing how tender and sweet these moments with her were—how precious. I searched her eyes and saw it—the love she had for me.

She wasn't giving me her keys. She was giving me her heart and her trust again.

"Mia St. James, I love you. You are more than I ever expected. More than I ever imagined, and definitely more than I deserved. Thank you." I kissed her sweetly, reverently. Wanting to hold this moment. It wasn't sexual. It was healing. It was the next level of us.

Then...

She leapt into my arms, straddled my waist, wrapped herself around me, and dug her hands into my hair.

Now it was sexual.

I stepped back at the sudden shift in our weight and laughed through our kisses, automatically turning to take her back into the house until there was an extremely obnoxious horn blaring. "Hey, Dipshit. Put my sister down and let's get going. I need food."

"I'm rethinking the need for the brotherly visit," she said, her mouth close enough for her breath to mingle with mine.

"I'll pay for a hotel room. Five star and everything," I said.

"I swear to God," Trick yelled. "I'll get the garden hose out on you two. Mia—I'll tell Dad if you don't get off that boy!" I was once again thankful I was the only child.

I slowly lowered her to the ground but didn't let her go.

"Trick, cool it or I will tell Davy you have a life-size poster of Dawson Shaw on the wall in your bedroom."

Even under all that hair, you could make out the redness on his cheeks. "It's not a life-size poster—it's a signed—"

"Do we need to talk about your Carolina bobblehead collection?"

His lips thinned and disappeared beneath his beard. But he turned his head and shut up and stomped off. "I'm hungry, let's go."

"That's all it takes? Just mentioning the Carolina team—oh God, does he know you dated Shaw? He will truly hate me if he knew Shaw was an option."

She shook her head. "He knows I know him. It's how I get him to do things—like tow my car down from Chicago."

I kissed the top of her head. "That's pretty clever—and devious."

She winked at me, and we walked to get in her car. "Haven't I taught you anything?"

I opened the door to her car but caught her before she got in, cupping her face in both my hands, and with the happiness that radiated from so deep inside it made me electric. I gave her a kiss on her forehead and then her lips. "You've taught me how to be happy, Mia. And I can't wait to see what other lessons the future will hold for us to learn together."

AFTERWORD

While I tried to stay as close to the sport as possible and give readers a true experience, I intentionally didn't delve too deeply into technical aspects of stock car to keep the story from becoming too dated if the industry adjusts its format or makes other changes. I also played with the schedule of the races for creative reasons, and each year can also be different.

Since writing A FAST WOMAN, the industry has already started to change. It is an exciting time for the sport and for women in the sport. Drivers, engineers, race officials, race announcers, trackside reporters, tire changers, executives—women are in every facet. So much inspiration for *Driven Women* to choose from!

ABOUT THE AUTHOR

Laralyn is a proud special needs mom and an autism and dyslexia awareness advocate. She lives in Maryland with her husband, three children, and three dogs.

She loves to write about witty, strong women, then throw sexy, charming men in their path and see the chaos it causes. It's a great distraction from everyday life and is usually done with lazy dogs at her feet, a chai latte or Diet Coke in hand, and the promise of a glass of pinot at the end of the day if the writing is worthy. She is often distracted by chatting on social media or found listening to an audiobook.

Sign-up for her newsletter and learn what she's up to next by hearing about new releases, freebies, events, and more at www.laralyn-doran.com

You can join her friends in the exclusive reader group, S.A.S.S. (Smart-Ass Scribbling Squad).

BOOKS BY LARALYN DORAN

DRIVEN WOMEN SERIES

A Fast Woman

Boss Lady

Clever Girl

Made in the USA
Middletown, DE
30 September 2023